PRETTY VENGEANCE
A Dark College Romance

MARLEE WRAY

I

SAWYER

Bitter cold bites into my skin like thorns.
Since I'm in the midst of a low-key hazing by Granthorpe University's Briar Club, the thorn-like chills are poetic justice.

The Briar Club is an exclusive organization of "powerful women of style and substance"—their branding, not mine—that believes beauty shouldn't be a woman's main currency. While I agree with the sentiment, it's not the reason I applied for membership. My reasons are personal, private, and *problematic*.

I shift from foot to foot inside the yard of a Colonial Revival house. The smell of cigarette smoke curls through the cold like vines. Burying my chin in my coat, I turn my head toward the front where the chain-smoking security guard is stationed in the shadows.

GU is so bougie sometimes. There's a student poker game inside the house, and the organizers hired armed security. It's not like this is Vegas and the pot is a million dollars, so the cloak and dagger is a bit much. Ditto for having me stand outside, battling frostbite, to greet the late arrival. It's all a bid to reinforce the host's sense of self importance, and I'm over it.

My fingers burrow deeper into my pocket where I'm clutching my phone.

Come the hell on, Silver Spoon guy. Get your ass here.

People might roll their eyes at my calling out my classmates for their wealth and privilege when my adopted family—the Allendales—have enough money to bankroll a war in Central America. The difference is I wasn't born rich. I still have memories of my chaotic life in foster care when I had nothing more than a garbage bag of old clothes and mangy stuffed animals. A time when my bio mom was allowed to contact me, but didn't.

Stale news. Gritting my teeth till my jaws ache, I try to resist the urge to dwell. It's hard to move on, though. Because my difficult start in life didn't end when I was adopted, it marks me like a scarlet letter. On the surface, I'm an Allendale. It's the last name I'm allowed to use. But the most powerful members of my family don't accept me. Which means that, because I'm eighteen, they could cut me out of their lives. Estranged. *Exiled.* The threat is so close I can smell it, like moth balls in the corner of an old attic.

That's why I'm on driveway duty tonight. I need to secure my membership in the exclusive club as proof I'm worthy of being a full-fledged Allendale. Since the loss of my adopted mom, Celine, to cancer, the future of my life literally depends on this.

Instead of grieving in peace, I'm locked in an elitist's game of survival worthy of a reality show. So fucked up. But I'll manage. One thing I got from my bio mom is the ability to adapt and persevere. "Your people are human cockroaches," my adopted brother Brad once said. It crushed eight-year-old me but barely stings now. Brad's opinion no longer matters.

The sound of a muscle car's motor fills the night. *That's different.* Moments later, a red vintage Camaro roars into the driveway, its headlights blindingly bright.

Wow. No Mercedes? No Lexus?

My internal thoughts have a bitter edge. I should probably work on that. There are a lot of foster kids who are never adopted, and they certainly don't end up at a university with ivy climbing its walls. While I'd never call myself lucky, I'm luckier than a lot of my former peers.

I watch, intrigued as the passenger door opens and the interior light flicks on, revealing a glimpse of a beautiful blond girl as the driver. So unexpected is the driver's gender, as well as her purple beanie with a yellow smile emoji on its front, that I only manage to notice two things about the passenger being dropped off—blond and male—before the car door closes and the interior lights go out.

The Camaro backs out of the drive as the security guy near the front door calls out, "Password?"

"Folklore," the newcomer responds, his deep voice lazy and amused. As if he too finds this whole set-up ridiculous.

As he nears, I hurry to turn on my phone's flashlight function, waving it back and forth as instructed by Clare Duffy, the Briar Club member who's evaluating my club suitability. She's super intense and definitely the type to ask whether I did my job *exactly* as specified. As a senior and the membership committee chair, her recommendation will make or break me.

Footfalls approach in the darkness. I turn, allowing my phone to illuminate the footpath to the back of the house. The guy's several feet behind but doesn't hurry to catch up. Reining in any outward signs of annoyance, I open the unlocked back door and wait for him, basking in the heat escaping from inside.

All thoughts of the temperature vanish when the guest steps onto the brightly lit landing. He's utterly beautiful. Bewilderingly so. Looking at him warms me up far faster than the heat pumping from the vents. Sparkling blue eyes, high cheekbones, washboard abs. Yes, washboard abs, which I'm able to admire because he's shirtless under the wool coat that hangs open even in this frigid weather.

And it isn't just his beauty and bare chest that are unsettling. He seems to have been in a fight. The corner of his lower lip is swollen and scraped raw, implying he got on the wrong side of a fist. A glance at his knuckles reveals his hands were thrown, too.

Swallowing past attraction and curiosity, I remind myself this is none of my business. *He is none of my business. I'm just here to do a job.*

"Can I get you something to drink?" I say, eyes focused on a burnished gold medallion pendant that hangs from an oxidized chain. I want to examine it more closely but don't want to get caught staring at his chest.

"Who are you?" He scans the kitchen. "The hostess?"

As if his looks weren't enough, he has an accent as pretty as he is. Irish, I think.

"Yes... Sort of." It's an accurate enough description for my job tonight, and I prefer hostess to minion. Shrugging off my coat, I set it on the back of a tall chair along the raised granite counter.

His eyes drop to my dark gray, v-neck sweater, lingering on my breasts. After a beat, he drags his gaze up to my face. "Are you playing cards?"

The brazen way he checks me out would be irritating if he were less attractive. Instead, my insides feel like marshmallows over an open flame. "No, not playing cards."

"Who do you belong to?"

My brows rise slowly. "Belong to?" The skepticism in my voice causes his damaged lip to curl into a small smile.

He leans back against the counter, seemingly settling in. "Someone put you on driveway duty. Who might that have been?"

Driveway duty. As though he plucked the words from my head.

Pressing my lips together in distaste but managing not to frown, I say, "That would be Clare."

"Ah." He scrutinizes my wrists, and I know immediately he's

checking for the Briar Club bracelet I don't have yet. "A new recruit, is it?"

Licking my lips, I nod.

He runs a hand through his hair and leans toward me. How the hell do his eyes sparkle like aquamarines? Is he a member of the fucking fae?

"What's your name?"

"Why?" I say slowly.

"The usual reasons. Plus some others." He winks at me.

When I fail to answer, one end of his busted lip twitches. I really want to lean in too... to taste his bloody mouth. Which just goes to show the Allendales are probably right about me. Deep down, I'm not one of them. I'm a girl who's drawn to actual bad boys. The beautiful ones who were born cool enough to make girls want to drop their panties from a sexy look.

God, I'm spiraling. Since getting to college, I've been envious of girls who are free to hook up with the handsome guys we meet at parties. That would be too risky for me, since I'm not the only Allendale on campus. If I did anything that would reflect poorly, it might get back to our family.

"I'll go first." He presses a hand against his bare chest. "Jamie O' Rourke." He blinks slowly, anything but innocent.

"Sawyer." My name's out before I can rethink letting myself engage.

"First name Tom?" He drops his hands, his blue eyes crinkling at the corners. "As a lad, I enjoyed your book."

Giving in to his charm, a small smile emerges. "Sawyer is my first name."

"Tell me, Sawyer, last name first, why do you smell like chlorine?"

"Do I?" After a beat, my surprise gives way to understanding. "It's hair dye. I was trying to even out my color." I tug on the ends of my processed hair, embarrassed at being called out on my moment of box-dye rebellion.

"Hmm." Reaching out, his fingertip touches a dark magenta strand that hangs over my ear. "You look like a cranberry."

I roll my eyes, embarrassment giving way to amusement. "Yes, I know."

"You thought the death of Delores left an opening for you?"

"The death of who?" I swallow hard and wonder how I failed to notice this guy on campus.

"Ah. Too American to know." His hand drops, and he takes a step back.

The distance allows me to breathe easier, but his dismissive tone hits one of my worst triggers.

"*You* look like you're auditioning for a *Fight Club* reboot. Bloody. No shirt." I fold my arms across my chest. "Too bad you're not pretty enough to play the Brad Pitt character."

A smirk emerges and warms me to my toes. "I'm not, no. Curse of my life being born so unattractive."

I love that he's so easygoing about being teased. My family is so stuffy. Sarcasm is completely wasted on them.

"Have any more constructive criticism you'd like to share?" The challenge in his eyes makes me want to slam my palms against his chest to shove him away, or grab his lapels to pull him closer.

I purse my lips into a fish pout. "How long have you got?"

His laughter raises gooseflesh on my arms. I love the sound of it so much.

"Look at you trying to rub the shine off me." He rests a palm over his heart, feigning that I've wounded him. "You sure you're not Irish? That's our way with each other, you know."

I smile but don't have a chance to respond because Clare Duffy enters the kitchen with a sharp green-eyed gaze. Her red hair is thin and stick-straight. I bet it dries in five minutes, which is something mine could never do.

"Jamie, you finally made it."

"I did, yeah." He turns in her direction, causing the gold

pendant to thump against his chest. He doesn't seem like the kind of guy to wear jewelry, but the dark chain does have a "fuck off" vibe that suits his overall lawlessness. "How are you, Clare?"

Clare's got the body of a coffee stir and a personality to match, complete with traces of bitterness. She's not afraid to spar over politics, history, or religion, no matter who's around. The Allendales would be appalled. But Clare has her acceptance to the country's top law schools. She can afford to be smug. I admire her accomplishments and the flashes of her "zero fucks given" attitude. She's not a blue-blooded GU legacy girl. Instead, she's proving what can be achieved by someone who's smart, driven and fearlessly assertive.

Turning her attention to me, Clare says, "Allendale, you're dismissed for the night."

"Hold on," Jamie says, accepting the way Clare leans in to give him a kiss on the cheek. "She's serving drinks, and I need one."

The fact that he's making excuses for me to stay causes my skin to tingle with anticipation.

"Jesus, James, you're freezing," Clare says, ignoring what he said. Instead, her hand slides down his side, touching his bare skin until he shifts out of reach. Her hand drops, but her expression is unchanged. She's not one to buckle under an awkward moment. "If you already lost your shirt tonight, it doesn't bode well for your getting into the game." She arches a brow. "You know the buy-in is ten grand, right?"

I nearly choke. Ten thousand dollars isn't a lot of money for most Granthorpe families, but as someone who only gets 250 dollars per month for incidentals, it feels like an insane amount to use to play a game.

"I'll manage," he says in a low voice. His eyes return to me. "I'll have a whiskey. Bushmills, if you've got it."

I start to turn. "I'll check."

"No Bushmills," Clare interjects, her voice growing haughty.

"Only Jameson's. But the Jameson's is top shelf, so I suppose you'll *manage* there, too." Her smirk is plenty sly as she links an arm around his to guide him toward the poker table.

A spark of jealousy burns through my chest, but I tamp it down. It's actually a good thing Clare came out and made her interest in Jamie O'Rourke evident. He's clearly wild and a world-class flirt... which is dangerous. Because, though I would never go out with a bad boy, nothing turns me on more. It's some kind of genetic flaw in my low-rent DNA.

Exhaling when they disappear into the sitting room, I try to regroup. The best thing I can do is leave as soon as I drop off the last round of drinks.

I won't interrupt the game for last call. I know what all five—now six—of the players are drinking. I mix the cocktails and carry a tray into the room. Switching out empty glasses, I make my way around the table.

The game's banker counts the one-hundred-dollar bills Jamie's given him and then sets stacks of chips on my tray for me to deliver. When I set the chips in front of Jamie, he lifts one and lets it ride over the backs of his scuffed knuckles as he plays with it. After I set his whiskey down, he passes me the chip.

"No tips," Clare says, reaching over with the intent of snagging the plastic disc.

Before her hand reaches mine, though, Jamie's fist closes around it, trapping the chip inside. And trapping my hand in his. The tightness of his grip conjures an irresistible ache inside me. This is the kind of guy who pins a woman down and makes her like it.

"No tips?" Jamie scoffs. "It's America. Your lot tips for someone saying good morning." He turns toward me, holding me prisoner with his attention as though he's some kind of hypnotist. "Keep it, Cranberry Sauce. For waiting in the cold for me."

His calling me by a nickname feels intimate. The way he's looking at me is, too. My lips part, and for a moment, I'm transfixed, my mind as much his captive as my hand. I should try to jerk free. But I don't want to.

What is happening? Between my legs I'm burning as though someone's lit a torch in my groin. Heat creeps upward, and I'm afraid his effect on me will show on my face.

"Jesus, James. What the hell?" Clare's voice snaps like a whip. "Let go of my terrified intern."

Jamie's eyes never shift from my face to Clare's. "Terrified, is it? Really?"

"No," I say, feigning casualness.

Yet, Clare's rebuke reminds me I should object to his grabbing my hand and keeping it imprisoned without permission. Even when I do pull my arm back, it doesn't free me because Jamie's grip tightens. Which sends a stab of lust through me the likes of which I've never felt before. I want more of this. Of *him*.

When Jamie finally releases my fingers, I force myself to set the hundred-dollar chip carefully onto one of his stacks.

"No tips," I say firmly, my heart jack-hammering against my ribs like I've run a marathon. "Have a good night."

"You as well." Undaunted by my refusal to keep his tip, he smiles at me before I hustle toward the door.

When I look back, it's not to get one last look at James O'Rourke's stunning face. The person whose expression I want to see is Clare Duffy's. And I do.

If looks could kill, I'd be pulseless on the floor.

Fuck.

I don't think she'd try to sink my application on the basis of the last few minutes. Not after I've spent five weeks as her personal assistant, hanging on her every word and running all her errands. The past few days, she even started to open up and offer advice. I was sure she planned to recommend me.

The memory of Jamie's strong fingers imprisoning mine raises all sorts of intriguing feelings. They're almost enough to make me not care whether Clare's angry.

Then, as I reach the front door, the reality of my situation comes roaring back. Despite the appeal of his "I'll fuck you senseless" vibe, gorgeous rebel Jamie O'Rourke is completely wrong for me.

There is no way I'll let him, or any guy, get in the way of my entry into the Briar Club. No doubt he'd be an awesome one night stand. But a one night stand isn't worth sabotaging the rest of my life over.

2

JAMIE

I'm ahead five hundred bucks when the game breaks up. The other players offer me a ride home, but I decline.

My motive for joining the poker game tonight wasn't social. I was trying to distract myself from an anniversary that drags my mind to dark places. There's no real escape from the old memories, but counting cards gives my mind short breaks.

Now, play time's over, and I have to face my demons. For that, I need to be alone.

I button my coat as we walk down the driveway. Despite having a Massachusetts driver's license and access to an SUV, in the US, I rarely drive anything other than a motorcycle. I reckoned there was no point getting used to driving on the wrong side of the road since I'd be going home soon enough. That's not how things worked out. I've been in America for more than two years, and my prospects for going home are as grim as ever.

Amidst the goodbyes, Clare catches my sleeve. "You shouldn't walk home. It's freezing out."

"I've got the Jameson's to keep me warm." I wink. "Besides, it's only half a block to the bus stop."

"The bus?" she scoffs. "Seriously? This from a man who carries bundles of cash in his pockets?"

Pulling my sleeve free, I exhale a small laugh. "What can I say? I'm full of contradictions." With a shrug, I stride away. The cold's not troubling me yet, but I don't fancy standing around on the sidewalk, either.

It turns out I meet the six-a.m. bus just as it pulls up to the stop. My timing couldn't be better.

Once on board, I ride toward St. Benedict's, a Catholic church near the southwest edge of campus. God and I are not on the best terms, not for years, but today I need to visit a church.

The short ride gives me a wee minute to wallow in my guilt. I came to America with one purpose in mind. Vengeance. But as my time on this side of the pond stretched on, I had to take a job in my cousin's criminal empire. The work landed me at Granthorpe University in a three-man gangster sleeper cell.

It's a prestigious university and, if you add in my rowing scholarship, from the outside looking in, I seem destined for wealth and success. None of that matters, though. Especially today.

With last night's whiskey wearing off, the corner of my mouth throbs as I exit the bus. I stroll to St. Benedict's and climb the church stairs. Pushing open the heavy wooden door, I'm greeted by a rush of warm, musty air. The dead likely feel at home when they pass through.

It's two hours till morning mass, so I'm alone, and the quiet swallows me up as I dip my fingers in Holy Water and cross myself.

Heading up the left center aisle, I glance at the stained glass windows. My scan stops on the seventh station of the cross where Jesus falls for the second time. I can relate. I came to the States with fresh leads to run down. When they amounted to nothing, I ended up stuck here, on a seemingly endless path of pain and sorrow.

Reaching the front of the aisle, I stand over the votive candles. I light one, the red glass shimmering like blood.

"Hey, Jude, it's me." The whisper is loud in the solemn silence. "I'm thinking about you today." *And every day.*

Normally, I don't talk directly to my brother when lighting a candle for him, but I'm short on the humility necessary to pray.

My attention shifts to the altar. It's been ten years since I sat in another church, miles away, and swore at God under my breath. On that day, with my brother's small coffin filling my vision, I promised God if he didn't avenge Jude, I would.

I didn't really expect God's help. If he'd wanted to give any, there would've been better moments. Like when I was nine and prayed to him with every drop of blood in my heart to help me get to Jude in time.

He didn't help me then or at any point after.

My phone buzzes, and I slide it from my pocket. A text from my housemate, War. He's probably wondering where the fuck I am. When he dropped me off at the pub, I'd told him I'd likely text for a ride around one or two in the morning.

Last night, I only intended to go to the poker game for a couple of hours. But being in the rhythm of drinking and playing cards helped me avoid reliving the details of the day Jude died. I needed the distraction, and time got away from me.

I should respond. Before I answer a friend's text, though, I need to give my young brother his due.

Opening my camera roll, I find a picture of Jude. In this one, he's eleven. The smile he wears is a lie. The picture was taken on his birthday, just fourteen days before he killed himself.

The back of my throat burns, and I swallow against it, ramming down the pain. He held on as long as he could. That's what he wrote.

Taking a wooden stick from the sand next to the candles, I lower the tip into the flame to light the stick. After a moment, I use it to light another candle right next to the first. A pair is always better, so one doesn't have to burn alone.

Closing my eyes, I recite a prayer. I direct it to Mary. She understands how loss can rip a person apart.

After raking open the old wounds, I keep my eyes closed, not wanting to face the day. I blame a lot of people for what happened to Jude. Including myself.

All that's left to do now is make amends. With a blood offering.

Finally opening my eyes, I shove a twenty-dollar bill into the donation slot.

I haven't found him yet, Jude, but I will. It won't be long now.

The last is wishful thinking on my part, but I figure it doesn't hurt to tell Jude that.

If I had to guess, I'd imagine waiting is easier on Jude than on me. After all, he's got nothing but time. Meanwhile, I'm in a self-made purgatory, hunting shadows in a country that's not my own.

Most days, all I want in the world is to go back to the island. To fish and surf and celebrate holidays in our family home. Maybe to row for Ireland in the Olympics. Before I left, I was invited to training camp.

First, though, I have to keep my oath. I can't go back yet, no. I promised the only thing that would stop me from avenging my brother is my own death. So far, God hasn't struck me down or let my enemies get a clear shot at me. It's the one advantage of God's neglect, I suppose.

Trying to shake off the blackness that threatens to choke me, I hustle out of St. Benedict's. The cold air is bracing, which makes it somehow easier to breathe.

On the church steps, I call War McCann. Half Russian and half Irish, he's about as cheerful as a Tolstoy-Frank McCourt mashup would be. His unpleasant disposition is one of the things I like about him.

War answers, sounding gruff as usual. "Where are you?"

"Mission and Main. Walking home."

"I'll roll your way and pick you up."

He's been out all night, too? Or is he coming out to get me? Either way, doesn't matter. I'm tired and I'll take the ride.

"Yeah, grand," I say.

My finger slides over the screen to end the call. Now that I've made it through the night and lit the candles, I'm ready to give up the cold in favor of a warm bed. I'm gonna try to sleep late. The more of the day I can kill with unconsciousness the better.

As the sun rises, salmon color paints the horizon. Too pretty and too pink. Like the girl with cranberry-colored hair and incredible breasts. She's worth a dark thought or two. The v of her tight sweater issued an invitation I hated to pass up. But since I've banned myself from getting laid on the anniversary of Jude's death, I ignored the temptation.

The next time we cross paths, though, she won't get away so easily. Fucking pretty girls is a great way to clear my head. And that one managed to make me laugh and give me a taste of home. No random girl's done that before.

Moving my neck to stretch my sore muscles, I consider the way Cranberry Sauce—*Sawyer*—looked at me. Dilated pupils and parted lips. The kind of look that implies a girl will give over control. Better and fucking better, I thought at the time.

Then again, she refused to keep the poker chip when I urged her to. Was that self preservation or rebellion? Maybe both. If she's rebellious, it'll take a lot more work to get what I want. Which is not a good thing.

I'm too busy to chase. Fun as it might be.

I've got a job, a vendetta, and a training schedule. My best course of action is the one I've been using. Engage in casual one night stands to hold me over between sex dungeon visits.

3

SAWYER

At six-thirty in the morning, I wake for the second time. The first was when my perpetually absent roommate came in around three—nearly giving me a heart attack—and got into the bed she's never slept in before.

At the moment, light streams in through curtains she apparently pushed open. God only knows why she did that. It's Saturday, for fuck's sake. We could've slept in.

Turning onto my side, I stare across the room at her. She's rolled up in her bedspread, facing away from me. Her burrito configuration exposes the mattress, which is bare. She never even bothered to put sheets on the bed.

At least she's still here. Honestly, I half expected Ash to disappear before I woke up... like a member of the fae, which is what she looks like to me. Honey blond hair. Impossibly symmetrical features with high cheekbones, china blue eyes, rosebud lips. She is *freakishly* beautiful. And also quirky and friendly, with an essence seemingly made of smoke. On move-in day, one minute, she was putting knick-knacks on her dresser and chatting up a storm, the next, she was gone for two months.

"Hey?" I say, testing out whether the blazing light has woken her, too.

"Hmm?" The response comes from somewhere deep in her blanket cocoon.

"Are you back?" My voice is hoarse from not having had enough time to wake up.

A slim hand grabs the curtain and pulls it across the window. Thank God.

Ash rolls over to face me. "Oh, hey. Sorry I woke you up and scared you when I came in. Couldn't remember which bed was mine. Did you move the furniture around?"

Around where? The room is too small for any other configuration.

"No."

Looking at the plastic tower of drawers at the end of my bed, she narrows her eyes. "Is there more stuff in here?"

"Uh... No."

As she bursts out laughing, she smacks her heel against the mattress for emphasis. "Wow, I guess it's been too long."

A small smile of acknowledgment forms. "Nine weeks."

She sits up, revealing an oversize black graphic t-shirt with a monster truck emerging from a cloud of dust. "You've had the room all to yourself till now. Would it suck if I wanted to move back in here?"

"*Back* in?" I mumble. "Your bed doesn't even have sheets."

After a shared glance, we crack up laughing.

When the laughter fades, I shrug, still smiling. "It's your room, too. You're still paying for it."

With a shrug and a devilish smirk, she leans forward. "Well, Scotty is anyway." Rolling toward the wall, she digs a giant purse out from where it fell off the bed.

"Scotty?"

"My brother."

"Wow. Your brother's paying your room and board at GU? He must've been *really* impressed when you got in." I feel a pinch of envy over the fact that she has a brother who gives a shit about her future. That's something I'll never have.

"Impressed? Nah, Scotty's a genius, so he takes academic success for granted. He wanted me to come to Granthorpe because it's only a couple of hours from his house."

"So he could keep an eye on you?"

"No. Well, maybe," she says with a smirk. "Big brother vibes for sure. But no, he would've paid for me to go wherever I chose. He just didn't want me to go away because he would've missed me. If he could, Scotty would have the entire family lined up in houses on the same block as his. I tease him he should've been a cult leader so he could start a commune." She laughs merrily and rolls her eyes. "As if."

Her brother wanted her to go to GU because otherwise *he would've missed her.* I can't even imagine that being a factor in a family's decision-making. I'm at Granthorpe because Allendales go to Granthorpe. And they come here because they believe it's the finest university in the country. If I hadn't gotten in, after my expensive prep school education and their investment in a college admissions consultant, the fallout would've been severe.

Ash's hands delve frantically through the contents of her bag and then she lets out a small shriek of joy and holds aloft a package of partially smashed raspberry Zingers. "I'm so hungry." She tears open the plastic wrapper and slides the squished processed pastries free. "Here. Split them with me."

My face scrunches in distaste. "No thanks."

Undeterred by my reaction, she eats all three of them. "So good."

Cocking my head, I flip my hand with flourish. "And so nutritious."

Her eyes twinkle as she smirks at me. "I wish I'd known you were funny."

"Why?"

"I'd have moved in sooner... Or at least split my time."

"Where have you been living?"

"I can't really say." Her tone is breezy as if it's totally normal to be cagey about whether one has chosen to couch surf like a homeless person rather than live in a dorm room that's paid for.

"You can't say because..." I make a "do go on" hand gesture. "You don't know?"

She chokes out a laugh. "No, nothing like that." Her eyes grow wide. "Wow, how wasted do you think I get?"

Sitting up, I look her over. Despite smudged makeup and disheveled hair, she beats most women on their best day. It shouldn't make me more forgiving of her weirdness, but it does. I'm such a sucker for wayward and beautiful. A lingering longing for my bio mom, no doubt. A therapist would have a field day with me.

"Do you like coffee?" Ash asks.

"More than life itself." My deadpan delivery causes her to do a double take.

"Hey, can we just go down and get coffee whenever we want? In the dining hall?"

My brows rise. "As opposed to what? Making reservations?" Is she for real? How does she not know how the dining halls work?

"Okay, cool. Wanna go?" She climbs from the bed wearing an extremely short, puffy white lace skirt. It's halfway to becoming a tutu. Ash scratches her leg before making an attempt to smooth down the skirt's layers. "So freaking itchy. Can't believe I forgot to take this off last night."

"I can't believe you forgot to take it off when you tried it on. What's up with that? You had a *Swan Lake* audition between classes?"

Her chuckles emerge in a staccato rhythm as she turns to her small dresser. "Man, if I could dance like that, I would wear this skirt into the ground. No, I was the worst kid in ballet class. At the Y's rec center, so we're not talking stiff competition." Chuckling again, she shakes her head. "Complete lost cause." Opening her drawers, she finds a pair of print leggings that could induce seizures. "It's cool that I have clean clothes here. Legit helpful."

Even in the slept-in t-shirt and crazy leggings, Ash ends up looking like the cover of a magazine. I grab jeans and a plain v-neck navy sweater. Once dressed, I don't look like I belong in a fashion magazine. Or like I've ever opened one. "Nondescript but never sloppy" is an Allendale signature look, and I've got it down.

As we leave the room, my phone buzzes.

I pull it from my pocket.

APPLICANT ALLENDALE,

I appreciate your efforts the past five weeks and hope you gained valuable insights into the Briar Club and its application process.

With regret, I won't be able to mentor you further as my schedule has become too full. Best of luck with everything.

Regards,
Clare Duffy

MY BODY STIFFENS WITH RAGE.

She promised she'd prep me for all the upcoming events and interviews, and I performed every tedious task that privileged swizzle stick gave me while never once complaining.

Now, after one random flirtation, she's dropped me?

Also, is withdrawing her mentorship as far as she means to go? Because if she wanted to, she could blackball me from the Briar Club. She *is* part of the membership team, after all.

"That fucking bitch."

4

JAMIE

The black SUV pulls up to the curb, and I climb in.

Heat blasts from the vents, and death metal blares from speakers. That's no surprise, but the fact that War's shirtless, too, and has a smudge of blood on his side causes my brows to rise. Not like him to lose a fucking inch in a fight, let alone have clothes destroyed.

At six-foot-six and ripped, War's got the body of a cyborg. If not for his wild black hair making him look like the leader of a motorcycle gang, he'd probably have been recruited by some secret military operation with a codename like Apocalypse.

"Lost mine in a fight," I say. "You?"

"How'd you lose a shirt in a fight? Was someone trying to fuck you?"

Huffing out a mirthless laugh, I take the gun from my inside coat pocket and toss it in the glove box. "You'd have heard from me earlier if I'd shot someone in the head."

It's too bad that wasn't what happened. Burying the body of an asshole would've been a much more satisfying way to end the night.

"So?" War asks. "What happened to your face? If there's somewhere we need to stop before we head home, tell me now."

War's always ready for action. When the bosses send him out for blood, he spills the maximum amount that the situation calls for. My friendship with War has made my own vicious plans feel almost pedestrian.

If I told him about the Jude mission, I wonder if he'd offer to help. That can't happen since we work for an organization that doesn't allow criminal moonlighting, but I'm still curious.

No one can know, I remind myself. *Not even War*.

This has always been something I need to do alone.

Jude and I were alone when he was taken. We were alone when I found him bloody and abused. And we were alone when I found him dead.

Rubbing the back of my neck, I exhale a sigh. "Nowhere to stop. Head home."

War's silent. He's waiting to hear the story from last night. I don't leave him in suspense.

"The fight was with a couple of dickhead frat guys who wouldn't leave my cousin Ash be." I shake my head. "In a bar full of men, that girl's always one second away from some asshole trying to kidnap her."

War's scowl is black and bitter. "What the fuck was she doing in a bar on her own? Bodyguard or locked down. That's it."

My gaze cuts to his profile. When it comes to girls, he never asks questions or renders opinions on how to handle them. He does what he does. And I do the same.

"Who said she was alone? I just said I was there," I counter to his implied accusation that by letting my nineteen-year-old cousin meet up with me for a drink, I'm shirking my responsibilities.

"I don't see her with you now. So, you parted ways sometime."

Despite the American spelling of her Irish name and the fact that she was born and raised in America, Ashling has full Irish blood in her veins. Under the beauty and quicksilver wit, there's a clever girl. Her older brother is a stone-cold killer with over a billion dollars to his name. If either of them thought she needed a twenty-four-seven bodyguard, she'd have one.

My eyes narrow as I study War's face in profile. Ash is a stunner, but I've never seen War give her more than a passing glance. "What's your interest in Ashling?"

There's a moment of silence as War's thumb taps the steering wheel. "We're on campus. The bosses aren't. If something happens to her in a Granthorpe bar, where will the blame fall?"

"If we're there and do nothing, sure. But no one's given us orders to keep an eye on her."

He says nothing more on the subject, but there's something unspoken hanging in the air.

I could choose to take War's words at face value, but our family legacy is pretty fucking consistent. Exceptionally pretty looks were passed down the McAuliff line to Ash's mother and my own. And when someone takes an interest in a girl with those looks, it's rarely casual. Obsession and bloodshed show up far more regularly in the family history than is typical for most.

When we reach our street, the factory that's been converted into a house looks like an asylum as we approach. Old brick. No windows. It's not until War passes the street-side of the building and enters the waterfront parking lot that its true potential can be seen.

As I climb out of the truck, my attention travels to the newly built dock. Our canoe currently rests against the side of the house, but knowing I have a place to launch a boat from the property lifts my mood. I've always loved the water. Just more of the Irish calling to me, I guess.

War carries his coat in his right hand, and I get a first look at the tear in the thigh of his jeans and a white gauze bandage underneath. For fuck's sake. It doesn't seem that his shirt was torn from another guy grabbing it during a fight, as mine was. The gauze means something more sinister went down.

"Did someone knife you?"

"No, caught a stray bullet." His tone is relaxed, but I swallow the news like it's arsenic. While I was nursing old wounds, War was caught without backup and ended up shot.

"I should've been there."

He shrugs. "Wasn't an op."

We work for a crime syndicate called C Crue. My cousin Trick is one of the founders, along with War's uncle Connor who's known as C. They sent three of us to Granthorpe University for an unspecified operation that's still being worked out. Until then, the three of us, War, Killian Callahan, and I are sent on intermittent operations that don't always directly involve the university town. For each operation we've been given, no man works alone. Two or three of us go. Always.

We enter the house through the downstairs door, which means War must be hungry.

"What happened?" I ask.

Just inside the door, War drops his wool coat on the floor. His t-shirt, which is saturated with blood, is crumpled inside. "I need to destroy those in the burn barrel tonight." From his pocket, he pulls a slug, also blood-covered. "Was on my way to a club and stopped in an alley to take a piss. A commotion started at the far end. Couple guys—not college ones, they looked street—were dragging a woman toward a car. Big blonde. Outfitted like a model. She broke away and ran down the alley past me. I didn't get a good look at her because I was focused on other things. Like the guns they had drawn. Russian pistols."

"Jesus. Did you have time to put your dick away?"

"Yeah, and got my gun out. Didn't need to use it, though. Someone on the roof fired at them. A slug ricocheted off the ground. Sliced a groove in my thigh. That's why no shirt. I didn't want blood all over, so I tied my shirt around my thigh."

"You haven't been home, but you're patched up. Did you go to a hospital?"

"No. Killian's."

Killian moved a few weeks ago, but I see him often. Either at rowing practice or when he comes here to our Crue headquarters on campus. As far as I know, War has only been to Killian's place once, when we helped him and his girlfriend move in.

The implication is clear. I wasn't home or reachable, so War was forced to go to Killian's where his girlfriend, a civilian, lives.

"You could've given me a heads-up things were urgent. Your text just asked where I was."

War gives me a bland look before he goes to the fridge. Yeah, that was a stupid thing to say. For War to label something urgent, he'd have to be incapacitated. The likelihood of that happening to him during a bar crawl on campus is nearly impossible.

"At the card game the bosses sent me to, phones were off-limits during play. Next time, fuck that. From here on, if you text, I'll answer immediately."

A nonspecific grunt of acknowledgment rises from behind the fridge door.

Good enough.

I head upstairs. After a stop in the bathroom to brush my teeth and smear some medicated ointment on my lip, I crawl into bed.

Sleep can't come fast enough. But it doesn't. The anniversary of Jude's death is still on my mind.

I close my eyes and try to let go of the thoughts that churn like whitewater. I've been in America over two years and all I've managed to do is eliminate hundreds of possible paths to my target. I've got no idea whether I'm even getting close. I might be weeks away from identifying the bastard. Or I might be decades.

Rubbing the space between my eyes, I concentrate on the inevitable truth, trying again to manage my frustration. This isn't rowing in a 2000-meter heat that's over in seconds. This is an ocean race covering thousands of kilometers. The mindset is different. As it must be.

5

SAWYER

"Who's a fucking bitch?" Ash curses with such innocent nonchalance it takes my brain a minute to catch up.

Ash doesn't wait for my answer. Instead, she walks down the hall, apparently sure I'll follow as I respond. I do the first, but remain quiet on the second. I'm hesitant to go on record trash-talking someone with power in my life. You never know who's friends with whom. Calling out someone's bad behavior can backfire.

To Ash's credit, she doesn't press as I remain silent. Running my hand along the ivory wainscoting trim as we walk, a part of me wishes she would, though. I'm upset and that makes me want to talk.

Our residence hall is the newest on campus and parts of it look more like a boutique hotel than a college dorm. In the elegant elevator, there's a large framed mirror. Considering how ragged we look most of the time as we head downstairs for breakfast, I'm not sure the mirror was the best idea.

Once inside, Ash bumps her arm against mine, reminding me

she's there. It's more reassuring than obtrusive, and I find myself desperate to spill the tea.

There's something refreshingly friendly and open about Ash. She doesn't seem the type to stab anyone in the back.

"Between us?" I ask, breaking down.

Her sparkly blue eyes lock with mine, and she nods. "For sure."

"So, I applied—actually, it's more like I'm pledging—this woman's club. Anyone who makes it through the initial screening is assigned an upperclassman mentor from the club. Mine used me nonstop as a personal assistant, which I accept. It's probably standard practice. But in return, she was supposed to help me prepare for things. Like after getting to know me, she suggested the theme for my second-phase essay, which was helpful—"

"Essay?" Ash's brows crinkle as she makes a face of distaste. "What kind of club assigns essays?"

"One that takes itself *very* seriously." My tone is grim, though to be fair, I'm not pissed at the entire club, just Clare fucking Duffy. "It was formed like a hundred years ago in answer to the male-only clubs on campus. It's called the Briar Club, and it leads the nation in the number of alumnae in high-ranking government positions and corporate C-suites."

I sigh, dropping my head back against the elevator wall. "My mom—a U.S. congressman—was a member. She wanted this for me. And my family expects me to get in. If I don't... Well, it won't be good." I grimace, thinking about warnings I've gotten about not measuring up to Allendale standards.

"Oh, wow." Ash reaches over and squeezes my arm, her grip surprisingly strong.

We're close to the same height. I'm five-five. She's probably five-seven. But she's willowy like a fairy, and I'm built like a mortal who occasionally eats a cheeseburger and fries.

"You said she wanted this for you? Past tense?" Ash tilts her head as she studies me. "You lost your mom?"

I actually lost two moms, but I'd never admit that out loud to another GU student. "Yes, my mom died."

"My dad," she says, touching her chest. "I was little." She shrugs her slim shoulders and then shakes her head. "Anyway, I heard a rumor GU is trying something where they match up freshman roommates with similar major life events."

"Really?" For some reason, the idea hits me in the gut like a punch. My background and family circumstances are my own business.

"Sorry." Ash grimaces sympathetically. "Does that make things weird and morbid?"

"No. But if they're running a psychology experiment with us as subjects, that is not cool. Seems like we should be able to opt in or out of that kind of matchmaking."

"Yeah, big institutions are sketchy. Especially this one." She blows out a breath. "I knew that going in."

In the dining hall, which is full of fall wreaths that create cravings for pumpkin spice, Ash spots the shelves of small plastic containers of Nutella and lets out a gasp. "Look at these!" She grabs two containers and a small bag of pretzels. "Are these on the meal plan?" The amount of wonder in her voice is comical.

A slow smile curves the corners of my mouth. "Haven't you been in any of the dining halls?"

"Not really." Her focus remains locked on the shelves. "Wow, I am so happy right now. Say what you will about their sketchy psych experiments, but the bougie GU dining halls are aces." Ash makes herself a coffee and congratulates herself on going to a school where peppermint mocha creamer is readily available before turning back to me. "So finish your story about the fucking bitch."

"There's not much to tell." I pour coffee into a to-go cup, adding nothing. The dining hall uses good beans, I'll give them that. "I played the part of this woman's minion for weeks. And then when some guy she's interested in paid attention to me, she dropped me as her advisee."

Ash's brows rise. "That's bullshit."

"I know." The bitterness in my voice isn't something I even try to hide.

Ash gulps down some coffee and licks her lips.

"It's a problem if I'm on her hit list. I probably need to reach out to try to smooth things over." My fists tighten reflexively at my sides. I'd rather swallow broken glass than grovel, but a "big picture" view of my life might call for it.

"Can I say something about this?" Ash's voice is gentle and earnest. Exactly what I probably need at the moment but not what I want. I'm craving outrage, emphasis on the rage.

"I guess so."

"When I was little, one of my so-called friends stabbed me in the back. She invited me to Disney World and got me all excited and then said she couldn't take a friend after all, because their travel plans had changed. The truth was that she took another girl instead, for a completely bullshit reason having to do with jealousy. I was so upset. I was fucking seven and thought I was going to meet Elsa from Frozen. And then I wasn't." Ash grits her teeth like the betrayal still stings and I find myself leaning in, surprised by her sudden ferocity—and loving it.

She taps a fingernail against the side of a Nutella container. "Anyway, my brother told me something that has always stuck with me. Scott said, 'This is good. Now you know she's not your friend. You can stop wasting time on her and get on with finding real ones.' Of course, at the time, I was a crybaby—'But I wanted to go to meet Elsa.' And he said, 'You are going. When school's out, *I'll* take you. Fuck that little traitor.'"

My jaw drops, and I choke out a laugh. "He actually said 'fuck that little traitor?' About a seven-year-old girl?"

She laughs. "I know, right? He's the best."

"I—you're not a GU legacy, are you?"

"God, no." She winks at me, looking like she relishes the fact that she's from what the Allendales would consider inferior stock.

"Are you on scholarship? I know you said your brother's paying for the dorm, but—"

"No scholarships. We're what the Mayflower kids would call *nouveau riche*." Her smirk is priceless, then it disappears as her eyes widen. "Wait, did your family come over on the Mayflower? If so, no offense. You seem cool."

I shake my head, inwardly pleased anyone could even make that mistake. The irony. "No, and no offense taken."

"Sorry, when it comes to my family, I'm 'ride or die' and I have a pathological need to prove it. Scotty's never gonna say 'fuck that little traitor' about me." She winks again and takes a two-ounce quinoa and cranberry salad from the grab-and-go cooler.

Having "ride or die" people in my life is what I'd kill for. I'm so sick of polite, pearl-wearing backstabbers. For a moment, I'm speechless as it sinks in that maybe GU's morbid roommate-matchmaking experiment is right on the money.

"Anyway, getting back to you," Ash says. "I've got my brother's take on things. When it comes to the girl from the club, best to know who your enemies are up front."

It's immensely satisfying to meet someone who allows herself to speak passionately and without remorse. Ash seems a bit insane, but in a way, that makes me want to be around her more, not less.

After we check out with our food, I say, "An enemy, huh? I wouldn't have labeled Clare that way, but maybe I should."

"Having enemies is time-consuming, but then you can plan."

That makes me laugh. "What are you doing today? Want to hang out?"

Ash tilts her head, assessing me. "I one hundred do."

Does that mean a hundred percent? Seems like it.

"Cool. Me, too."

She sips more coffee and gives me the side-eye. "After I shower, I've gotta check on some guys. It shouldn't take long, but it's priority one. You up for a ride-along?"

As opposed to bailing on the first person on campus I've been able to laugh with? So I can sit alone in a tiny dorm room, sulking? No way.

"Sure, Ash, whatever." I press the elevator's call button. "What does 'check on some guys' mean?"

"My cousin got into a fight last night. Protecting me, actually. Which was totally off book since I was supposed to be the one supporting him. Anyway, I need to show concern and take him a breakfast taco or something."

I stare at her perfect face, stunning blue eyes, and blond hair. "Your cousin who got in the fight, what's his name?"

"Jamie O'Rourke."

For fuck's sake.

6

JAMIE

"The fuck?" War's voice roars from down the hall a second after alerts begin blaring from our phones.

Other than War, Killian and myself, only our bosses and my cousin have the security code. We need to get up.

Far more quickly than I want to move at this hour, I pull on a pair of jeans and stride out of my room, meeting War in the hall. He's wearing a pair of black boxer-briefs and has an automatic pistol behind his back. His shoulder-length black hair looks like a crow's nest in a Tim Burton movie.

I note the bandage wrapped around his thigh before he tosses me a gun, and we head down the steps.

Here's hoping the interloper is one of the bosses dropping in unannounced to check on the state of us after we reported in about the fight and gunfire last night. Because the alarm doesn't sound in the whole place, someone entering might not realize it's armed.

Downstairs, instead of finding Crue leadership, War and I are met with a pair of pretty girls in the first-floor kitchen. One is my cousin Ash.

The other is Cranberry Sauce.

I tuck my gun into the back of my jeans before they see it.

"Hey," Ash says, her eyes dropping to War's leg. "Pull a hammy?"

War glares at her, which causes Sauce to step back. Ash, on the other hand, could hold an ice cube in her hand without it melting. She is that much a C Crue boss's little sister.

War turns, shifting his arm to keep his gun out of sight. As he passes me, he says, "Get them the fuck out."

"Charming, as usual," Ash says, searching through the kitchen cabinets as though she lives with us.

My gaze locks on Sawyer's navy sweater, which is stretched out in all the right places. I'd gladly blow off sleep today to unveil the contents of her clothes. Dragging my eyes away from temptation, I return them to my blood relation. "What are you doing here, Ash?"

"Got it." From beneath the quartz-topped island, she holds up a pair of cookie sheets "Brought some dough for rhubarb scones. You like scones, right?" She inclines her head at a bag of pre-made dough.

Touching the edge of my lip to be sure it hasn't started to bleed again, I sigh. "We were out all night, Ash. So, a visit before eight am makes me want to tell you what you can do with your scones." I keep my voice low. I'm tired, but I'm not raging. Ash is a friend, as well as a cousin. Also, while no one has ever said it would be unwise to be rude to her, she's a favorite of two of our straight-up gangster bosses.

Ash tosses her hair over her shoulder. "C'mon, James. No one told you and the minotaur to stomp down here. I was gonna make these magically delicious scones for you and put them in a container so they'd be fresh when you woke up."

"Yeah, right." I shake my head with a disgruntled expression. "Because you expected us to stay in bed while the house was infiltrated." She knows better.

Ash pauses to stare at me with a skeptical expression. "I

didn't think the security system was on. How did you even know?"

"We always know." I circle around the island to where Sawyer stands. "Morning, Cranberry Sauce. Didn't realize you and my cousin were friends. How did that happen?"

The expression in her brown eyes suggests she wants to dismantle me. I would very much like to see her try. A struggle of that kind would end with her naked and trapped beneath me.

Her brows wrinkle suspiciously, as though she can read my thoughts. "Roommates."

"Roommates?" Looking between the two of them, I say, "Since when?"

Ashling is practically a gypsy with her souped up 1969 Camaro as her caravan as she bounces between residences, staying with friends who live off campus. Ash refuses to live in a dorm room because freshmen aren't allowed to have cars on campus, and "her car is her life." Leaning toward dramatic, that's my cousin.

"Since now," Ash says cheerfully. "How are you feeling?"

My eyes cut to her. "Grand." The sarcastic edge in my tone can't be missed, and she doesn't miss it. Pulling out a chair at the island, I sit.

Sawyer smells like berries and spice, and in a perfect world, she—far more than scones—is what I would like to have for breakfast.

In the middle of dropping dough onto a baking tray, Ash's brows rise. "Go back to bed, Jamie. Sorry I woke you up." Her tone is unusually flat, proving there's a darker edge beneath Ash's bright surface.

I give her a meaningful look. "Can't go to bed with guests in the house. What would the relatives say?"

Ash glances fleetingly at her new friend and then back at me, finally taking my meaning.

This house doesn't belong to me. It's Crue property, and War and I are responsible for keeping its secrets. Leaving Ash's friend to be supervised by her alone is not happening. The girl might force open the wrong closet door and find an illegal arsenal.

"You know, the dough will keep." Ash ties a twist around the bag and sets it in the fridge. Then she dumps the uncooked dough from the pan into the trash. Yeah, dramatic.

"Aw." With a frown, Sawyer gives me a disapproving look. "You're like a bad penny."

Raising a brow at the challenge in her tone, I reply in kind. "Is that so?"

"Yeah, it is." She doubles down by narrowing her eyes at me. "Your girlfriend Clare abandoned me to my fate over your bad behavior. Now, your cousin brings fresh, handmade pastry dough to bake for you, and you bounce her? You look like a gold medallion, O'Rourke, but no way. Straight up bad penny.' When her full lower lip pushes out in a quasi pout, I want to bite it. Is she fucking French? In my experience, American girls don't know how to pout.

"I don't have a girlfriend. And if I did, it would not be Clare Duffy."

She shrugs, causing the contents of her sweater to work on my groin. For fuck's sake, why did God give a pain-in-the-ass girl tits like that?

"Are you fishing for my help?" My gaze moves to her mouth again. "If so, offer me better bait."

"Am I *fishing*?" She leans closer. Another wave of the spicy berry perfume hits me, to full erotic effect.

"Whoa," Ash interjects. "Hang on." She frowns at Sawyer. "The enemy declared herself because of a crush on my cousin?"

What enemy? Does Ash mean Clare Duffy?

"That's something you should've shared, roomie." Ash turns her frown on me. "And, Jamie?"

It takes a moment for me to peel my eyes from Sawyer to look at Ash. "What?" My tone lacks its usual friendliness.

"I know this is a bad day," Ash says softly.

I'm thrown off kilter for a moment, until what she means sinks in. In a warning tone, I say, "Ashling—"

"Never mind," she murmurs, grabbing her luggage-sized purse and then Sawyer's arm. "Sorry again for waking you."

With a sharp tug on her friend, Ash pulls Sawyer away and marches them both to the door and out.

I rise and circle the island to watch as they walk to Ash's car. Neither girl looks back, so points to them for acting like they don't give a shit. A bit of guilt hits me over causing Ash to leave in a temper. The other one, though...

The Camaro's motor roars to life, loud enough to wake the fish at the bottom of the river.

As the car zooms out of the parking lot, I smirk. Should I have used some restraint in front of my female cousin? Probably. But Sawyer's the best distraction I've ever had on this fucking anniversary. Which makes her difficult to resist.

I don't intend to pursue her in the conventional sense. No time.

But am I going to back off if she's in my own damn house? Not while I have a set of working balls.

7

SAWYER

As Ash pulls out of the lot, she purses her lips between her teeth and shakes her head. "So... *that* was awkward."

The tension in my roommate's usually "devil may care" posture makes me annoyed at myself. *And* at the golden boy. I like Ash and don't want her to disappear again.

"Agreed. Sorry. But why *couldn't* he have just gone back to bed?" I scoff. "You're his cousin. Did he expect us to loot the place?"

Her small smile is gratifying.

"Not that I wasn't tempted." I hold up my index finger like I'm making a note to go back to rob it. "That place is incredible."

Ash's grin widens. "You should've seen the before pictures and the upstairs. It was originally a rundown factory. Rusted equipment with jagged edges all over the ground floor, as in 'welcome to your highest risk of getting tetanus ever.'"

Glancing back in the house's direction, I ask, "You said something about it being a bad day for him?" I grimace, immediately regretting having asked the question. "Never mind." James

O'Rourke is trouble, and no one needs to know I'm interested in him because I shouldn't be.

Ash draws in a big breath, looking pensive. "Jamie wouldn't want me to talk about it with someone outside the family, so I've gotta hold back a little." Ash swivels the wheel to take us into a residential neighborhood. "How interested in Jamie are you?"

With a shrug, I peer out the passenger window to avoid eye contact. "I don't know him, so not very."

"He's interested in you," she says firmly. Her head bobs in a nod.

An annoying ripple of satisfaction runs through me.

"Though," she continues, her tone less certain now. "I can't tell if that was him falling into his usual routine or something more." Her thumb taps the steering wheel. "When he and I hang out, it's usually in a pub, and he's not hitting on anyone because I'm there. But a couple of times I've gone into a bar where he's out with his friends, and from across the room, he seems like a player."

"I'm sure he is one." I say it as if I'm some kind of expert. Which I'm not. At all. The boys at my prep school were no playboys. They were kind of clueless, actually, including the ones I dated.

Ash gives my shoulder a playful shove, before returning her hand to the gearshift. "You're *sure*? How are you sure?"

"Because he said he doesn't have a girlfriend. Someone who looks like you guys do is never without a girlfriend or boyfriend except by choice."

A slow smile spreads across her face. "Things aren't always as easy as people think. Plus, Jamie and I are different. Pretty sure he's got game. I don't. I'm actually kind of a misfit toy. Though, a decently pretty one, I guess, thanks to DNA."

Decently pretty? Insane understatement.

She pulls up to the curb of a candy-pink Victorian with white trim that looks as though Historical Barbie should come with it.

Blowing a strand of hair from her eyes before tucking it back, Ash turns toward me. "I need to ask for a bullshit favor."

"Go ahead."

Ashling's fall-festive rose gold nails with leaf decals catch my eye as she taps the gearshift. I really need to find a salon around here before Thanksgiving. Because of Briar Club, doing my own manicures doesn't cut it anymore. And beyond that, my grandmother will notice immediately if my appearance isn't up to snuff when I visit. She didn't want them to adopt me, so she's quick to point out my shortcomings in that grim "I told you so" tone.

A small pang hits me in the stomach. Holiday facials and manicures were something Mom and I always did together. Usually before the annual winter shopping trip. Purchasing a few new "Allendale appropriate" outfits and hand bags were *necessary*. One could not show up to Thanksgiving in the big house looking like a slouchy student.

Ash bites the corner of her lip and finally admits, "I need to go in alone. You okay waiting out here?"

"Sure, no problem." I reach for my phone in my pocket. "I've got an assignment due Monday that I've been meaning to submit. I'll log in on my phone." I gesture to the house. "Take your time."

"Awesome. Be right back." Ash hops out of the car and slams the door closed before running up onto the porch.

I turn in my Poli Sci assignment and jot some notes on a Philosophy paper I need to write but become distracted when two men, dressed completely in black and sporting buzzed hair and five-o'clock-shadows, pass in front of the car.

Something about them gives me pause. They aren't young hoodlums. They're more put together than that and are maybe in their thirties. It's the swagger and the scowls. And how they're walking toward the house like they mean business. *Bad* business.

Unsure if I've seen too many thrillers or if there's real cause for concern, I lean across and honk the horn in warning.

The men slow and look back at me. My stomach drops. Oh

yeah, I was right to be worried. No one's eyes are that dark unless they've seen some stuff. And done bad things.

Holding their stares, I lock myself in, and then depress the horn again. Longer this time.

The front door opens and my anxiety is further justified when, after a glance at the men who are still distracted by my honking, Ash slams it shut.

The men jump into action, wrenching open the screened storm door and shoving themselves against the solid door behind it.

Holy shit.

Thankfully, Ash must've managed to secure it in time, and it holds.

A loud thud cuts through the air as one of them slams the sole of his boot against the door. I jerk, my phone bobbling from my hands and landing at my feet.

I grab for it just as the sound of wood splintering sends chills down my spine.

My fingers fumble over my phone's screen, desperately trying to call 911.

But just as I manage to bring up the keypad, a bang against the driver's side door causes me to jump and jerk my head up.

Ash.

She's here and safe. She must have gone out the back door and raced around the house.

Because it's a classic car without power locks, I dive across to pull the button up to unlock the driver's door. She's quick to get in, but by the time she puts the car in gear, the men have seen her and are running toward us.

Ash throws the car into reverse, backs up half a foot, slams the brakes, and then puts the car in drive. Careening down the street, it's like a Nascar race.

We make a hard left, and it feels as though the passenger wheels leave the ground.

I'm no longer breathing. All my energy is concentrated on staying in my seat and not interfering with Ash's ability to drive.

Eyes flicking back and forth between the rearview mirror and the road in front of us, Ash leaves the residential area at about seventy miles an hour and bursts onto a highway. We weave in and out of traffic, crossing lanes as though we're in a video game.

This is crazy.

Ash downshifts to avoid rear-ending an SUV and then peers in the rearview mirror, as if to plan her next high-speed maneuver. "All good." Her grip on the gearshift eases, the tension leaving her.

I look over my shoulder and don't spot the men behind us.

Dropping back against the seat, Ash turns down the street we drove this morning. The one leading to the waterfront building where her cousin and his roommate live.

Within moments we're sitting in their small back parking lot, completely out of view from the street because of the big factory building.

The river looks serene and quiet, but even if it was full of white caps, I wouldn't hear the roar. Not because of the powerful motor still humming under the hood, but because of my own heartbeat banging louder than all the hundreds of cylinders and horses of the Camaro's engine.

Ash scans the area. "We'll give it a minute. I didn't see them following us. Their sedan was halfway down the block." She studies her manicure, as if wondering if she needs a new set. "And I drove away pretty quick."

"You don't say." I'm surprised by my dry tone, but it's as if her unconcerned demeanor has fooled my brain into thinking that nothing is out of the ordinary.

I'm not the only one surprised; Ash bursts out laughing at my response and then winks. "Still wanna spend the day with me, Sawyer?"

"I don't know." My tone is deadpan, but I'm questioning things. Taking a deep breath, I run my hands down my thighs, trying to rid myself of the shakes now that my brain has decided I'm not facing imminent death. "Who are you really? CIA Barbie?"

That makes Ash put her head back against the headrest as she laughs. "That settles it. Jamie can't have you because you're mine."

My brows furrow as my heart finally remembers how to beat at a normal rate. "In all seriousness though, what's the deal? Who were those guys?" I bite my lip. "If you're a drug dealer or involved in something illegal, I can't be a part of it. My family would—"

"I'm not a drug dealer." Ash rests a hand on my shoulder, and for some reason, I believe what she says. "And those guys are not after me. They're looking for my friend. Who is *also* not a drug dealer." She holds my eye. "No drugs."

I nod, signaling I accept that as truth. "So then, who were those guys?"

She drops her hand, looking out toward the river. "I'm not totally sure." She sucks on her lower lip for a few seconds before shaking off her uncertain expression and navigating the car back onto the street. This time at speeds of closer to ten miles an hour. It's quite a change. "The girl I was staying with said she was in some kind of trouble, but I don't know the details."

I watch Ash, noticing the way her brow furrows and her hands tighten on the wheel. "You're not sure, but you must have a theory."

Ash's shoulders lift. "No, but those guys looked..." She cocks her head thoughtfully. "It's possible they're Russian Mafia from New York."

Russian Mafia?! I continue to stare at her, unblinking. "What?"

"But don't worry about it." Pulling to a stop at an intersection, she looks both ways before moving forward again. "We're not going back. The girl renting the house left town. She told me she was planning to." Ash drops a hand to the gearshift. "Now that she's gone, they'll leave, too. So, all good."

It doesn't feel all good. It feels off. "If she was a student, how could she just leave town in the middle of term?"

"I don't think she was enrolled this semester. She's the older sister of a high school friend. I was sometimes crashing at her place because it's off campus, so I could use my car." Looking over at me, she inclines her head for emphasis. "We weren't close."

We drive in silence. Part of the reason I like Ash is because she's so refreshingly different from everyone I know. On the other hand, I can't afford any guilt-by-association connections. During the short ride, I watch the passing houses as I battle myself over whether to pull back from the friendship.

Ash parks beside the local coffee shop, Espresso Yourself. Turning to me, she flicks her hair over her shoulder. "I'm gonna run in and grab us both a pumpkin spice latte. We earned it."

Still processing the surreal events of the past hour, I stare at her.

Finding me speechless, she winks at me. "Be right back, Seesaw."

"Wait." I shake my head, ridding my mind of all the things that I can't figure out. "What did you call me?"

"Your nickname." She tilts her head, looking one hundred percent like a typical pretty college student and nothing like the death-defying stuntman from fifteen minutes ago. "Cranberry Sauce is too long. C-Sau for short. It's better." Without waiting for a response, Ash climbs from the car and heads into the coffee shop.

So, she's adopted Jamie's nickname for me... Inexplicably, that makes me feel closer to her. And I can't deny that her breeziness is like breathing fresh air.

Still seems risky to be around her, though.

Get out of the car and start walking, I tell myself.

My movements are robotic as I open the car door, shut it and shuffle toward the sidewalk. Toward the bus stop that will take me back to the dorms, and away from thugs and high-speed chases.

And yet, like a lunatic, I bypass the oncoming bus and the line waiting to get on. Instead, I join my new friend, and possible criminal associate, in line for a much needed dose of caffeine. "Hey, I don't like pumpkin spice."

"So, *you're* the one."

Unbidden, a small smirk emerges on my face. She really might be a fucking faery. In books, they're always irresistible.

Pointing at the chalkboard menu, she wiggles her finger. "How about a peppermint mocha?"

I nod.

"Sorted." She links her arm around mine companionably. "After this, let's go get our nails done."

Since losing Mom, I haven't had anyone to get manicures with. A warm wave of nostalgia washes over me. And just like that, I'm glad I didn't get on the bus.

8

JAMIE

At two in the afternoon, I drag myself out of bed and head to the training center. Three other rowers meet me at the pool. The guys are loud and rowdy. A late night, a hangover, and the Jude anniversary slow me down, but muscle memory kicks in once I get moving.

Growing up, the water was always the best place for me. When you're in the Irish Sea—or even seaside as a lifeguard—you have to be vigilant. It was then that I was most free of my guilt. The times I had to focus attention elsewhere were the only thing that kept me from beating my head against the wall in my teens when my anger unhinged me.

Later, I learned to harness and channel my rage into violence, and things improved. It's ironic that, as I became more of a menace, I must've seemed calmer to the outside world.

Ten laps in, I begin to dominate and win our races. The others are just as strong and fit, but I'm more efficient. My experience fighting currents was a training like no other. Nature never wears out. I learned to make the most of every stroke and how to recover quickly during moments of rest. In a rip current, there's no place for doubt. Pain and fatigue are things to be managed. So you can keep fucking going.

A good metaphor for a troubled life.

I find my rhythm and swim so long I'm the last one in the pool. Counting strokes drops me into a meditative zone where I'm dissociated from the burn in my muscles or lungs.

When someone calls my name and draws me out, I wonder again if what I feel in the water is anything like what submissives feel when they reach subspace. From things some have explained about it, I think it might be.

After a shower, we emerge from the center as a group. There's talk of going for food and one of the guys' girlfriends is bringing a friend.

I'm always in the mood for company, if only to help drown out dangerous thoughts, but there's a text from War. He has to go to Boston for work and plans to stop in a dungeon on the way back. I'm tempted to go along. Wild sex is another great way to distract myself, and I was already celibate yesterday in observance of Jude's loss.

Before I can reply, someone steps into my personal space. A cloying perfume overwhelms my senses, and I look up. Clare Duffy's standing a few inches away.

"Ride with me to Bruno's, Jamie. I've got a proposition for you."

Oh, hell. Clare's the friend. Hard pass.

One of my teammates gives me a wave as he and his girlfriend head toward the parking lot, probably thinking he's done a good deed by leaving me with the clever girl whose family has Irish roots. It's a shame I'm not attracted to Clare because she's after me like a queen bee looking to colonize her hive.

My tone is less than pleased when I respond. "What are you doing here, Clare?"

Her thin brows rise over green eyes that are set a fraction too far forward. She studies me in cool assessment with her bug eyes. "My friend and I were working on club business, and she mentioned dinner with her boyfriend and some of his teammates. Is my being here a problem?"

The challenge in her voice is a mistake. Not that she had a chance of getting anywhere with me anyway. Razor sharp banter is fun during a poker game, but it doesn't get my dick hard.

"The Briar Club business you were working on, was that to do with incoming members?"

I've been wondering what Ash meant when she said a girl with a crush on me declared herself as Cranberry Sauce's enemy.

There's the tiniest hesitation before Clare speaks. "No." *She's lying.* "Event planning," she adds firmly.

"Hmm. The girl you had helping out at the game last night, she's a potential member, right? How long until she's fully in?"

Clare's expression hardens. "Induction into the club is very limited. Only five percent of applicants make it through both rounds of screening."

"But she's got you as an advisor, right?" I cock my head, appraising her. "I bet the ones you choose make it through."

She stares in the direction the others have gone. "So, about dinner... I'm hungry and you must've worked up an appetite. Let's head to my car."

"I drove here."

Her eyes widen. "I thought you didn't drive?"

"Little known fact," I say with a shrug. "So, about Sawyer. You're not dropping your support for her, are you?"

Clare's expression shutters. "As I said, I'm hungry. I hope you'll be at the tavern. There's something I want to discuss." With that she stalks away.

If petty jealousy wasn't what drove Clare to drop Sawyer, Clare probably would've pointed out some of her shortcomings to me just now. From the look on her face at my bringing Cranberry Sauce up, Clare cut ties with Sawyer on impulse for the exact reason Sawyer suspects.

Normally, I've got no interest in this kind of petty shite. But there are reasons I might decide to take an interest. Because *she* —Cranberry Sauce—interests me.

I get in the truck and let out a slow breath.

C Sauce is a poor prospect for me if my cousin plans to strike up a close friendship with her. The rough way I'd like to use her means things could get messy. And I don't have time to deal with complicated situations.

Plus, there are plenty of other attractive women on campus. And in the Boston dungeon.

Right, stay focused. No messing about with Sawyer.

That settled, I bail on dinner with the team and pick up food on the way home for War and me. We'll eat and then head to the sex club.

9

SAWYER

Ash and I sit on couches in the lounge, hanging before dinner. We're both on our phones, but she's the only one of us who's having fun. I'm keeping tags on Briar Club socials.

One of the women from the club posts a picture of members of the rowing team near an indoor pool. The caption is *when swim team is away row team can play. #gurow*

In the shot's background, Jamie seems to have just climbed out of the pool because water streams down his perfect form. *Jesus, he's beautiful.*

Wait, does this mean he's on the rowing team? Because then, my family would not object to him in any way. Rowing crew is the only sport they care about. When my brother made the GU team, they threw a party.

After the pool photo, the girl posts a carousel of pics that includes a group at Bruno's Tavern. In one of them, Clare Duffy's making a duck face. I scour the pics for another glimpse of Jamie, but I'm disappointed to find he's not in them.

Next in my feed, Clare posts an image, which is something

she rarely does. The vibe from her socials is that she's too busy to attend to them much. Her pic is an off kilter shot of her Briar Club cuff bracelet that has briar roses with their thorns etched into the gold. The caption is *hate when would be briars think they can get away with things. i love proving them wrong.*

I reread the words, my body stiffening. Is she talking about me?

Trying not to freak out from a fit of paranoia, I scan the tavern images again. I'm hunting for any prospective Briar Club inductees that might be nearby. I'm praying some other girl pissed Clare off.

After rising from the couch, I start to pace.

"What's wrong, Seesaw?"

"What?" My movements are jerky as I turn toward Ash.

"You're looking pale. What's up?"

I rub the pinched skin between my brows, trying to drag myself back from the edge of panic. "I think Clare Duffy from the Briar Club might have it out for me now, which—"

The world fades as my eyes unfocus from my intense concentration. Clare and Jamie were together. If so, did he mention I'd been at his place this morning and imply I'm making a run at him?

Because I'm not paying attention as I pace, my leg bangs against the edge of a low table, making me stumble. *Fuck.* Catching myself before I land on my knees, I have to release my phone, which clatters across the tabletop.

"Whoa!" Ash shoots to her feet and grabs my arm to steady me.

"I'm okay," I say, focusing on Ash's concerned face.

Her grip is surprisingly strong as she pulls me to the couch. "Sit, Seesaw."

Dropping onto the cushions with a *thwap*, I touch my forehead. I'm surprised it's not covered in sweat.

As if on cue, I get a text from Clare. She wants to know who I've been discussing private club business with.

Sucking on my lower lip, I try to decide how to respond. What I'd really like to do is talk to her face to face. Maybe I could smooth things over before she decides to destroy my chances.

I look over at Ash. "More Clare Duffy trouble."

"Fuck's sake." Ash scowls. "What now?"

When I don't answer, she cocks her head. "Why do you want to be in that club anyway? Sounds like a pretentious drag."

"It's a really big deal to my family. My mom and grandmother were members." I lick my lips, picking up steam. "Becoming a Briar is critical for me. It's not just that I need to prove something to the older members of my family—which I very much do because my grandparents expect it and they decide—" I bite off my words, hands shaking. Ash doesn't need to know everything. "It's also my last connection to my mom," I whisper.

Tears burn in my eyes as I try to blink them away. "She used to put her beautiful vintage Briar Club bracelet on my wrist when I was little and tell me about how she'd had big dreams and made them come true. She said I would do the same." I swallow. "My older brother is the one everyone else pins their hopes on, but my mom believed in me. *Completely.*" My breath stutters out of me. "In the beginning, I had some problems and she's the only reason I've made it this far. I don't want to call my getting into the club her dying wish, but... I need to do this."

Ash's face takes on a determined expression. "Okay, understood."

"Look, I want to go to Bruno's Tavern to talk to Clare before she says something she can't take back and ruins my chances for good. Can you drive me?"

"Shit, I've got a video call with my brother to talk about my mom's birthday in half an hour. We could go right after."

"I can't wait." I shoot to my feet and Ash follows. "I don't know how long she'll be there. Plus, she could be trash-talking me right now." The last words explode from my lungs like I'm trumpeting them.

Ash's eyes widen to saucers, then she gives me a tight side hug. "It's okay. Calm down. Can you drive a stick?"

My brows rise. Ash's car is her baby and she barely knows me. "I can, but... Are you sure?"

"Yep. I've got you." She grabs my hand and pushes her keys into my palm.

With a rush of emotions, I throw my arms around her, hugging her in a way I haven't hugged anyone in years. "Thank you so much."

"If you can, try to be chill when you talk to the bitch. A shark who smells blood in the water just wants to feed more. Be calm, okay? And maybe imply—lightly and with a friendly smile—that you have powerful friends who will not take it well if she fucks with you. That should buy some time."

Blinking, I open and close my mouth. I'm about to say I'm not sure I'm good enough to bluff Clare who's a poker player, but then I stiffen my spine. I will be convincing because I have to be. "Right."

"Good. You've got this."

I nod as she squeezes my arms in support, making me want to hug her all over again. Then, she turns me toward the doors and gives me a small push.

Once I've zipped my coat to my chin, I hustle out to the parking lot.

Even in the low light, the Camaro's gorgeous bright red paint gleams. The thick white racing stripes on the hood are blocky and retro and seem to be trying to push me toward ballsy confidence as I get behind the wheel.

"I've got this." I whisper the words over and over like a mantra.

It's a quick drive to the tavern, but the parking lot is full. When I see someone pulling out, I pause in the aisle to take their place. Then I recognize the elegant, eggshell-colored sedan and its driver. Clare Duffy is leaving.

Fuck, I'm too late.

In an instant, I backtrack on my thinking. At least she's not inside cutting me down to other Briars. And I haven't gotten any texts telling me I've been removed from consideration, so that's a decent sign I hope.

I'd really like to know what's going on.

I scrutinize the area, looking for the black SUV from Jamie's place. Not finding it, I press my lips into a thin line.

After I park, I head inside. But I don't spot anyone I know in the tavern and head out just as quickly.

Now what?

Go after Clare? No, because she lives in the Briar Club house, and I don't want people asking why I'm showing up to request an emergency meeting.

Instead, I send a text, asking if I can speak with her.

Clare ignores me. As time ticks by, I grow more agitated.

Maybe the best person for me to talk to isn't Clare. Jamie was with these people tonight. He not only knows what he and Clare discussed, he probably overheard whatever she said to the others.

Pulling out of Bruno's parking lot, I exhale a breath I've been holding.

I'm going to see *him*.

༺༻

JAMIE

MY BELIEF THAT MY EVENING ACTIVITIES ARE SET IS SHORT-lived. When I arrive at the house, Ashling's Camaro is parked in the lot. And worse, as I pull up beside it, I see it isn't Ash in the driver's seat.

For fuck's sake. Sawyer, the stuff of wet dreams, climbs out of the Camaro just as I throw open my door.

As I round the hood, she eyes me the way one would a dangerous animal. "Hello, Jamie."

"Cranberry Sauce," I say in acknowledgment, knowing my tone needs to get much rougher. We can't have an innocent college girl turning up on the property without warning. Too many secrets here need keeping.

She rolls her eyes at the nickname, some of the wariness leaving her.

Not good.

I harden my voice. "What do you want?"

The harsher tone registers, and her expression falters. "I, uh..." Her eyes focus on the take-out bag in my hand. "You're about to have dinner." She steps back toward the Camaro. "I didn't intend to interrupt."

"Get to the point." Again, the hardness.

Her shoulders slump. "I would've sent a text, but I don't have your number. I didn't want to ask Ash for it."

"But you asked for her car?" I can't help but scoff. "I guarantee she guards that Camaro more fiercely than my mobile number." My brow cocks. "Is she dead? Because I can't see how you pried the keys from her hands, otherwise."

An uncertain smile plays on her lips. "Ash took pity on me."

I wait her out.

Sawyer swallows but keeps her tone even. "I wondered if I could talk to you about something?" She glances at the food again. "Maybe not now. Later tonight?" Her determination is ironclad. I'll give her that.

My body clocks the way the wind is whipping the magenta hair around her face. She's a gorgeous one all right.

Drawing in a breath, I peer at the house. Downstairs is a safe zone these days. Since we use it less, we moved the weapons upstairs. War won't be keen on an unexpected visitor, but I prefer to get this meeting over, so there's a clean end to things and I can warn her to never show without warning again.

"Come inside with me."

"Are you sure?"

"When I give a girl an order, I'm always sure."

10

SAWYER

When I give a girl an order... Things low in my body throb at his tone and the undercurrent of sex radiating from those words. It's the same response I had to his tightening his grip on my hand when I tried to pull away at the poker game.

There's a dangerous edge to him. Which I'm obsessed with.

I follow Jamie up the outdoor metal staircase to the second floor of the converted factory. The air is damp and musty, like old newspapers left out in the rain, but being so close to the river is worth it.

He unlocks the door and steps inside, calling out, "Me. And a guest."

After punching in a code on the keypad, he strides past a wall of enormous vertical windows that overlook the water. The sky is a muddled gray today, but the view is still amazing. What must it be like when there's sunshine?

Jamie sets the bags of food on the upstairs kitchen counter. There's an entire second floor apartment.

I stand near a smooth honey-stained wood bench in front of

the middle window. The choppy surface of the dark river is a chaotic Jackson Pollack painting, with thick streaks of white and gray creating a menacing mix as the sun sets.

Jamie's black-haired housemate emerges from somewhere in the back. He's wearing jeans and a t-shirt now, but he's so massive they don't make him look less intimidating.

Earlier, as soon as he saw Ash and me, he turned and went back upstairs without saying a word to us. This time, he doesn't disappear.

"Just this one?" the guy says in a baritone a trombone would envy. He stalks over to the windows and looks down. Is he checking to see whether we left Ash in the parking lot? Why would we?

"Just this one." Jamie unpacks food and divides it. "Her name is Sawyer."

The housemate's dark eyes sweep over me. He doesn't introduce himself. His expression's the perfect pairing of rude and condescending. I'm used to condescension from the Allendales, but they are never rude with regard to greetings. Good breeding requires introductions. Without exception.

My hand itches to offer a handshake, but I resist the urge. This guy looks like an MMA fighter, not a GU student. Different rules apply here.

The giant rolls his massive shoulders as he scans the parking lot again. "The other one let her drive the car?"

"Apparently," Jamie says, repacking a few things into one of the bags. "Haven't confirmed it, though. Could be grand theft."

The corner of the big guy's mouth curves up. So, he does have a sense of humor buried under all that surliness. Unfortunately, it vanishes just as fast as it came. "Gotta roll soon."

"I know." Jamie strolls past his roommate and waves for me to follow him.

"Bye," I murmur as I jog down the indoor steps. Apparently, we only stopped upstairs to drop off the guy's dinner.

Now, we're back on the main floor, which has smaller water-facing windows and a gigantic footprint. It must be ten-thousand square-feet. There are several seating arrangements of expensive modern furniture. It's a house that looks like it should belong to rock stars, not college kids.

Down here, we can talk privately, which I appreciate.

Jamie sets his food out on the white stone island and nods for me to take a seat. He gets out two plates and forks. "Do you like fish tacos?"

"Yes."

"Dig in. But also, say what's on your mind, because when the food's gone, so are you."

I frown. He's been so fucking unfriendly since I got here. Not that I can completely blame him. He didn't invite me to come.

Best for me to get right to it. "I got a text from Clare Duffy a little while ago. She wanted to know who I'd talked to about the club. I've only talked to you and Ash, and Ash hasn't even met Clare."

Jamie glances at me. I haven't taken him up on his invitation to eat. My eyes drop to where he's set a taco and some chips onto a plate. He pushes it over to me with a single terse word. "And?"

My fingers rub the muscles of my neck, and I look up at him through my lashes as my heart thuds in my chest. This is so freaking awkward. "Another Briar Club member tagged some people in a post that included you and Clare. By a swimming pool? I didn't realize you were on the rowing team."

I wonder where Jamie falls on the roster. Even though my so-called brother Brad made the team, according to my dad, Brad doesn't think he's likely to get into the top Varsity Eight boat or even the second.

Since Jamie doesn't volunteer to make small talk about his being an athlete, I exhale a small sigh. Leaning forward, I dip a chip into avocado salsa. "Did you say something to Clare about what I said this morning?"

"No." He takes a bite of a taco, chews and swallows. "But I asked about you. Your prospects for getting in."

My nerves are live wires. "What did she say?"

"She wouldn't answer." He flips his hand over in a "there you go" gesture. "Which is an answer in itself."

The chip cracks from the pressure of my fingers and falls onto my plate. I set the rest down, and after wiping my hands on a napkin, I sit back and push the plate away.

My silence drags on. He eats two tacos and a handful of chips with queso.

Blowing out a breath, I feel myself deflating. This is so fucking unfair. With my pedigree on paper—Allendale last name, Briar Club legacy, graduating with honors from an elite prep school—I should have had no problem getting accepted.

If Mom were still alive, this wouldn't be happening. She was too influential for Clare to get away with this bullshit. I consider talking to Dad, but I know he couldn't really help. And it would mean admitting there's a chance I might not make the cut. That would just add stress to us both, since getting into the Briar Club is part of our strategy for winning over his family about my continued existence as an Allendale.

Beyond Dad, there's Brad, my so-called brother. He knows plenty of people, but he wouldn't lift a finger to help me. He wants me to fail. In fact, I think he wants my failure more than his success. And as a legitimate Allendale, that says something.

"Why did you mention me?" My frustration leaks into my tone. "You made things worse."

Jamie's jaw sets. "I was curious about whether you were right about her."

"I hope your curiosity doesn't cost me the most important thing in my life." I huff out a sigh. "What else was said—about me?"

"The most important thing in your life? *Seriously?*"

He thinks I'm being melodramatic. There's no point disavowing him of his beliefs. When I don't answer, Jamie leans back and crosses his arms over his chest. His shoulders flex, and I can't keep from noticing again what a great body he has.

"What do you want from me, Cranberry Sauce?"

I stiffen. That's a good question. The answer is obvious. "Nothing, I guess." Sliding my butt off the tall chair, I stand next to the island. "When I told you this morning that Clare dropped me because you flirted with me, the last thing I thought you'd do was double-down by asking her about my club candidacy."

He leans back, studying me the entire time. "Again I ask, *what do you want?* My help? Because that would cost you." The words are like a knife in my kidney.

"I don't have any money."

"If you did, I wouldn't take it. You have something better than money."

Rolling my eyes, I shake my head. Is he seriously propositioning me right now? After pissing Clare off even more? "I have to get into the Briar Club. That's the kind of help I need."

"Right, I know." The words roll off his tongue because of his accent. For some reason, goosebumps break out over my arms. "Ground rules first. You're friends with my cousin who couldn't know about our arrangement."

My brows furrow, and I cock my head in confusion. "What arrangement?"

"As I've *just* been saying, if I agree to get you what you want, I will want something in return."

I guess I shouldn't be surprised. Growing up in the Allendale household means I know all about exchanging favors. "I could keep an arrangement secret if—"

He points at me. "Will you swear to it?"

"As *I* was just saying, *yes.*" Crossing my arms over my chest, I tip my chin up defiantly. "But you're assuming I believe there's something you could do to actually help me. Other than Clare Duffy, who do you know in the club? Because a guy's opinion won't have much weight. The Briar Club is run by women."

"The club is run by *school girls,* no offense, and I can get school girls to do what I want."

"How?"

"Leverage." He settles back in his chair, and there's a smugness to his expression. He certainly believes what he's saying. As I open my mouth to speak, he holds up a hand. "No questions. Stay in your lane, Sauce."

Sucking in my cheeks, I lean back. "What's my lane?"

He watches me with a predatory air. "Feel free to say no to what I propose. Unlike Clare Duffy, I'm not vindictive about petty bullshit."

As my fingernails dig into my thighs, I wait, my mind racing with possibilities. My brother's friends, who are Jamie's age, like to use girls and use them up. Humiliation is par for the course.

Jamie sits forward. "Our arrangement will include sex and nothing else. No commitment or obligations on my part, other than to help you get into the Briar Club." His dark smile ignites the forbidden ache he seems to constantly inspire. I don't want him under my skin, but he's there. "And unless it's pre-specified as a 'hard no' from you, I can have you however I want."

I knew he would want sex, so I shouldn't break out into a cold sweat over his saying the words, but I do. This would be a kind of prostitution. I'd be paying for his help with my body. *Quid pro quo.* Am I actually willing to do that? Sucking on my lower lip, I look away. He also said he gets to have sex with me in any way he wants, which covers a lot of ground. I rub my palms against my jeans.

From upstairs, the giant's deep voice bellows, "J, you ready?"

I jerk in surprise. Oh, right. They're going out. I peer in Jamie's direction and find his entire attention fixed on me. I like the way that feels.

"You can think about it, Sawyer." He starts to rise, and my hand darts out to his thigh to stop him.

"I need to clarify some things." My mouth is suddenly bone dry. Even licking my lips doesn't quite work.

"Fair enough. Give me a minute to send my mate on his way, and we'll talk it through." He rises and gives me a slow once-over.

The way he looks at me is fire. As my flesh hums with anticipation, something startling jars me. "Hey, Jamie?"

Turning back, he says, "Yeah?" His voice is so much warmer than it was outside.

I guess I'm no longer an unwanted intruder. Now, I'm the girl who may give him something he wants.

"It's our secret from everyone, right?" My gaze drifts meaningfully toward the stairs.

"He lives here, so he'll figure out pretty quickly that I'm fucking you. But the terms of our agreement can be just between you and me, yes."

I nod. "That's what I want. If I decide to—"

"Grand. That's settled."

As he walks away, my head is filled with a jumble of questions and, yes, a few recriminations. Am I really considering this?

I have to admit—if only to myself—there are several compelling reasons that I am. First, I'm out of options. If he really does have a plan that would get me into the Briar Club, I need him to put it into action.

And, just as importantly, a part of me *wants* to do this. I've never been with anyone who makes my heart pound half as hard as James O'Rourke does. Every inch of him is fucking delicious. And the glint in his eyes when he said he will have me however he wants made my pussy clench.

I've had to be so careful all the time. Choosing the right boyfriends. Keeping things so sedate and safe. And the entire time, I'd been wishing for something hot and dirty. I always wondered if it might be because I wasn't born a cold fish Allendale. Here's a chance for me to experiment and find out.

Keeping our arrangement a complete secret means no one will know if I let him do every thing I've fantasized about.

My heart is like a jackhammer cracking my ribs. I stalk over to the sink and fill a glass with slightly shaky hands.

Careful! the cautious voice in my head screams.

I need to make sure there's no catch. Someone with Jamie's looks doesn't just want a few blow jobs from a girl with double-D boobs. He's a handsome athlete at an elite school. Plenty of women would have no-strings sex with him.

Or *maybe not*. Hookups are super common, of course, but Jamie's hookups probably want to be more. Landing him as a boyfriend would mean a lot to plenty of women.

When he returns, he glances at the food on the island. "Finished?"

"Yes."

"Right, okay. Let's sit over here." He moves to the sleek, black modular seating arrangement.

I slip off my shoes and sit sideways on the couch facing him. "You said you could have me however you want. What does that mean?"

His lips curve into a small smile. "It means I can have you anywhere and anytime. If I tell you to drop your knickers, they'd better be around your ankles by the time I lower my zipper."

My lips part in shock, but my nipples bead, too. He's bad, and my body finds bad very attractive.

"In front of other people? On camera?"

"Not on camera. Maybe in front of others, but only under special circumstances where privacy is assured."

"You can't assure privacy anywhere."

"There are places where cell phone jammers are in use, and masks can be worn."

I blink and tilt my head. "I can't agree to sex in public. It's too risky. If it got back to my family, they would cut me out of their lives."

His bright blue eyes bore into me like lasers. For a moment, I expect him to call off the deal.

"Right, sure, not in front of other people or cameras. What else?"

I'm sure there are sick, perverse things I should list, but I don't exactly know what all those things are. "That's all for right now."

"To be that innocent again." Jamie winks at me. After a moment, he runs a finger along my cheek. "You need to know, when it comes to sex, I'll own you."

My pussy clenches. My panties must be soaked. "Like a slave?"

"Exactly."

Maybe it shouldn't be, but that is the hottest thing I've ever heard. Licking my lips, I give a tentative nod. "In secret, I would try that."

"How many men have you been with?" His tone is merely curious.

"I don't know that I'd call them men." I let out a small, nervous laugh. "Two long-term boyfriends in high school."

His thumb strokes mine. "But you've had sex?"

"A few times."

"This will be more intense." I'm not sure how a pretty smile can also look sinister, but his manages it. When he stands, there's an air of danger crackling around us. "And more satisfying for you, if you're suited to it."

I'm not sure what he means. Suited to being a slave? Is anyone really suited to that? "It's a game, right?"

Jamie nods. "During our sexual encounters, we'll each play a role. I'll have control. You won't."

How can something scary also seem appealing? A shiver runs through me. This could be a trap. He's handsome, but maybe he's also vicious.

His hand takes mine and squeezes it. "You'll always have an out. Do you know what a safeword is?"

My eyes widen, but I nod slowly. A safeword is for sex at its wild and darkest. Maybe bondage. *Maybe pain.* My heart thumps like a rabbit's foot, sensing the ultimate danger. And yet, I don't immediately call an end to things. I can't seem to stop staring at him.

"We'll use *red* to start." Jamie watches me closely, as if he's trying to read my mind. "What questions do you have?"

Licking my lips, I shrug. "I think I get it. Red is the word for calling a timeout?"

"Exactly."

At least he's promising things will remain consensual. He curls his fingers in a gesture for me to follow him.

"Wait." As I stand, my brows furrow. "You want to start now?"

Giving me a once-over, the corners of his mouth curve into a smirk. "I wanted to start the second I laid eyes on you."

The flames consuming my insides burn brighter. James O'Rourke is officially *the king* of right answers.

"Lead the way."

His smirk widens into a breath-stealing smile. "That's the plan."

※

JAMIE

M<small>Y</small> <small>COCK IS MADE OF QUARRY STONE AS</small> I <small>GUIDE</small> S<small>AWYER</small> <small>UP</small> to my room. Cranberry Sauce is calm, at least outwardly, which is unusual. It may mean I'll be able to take her farther faster. My muscles twitch with anticipation. Everything about her draws me in until all thoughts disintegrate in the face of stripping and fucking her.

Sawyer rests a hand on the charcoal-colored fabric of the headboard before lifting her eyes to the painting above it. "Pretty."

The horizontal abstract is indigo and gray, reminiscent of a stormy sea. The magenta of her hair complements it, bringing some heat to the cold. Apparently, I'm determined to see the rightness of her being here in every small detail.

As she continues to admire the art, she says, "It reminds me of the ocean you find in books."

That's my feeling, too. Melville and *The Perfect Storm*. I enjoy that she sees it, but conversation isn't what we're on about right now. "Take off your clothes, Sauce."

Her head turns to look at me intently. "You first?" Her voice is steady enough, but the way she swallows tells me she's playing at bravery rather than owning it.

"No." The word's sharp as a smack.

She exhales a breath as her fingers fondle her zipper, courage faltering.

Reaching out, I grab her waistband. I jerk her closer to me, offering the reassurance of physical closeness at the same time I'm wresting control. "This is the game we're playing, Sawyer. I own you. You in or not?" My tone is commanding but not rough.

She must take it that way though because she winces. I don't backpedal. She's no good to me as a play partner if she stands in the corner like a reluctant virgin.

With quick breaths, she unfastens her jeans.

Good girl.

My lips brush her temple, imparting my approval. I take a step back to give her room to undress. "Keep going, Sauce."

The way I want her burns inside me. This kind of pent-up desire is something I haven't felt before. Pushing my sleeves up, I flex my forearms impatiently.

The pulse in her neck jumps. Points to her for not outright balking. She's curious, which is the best thing a new toy can be.

She pauses, taking a heavy breath. For a moment, I think she might bolt for the door. Then, something angry and rebellious flashes in her eyes. With jerky movements, she strips down to skin.

Suddenly, I'm faced with a girl who's exactly what nature intended to bring about the fall of man. Full breasts, protruding nipples, smooth skin, a small waist flaring into round hips, and a thatch of chestnut curls over her sex. Not a single girl I've fucked at GU has had hair on her pussy. I'd forgotten what it looked like.

On this girl, I like it.

Her flushed cheeks make my cock jerk with errant hunger.

My instinct is to praise her for taking the first big step into the scene, but that might cause her to falter. Instead, I keep my voice firm. "Lie on the bed on your back."

Her silence is almost hostile as she obeys. Which doesn't give me pause. An air raid couldn't give me pause at this point.

I consider keeping my clothes on to emphasize the power differential, but a deep compulsion pushes me to shed my clothes. Though we've only just met, I feel like I've been waiting forever for this, for her. And I want the maximum amount of skin contact.

After digging a condom from the drawer of the nightstand, I roll it onto my cock. She stares at the ceiling the entire time.

I almost smile.

The thumping of my heart is like a bass drum. There is something about this girl that sets her apart. And I'm here for it.

I lie on my side next to her and lower my hand so it rests on her belly. She shivers then stiffens, trying to control her reactions. Which is the opposite of what I want, though her innocence and uneasiness are a turn-on.

With practiced ease, I move my fingers lower so the tips get lost in her curls. Moving my mouth to her ear, I whisper, "Are you already wet for me, Sauce? Or are you going to make me work for it?"

She swallows. "I don't know." Her voice is barely audible.

"You actually don't? Or you want me to think you don't?" My fingers slide lower until I'm parting her lips with them.

Circling her clit with the pad of my index finger, I scrutinize her face. The flush in her cheeks darkens. *Good.* And also, fucking beautiful.

My hand slides lower to her slippery inner lips, which makes my balls ache. Going slow has never been so hard. Slapping her pussy with three fingers creates a lovely wet thwack that causes her mouth to open in surprise... and something more.

"Spread your legs."

Her knees part, tentatively.

"Wider."

With maddening slowness, she complies. If we were further along, I'd punish her for testing my patience, but this is new for her, so I restrain myself.

"Reach above your head and touch the headboard."

After a moment, she obeys. Her gorgeous tits rise and shimmy.

"Some nights, your arms will be bound."

Her gaze drops to meet mine, and from her dilated pupils, she finds the prospect intriguing.

"For now," I say, spreading her pussy open with my hand, "Let's see how well you can hold them in position."

SAWYER

Past sexual experiences make me expect Jamie to shove his cock into me immediately, but he holds his own lust in check. Instead, his fingers spread my lower lips, exposing my pussy to his scrutiny in a way no one ever has before. I shudder at his deep intake of breath.

Subconsciously, I've started to close my thighs, but he slaps the soft inner flesh and then shoves them apart so far my tendons ache.

Jamie raises his head. "Look at me, Cranberry Sauce."

It's tough to make eye contact when his hand is still splaying my pussy open. After biting down on my lip, I lift my eyes to meet his.

"I'm going to look at your body for as long as I want, especially what's between your legs. Don't make your discomfort with that my problem because I will punish you and then tie your legs open, so you're powerless."

Things deep inside my pelvis clench, and the darkness in his voice makes my nipples ache. Do I really want him to be harsh? *Maybe.*

"I'm not trying to resist. It just happens."

The corner of his mouth curves into a smug smirk. "If you can't control it, you've heard what will happen." His thumb swirls my own juices over my clit.

The sensation is electric, and my body jerks as though its been touched by a live wire. My eyes shift to the ceiling as I shiver.

"Close your eyes, Sauce, and concentrate on giving yourself to me."

My lips part, and I almost protest that I already am. Then he rubs my clit again, and I don't want to fight. I just want him to keep touching me right there.

When my lids drop, so do my defenses.

"Your body's exactly what I want." His voice is rough and beguiling. "It's like I ordered you from a menu."

Warmth courses through me. Yeah, he's definitely the king of saying the right thing.

As he teases me, his breath scalds my hip. The intimacy is almost too intense. His hand slides up to cup my breast, and he squeezes until his grip turns painful. In a way that's strangely delicious. My hips twist from the gnawing desire. I need him to fuck me.

"You should expect to be naked and spread open for hours when you're in my bed."

Hours? A small groan escapes my throat. Could I last that long with him playing his games?

A couple of his fingers push into my pussy, and it sets off a primal need. My hips circle and pump.

As my soft moans grow louder, I'm tempted to beg.

I want this man inside me. Fingers. Tongue. And especially cock.

※

JAMIE

HER WRITHING IS SO FUCKING EROTIC ALL MY BEST intentions dissolve. I move above her, so I'm staring down at her pretty face and perfect tits.

"You're too beautiful for your own good," I whisper gruffly.

Warm brown eyes open and stare up into mine. "I want you."

"Likewise." As I enter her, she raises her hips. Even with a damned condom on, this feels fucking amazing. She's hot and tight and wet. "Christ," I murmur, concentrating on the sensation of her walls squeezing my dick.

Her eyes close as I sink into her, and her mouth opens wider, as though she needs more air. That expression is what I want burned on my retinas for the rest of my life.

When I pull back and drive forward, her hands close into fists. *Fuck, yes.* There is nothing contrived about the way she moves.

As I fuck her in slow, deep strokes, her gasps mix with my groans.

We are so good together. I concentrate on dragging things out, making the tension build in both our bodies.

The way her tits shake makes my mouth water. The body of a goddess, truly. I slow and drop my head to suck on a nipple that would take a clamp perfectly. Biting down with my teeth causes her to buck beneath me.

A slow smile of satisfaction curves my lips. Her body is going to be so much fun to play with.

When I pull out, her eyes pop open.

"What's wrong?" she whispers as she lowers one arm so she can reach for my shoulder.

I push her hand away. "Nothing, you're perfect. Lie on your side."

She blinks and, after a breath, rolls onto her side, facing away from me. I lie behind her, moving a thigh between hers and then entering her pussy again.

After pushing my right arm beneath her head, I grip her throat with it. Then I move my left hand in front of her hip and down to her pussy. As I thrust into her, my fingers stroke her clit just above where I'm entering her.

"Oh, my God," she whimpers.

My breath husks harshly in her ear. I'm close, but so is she. I can get her there first, and I want to.

"Like that, baby girl?"

"Yes." Her hand slides along my left forearm. "Please... Right there."

My grip on her throat tightens, making her breath catch.

"Jamie—?" The hint of fear in her voice causes me to put my lips against her ear.

"You're safe, Sauce. Stay quiet, and feel what I want you to feel."

With our bodies connected, I know the moment she decides to trust me. *Good girl.*

Her back presses against my chest as she literally leans into the way I'm fucking her. My body has its own rhythm now, my hand pressing against her windpipe as I thrust, then easing off as I retreat.

As she comes, her moans are cut in two by my grip. I rub harder against her clit and clamp down on her throat. Her pussy convulses around my cock. I let her ride out her orgasm until I've milked it for all she's got.

Then I roll her facedown and grab her hips, dragging her ass up to my groin. I fuck her in hard, punishing strokes as she gasps into the sheets. When I finally blow, my mind is wiped as clean as a white board.

This is what life is about.

When I release her hips, she crumples like the sheets beneath her, limp and sated. I stare down at the curve of her ass. More luscious than a fucking trifle.

My ringing phone causes me to back off the bed reluctantly. I don't know when it started to ring.

Sawyer, God bless her, doesn't move an inch.

When I lift the phone, I see it's Ash. I'm tempted to let it go to voicemail, but my cousin is a wild card. You never know what she'll do if left to her own devices.

I swipe to answer. "Yes?"

"What's my car doing at your place? Is Sawyer there?"

For a second, I consider lying. I don't. "Yeah, she needed to talk to me."

"All this time?" Ash says suspiciously.

My tone is terse. "Apparently."

My private encounter with Sauce suddenly seems decidedly less private. Which means, I should let her go for now. It's not what I want to do. *At all.*

"We're done talking. She'll be on her way back in a few minutes." I don't wait for a response before ending the call. Tossing my phone on the nightstand, I continue to stare at Cranberry Sauce.

"I heard." Her voice is muffled by a pillow.

Leaning over the bed, I bite her ass.

She sucks in a breath and jerks forward. "Ow!" Looking over her shoulder at me, she rubs her ass cheek. "I said I was getting up."

"I know. That's not why I bit you."

"Then why?"

"To see if you taste as good as you look." A smile tugs at my lips. "You do."

11

SAWYER

My body continues to tingle as I climb from Jamie's bed.

While I've always liked the anticipation that comes with starting to have sex with someone, I never actually had an orgasm *during* sex before. In the past, I treated sex as foreplay.

Being stroked and choked by Jamie was a whole other level. One that *worked* for me.

Is this what I like? When he first put his fingers over my neck, I was scared. I can't understand how that turned into my coming.

I collect my clothes from the floor.

"What's your mobile number, Sauce?"

As I hook my bra, I rattle off the digits. Jamie programs my number into his phone, then drops it on the bed so he can pull on his pants.

When I finish dressing, I check my phone. No messages. Not even one from him so I'll have his number. I want to ask him about it, but hesitate. There's something deeper at play that

I want to talk about first. Things like... what's in store for me when we have sex again. And can that happen soon because the anticipation and suspense might kill me.

I stare at his bare chest. He's like a piece of art.

What in the AF do I say to him? *I had a really good time as your sex slave. Can't wait to do it again.* For fuck's sake.

Be casual. Like him. As I stroll to the door, I don't make eye contact. "Okay, see you later."

"Hold on." He moves in my way, putting an end to my awkward escape.

My eyes lock on his throat, causing heat to rush to my face. He choked me, and I liked it, and he knows. It's *a lot* for a first hookup.

"Look at me, Sauce."

I raise my gaze, so my browns are staring into his blues. "Yes?"

His hands slide down my arms to encircle my wrists and then move to trap my hands behind me. "How are you?"

"I'm fine." I try to infuse my tone with cool and casual, but I'm not sure I nail it.

"Are you, then?" That accent... delicious. He lowers his head and kisses my lips. No tongue. No pressure. It's more like a caress.

Which is unsettling.

There was nothing sweet about the sex, so I'm unprepared for this.

His thumb strokes my skin. "I don't like you leaving when I could've made good use of the night. Next time, you'll stay over."

I lean closer, enjoying the thought of sleeping with him. Though... I need to be careful. I don't want to read more into his words than he intends. "I thought—are we doing that?"

He nods. "The kind of sex we're having requires us to forge a special connection. It's not a romance, but it's intimate. I'll use your body, but I'll also make sure you're all right after we try new things." His hand rises and touches my throat. "You trusted me with breath play. I don't take that lightly. Unfortunately, Ash is waiting for you to return her car, so this time, I've gotta send you back."

Licking my lips, I nod. I wish I had my own car.

"There will be rules when you stay the night in this house. And you *will not* break them."

That causes me to shudder. There's an ominous sensuality to his voice when he's giving orders... as though my spine is a bowstring he's plucking.

Jamie steps back, which I'm sorry about. What I really want is for him to push me back onto the bed and pin me down. While we have sex again. Being bound... somehow I know that will be the hottest thing ever. I *know* it.

"Wait a moment," he says. "I'll walk you to the car."

As he dresses, I glance around, taking in details I missed earlier. His bedroom is a gorgeous mix of light gray, beige, and various shades of blue. And while there's nothing specifically nautical about it, it's all about the sea somehow.

Jamie puts a thick scarf around his neck. It hangs over his chest, not completely matching his sweatshirt. "Right, we're ready." He leads me out of the room, outside, and down the metal stairs.

His wearing a scarf but no coat makes him look very European. Again, the novelty is attractive.

After I unlock the car door, he opens it for me. If this is part of the sex slave treatment, I'm down for it.

"Listen," he says as I lower myself into the driver's seat. "The car's a hot rod, but you don't need to drive it that way."

I smile. "Noted."

Jamie's expression sobers. "That's not me going soft and sentimental over you. I just don't want you damaging my property." He inclines his head at my body.

Cocking an eyebrow, I repeat, "Noted."

I'm into this insane construct where he both objectifies me and tells me to drive carefully. It's been a long time since anyone worried about me, and for some reason, it means more coming from Jamie. He claims we're not going to get attached, but I wonder if it's possible to remain detached after sex like we just had.

After sliding the key into the ignition, I look over at him. "You took my number but didn't give me yours. Is that part of the rules?" Trying to keep the challenge out of my tone, I ask, "You're the only one allowed to initiate contact?"

"With some exceptions. We'll talk about it." He reaches out and rubs my lower lip with his thumb. "I'll text soon so we can get time together on the schedule." His hand slides up the back of my neck, and his fingers close around a handful of hair. With a tug, he forces my head back, so I'm staring up at him. "Right, okay." He murmurs the words as if he's actually addressing himself rather than me.

I think he might kiss me. Instead, he releases my hair and steps back.

"Go on, Cranberry Sauce. Before I drag you back to my bed." The words cause a surge of satisfaction. I don't really understand our chemistry, but I love it.

Driving back to school, I can't stop thinking about Jamie. For the first time since I've gotten to Granthorpe, I think college could be more than just a stepping stone in my career.

I pull into the campus lot with the most direct route to our dorm. Once I'm on the path to Central Residence Hall, I realize I need to formulate what I'm going to say to Ash about how I ended up at Jamie's.

I run out of time when I'm within sight of the dorm, however, because Ash is sitting on top of a picnic table with her phone in hand, eyes fixed on the screen. On the opposite side of the table, there's a path to the quad and, approaching from that direction, are my horrible adopted brother Brad and his friend, Crosby Bergmann.

A glance at the men reveals their attention is locked on Ash.

Uneasiness engulfs me. Quickening my pace, I crunch over leaves until I'm practically jogging.

For some reason, Crosby, the stocky power lifter, always makes the hair on the back of my neck stand on end. But, as far as I know, he's the lesser of two evils. My brother is the real menace.

I reach the patch of grass in front of Central before the guys do.

Brad spots me and narrows his eyes as I move to the end of the picnic table to block their access to Ash.

"Hey," I say, more loudly than necessary, letting Brad know I'm prepared to draw attention to us if they cause trouble. Not that I expect them to with CC cameras all over.

They're more the type of guys I never want my friends to cross paths with after dark. Clean cut and well spoken, they *seem* trustworthy. But more than once my brother's high school friends plied some girl with so many drinks she passed out and had little recollection of what she did at a party. After, there would be rumors she'd been screwed by some jerk—or more than one. So sleazy.

Brad was never the one accused, but the company he kept was. And he definitely never criticized what any of his rich, powerful friends did. Bullying people. Using people. Humiliating girls. All fair game.

On top of my general reasons for disliking him, there are more specific ones. He's always treated me like a charity case who got lucky by landing in his family. While that's pretty much true, I don't need to be constantly reminded of it.

As we make eye contact, my stomach lurches with a sick feeling. My pseudo brother's scowl triggers horrible memories. The way he viciously taunted me over everything... my Southern accent, now gone, the gap between my front teeth, now gone, and my sensitive nature, definitely gone. At times, his anger even turned violent.

It was a relief when Brad went away to college. So much so

that knowing he would be here, I almost didn't apply to Granthorpe. But it was something my mom really wanted. And the GU Briar Club is a way to prove myself to my Allendale grandparents who consider me fruit of a poisonous tree.

The older Allendales forbid Robert—my dad—from adopting me, threatening to cut him off if he did. I didn't know the truth until Brad told me when I was eleven. Dad was calm when I went to him in tears. I felt betrayed, but he assured me the delay was just part of his plan. We would bide our time. Eventually, he would control the massive family fortune himself, and he'd make the adoption legal and official. Until then, I needed to be patient. Sometimes, I was frustrated he didn't take a stand, but he always treated me like I was his real daughter, which meant a lot to me.

Dad formally adopted me at seventeen, just before I aged out. In other words, just in time. Maybe I should've been annoyed that he didn't announce it to his family, but I was just happy and grateful he did the right thing in the end. I'd started to think I might turn eighteen and be on my own.

Standing at the end of the picnic table, I study the pair of men when they reach us. Crosby is stocky, with a barrel chest and a surprising layer of fat across his middle, despite broad shoulders and muscular arms that strain against his shirt. His legs are as thick and sturdy as tree trunks, and his cloying aftershave barely covers the musky smell of male sweat as he starts to sidestep me.

We nearly collide, but Brad grabs my arm and jerks me out of his friend's way, freeing Crosby to move in front of the bench where Ash's feet are resting.

Trying to pull my arm free, I glare at my brother and notice there's a raised reddish bruise on Brad's cheek. My eyebrows rise. What happened? Did he fall down while drunk? That isn't like him. He always wants to be in control.

"Ashling." Crosby's voice is excessively New England blue

blood, which is crazy since his physique makes him look like a thug who went shopping at a yacht club.

Ash lowers her phone to her jeans-clad thigh. "Hello." Her gaze cuts from Crosby to my brother, her blank expression resting where Brad's hand grips my bicep before lifting to Brad's face once more.

I aspire to that level of cool.

"You're not manhandling my friend, are you?" Her head tilts, faux casual, to match her tone. "Hands off, please."

"Your friend?" Brad scoffs, his incredulity fading when he notes Ash isn't joking. "Since when?" His hard eyes ping-pong between us.

"Brad," Crosby says with a side nod that signals Brad to let me go.

My tormenter releases my arm and gives me a small shove away from him.

"So, Ash, how's your cousin?" Crosby's tone is surprisingly facilitative, like a cat trying to lure a canary from its cage.

"He's as pretty as ever. Lucky for you." Ash's tone is cool and faintly amused.

My brother's bruise suddenly makes sense. Are these the guys Jamie got into a fight with? Given that Crosby has bowling balls for shoulders, I'm surprised Jamie doesn't have more than a swollen lip.

"Glad to hear it." Crosby steps onto the bench, causing the legs of the picnic table to sink deeper into the grass.

The movement causes Ash's phone to slide off the edge of her leg. Her hand shoots out and catches it before it drops. Reflexes for days.

Crosby sits next to her. "Hey, listen, I shouldn't have been so aggressive. Too many drinks. I misunderstood what was going on in the booth. Sorry about that." His fake friendliness causes my spine to stiffen. "But Ash." His meaty paw touches his side. "He cracked one of my ribs with that pool cue."

Ash cocks her head, eyeing him speculatively and seemingly unmoved by his snakelike smile.

"A cracked rib means I can't lift." He clucks his tongue in admonishment. "And if I can't lift for a couple weeks, I have a hole in my schedule." His index finger points at her. "A hole I want you to help me fill. That's only fair." He chuckles, sounding like a rhino with a stuffed nose. "Wouldn't you agree, Allendale?" He looks to my brother for back-up.

"Allendale?" Ash's eyes give us a once-over. "Are you related to this guy, Sawyer?"

"She's not a real Allendale." Brad crosses his arms, as if to put up yet another barrier against me. "Adopted by my mother, who was only an Allendale by marriage."

Only by marriage, so less than? I glare at him. This is the way he speaks about his dead mother. Celine was worth twenty of any blood Allendale. She was amazing.

Ignoring our family dysfunction, Crosby turns back toward Ash. "Look, things were going well. I don't want last night to get in the way. Let me make it up to you. How about dinner in New York?"

Her exhalation of breath is a scoff. "Definitely not." As she starts to rise, he reaches for her arm but then thinks better of it.

"All right, not New York. Anywhere you want. Name the place."

Climbing down, she tucks her phone in her pocket. "You were jealous, Cros. That I get. But your friend is an asshole." She tosses a withering look in Brad's direction before returning her attention to Bergmann. "For you to have any shot at all, when I see your face next, I shouldn't see his."

I tilt my head down to mask my smile. Anyone seeing Brad for who he really is and casually taking him down a peg has my undying admiration.

From his expression, Brad's apoplectic with rage. "Fucking bitch," he mutters.

"Got it," Crosby says to Ash, trying to drown him out.

Ash hooks an arm through mine and tugs me along with her. I allow myself to smile.

When we're far enough away, I say, "I didn't realize you knew my brother."

"I don't really. But he's not going to treat you like shit in front of me and get away with it. Fuck him."

The urge to hug her seizes me, but I resist since we're walking. "Are you dating Crosby?"

"No, I went on two dates with him after he intervened at a bar when someone was hassling me and a friend. I thought Crosby was a decent guy."

"And now?"

She smirks darkly. "I think he doesn't realize how lucky he is that Jamie brought him to his knees with that pool cue."

I peer over my shoulder at my brother and his friend as they stroll away in the opposite direction. "You don't scare easily, do you?"

"Not easily, no." Ash shrugs. "It's not that I'm never scared. But I don't let myself show it. What would be the point? And also... Fuck that," she whispers with a small smile that hints at a multitude of secrets. The girl is an enigma. "Anyway, forget about Crosby and your dickhead brother. Listen, I was getting claustrophobic in the dorm room." That explains what she was doing sitting outside. "Want to go get a drink somewhere, Seesaw?"

"I don't have a fake ID."

"Me neither. Can't figure out where I lost it." She licks her lips thoughtfully and looks at her oversized handbag. "It's fine though. I never get a chance to buy my own drinks anyway."

I don't doubt that. The thing is... I can't afford to get caught drinking while I'm underage. Brad's nasty reminder that I'm a second-class member of the family is an implied threat. Anything he catches me doing will be reported back.

Also, Ash has shady armed guys after her and her friends. Also, I don't want to talk about what I was doing at her cousin's house just now, which is bound to come up.

Extracting my arm from hers, I say, "You know, I think I'm going to stay in."

She slows, glancing over at me. I expect her to ask how things went with Clare. And what I found out from talking to Jamie. Instead, she shrugs with a friendly smile. "Okay. Glad you feel better."

"Thanks." Warmth burns in my cheeks. Has she guessed the reason I'm feeling better is because I got laid? With a jolt, I realize I've haven't obsessed over Clare Duffy's disapproval once since I fell into bed with Jamie. Logically, I know Briar Club membership is still crucial for me, but that's not how it feels at the moment.

Ash opens an app that has a map with a twirling red car in the center. Apparently, Ash has a "find my Camaro" app on her phone. *Nice.* Since it's vintage and pre-dates smart technology, I guess she installed her own GPS.

"All right, I'm off," she says.

"Are you sure you want to go out alone? That's not the safest."

She smiles and gives me a firm hug. "Night, Sawyer."

"Be careful," I call out as she strolls toward the parking lot. She raises a hand in acknowledgement before disappearing into the dark.

12

JAMIE

On Saturday morning, I'm getting ready to leave town when my phone rings with a call from Ireland.

I'd been on the hunt for an Irish cop willing to do favors for money and finally got a name.

Having already hacked the local police's computer system years ago to look at the file on my brother's case, I'd assumed there'd been no real investigation. But I recently learned that while details in the electronic record are sparse, there could be a lot more on paper.

I swipe to answer the call. "Hello?"

"O'Rourke, is it you?" The accent makes me homesick.

"It is, yeah. Find anything?"

The cop is in his thirties. He was new to the force at the time of the incident with my brother. Although he never heard about the case at the time, he has access to the case file.

"Yeah, I found the file. It's got interview notes and some printed reports that weren't entered electronically. But even in the paper records, there's nothing concrete to point the finger at anyone." The sound of papers shuffling comes through the line, as though he's thumbing through the file as we speak. "I did find out why the case was designated as closed."

My body tenses. Any mention of the fact that local law enforcement closed the file on my brother's assault makes me want to gun down the asshole who led the investigation.

"It was actually not their idea to stop the inquiry." He pauses, implying I should brace myself. "Your da wouldn't let them talk to your brother or you. He said it was a misunderstanding. The local detective wanted to force your family to turn over the clothes for evidence, but the crown prosecutor wasn't of a mind to push forward. He thought the parent's wishes should be the priority, especially as it seemed like it was a foreigner who did whatever happened and he'd likely left afterward."

If my father was in front of me right now, I might shove him against a wall and pummel him. That old school way of thinking—pretend it never happened, don't think about it, move on with your life—directly contributed to Jude's death.

I followed my father's orders to never talk about it, even when Jude tried to bring it up. I trusted it would be better for my brother in the long run. But all the gag order really did was leave Jude to face his nightmares alone.

Our refusal to talk didn't help him forget what happened. The things he wrote and drew in a secret notebook he kept under a loose piece of carpet were proof that, despite our silence, the memories of that day never left him. *Never.*

"I understand." My voice is surprisingly level. "My father thought it was best to sweep it under the rug." Irony has a cruel sense of humor since that's exactly where the memories ended up.

No words pass between us for a moment.

"You sure you want to keep on, Jamie?" The man's tone is kind, as if he senses there's a part of me that's tired of living with it and would like to finally let it go. "Nothing we do will bring the poor lad back, God rest him."

Right, sure. God rest him, I think bitterly. I don't believe Jude's resting. Neither of us will until I see this through.

"Make a copy of everything." It's tough to keep my tone neutral when I want to smash something. "If there's any physical evidence you can't send, take a picture and send that instead. I want it all."

"Not a problem." He pauses. "And you have my account details? For the risks associated with this sort of favor?"

"As soon as I have the file, you'll have the money. With thanks."

"Fair play. Good luck to you."

13

SAWYER

The weekend passes in a blazing fire of "for fuck's sake." When I wake on Saturday morning, Ash isn't in our dorm room. At first, I'm not worried and I spend more time wondering what Jamie's doing than where Ash ended up crashing. But I'm upset Ash and I somehow forgot to exchange numbers because I want to text her. I search for her on social media. All I find is a photogram account I think is hers, but it's set to private, so I can't DM. I send a follow request and tell myself she's fine.

On Saturday, I spend most of my time thinking about Jamie and hoping he'll text. I study in the library as an excuse to walk around campus. Whenever possible, I take the paths near the athletic training center. I'm hoping to bump into the rowing team on their way to practice, but I don't.

When Ash doesn't sleep in the dorm on Saturday or Sunday, my mind starts to spiral in dark directions. The last time I saw her she was heading to a bar alone. Is she okay? Or has something sinister happened to her?

On Sunday, I take the bus to Jamie's neighborhood and walk to his house. No one's home, so I leave a note in the mailbox.

Either he doesn't find it or he's decided to ignore it because neither he nor Ash bothers to text on Sunday or Monday. Finally, early on Tuesday morning, I go to campus police, sweating and freaking out, to tell them I'm worried about my roommate. Because the campus had a problem with kidnapping-murder events in the past, campus police takes any mention of a missing girl very seriously.

They have me wait in a lounge area while they make calls, offering me decent coffee that almost rivals what we have in Central Dorm.

Within ten minutes, my phone's ringing from an unknown number.

I answer immediately. "Hello?"

"Seesaw, *what* are you doing?" Ash says with a laugh.

I exhale, falling into a chair near a window. "I'm losing my freaking mind. It's been three days. Where have you been?"

"Coins."

"What?"

"I'm in Coynston, Massachusetts. Family stuff and work." There are high-pitched children's voices yelling in the background, presumably playing.

"You work in another city? While school's in session? Why? And, for fuck's sake, why didn't you or Jamie text to tell me that?"

"Jamie? Why would he text?"

I fall silent.

"Did you text him?"

When I answer, my voice is slightly bitter. "I don't have his number, so no." Chewing on the corner of my mouth, I shake my head at myself.

Ash must be walking away from the kids because their voices fade and then disappear. "If you didn't text, how would he know to text you about where I am?"

"Just forget it. I've gotta go."

"Hey," she says, her voice becoming serious. "Did you go back to his place?" When I'm silent, she curses. "Aw, Sawyer, come on." She huffs out a sigh. "I should never have taken you over there. I didn't think you'd—never mind. Look, I'm sure when you went there on Friday he warned you not to visit uninvited, but apparently that wasn't enough, so I'm telling you. Do *not* go over there unannounced."

A flash fire of anger lights up my brain. "Right. Glad you're all right. From now on, I'm out." Without waiting, I tap to end the call.

I feel like an idiot. Free-spirit Ash doesn't live the way the rest of us do, so I shouldn't have panicked about her disappearance these past three days, but *hello*... menacing guys are chasing her.

I'm also angry at Jamie for not getting in touch. We slept together four days ago. He promised he'd text. Even if he got busy over the weekend and was planning to reach out later in the week, when I left a handwritten note two days ago, begging him to at least let me know Ash was all right, someone should've put me out of my misery.

Walking out of the lounge, I stop by the campus police's front desk.

"She's fine," I say to the officers who were helping me. An embarrassing flush burns my cheeks. "Sorry I bothered you."

The police guys look sympathetic. "It's not a problem. We'd always rather have a false alarm than not get notified until it's too late."

"Thanks." I hold up a hand in a half wave as I exit the office.

Outside, sunlight blasts my retinas, blinding me. Worry kept me from sleeping well the past couple of nights, and now my head throbs. I fumble through my backpack for my sunglasses. Once I shove them on, I sigh heavily.

Deep down though, I don't feel calm and I don't understand why that is. I desperately wanted Ash to be all right, and she is.

If anything had happened to her, I would've felt sickeningly guilty for waiting so long to report her missing. Knowing she's okay should make me ecstatic.

A niggling irritation is like pinpricks into my eyeballs. I realize it's because I haven't recovered from feeling alone and afraid I'd lost another person I care about. It's happened over and over... Entering foster care meant losing touch with my bio mom and everyone I knew. In middle school, my best friend moved away, and finally, Mom died.

By now, I know that no matter what happens, I'll make it through to the other side. It's what I do. But I guess there's a part of me that doesn't want to go through another round of that hurt.

I pass the building where a class I'm going to skip today will be held. All I want to do is get back to my room, close the shades and bury my face in my pillow for a twelve-hour nap.

Stomping back to Central, I tell my brain to calm down and get ready to rest because there's no way I'm losing any more sleep thinking about this.

Fucking Ash. Why the hell do I already care so much about her and her damn cousin?

❧❦❧

"Sawyer!"

Trying to fight my way out from under my blanket, I mentally—and groggily—curse my life. "*What?*"

Somewhere above me, Ash's amused voice pierces my surly mood. "Hey, babes, you better get up."

I'm silent.

"Seesaw—"

"What?" I fling the covers back and open one eye. "What day is it?"

"Still Tuesday. And hey, sorry you were worried about me."

She bends down and kisses the top of my head. As though I'm a toddler. "You need to call Jamie."

That brings me to an upright, sitting position. Bright hair hangs over my eyes, and I peer at Ash through the tangled mess. She's wearing a manga t-shirt with a kitty on the front, along with a dark pink miniskirt. If I wasn't so tired and annoyed, I'd question her fashion choices. "What did you say?"

Ash's smirk makes me feel like punching the wall. "Call my cousin back, you little psycho." She sits on the edge of her bed. "He's in Coins, by the way."

He was gone and still hasn't come back even though the weekend's long over?

"'Little psycho,' your words, Ash? Or his?"

She laughs. "Mine." Ash hops up and goes to her dresser where she unpacks a small duffle. So, she really is moving in? "Call him back and then get your ass in the shower. We have to go shopping before the boutiques close." She pulls the curtain back, letting light in and opens the window a crack. "I'll wait down in the lobby cuz this room smells like Pumpkin Spice gym socks. Jesus." Flinging the door open, she marches out of our dorm room.

"What the AF?" Grabbing my phone, I open the messages I got while I was asleep. One's from Ash announcing she's on her way home. Another is just one word, *Jamie*. And there's a voicemail from Jamie's number. I play it.

"It's me. Call me." He sounds pissed.

The guilt I feel about causing trouble is brief as defensive anger quickly takes its place. If Ash and Jamie had just given me their numbers from the beginning, I wouldn't have had to go psycho-worrier on them.

I take a deep breath to calm down before hitting the call-back button.

By the third ring, I'm angry again.

"Sawyer." His tone is measured.

Mine is clipped. "Hey."

Silence stretches on for several moments, and I'm becoming exasperated. "Well?"

"Well what? You're the one trying to reach me. What do you need?"

Rising to my feet, I start to pace. "Didn't Ash tell you? I was worried about her. I didn't have her number or yours. I left you a note."

"I heard."

I jerk to a stop. "You—?"

"War found it. Don't go to the house again unless I've told you to come over."

If spontaneous combustion were possible, I would go up in a blaze of white hot flames.

"No need to worry about that happening." My phone case creaks in my grip. "*Ever* again."

"Grand."

Clenching my jaws, I count to three. "What I'm saying—"

"Hey." He cuts me off with a curt tone. "Whatever you're planning to say, do yourself a favor and don't. You're already in trouble with me, little girl."

His words have me wanting to throttle him. But his accent and dominance have me wanting to *be* throttled.

Memories of Jamie's hand on my neck while his cock drove into me spread goosebumps down my spine, lighting up places that are now very much awake—and itching to relive certain experiences.

Maybe Ash is right. Maybe I *am* a little psycho.

"I'm driving back," Jamie says. "We'll see each other tonight. Until then, behave yourself."

My silence is half rebellion, half excitement.

"Cranberry Sauce?"

I lick my lips, knowing the cup of water by my bed won't quench this particular thirst. "Yes?"

"I want to hear you understand me about the house." At my continued silence he growls. "*Sawyer?*"

A twisted part of me likes being able to get a rise out of him. But self-preservation wins out. "Yes, I understand." My mouth opens to explain why I felt compelled to drop by, but he's already disconnected.

The call's abrupt ending leaves me wondering when he's getting back and just how he expects me to get to his place. I'm not taking the bus to that part of the waterfront after dark.

Before I can figure out this latest in a long list of conundrums, my phone buzzes.

> Ash: Get down here! b4 stores close. ffs

Right. Shopping. Do I even want to do that?

Yeah, actually. I want to hang out with Ash.

Also, she's probably the only person on campus whose personality is big enough to distract me from thinking about Jamie.

I grab my hairbrush and drag it through my hair and then snag my toothbrush and bag of toiletries. After shooting her a quick text that I'm coming, I launch myself out into the hall.

14

JAMIE

The Porsche 718 Cayman handles well as I make my way out of the city toward campus. While my weekend purchase was available in a reddish purple color that reminded me of Sawyer's hair, I bought the graphite grey instead. Didn't help keep Cranberry Sauce off my mind, though. After all, wanting my own vehicle is mostly due to the fact that I didn't want to use the Crue SUV when I needed a passenger seat to put her in.

After fighting through Boston traffic, I reach the house in Foxgrove at half-past six. Wind churns the Tyne River, and I stand in our lot and admire the white-caps.

When I finally jog up the metal stairs to the second-floor apartment, the door opens before I get my key out.

"A Porsche?" War shakes his head. "She really needs that much of a push to deep-throat your cock?"

Rolling my eyes, I walk inside and set my duffle on the kitchen table. "I didn't buy it because of her."

"Sure." War throws a balled-up piece of paper at me.

I ignore what I assume is Sawyer's note because there's a thick cardboard envelope from Ireland at the table's other end.

War gestures to the mail. "Yeah, that came, too. What's up?"

"Divorce papers." I shrug my brows and lift the envelope. "Gotta get rid of the wife before my cute American schoolgirl finds out about her."

"Right." War lowers himself onto a couch and puts his feet on the coffee table. "Did Trick go over tomorrow night's operation?"

As I was in Coynston, home of all three of the C Crue founders, you'd have thought one of the bosses might have wanted to talk to me about work, but the weekend's chaos prevented it. There was a party to celebrate my aunt's birthday, and when you come from a popular Irish family, friends and relatives pour in from the surrounding area. Even Trick's massive house overflowed.

For a moment, an image of his young sons yelling and racing through the house springs to mind and makes me smile. Only a year apart, the lads are best mates. The little one, Finn, looks so much like Jude did as a toddler that seeing the brothers together, thick as thieves, hit me in the chest more than once.

When my attention jerks back to the present, War's scrutinizing me.

Running a hand through my hair, I clear my throat. What were we talking about? Oh, right. "No, tomorrow's op didn't come up. At first, the house was practically under construction. So many decorations going up, you'd have thought it was the Queen's Jubilee." I shake my head. "Honestly, my aunt seemed to think the light show was overkill, too. But when Trick and Ash throw a party for someone, a party is *thrown*."

War exhales a mirthless laugh. "Apparently. Surprised no one's roof caught fire. Those fireworks, definitely not street legal."

"No." I smirk. "C Crue's got the Coynston town council in its pocket."

War and I drove to Coynston together on Saturday, but he stayed at his uncle's place. Didn't even put in an appearance at the party. The guy can be pretty fucking antisocial sometimes. All three of our bosses, Trick, Connor—aka C—and Anvil were there. Anyone else would've at least shown his face for an hour, but War didn't.

I lower myself onto a chair. "What happened to you? The steaks and Scotch alone were worth a drop-in."

War's expression remains unmoved. "Working."

Cocking an eyebrow, I stare at him. We both know his excuse is about as true as me saying I have a wife. War could've made the time, but he seemed to want to make a statement, instead. And the statement was *I'm not here to socialize.*

Fair play. His choices are his business.

I turn my hand over in a gesture of acquiescence. "Right."

C Crue has us scheduled to run a pop-up rave at a place called The Ruins, an abandoned mansion on the southwest edge of town not far from the house.

The event is actually the bait to draw out two students who work in the university's IT department. Both guys are fans of Tronex, the celebrity DJ who'll be spinning. C Crue apparently owns a piece of him. For a crime syndicate, their investments are surprisingly broad. This isn't your grandfather's Irish Mafia.

Once the IT guys arrive, we'll make sure they're well lit—whether that's of their own accord or because we've had the bartender mickey their drinks. Then Killian will break into their townhouse to plant keystroke analyzers on their computers.

War stretches his arms overhead, and the pop of his shoulder joints is like walnut shells cracking. "Grab your laptop. I uploaded schematics."

My brows rise. "You think we need floor plans?"

He shrugs. "C gave me a mechanical pencil and fucking graph paper. Said Anvil wanted to know how I would stage things if I were planning it."

By his appearance and manner, you wouldn't guess War's

potential as a strategist. He looks like a guy who only steps out of the gym long enough to kick people's asses on enforcing gigs. But Connor, C Crue's leader, has been grooming him for bigger things, and C doesn't waste time on lost causes.

After grabbing my computer, I drop onto the couch next to him.

War pops his knuckles. "Frats have used the Ruins for parties they don't want associated with their own houses. And yet, they still get raided. I looked into why that happened so it won't when we're there."

My eyes skim over the marked-up floor plans and photos in our shared, encrypted folder. "Noise?"

"You'd think, but it's set pretty far back on the property. Well away from surrounding houses. Still, we'll cover the walls with packing foam to muffle the noise." He taps the screen, indicating areas for sound-proofing. "I checked last year's newspapers. Turns out online chatter and light pollution were the key tip-offs. People posted photos of themselves, and police started combing the area until they spotted signs of life where there shouldn't have been."

"Typical," I scoff. Choosing a clandestine location and then fucking things up by outing themselves digitally.

War makes a dismissive hand gesture. "Last night, Killian and I covered the street-facing windows with blackout film. And we're gonna have jammers to keep people from fucking live-streaming themselves."

"How is the DJ gonna spin? His equipment is wireless."

"Not tomorrow night." War smiles. "We're using cable fibers. Killian said you guys could hijack a feed."

I nod, thinking through what that will require. "Yeah, we can do it. Power?"

"Portable generators." He taps the screen again. "Already on site."

I point at one of the skull-and-crossbones symbols marking different points on the schematics. "What are these?"

"Muscle." War makes a dismissive hand gesture. "C's sending two truckloads of Crue to help keep the peace in case we need it. Seven guys, not counting us. But those hardcore Crue guys are used to pulling their weapons immediately when there's trouble, and we can't have gunfire flying inside the mansion. If some rich college kid catches a bullet, all hell will break loose."

Smothering a smile over the fact that War's implying that anyone other than a rich college kid getting shot wouldn't cause problems the Crue couldn't handle. It's also funny that War talks about students like they're another species, when in fact, we're GU students ourselves.

War flicks a finger at a skull marker. "I'm putting them outside on the perimeter to stop any local bangers with thoughts of crashing. You and I will handle anything that goes down in the house."

"Sounds right." My eyes rove over the screen.

War rises, stretching. The stitches in his thigh must pull because he scowls down at his leg.

Taking his standing as a signal the conversation's over, I close my laptop. "By the way, Sawyer's gonna be here tonight." I nod toward the stairs. "I'll use the first floor bedroom in case things get noisy."

He shrugs. "Like I give a fuck about that kind of noise. You do need to lock her down when you go to sleep, though. 'Cause if she snoops where she shouldn't, I'll kill her rather than report to the bosses that we've had another pussy breach of our pad's secrets."

I scowl. The thought of anyone hurting Sawyer causes adrenaline and testosterone to pour into my blood. My muscles contract reflexively. Yeah, no one's touching her. Which isn't to say I don't understand War's concerns. Pressing my lips into a thin line, I frown more deeply. This time I'm angry at myself. Cranberry Sauce isn't my girlfriend. If she doesn't behave herself, by rights, she should be subject to the consequences.

My pulse, however, registers a sustained objection. "She won't get into trouble, War. Everything's under lock. Same as when we've had girls here in the past."

"Whatever. My warning's on record." He walks away but pauses halfway to the hall. "Speaking of that, neither she or your cousin are welcome at the rave. No distractions while we're working."

"Agreed. Killian's girlfriend should stay home, too."

"Killian's preoccupied with her whether she's in the fucking room or not. I'll let him make up his own mind where he wants her." War inclines his head to emphasize what he says next. "Besides, Killian's girl knows better than to misbehave. Being chained up makes an impression."

15

SAWYER

The boutique I visit with Ash carries high fashion vintage clothing that makes my mouth water. There's a black 1990's Chanel cocktail dress with signature fringe that would be perfect for the Briar Club mixer. The excitement I feel when I realize it's in my size is quickly dashed when I learn that, at 1800 dollars, it's way out of my price range.

Ash wrinkles her nose from across the aisle. "Plain black?"

"*Chanel*. Always a classic."

The corner of her mouth curves into a smirk as she throws a Gucci belt over the stack of items she's carrying.

"It would be perfect for an upcoming Briar event."

A brilliant multi-colored scarf flutters over Ash's arm. It's Versace, which I adore... from afar. I've always wanted a Versace piece.

"If you need it, get it, Seesaw."

Forlornly, I set the dress back on the rack. "If I emptied my bank account and sold my plasma, I'd still be about 1500 short."

With price apparently not an object, Ash picks out an

emerald green beaded flapper dress and a black-and-green lace mask.

I finger the suede inserts of a cowboy-style leather jacket. "Are you going to a costume party?"

Ash assesses the *Gatsby* beadwork. "It's not strictly costume, but girls in sexy dresses and masks get in for half price. It's an underground party, which says speakeasy to me, so I'm feeling flapper vibes."

Pulling out her phone, she opens a text that has a sexy black-and-white image of a girl leaning against a brick wall, wearing a sleek dress and Venetian carnival mask. In block letters, the announcement reads: Let Tronex Vibes *Ruin* You.

Admiring the pic's erotic undercurrent, I say, "I love Tronex."

"He's gonna be there in person."

My head jerks up, and I gasp. "Shut up."

I've been obsessed with Tronex since I saw him at a festival before he broke out. He has one song that summarizes my whole life. I played it on repeat for two straight years.

Ash smiles and winks.

She has to be wrong. Tronex plays stadiums, not little parties in college towns. Cocking my head, I study her. "How much is it to get in?"

"Fifty is full price for girls." She holds the dress up to the light, smiling at the beads' kaleidoscope reflection. "A hundred for guys, I think." With her free hand, she grabs a hanger holding a maroon satin slip dress with embellished gold crocheted trim along the plunging neckline and hem.

"Gorgeous," I say, leaning closer. "That silk lace edging looks hand-sewn."

Ash smiles at the dress before holding it out to me. "Here."

The piece, while beautiful enough to stop me from longing for a Tronex fix, is also so delicate and light, I bet I could ball the whole dress up and put it in my pocket.

I take a step back, shaking my head. "I can't wear a lingerie dress."

"Why not?" Ash frowns at the outfit, then me. "You'd look amazing in this." She eyes the lace top. "If you're self-conscious, just wear a mask. No one will even know it's you."

"Even forgetting what my family would say if they spotted a pic of me in that, I mean I literally *can't*." I grip my boobs. "I'd need to go braless, and unless I'm going to take up sex work, I can't go bare under a crochet bodice."

Ash pouts. "Why couldn't you, Seesaw? You would slay in this." She jostles the hanger, throwing me an imploring look. "At least try it?"

I shake my head, now thinking less of nip slips and more of the complications my going to an underground party could cause. "I wish, but no. A party where illegal stuff may happen is too risky for me. Between Briar Club and my uptight extended family..." Shrugging, I turn toward a rack of little black dresses. Still expensive but less dangerous to the strict reins I've held tight to all my life.

Ash's pout purses. "Okay, no worries." Now seemingly unconcerned, she secures its hanger back on the rack, the satin dress rippling like liquid chocolate. "Truth be told, I probably shouldn't go either, for reasons, but there's no way I'm gonna miss the chance to hear the new Tronex tracks before they drop."

My head snaps in her direction again. New tracks? For that, he'd *have* to be present. "Were you serious about his being there in person?"

Acting a little too blasé to be believable, Ash fingers the feather curling over the brow of her mask. "I am. He likes to test new material live. My brother and his friends are longtime investors in Tronex's career, so—" She flips her hand in a "there you go" gesture.

At my following silence, Ash's smile widens.

Knowing I'm probably being played, but not caring, I step closer. "Your family is in the music business?"

Ash moves along the aisle. "Not specifically, but my brother and his partners used to throw big warehouse parties in Boston, New York, and Jersey. That's where they met Tronex, back when he was up and coming."

I follow behind her, still reeling from the news of her celebrity ties.

She lifts the lingerie dress again. "In this, they would put you right in front of the stage. Hey, what if we wore wigs, too? Full disguise?"

The temptation of being in the center of the action proves too much. "How much is it?" The price tag flutters to a stop over the bodice, and I gasp at the handwritten number. "Twenty-three hundred?" For fuck's sake. I push it away like it's burning. "Ash, I don't have that kind of money."

Her eyes narrow. "Then how come your dickhead brother wore a Ralph Lauren suede and cashmere jacket to a tavern?"

"Well..." I try and fail to think of a way to explain without sounding pathetic. While we might use the same last name, that doesn't mean we both get the financial benefits from it.

Ash raises her index finger. "That coat retails for three-grand."

"Three-grand? God." Leaning against a rack, I shake my head. "He must be charging things my dad doesn't know about."

Or, at least I hope my dad doesn't know. Because while I don't want or need a three-thousand-dollar coat, the monumental disparity between what Brad is given versus what I'm allowed only highlights how much of an unwanted burden I am.

"If he's charging stuff, you could, too." She waves the dress at me. "Daddy's not going to refuse to pay the bill, right?"

"That's not—" I heave a long-suffering sigh. "Listen, my dad is nice, but he's not *that* nice."

From Ash's flat expression I can tell I'm going to have to be more convincing.

"Plus, Brad will be getting access to some trust money pretty soon." I lean back, arms cross, pleased I remembered that little detail. "That's probably how he plans to pay for his charges."

Before Ash can respond, my phone buzzes.

> Jamie: Coming to campus to get you in 30.

"Oh shit. We have to go back."

"We do?" Ash leans over.

"I'm... going out."

"With?"

I try to back away before she can read the text, but her hand grabs my arm to keep the phone's screen close.

"No one." I jerk my arm free and put my phone behind my back.

From the smirk curving her mouth, I know I was too slow. Ash lights up. "Jamie. Good." She continues toward the cashier, heaving the expensive dresses onto the counter like one would a cart of groceries. "So leaving that note worked to get his attention and he asked you out. Silver lining."

I wince, recalling Jamie's anger on the phone. I'm not sure which annoyed him more, my going to his place or my inadvertently revealing to Ash that I'm in touch with him. FFS. "Ash, we're trying to keep things low."

"His idea, I'm sure. Screw that." Slipping her phone out of her pocket, Ash's fingers slide across the screen before lifting it to her ear. A second later, I hear a familiar Irish accent on the other end.

"What?" I feel the blood drain from my face. "No."

Ash holds a finger up to the stunned saleswoman before strolling a few feet away. "Hey, 'Mr. I'm so flush I just bought a new Porsche', your new girlfriend is broke and needs you to buy her a pretty dress."

Oh, my God. "I do not!" I lunge for her phone, but Ash is quick to dodge. "I don't!" I pursue her as she weaves in and out of the clothing racks. "Ash, what the fuck?"

Ash ignores me and continues to speak to Jamie. "The tag

says twenty-three-hundred, but I'm going to haggle and get them to come down."

A glance at the saleswoman makes me begrudgingly agree with my asshole roommate. The poor woman looks like someone Ash could eat up and spit out before speed-racing to the nearest coffee shop for a pumpkin spice latte.

Giving up on stopping Ash from mortally embarrassing me, I stand still, waiting for the heat radiating under my skin to combust.

"Oh, fuck off, liar." Ash laughs at whatever Jaime says. "I'll buy her the dress myself, and she can be my sugar baby instead of yours." After a moment, she laughs again. "Yes, she loves it. You will, too, if she lets you see her in it."

Face flaming, I take a few more steps backward. I can't even believe her right now. He must be furious.

Ash grabs a gold mask from a jewelry rack. "Good man."

Apparently not combusted, though kind of wishing I had, I stare, slack-jawed as Ash approaches the cashier.

Ash waves away my bewildered look. "He's getting it for you."

"Ash, what the hell?"

She grabs a black leather skirt with a row of shiny metal buttons down the front. "Look at this. Perfect for my sister. Kat's going to be so pissed." Ash laughs merrily. "Unofficially, Scotty made me my family's personal shopper because I'm the only one who loves shopping." Ash runs a hand over the buttery fabric. "Even if she's annoyed, Kat will totally wear it. I know her style."

I'm speechless. Is this for real? She just goes on a spending spree whenever she wants, and her brother is cool with it?

The saleswoman looks between us and the heap of clothing on the counter. "You have some really great pieces."

"Yes, and I'd love to take them all, but…" Tossing her hair over her shoulder, Ash smiles like the spoiled shopaholic I'm starting to suspect she is. "But I need a 'good customer' discount. I'm thinking thirty percent."

"Ash, the slip dress is going back," I hiss, my discomfort blossoming into a panicky feeling. I'm not Jamie's girlfriend. Pushing him into buying me clothes is totally sketchy. I retrieve the lingerie dress from the collection. "Even with thirty-percent off, this would still be over a thousand."

"Sixteen-ten," Ash says with a click of her fingers as she grabs the hanger. "And no, it's not going back."

What the what? I blink at Ash doing the math in her head like Barbie Savant.

"Okay, *Sixteen hundred.* Jamie won't—"

She turns, pinning me with her china blue eyes. "Listen, Seesaw." Something in her voice snaps me out of my downward spiral. "Jamie makes a ton of money now. Way more than I do." She gestures toward the clothing. "He can afford to buy you a dress, and he *should* because you make his eyes light up, which is not something that usually happens with him."

My spirits lift, and a small smile threatens.

"Life is so fucking fleeting." A rare, stoic expression flashes across Ash's face that makes me wonder what she's seen to feel that way. Then I remember her dad died young.

The saleswoman clears her throat, breaking the moment.

Smiling once more, Ash clasps my shoulder. "Jamie needs to enjoy his money, and buying you a beautiful dress will make him happy. *Especially* if you act all sweet and grateful." She rolls her eyes. "That's what guys crave. Trust me."

The cool satin warms in my hands by the time she stops talking. She takes the dress and lays it firmly on the pile.

Ash gives the saleswoman the full-force of her charismatic presence, leaving me speechless while she negotiates a ridiculous deal that leaves me feeling one more thing—guilt over the way she steamrolls the saleswoman.

"Here." Ash hands me one of her bags. "Take this." Grabbing the others, Ash hustles to the door.

"Why are we running?" I brace against the cold as we exit the shop and head toward Ash's Camaro parked out front.

"*Because...*" Ash opens the door and tosses the fortune in designer clothing onto the back seat. Pausing to rest her arms on the roof, Ash smirks. "While guys like Jaime have no problem throwing down cash for pretty things, they *hate* to be kept waiting." She winks. "Trust me."

When I leave the dorm with my overnight bag, the sun has set, so the path lights are on, casting moody shadows around the campus. I'm anxious about the reception I'm going to get from Jamie.

If he's furious, it doesn't show as he stands a few feet from the resident hall's main door. Passing girls look over their shoulders to check him out. I want to flip the gawkers off, but he doesn't really belong to me, so I don't.

Looking like a Ralph Lauren model, Jaime takes my backpack and guides me toward the parking lot nearest the dorm.

"I'm sorry about the phone call. I swear I didn't tell Ash I was seeing you tonight. Or that I wanted you to buy me a dress." My nerves, getting the better of me, have gone full babble mode. "We were shopping *for her*, but when I told her I needed to go home because I was going out, she grabbed my phone. She's so—"

"I know all about my cousin. Enough about her." He hefts the bag. "So, did you bring the dress to model it?"

"No, it's up in the room." Does he think I'm insane? I would never wad up a sixteen-hundred-dollar designer dress and shove it in my backpack. "And you don't really need to pay for it. I'm going to take it back."

As we reach the lot, one of his brows rises as he scrutinizes me. "Because you're not sure you want it?"

"No, I do. But it's too expensive, and the style's really bold.

There aren't many places I could even wear it." I worry my lower lip with my teeth. "Gorgeous, though."

The way he stares at me makes me shift from foot to foot.

"Honestly, I got caught up in the moment. Ash was moving so fast..." My laugh sounds strangled. "If anything, I should've gotten a dress for the upcoming Briar Club event I have to attend. That's a place where everyone will be judging what I wear and making decisions that affect my entire future. So, getting a slinky party dress was... crazy." Shaking my head, I pause to take a breath.

"Sawyer?" Jamie rests a hand on my shoulder.

"Yes?"

"Why are you talking a hundred kilometers per minute?"

"Oh, um—" I glance back at the dorm, which is a lot farther away than I thought it'd be. "I guess I got worked up. I don't want you to think I'm *that* girl. The one whose family has money, so she's got a terminal case of affluenza."

"Affluenza?" While the pinch between his eyes suggests confusion, the upward tilt of his lips gives away his amusement.

And for once, instead of someone's amusement at me flipping on my internal defensive switch, I find myself smiling back. "Whatever." I huff out a small laugh. "What I'm saying *is* that I don't have an overblown sense of entitlement. *At all.* I like to consider myself more down to earth than the quintessential Granthorpe elite, and while living on a tight budget is not something I love, I can deal."

He studies me for a moment. "A tight budget, is it?" Continuing to eye me, he finally says, "Flash—in terms of cars and clothes—is not something that ranks highly with me. But money's a means to an end, and that does matter to me, as it does to anyone." His fingers tuck a strand of my hair behind my ear. "My American cousins burn through money like the world's ending in five days. Half the time when Ash gets into a spending frenzy, it seems like she's overcompensating for something. Not sure what that might be, but..." He shrugs. "One thing about our

Ash is she reads people *really* well. I can't tell you the number of times since I came to the U.S. that she's rung me and pulled me into the family fold when I needed it. So if she says you need someone to buy you expensive dresses to keep up with these other girls, I'm inclined to listen." He strokes my jaw with his thumb. "From what I'm hearing from you about budgets, sounds as though she's right."

I open my mouth to protest, but he shakes his head.

"Don't know what a slinky dress is, but I'd wager I'll enjoy seeing you in it, so we'll call that settled." Waving his fingers, he beckons me to follow him.

His casual attitude leaves me sort of stunned. "I thought you were mad at me. And I assumed the dress would make things worse."

Jamie shrugs. "I'm not best pleased by your behavior the past couple of days, no. But I don't blame you for Ash's call. That would be like blaming a person for not being able to lasso a tornado."

The tension in my shoulders easing, I chuckle. "She *is* hard to contain. And you're sure you don't want me to return the dress?"

"I wouldn't have given the green light, if I wasn't." A minute later, Jaime opens the passenger door of a shiny new Porsche, the one Ash mentioned earlier.

I sink into the leather seat. Unable to keep the awe from my voice, I say, "Who needs designer dresses when there's this?" My fingers slide over the buttery fabric. It's such a beautiful car.

He smirks. "Fasten your seatbelt, Cranberry Sauce. This thing rolls a lot faster than a handful of dress beads."

16

SAWYER

When we reach his place, Jamie leads me inside on the main floor. My eyes shift to the stairs where rock music pours down like an avalanche. My spine stiffens. For no good reason, I assumed his housemate would be out.

Jamie strides past the seating arrangements. "This way, Sauce."

I'm relieved when, rather than heading upstairs, Jamie cuts to the left down a hallway.

He opens the door of a guest room and flips on a light. The room's large, accommodating a king-sized bed with an impressive burgundy leather headboard, chest of drawers and end table.

After swinging the door closed, he sets my backpack next to the dresser and turns to face me. "There are some issues we need to deal with, but first..." Bending his fingers toward his palm, he beckons me closer.

Once I'm directly in front of him, he pushes my coat off, so it drops onto the bed's silky silver duvet.

His hands rest on my hips, and he licks his lips. "I had a good time over the weekend, except..." Deep blue eyes trap my gaze. "I wanted to see you."

"That's unfortunate," I murmur with a small smile forming.

"Yeah, I see you're all broken up about it." He draws in a slow breath and exhales, his hands sliding up to my sides.

"Would it help if I told you I missed you, too?"

"Hell no."

My smirk widens. "Then, I won't." My brow cocks. "And, you know, why would I?"

He flashes his gorgeous smile for a second, and then it disappears. "I'll take a kiss before we get into what happens next." His intent expression makes me shiver, and I wonder what is coming next.

Putting my hands on his shoulders, I rise onto my toes. He lowers his head, so I can press my lips against his. A low growl emerges from his chest as he pulls me against him and sucks my tongue into his mouth. Tasting cinnamon and mint, I lean into him.

It's the longest kiss I've ever had, and it's not long enough.

Jamie takes my arms and sets me back away from him with a low curse. "You make me forget what I'm about, Sauce." Exhaling a slow breath, he squeezes my arms then releases me. "Right, okay." His Irish accent sends chills down my spine. I swear it's become more potent every hour since I've known him.

I extend my arm so my thumb can rub my plum-colored lip balm from his lips.

He crosses his arms over his chest. "You were supposed to keep our relationship quiet, especially from my cousin."

"Tried." I shrug. "I haven't told her the nature of the arrangement. That's the main thing I'm supposed to keep secret, right?"

"Mmm. True enough. And you haven't spilled details?"

"Of course not."

"Nor even hinted?"

"No."

"Which I suppose explains why she's tried to put me on notice that I need to buy you presents."

Rolling my eyes, I make a derisive sound in the back of my throat. "You could've just said no."

"I could, yeah." His thumb rubs his lower lip and then he sucks the tip, as though he's looking for traces of our kiss. "Ever been spanked, Cranberry Sauce?"

My brows rise. "Never." As my heart kicks into high gear, I tilt my head.

"Normally, the thought of punishing someone doesn't turn me on much, but in this case..." His predatory look provokes both anxiety and arousal. "We'll try it, then decide if it's right for our arrangement." He rolls up his shirtsleeves to the elbow, showing off toned forearms. "Take off everything except your knickers."

His cool blue eyes make it clear he intends to bend me to his will. Deep inside, things clench and ache with need.

I rub my upper arms, giving myself a hug.

One of his brows rises in a stern, slightly mocking expression. "Are you stalling? After popping up at this house uninvited to leave a note, when I made it clear I would reach out when I was ready?"

Blowing out a breath through pursed lips, I shiver. "Special circumstances."

"No." The finality in his tone makes me wince. "You could've gone to the dorm's RA, right? And you did go to the campus police. So, coming 'round to my place, not necessary."

Warmth burns my cheeks. He's right. I had alternatives. My subconscious—and not so subconscious—motives are clear. I wanted to connect with him.

"Strip, Sauce." He inclines his head for emphasis. "Or use your safeword, and I'll drop you home."

With a shudder, I jerk into action, tugging the sleeve of my sweater to free my arm. He steps back, giving me room to undress. He's so businesslike I wonder whether agonizing over my lingerie was a waste of time.

Spotting the hunger in his eyes as I raise the hem of my sweater, though, makes me decide it wasn't. Pleasure courses through me as he watches my every move. I pull the sweater over my head slowly.

Sitting on the edge of the bed, I remove my shoes and socks. As I peel off my leggings, he licks his lips, apparently enjoying the show. When I stand again, I pause in a subtle pose. My indigo satin lace bra and panties look great with my skin and hair. Since I wore the set for him, I want him to get his fill.

He doesn't disappoint. "Christ, you're gorgeous." When his gaze locks on my body, his breathing deepens and the heat in his eyes could burn the house down. "Bra off."

After reaching back and removing it, I set it on the dresser.

He's already seen me topless, but you'd never know it from his unblinking countenance. There's gravel in his voice as he says, "Come over here."

When I do, he brushes his thumb along the curve of my breast.

"Your nips would look great in clamps."

My pussy clenches. Nipple clamps? That sounds like it would hurt, and yet... I can't explain why I'm so intrigued. "Do you have them here?"

"Yeah." A slow smile emerges. "Curious, huh, Sauce? Always a great thing to find in a play partner."

In a fluid motion of pure athletic strength, he grabs me and carries me to the bed. Sitting on the edge, he tips me over his lap. All the air rushes from my lungs as my head and upper body tilt toward the floor.

Jesus, he's strong. Which causes another blaze of lust in my pelvis. But also, I'm now positioned over his thighs with my ass pushed up. Unable to keep from squirming with embarrassment, I start to slip from his lap.

Instantly, Jamie's arm snakes around my waist and hauls me

closer, so my hip is pressed against his hard abs. And it's not the only place he's hard. His erection beneath my belly causes my pussy to cream.

"Be good." The warm masculine tone draws out another small shiver from me.

Then his strong hand lands on my ass in several swats. It isn't until the third smack that my body registers the sting.

At first, the pain doesn't bother me. I'm too enthralled by his show of dominance.

When his fingertips catch the elastic of my panties and pull them down to my knees, I gasp as my vulnerability increases exponentially.

Suddenly being naked from the waist down, with my whole ass and between my legs exposed causes me to squeeze my thighs together. "Hold on," I whisper.

Jamie pauses, but when I reach for my undies, he grabs my wrists and pins them against the small of my back. That easy show of power causes my breath to catch. I can't stop him, not physically. As I squirm, he moves a leg to trap me, keeping my bare upturned ass in perfect position.

"You're not in control, little girl. Relax and accept it."

Shivering uncontrollably, I exhale. "I need a minute."

"No, you don't. Try to get out of your own head. There's freedom in giving up control. Remember?"

My mind races, and I realize he's talking about when I didn't resist his squeezing my throat during sex. He's right... I completely let go, and that blind faith felt amazing.

His thumb strokes the skin of a wrist he's holding captive. The small touch is reassuring. "Lean in to your helplessness, Sawyer. I'll take care of you. All you need to do is feel whatever feelings arise."

It's tempting to relinquish control. Sometimes, I'm exhausted from always holding myself in check. "Okay, I'll try," I whisper. Concentrating, I force my body to go limp.

"Good girl."

The spanking begins again with a slow, steady intensity until heat blossoms throughout my ass and pelvis. Arousal brews in my core until at least half my focus is on his erection and how great it would feel to have it inside me.

When his hand lands the next time, the real discipline begins. Spanks ring out as sharp cracks, and the burning pain is unnerving. After one hard swat, I gasp and try to twist free. *And fail.*

Jamie pauses to squeeze my flaming ass cheeks possessively.

"I'm—"

"Unless you need to use your safeword, stay quiet." His tone isn't brutal, but it doesn't need to be to cause my lips to part in shock. He's got all the power now, and he wants me to know it.

With something explosive building in my body, I'm not ready to stop yet. Pressing my lips between my teeth, I force my ass and limbs to relax. Instead, I focus on each sensation... My hips grinding against his thighs, his hard cock that's hungry for sex with me, the flames that ignite every time his palm compresses my soft flesh.

The game stretches on until my body is vibrating on the precipice between pleasure and pain. My thoughts start to unravel. The pain is a key that unlocks... *something.*

My body gives up its struggle. I'm breathless and bite my lip as my eyes brim with tears. But my mind floats, aware of the humid heat between my thighs, aware of the way his hand strikes a spot that causes my hip to rub against his hard-on over and over.

When he finally stops and rubs my blazing ass, I can barely catch my breath.

How can anything that hurts so much also make me so hot for him? I want him to bend me over the end of the bed and use me hard.

"Good girl," he whispers. He repositions me, so I'm on my knees, my crying face in front of his groin. Leaning forward, his lips graze my scalp. "You're all right."

I look up through wet lashes as he unzips his expensive trousers. "I need you," I whisper. Shaking as though I'm outside in the freezing cold, my teeth chatter. And yet, I'm not cold. In fact, my ass is scalding the heels of my feet.

Jamie's cock springs free, and he grips it in his fist, pumping it several times.

I open my mouth. Instead of shoving his cock into it as I expect, he puts his fingers onto my tongue. I suck them, and the look of satisfaction on his face ignites a wave of pleasure inside me.

He pulls his fingers free of my mouth. "Stand up," he orders, towering above me. His voice is pure dominance and masculine need. The part of me I've hidden for so long revels in it.

Rising, I lick my lips. His right hand grips my hair and tips my head back. When he kisses me, I cling to him.

"Lie on the bed and spread your legs."

I crawl onto the mattress. When I lie back, the sheets are cool against my swollen ass.

When Jamie joins me, he pushes my knees apart and kneels between them.

Lowering his head, he tastes me, causing my body to vibrate with desperation. His tongue on my clit makes me writhe and moan. I lift my hips to press against him.

In the grips of some kind of primal need, I abandon my senses.

He sucks while penetrating me with his fingers. When the orgasm hits me, my pussy clenches over and over until my legs shake. The air in my lungs emerges as a long, slow shriek.

When my body goes limp, Jamie crawls up the bed and rolls me onto my side. Rubbing his cock against my lips is all the guidance I need. My lips part.

As he feeds me his cock, the smooth head passes my lips and glides over my tongue. Salty pearls of pre-cum trigger a need to eat him alive. Hollowing my cheeks, I suck on the length of him.

"Fuck," he groans.

My fingers grab the back of his thigh in an attempt to pull him in even closer. Jamie thrusts, giving me what I want—more of him. His hand slides into my hair, tangling and twisting until my scalp stings from his grip.

"Christ that's gorgeous." He drags my head forward on his cock, so I'm taking him to the root.

My throat convulses, and my eyes water. Moaning, he eases his grip long enough for me to pull back enough to take a breath. Then he drags me forward again. I fall into the rhythm he sets.

It's gritty and raw and out of control. The world blurs, until there's nothing beyond the way we're joined, the way I'm consuming him.

"Swallow it," he orders in a harsh rasp. Thick strands of cum fill my mouth, and my throat spasms as I struggle to keep up.

My nails dig into his thigh.

By the time he releases my head, I'm dizzy. A little liquid has escaped the corner of my mouth. He catches it with his thumb and smears it on my lips. We lock eyes, and I suck the cum into my mouth.

The bed creaks as he lies down on his side and pulls me against him. Being skin to skin feels so right. Every time his chest expands, his muscles graze my soft flesh.

His panting breaths gradually slow. "Jayzus. Are you all right, C Sauce?"

Hugging him so tightly that I'm risking osmosis, I press a kiss into the hollow of his throat. Moving to the muscles under his jaw, I suck on his flesh. His fingers stroke the back of my neck soothingly.

Jamie cocks his head and pulls back from the vortex of my mouth. "Easy there, baby vampire. If my teammates spot your marks on me, I'll never hear the end of it."

"Not my problem."

That tears a small chuckle from deep in his chest. He rubs my lower back and then rearranges me so I'm under the covers. After he strips out of his clothes, he climbs under the covers and lies on his side, so we're facing each other. His left hand slides over my hip to fondle my still-warm ass.

"How are you, Sauce?"

"Great," I say, leaning closer.

The warmth of his body and our blanket cocoon feel lovely. And strangely safe, in a way not many things have since I lost Celine.

"You can tell me anything." His lips graze my forehead. "More importantly, tell me if something isn't a good experience for you. These kinds of games rely on honest communication."

Tipping my head back so I can see his face, I say, "I don't understand why something that hurts makes the sex even better."

With a rueful smile, he shrugs. "When the tension is higher, so is the release."

Lowering my head onto his outstretched arm, I close my eyes. "I guess that must be it." Raising my lids to half mast, I stare at the pulse in his throat. "I had no idea I'd like this kind of thing. Important discovery for me." My breath blows against his skin. "Even though the arrangement's temporary, I'm really glad we met and hooked up."

His thumb strokes my spine. "Same."

A small dagger of disappointment pierces my heart when he doesn't suggest making things more permanent. I manage to keep from pressing him. We made an agreement, and so far, I'm getting as much from his side of the bargain as he is.

It's enough.

Because it has to be.

17

SAWYER

We have sex twice more before dawn.

As I dress, I'm sore. In the *best* way.

The rowing team has an early morning workout with their coaches, so Jamie drives me back to campus and walks me to the residence hall at six-thirty.

"I'm working late tonight, Sauce, so I can't play with you. Hold tomorrow night for me, though."

"Done."

He winks with a smirk.

"Bye, Jamie." I wait, intending to watch him walk away, but he doesn't move. "You're waiting for me to go in?"

"It's still dark out, so yes."

"Okay." With a wave, I head to the security keypad and swipe my ID. I love that he's watching me get inside safely. I'm not used to having anyone act protective toward me.

As the door closes, he turns and walks away.

I smile the entire elevator ride up to the room. When I unlock the door and enter, I wake Ash who sits bolt upright with her hair flying everywhere.

"What? What's wrong?"

Laughing, I sit on the edge of my bed to take my shoes off. "Nothing, weirdo. Go back to sleep."

She rubs her eyelid with the heel of her hand. "What time is it?"

"Like seven-ish."

"In the morning? What is *wrong* with you guys?" Falling back onto the bed with a thud that drowns out the squeak of the bed springs, she groans.

Smiling, I strip down to my underwear before crawling under my weighted blanket.

A couple of hours later, I'm drifting in and out of sleep when Ash sits up again. "Seesaw, you awake?"

"Yep."

Rising to her feet, she says, "I can't sleep on this prison-issue bed another minute. Wanna go to Boston?"

Pushing up onto my elbows, I look at her. "I have class at eleven."

"Skip."

Chewing on my lip, I consider. Literary Criticism is one of my toughest classes, and participation factors into the grade. I never blow it off... normally. "Should be okay this once."

"This once?" Ash pauses as she drags clean clothes from her drawers. "You go to all your classes? In the actual lecture halls?"

Laughter bubbles out of me. "Yeah, I like our campus. Besides, it's an upper level course, and the professor is really tough. Doesn't want people thinking it's an easy road."

"Subject?"

"English."

"Are you going to be a tortured writer when you grow up?"

"No."

"What then?"

"Lawyer."

She wrinkles her nose in distaste. "DA or defense?"

"I don't know."

"Don't think. Just answer." She fires the words at me like we're in a movie scene courtroom battle. It's odd and strangely amusing.

"Politician."

A slow smile forms. "Fair play to you," she says in a mock Irish accent. Gathering her clothes, she gives me a pointed look. "Do you need a shower this morning? If so, haul butt, babes, cuz as soon as I'm ready to go, this train is leaving the station with or without you."

"Maybe you should roll without me then," I say, falling back onto the bed. "I'm tired."

Without warning, she hits me in the face with her pillow. "Get your lazy bones up and come on." Then, she stalks out.

My smile stretches wide. I like the way Ash does friendship. Things are never stilted and circumspect. Unlike at my prep school or the Briar Club, there's no careful consideration of whether forming a relationship with someone would be an asset or a liability.

Ash's 'no holds barred' manner is the way I imagine things would be between sisters.

※

WHEN WE'RE ON THE EXPRESSWAY, ASH SINGS OUT OF TUNE TO every song blaring from the enormous speakers.

"Ash!"

She swivels the volume dial down. "Yes?"

"Can you stop splitting my eardrums? Seriously!"

"Music too loud? Or is it my bad singing?"

"Both," I say.

She laughs. "Yeah, the Patricks aren't the best singers. My ma always says she 'couldn't carry a tune in a bucket.' To which Scotty says, 'who carries buckets anymore?' And so, my sister Kat started saying, 'Couldn't carry a tune in a backpack. It's a real shame.'" Ash smirks. "It's our worst thing, and it's genetic.

We all three look like my mom—which is good—and sing like her, which is really, really bad."

"If you know you can't sing, why were you screeching at the top of your lungs for the past twenty minutes?"

"I like to sing and thought you might be too polite to call me out."

"Oh, my God. Such a bitch move."

"Really?" Her eyes widen, and there's a hopeful note to her voice. "I'd really like to be a bad bitch in public occasionally." She makes a fish-lips pout. "But I haven't really got it down. I'm sunny on the regular. And a rebel, quasi-outlaw, on the down-low. But bitchy? Nah."

"Rebel quasi-outlaw? In what way?"

"That's a 'been friends a year' kind of a question. But I will tell you this, because you need to know, the underground party with Tronex? Jamie and his asshole housemate will be working security, and they don't want us there."

"What? Why?"

"We might become—" She lifts her hands from the wheel long enough to make quote marks. "A distraction." Dropping her hands back into position, she lowers her voice a couple of octaves to mimic a guy's voice. "They're very *serious* about their work."

I smirk for a beat and then sober. "Are you still gonna go?"

"Yeah, but I'll understand if you want to stay home so you don't piss off your new boyfriend."

"He's not my boyfriend, exactly." I suck on my lower lip. "And I was a Tronex fan long before I was a Jamie fan." Tilting my head, I shield my eyes from the sunlight pouring through the windshield. "If he's working, I'll steer clear. We won't be a distraction."

"Exactly." Ash offers me her big white-rimmed square sunglasses. Where does she find these things?

I slide them on, and they're so big they hit my cheekbones.

"If it was just War working the door, I'd tell him to fuck right off. His inability to focus is his own problem. But Jamie's my favorite cousin, and we... kind of watch out for each other. That's why you and I are headed to Boston to get wigs. Between them and the masks, done and dusted. Can't be a distraction if we're unrecognizable."

"What's the deal with War?"

"We got off on the wrong foot because..." Ash blows out a breath, squinting in the sunlight. "He's a raging asshole who despises everything about me. And he's worked hard to earn my complete loathing." She nods and flips her hand over for emphasis. "Other than that though, we could've been besties."

Chuckling, I cock my head. "Are you sure he despises you in particular? The guy's resting face is a glare. Seems like he hates the world in general."

Ash chuckles. "That's on the money." Lifting her hand from the gear shift, she gestures toward the glove box. "Grab my spare sunglasses for me, Seesaw."

I open the glove box and find a pair of aviator glasses. After passing them to her, I watch her out of the corner of my eye.

"I'm not sure what War's damage is." Ash pushes the glasses up the bridge of her nose. "He wasn't raised in Boston or Coynston, so none of us were around for whatever went down while he was growing up. But I know his dad wasn't murdered, like mine was." Her tone carries the most bitterness I've ever heard from her. "And I know his happy family wasn't ripped apart because they were broke, with one sister having to live with relatives in Ireland and a brother forced to live an hour away with a jerk uncle. And a mom so grief-stricken she could hardly get out of bed." Ash purses her lips, then blows out a slow breath.

Grimacing at her pain, I put a hand on her shoulder.

Ash reaches up to squeeze my hand before dropping hers back to the stick-shift. "Sorry, Seesaw." Her tone lightens. "Didn't mean to make it sound so grim. I'm fine. I was only three when my dad was killed, so I don't even remember that. My family did their best to shield me while I was growing up. The hardest thing for me is that I wanted us to all live together again. Sometimes, it was just my mom and me at the house, and I missed our other three. *So* much."

"You were really close, huh?" The pang that hits me nearly brings tears to my eyes. My own losses were so tough that any tragedy that causes family separation is like a knife twisting in my chest.

"Yeah. We're still close." She shrugs. "I'd do anything for them. Need a kidney? Here you go."

And this is the girl War despises everything about? Ash's right. He's a raging asshole.

18

SAWYER

The party is lit, literally. Crazy flashing lights shift into neon colors and swivel between Tronex's turntable and out onto us—his worshippers.

Ash and I bounce up and down in front of the stage, giddy with excitement. We're both wearing black wigs, mine flows like a mermaid, hers is a chic bob.

Tronex wears a black bunny mask from his early days, and his spinning is on fire. With people crammed into every inch of space and dancing wildly, the temperature inside the house has risen ten degrees. The organizers should turn off the space heaters.

Ash says sagely, "They won't. The heat encourages people to lose their clothes."

By midnight, half the men are shirtless and a third of the women have stripped down to their bras, some even to bras and panties as though their lingerie is a bikini. Wearing masks squashes our inhibitions.

To quench my thirst, I slip off the dance floor to drink a Virgin Cape Cod. Ash, a seasoned party girl, drinks real cocktails while dancing erratically. I guess she manages to not spill her drinks because she downs half the cocktail before coming back onto the floor. For some reason, every time she bumps into me, I can't stop laughing.

To add to the wild atmosphere, a pair of young women spray paint that glows in the black light. Most of us have some paint decorating our skin. We blend together and into the walls. It makes me feel insulated and more a part of the college community than anything else has.

Two guys in emoji-print hoodies sell designer pills to people. Ash and I avoid the free-flowing drugs. Because of my bio mom, I find those about as appealing as a traumatic brain injury. The house's frenetic energy is fun, though, and for once, I understand the appeal.

Jamie and the other guys who are part of the security force wear Batman masks and black shirts with a silver barbed C on the chest. The sinister logo fascinates me, but I keep my distance. Jamie's eyes constantly scan the room, but we must be unrecognizable because his gaze never lingers.

At twelve-thirty, on the stairs to the right of the DJ stand, a couple has sex with no interference from the security force. People cheer them on loudly and encourage more groping. A girl removes her bra, and her boyfriend splashes his drink on her breasts, so he can lick it off.

The mayhem intensifies.

Guys have been grabbing us all night, sometimes to avoid falling over in the crush of bodies, sometimes just to touch us. We take it in stride, pushing them away with a laugh and centering ourselves in packs of girls.

When I head to stand guard as Ash uses one of the bathrooms, Jamie appears in the hall. He stalks down the line of women before stopping in front of me.

Without warning, he grabs my wrists, pulls my arms over my head and pins me to the wall. My gasp can't be heard over the music as he leans down and kisses me, crushing my body with his.

His cherry Coke-flavored mouth tastes sweet. With a hammering heart, I open to the brutal kiss. Through a haze of adrenaline and lust, I slide my thigh forward to stroke his groin. He raises his head and moves his mouth to my ear.

"Go ahead." His voice is a snarl, and one hand drops to pinch my nipple. "Dare me to fuck you against this wall. See what happens."

I should resist. Or possibly apologize. But wild rebellion and the need to be close to him win out. I don't pull my leg back. Instead, my back arches, pressing my breast, bare beneath the satin, into his hand.

A crashing sound causes his head to jerk in the direction of the main room. "I'm not done with you." He turns and stalks away, leaving me breathless.

The girls in the line gape at me. The one standing next to me asks, "Do you know him?"

I nod. Thankfully, Ash emerges from the bathroom before more conversation breaks out. She loops her arm through mine and tugs me back toward the party.

Everything appears in order, so the source of the crashing sound must have been people falling down. There's an entire group of drugged and dazed partygoers sitting against a far wall, swaying like they're listening to Enya rather than Tronex's driving beats.

Our spot close to the stage has been claimed. Without making eye contact with Jamie, I follow Ash and melt into the crowd on the dance floor.

We cheer Tronex on when he plays his new tracks, shaking our fists in the air as we jump up and down. Then, my favorite track, *Burn Down*, comes on and I lose my mind, yelling to Ash that it's my theme song.

I don't so much sing as shout the lyrics, lost in the moment. All those lonely days and nights that tore me down and made me feel broken—that made me wonder if a bonfire might not be the best thing that could happen to my life. And now, feeling the opposite emotions. It's cathartic beyond belief.

As the song winds down, I throw my arm around Ash's shoulders, and we dance together. Even under her heavy makeup, I can see her face's happy flush. Mine must be the same.

When a tall guy in a wolverine mask stops in front of us, at first I think it's to flirt. Then I clock the rage in his eyes and a second later recognize them and the small mole above the corner of his mouth. It's my pseudo brother, Brad.

"Sawyer," he snarls, grabbing my face.

I break his grip, but when my chin slips free, he grabs my arm and rips the mermaid wig off, tearing pins from their positions in my real hair. My gasp rings out as he shoves my mask halfway up my forehead and raises his phone.

I recoil but can't free myself in time. He's shooting video of my face, with its smeared makeup and disheveled sweaty hair framing it, along with the bodice of the slip dress where my breasts are partially exposed by the plunging neckline and whisper-thin fabric.

Ash's slim fingers snatch the phone and dislodge it from his grasp.

Brad turns and grabs her, but she twists away and focuses on the phone, clearly trying to delete what he's captured. As he wraps an arm around her throat from behind, he drags her backward, knocking into people. I claw his arm, trying in vain to get him to release her.

Then, suddenly, we're not alone. Bodies go flying as War shoves people out of his way. His massive hand grabs Brad's throat, and Jamie appears and shoves me behind him.

Then things happen in a blur. Jamie plants a foot in the back of Brad's leg, causing Brad to drop to his knee. As he goes down, War releases him. Because of Brad's hold—though loosened—around Ash's throat, she buckles backward as he falls. Before she lands on Brad or the floor, though, War grabs Ash around the waist. He yanks her away from Brad, lifting her several feet off the floor so her side is flush with the sweat-drenched t-shirt that's stretched across his chest.

My heart hammers like I'm sprinting for an Olympic record, but Ash doesn't even bobble the phone when she's wrenched out of my brother's grip. Instead, she slides her fingers over the screen intently.

When she looks up, she locks eyes with me. "Deleted. Nothing to worry about, Seesaw." Holding the phone in her right hand, she reaches out with her left to tug my mask back into position.

"Give me my phone," Brad snaps as he rises to his feet.

"Go fuck yourself." Ash's smug tone causes him to stiffen and ball his fist.

"Skinny cunt—"

Jamie hauls Brad backward. In the same instant, War's left fist shoots out and slams into Brad's stomach, knocking him farther into Jamie.

Brad's breath wheezes out of him as he doubles over and lands back on the floor. I don't think he got the full effect of the punch though, since his momentum was away from it, but he's shaking from more than rage as he retches.

Jamie signals two other security guys who are hovering nearby. "Outside and slow his roll," Jamie orders.

The men grab a startled Brad to haul him away. "O'Rourke, you don't want to do this. You'll lose your scholarship and your spot on the team."

Jamie's blue eyes are deadly cold, but he remains silent.

Moving into our orbit, Crosby Bergmann appears from nowhere. He's not wearing a mask or costume. His black shirt hangs open revealing thick pecs and a barrel-shaped torso. "Hey, what the hell's up? Ashling, is that you?"

"Fuck off," War says, still holding Ash against him.

"Hello, Cros. Did you come with Asshat Brad? If so, I hope

you drove because he's been bounced, and if he's your ride, you're walking."

"Allendale's not with me," he says quickly. "Not after a certain girl made her feelings on him crystal clear. Hey, Andre the Giant, you can put the princess down now."

I expect War to drop Ash so he can hit Crosby, but he doesn't rise to the bait.

Still, there's a toxic cloud of testosterone and rage swirling around us. I don't want Ash and I caught in the middle of a fight if one erupts. My muscles tighten as I pick up my wig and yank it into place, trying to figure out how to get us away.

"Princess Bride. I love that movie," Ash says in an easy tone as if her feet aren't dangling well above the ground. She looks War in the face and gives him a pretty smile that's mock flirtatious. "If you wanted to dance, all you had to do was ask."

Oh, my God. He is not someone to taunt—

"For fuck's sake," Jamie says.

Ash grimaces, and I guess at the cause because of the way she looks down at her side where War has her in a vise grip.

Jamie moves forward, but before he intercedes physically, Ash's voice changes again. Now she's calm and serious. "War, truce." As their gazes lock, something passes between them. Her voice implores him. "For the night, truce."

"You shouldn't be here," War says as he sets her on her feet.

"Not up to you."

"Your cousin banned you."

"Not up to him, either." Her eyes flick to Jamie. "No offense, James. I love you, but if you want me to respect a ban, it needs to come down from the top."

Jamie's lips tighten into a frown. "If that's the way you want to play it, all right."

She wrinkles her nose. "Still friends?"

His angry expression eases and he nods grudgingly. "Always."

Stepping forward, she gives him a hug, which he doesn't return. "The party was great." She turns. "I'm ready to go." Her hand catches mine and holds it, claiming me as hers. "Cros, walk us out?"

"No." War's arm stretches between them, blocking Crosby's access to Ash. "That's J or me."

Ash cocks her head. "Can they really spare you, Security Monster?"

"Get moving," he growls, giving her shoulder an impatient push that propels her forward. "You, too," he says to me before taking the lead.

Jamie's hand slides down to tap my ass in a subtle threat. "I'll see you later." His gaze traps mine.

I try to keep the rebellion from my eyes. And fail. It's not my fault Brad is an asshole.

Jamie's lips flatten into an annoyed line, but I don't wince or shrink back. Ash and I had an amazing time. I don't regret coming, despite how badly the night ended.

War forces people to clear a path.

Ash tugs me along, still holding my hand as though we're five years old. Glowing and completely unruffled, she walks directly in War's wake. "This is the most fresh air I've breathed all night." Her tone is faintly amused. "Having a human tsunami lead us out is helpful."

※

In our dorm room, we're in the middle of changing clothes and removing makeup when my phone rings from an unknown caller. When I don't pick up, I get a text.

> Unknown: Come down with phone now or later you get what you get.

Realizing it's Brad, I stiffen and all my earlier bravado falters. Even without video evidence, he'll probably give a full report to our family. The slutty lingerie outfit and wild dancing... He might even claim I was drinking and using drugs.

Most people were. There would be no way for me to prove I wasn't.

"Fuck," I say, scrubbing off my makeup and pitching the wipe into the trash. I need to tread carefully.

"What?" Ash pulls pins from her hair, and blond waves tumble down.

"Give me Brad's phone." I send a text to the borrowed phone he's currently using.

> Sawyer: I'll bring it down.

Ash's eyes narrow, but she makes no move to dig his phone from her bag.

Extending a hand, I bend my fingers in a "c'mon" gesture. "He's threatening to make trouble if he doesn't get it back right now."

"Threats," she murmurs with a roll of her eyes. "Idiot." She shrugs. "But I'll give it back."

"Oh no, I'll do it."

As much as I love Ash's attitude, I'm concerned about how wrong things could go if I let her do the handoff. If she lets him get too close, he could do something to hurt her. It would be subtle and something he could deny... "No, I didn't twist and break her finger. She must have injured it earlier and is blaming me out of spite." He has a psycho personality that allows him to go from menacing to blank-faced in an instant. In my experience, people always give Brad the benefit of the doubt.

Ash pulls on an oversized black sweatshirt. "We'll go together. Safety in numbers."

It is smart for me to have a witness. "Okay," I finally say. "But you hang back. I'll do the handover."

"Sure." Ash pulls his phone from her purse. "I don't suppose you'd let me wipe it?" The twinkle in her eyes drags a nervous laugh from my lungs.

"Why do you wanna cause more trouble?"

"Because family doesn't try to get dirt on each other to keep in a camera roll." She clenches her jaw and, for an instant, looks halfway menacing. "Fuck that little traitor."

I give her a hug. "Thanks for grabbing his phone and deleting the video."

"You don't need to thank me." She drops the phone into my hand. "I wanted you to come out and you did. No way would I let anyone mess with you at a Crue party."

A crew party? Was the event put on by the rowing team? No... because Brad's on the team, and he wouldn't threaten to get a teammate in trouble if it was the whole group's underground party.

I fall silent as we leave the room. My heartbeat races, though I try not to show my anxiety at facing off against Brad.

Would the Allendales believe me about him now? As a child, I told our parents he punched me and shoved me down the two-step landing. He claimed I'd tripped and was blaming him because he wouldn't give me some toy I wanted. They believed him, making it clear I hadn't lived down the lies I'd told when I first arrived as a desperate foster kid. I'd been branded a liar, and he was not.

Worse than our parents sweeping aside my plea for help against a much bigger brother was that the Allendale grandparents were outraged I'd accused Brad of anything. They told my parents it was dangerous to keep me in the house, as though I were a dog who'd bitten someone and clearly needed to be dropped off at the pound to be put down.

When Mom and Dad didn't immediately toss nine-year-old me out, the Allendale grandparents waited for an opportunity to talk to me privately. I remember standing in the corner of their library with the enormous Christmas tree's bows and shelves of leather-bound books looming above. They said if I ever made up another damaging story about their grandson, they'd see me "exiled." They reminded me my dad hadn't adopted me because they forbade it and claimed my mom could be pressured to return me. They were her most important financial backers, so she'd lose her political career without them and their friends.

I knew my mom's career was the most important thing to her. If they could ruin that, she'd never be able to stand up to them. Their words haunted me for a long time. "You'll be sent back into the foster care system where you belong." The sting of their disgust and the threat of being cast out paralyzed me.

For a while, I didn't stand up to Brad. If he took something from my room, I let him. If he broke something of mine, I accepted it. When he belittled me, I swallowed it. My goal was simple. Withstand him. Persevere. Keep his parents as my own. That was the best way to beat him.

As we grew up, his anger at my presence in the house seemed to lessen. His focus was elsewhere, and my life got easier. Until now.

At the front door, Ash lets me walk out first and remains just behind me in the open doorway.

Brad's red-faced from anger and the cold. One eye is swollen nearly shut. I recall Jamie's words. *Slow his roll.* Was that a suggestion to the other bouncers to beat Brad up? If so, I have mixed feelings about it. I don't care if Brad gets hurt. He hurt me plenty of times when we were young. But humiliating him will make him more determined to get the upper hand. And I'm the one who has to be in the same house with him over the holidays.

Brad's angular features are so pinched even his good eye is a slit. The weight of his hatred makes me want to draw back, but I don't move. He shoves limp strands of brown hair back from his forehead. "You're nothing," he spits, his voice dripping with disgust. "And if you keep pushing me, I'll make sure everyone knows it."

Why his fury has flared again so darkly isn't clear. I suspect it's because I'm not trying to make myself small at the moment. Plus, I'm keeping company with a girl who openly despises him.

Women disrespecting him—or taking up space in a big way—isn't something he can stand.

"Here," I say, tossing the phone the few feet to him.

He catches it with a glare and checks it.

While he's distracted, I backtrack to the door. I tap my ID against the security pad. At the sound of the doors sliding open, Brad looks up at me with an expression that implies he'll be eviscerating me at the earliest opportunity.

"Listen—" I start, in a conciliatory tone.

"No," Ash says, dragging me inside.

The doors close, ending the possibility of any more conversation with Brad. Glancing over her shoulder, Ash raises her middle finger at my brother.

A part of me likes that she does it.

Another part winces.

19

JAMIE

When I wake around four in the afternoon the day after the rave, my first thoughts are of Cranberry Sauce in her delicious disguise. Satin nightgowns are the only thing I should ever let her wear.

Grabbing my phone, I review the blurry snaps I took of her. Fake sable hair spills down her incredible body. She would look good with dark hair. Or any color, I reckon.

My fingers enlarge the picture so I can admire the way her nipples tent the fabric. That body. She's too fucking gorgeous.

Licking my lips, I draw in a slow breath. I want her in my bed right now.

Then, I remind myself she's already distracted me way too much.

Setting my phone on the nightstand, I ignore my sexual urges. After a moment of rubbing my eyes, I tell myself, *Work first, then you can have the girl.*

Rolling onto my side, I open the nightstand's drawer and retrieve the envelope from Ireland.

Sitting up, I brace myself. At times, I can maintain the

detachment I need when facing the facts surrounding Jude's case. Others, the details hit me as though I'm still a broken-hearted lad who couldn't save his brother.

Tugging the papers from the envelope, I drop them on my lap.

Here we go.

I flip through handwritten pages first, skimming some of the interviews they did at local inns. No Americans fitting the description we'd given were identified. The detective on the case had planned to expand the radius of their inquiries. But, just as the cop told me on the phone, when the detective followed up with our father, Dad wouldn't let us participate in additional interviews. And the local prosecutor said let it go.

For fuck's sake.

With a few days to contemplate my dad's role in shutting down the investigation, my anger has evolved. It's not sloppy now, like snow trodden into dirty slush. It's more like the invisible black ice that forms in the bitter cold of night. The old man did what he thought was best, and so did the other men involved. They were wrong, but a lot of things are clear in hindsight.

As I flip, Jude's drawing of the man's ring falls out. I've seen several pictures like it in his journal, but this one has the most detail. He's captured the guy's right hand and the ring on its fourth finger. It was burned into Jude's mind while the man was behind him, looming over him, holding down Jude's arms whenever he tried to pull away.

The signet ring tilts to the right, showing part of the top and left side. The uppermost portion has a scripted *R*. On the left side, there's a school crest with a vine above an open book. *Est. 1898*

By the time I began researching the school crests of hundreds of American universities, Jude was gone so I couldn't ask him whether he was sure about the date.

When I found the Granthorpe crest on its class rings, it was a perfect match down to the date it had been founded. Feeling pretty certain I'd found the correct university, I tried to learn the man's identity through digital sleuthing. Unfortunately, photo rosters weren't available to outsiders and the system was too difficult to hack. Ironic that I'd had a much easier time getting into police databases.

Thwarted online, I followed the lead to the United States.

Pretending to be interested in enrolling, I took a tour of the campus and slipped off during lunch to visit the library's collection of yearbooks. I went through class rosters from the years I believed the man may have been enrolled. A hasty and fruitless search.

As soon as I became a GU student, I went back to the library. This time I spent days pouring over the yearbooks, which stretched back for decades. Unfortunately, some of the collection had walked off over the years.

Whether the guy was in an edition that someone had stolen or whether he just looked too different as a young man, I couldn't identify him. After a frustrating few weeks of trying to get the missing editions and failing, I had to concede that I'd taken the yearbook investigation as far as I could.

As I stare at the picture my brother drew, another way to investigate occurs to me. When schools designate a company to produce their class rings, students place their orders. And while digital mockups for a twenty-year-old edition of the yearbook aren't maintained, spreadsheets of purchase orders might be.

A place like Granthorpe is all about tradition. They would use a reputable company and stick with them if they did quality work. How many ring companies could there have been over the years? Two? Three?

If I could get the records for all the rings ordered by male students in the twenty-year window I'm interested in, maybe I could narrow down the list by identifying the men who ordered signet rings with the letter R on top. There can't have been that many. From looking at the past few years of class ring designs, I know signet rings are the least popular choice. Usually, there's a gemstone with the university's name surrounding it or the school crest sitting atop the ring, and the sides have other logos or symbols.

My phone buzzes with an incoming text message. I pick it up.

> Sawyer: U awake?

I respond that I am, and she sends another text in quick succession.

> Sawyer: Am I coming over there? Ash can drop me.

The girl is more anxious to face me than she should be. I'm pissed she and Ash crashed the rave after I said they shouldn't. With Ash, there's no recourse. But Sawyer's mine, and we've already established I'm allowed to punish her.

My cock twitches at the thought, and I clench my jaw. I'm becoming way too invested in this temporary arrangement. Then, I think about the way she looked in that satin slip and accept I need to keep going until I've had my fill. It's the only way I'll be able to get my head clear again.

I glance at my bedroom door. War's heavy footfalls can be heard beyond it. I climb from my bed and open the door.

"War?"

He appears in the hall in shorts and covered in sweat. Apparently, he's been working out. "What?"

"You talk to Killian or the bosses?"

"Both."

"And?"

"Mission accomplished."

I pop the knuckles of my right hand. "Any blowback from the bosses about the rough bounce of a GU student?"

War shakes his head.

"Did you tell C that Ash and her roommate were in the thick of the trouble?"

"I mentioned it. I also asked the question." His jaw clenches. "Can we ban little Patrick from this house and any public op we're running?"

I wait.

"He asked why we would need to ban her. Told him I assume there are things she shouldn't see. And also that if we've gotta keep her out of trouble, I need to plan accordingly cuz she's a live fucking grenade on the regular." A muscle in War's jaw twitches. "C, Trick, and Anvil wouldn't let one of their wives wander through the middle of a fucking op. Anvil's house is practically on fucking lockdown twenty-four-seven."

Not from everyone, I think. Ash is the designated babysitter of Anvil's little girls. But my saying Ash has an "all access" pass into even Anvil's house will just annoy War more.

I lean back against the wall. "So, what was the word from C?"

War scowls. "He reiterated he doesn't want us sharing operational details with anyone, not even other Crue members. What's between the three of us—you, me, and Killian—stays between us and the bosses. But when it comes to the house and campus parties, Ash can go where she wants. Fucking bullshit." His tone is the snap of a whip. "She's reckless, and they let it roll. My question is why? Maybe C or Anvil is fucking her."

My brow cocks.

"Right?" His black glare is a knife trying to slice me open so the truth pours out.

"If I knew that I wouldn't confirm it. And I strongly advise you not to ask questions whose answers could get you killed."

"Me killed? Fuck no. Why would it?" War growls.

"One of Trick's best friends fucking Ashling could blow up the Crue leadership and hence, the Crue itself. If C or Anvil were involved with Trick's baby sister, they would not let that secret surface without a fight."

The black expression on War's face causes my eyes to narrow. Challenging this set of bosses—relatives or not—is straight-up insane. And yet he seems ready to double down.

I lean forward. "Why do you care, mate?"

"I don't," he barks. "Except when she's making trouble on a job site." An oven timer dings, causing him to turn and stalk away.

Shaking my head, I frown. War's interest in Ash is not going to end well. He likes control, and she's a human stick of dynamite.

The image of War slamming through people last night when Allendale put his hands on Ash rises in my mind like smoke. I was close enough to handle it, but that didn't stop War from charging forward and snatching Ash up, effectively taking her off the board. I've rarely seen him move that fast. And he didn't just get her out of harm's way. The minute he had a hold of her, he didn't want to put her down. To someone who knows him, that was very clear.

Ash is no help. He clearly did something to piss her off because that girl pokes the bear every fucking chance she gets. Even while calling for a truce, she was testing him. Asking that asshole Crosby to walk her to her car... She knew that wouldn't fly. But she didn't glance my way or even Bergmann's when she said it. Her eyes were on War.

Shaking my head again, I scowl. They could've been a good match if their chemistry wasn't so volatile. A McCann and a Patrick together would've united the families, which C and Trick probably would've welcomed. But when War gives a girl an order, he expects to be obeyed. And Ash clearly doesn't want to take orders from him.

Given that, it seems like the best thing I can do is keep them apart. Which means I'm not going to greenlight Ash coming by to drop off Sawyer. If she did, Ash would come in to say hello to me, thereby crossing paths with War again.

Raising my phone, I type a text to Sawyer.

> Jamie: I'll come to get you. 1 hour.

20

SAWYER

When Jamie collects me from the dorm, his mood isn't exactly upbeat. He takes the overnight bag from my shoulder, so chivalry is not dead, but there's no kiss.

As we settle in the Porsche, I glance at him as I click my seatbelt. "How are you?"

"Well enough. You?"

For some reason his response casts me into the role of an Allendale. My tone is cool and pitch perfect. "I'm well. Thank you."

Our seven-minute drive to the waterfront house is silent. I stare out the windshield, waiting for the other shoe to drop. If he's angry Ash and I attended the Tronex event, why is he bringing me to his house?

In the guys' parking lot, there's a Honda compact next to War's SUV.

"Whose car is that?"

"War's got company." Jamie leads me into the house through the main door.

As soon as we enter, we face the onslaught of music blaring down from above at an ear-splitting volume.

"Guess he's not planning to have a conversation with him or her." I glance toward the stairs to the second floor apartment. "Jesus, that's loud. How are their ears not bleeding?"

Persistently silent, Jamie guides me toward the hall that leads to the guest room we used last time I was over.

Between tracks, a girl's wail pierces the quiet just before screaming guitars resume. The female's distress brings me a up short and causes my head to jerk so I'm staring at the rafters.

"Is—do you think everything's all right up there?"

"It is, yeah." Carrying my bag, Jamie takes my arm and guides me the rest of the way down the hall.

In the guest room, a collection of sex toys sits atop the nightstand, and black leather restraints with silver chains rest on the mattress.

I stare at the chains, my body suddenly on high alert. "Umm..."

Jamie drops my bag unceremoniously in the corner. "I've got a question for you, Sauce."

Licking my lips, I drag my gaze from the bed to his face. "Yes?"

"Did Ashling tell you I sent her a text saying you guys weren't to attend the party last night?"

My body goes rigid but my voice remains steady. "She was a little vague on details, but yes."

Jamie leans back against the dresser, his muscles flexing. "So, you ignored what I said." His tone is calm, but his cool eyes rake over me in an unfriendly way. "If you ever follow her lead in breaking an instruction I've given again, you and I will be done."

His "matter of fact" tone sets my teeth on edge, even as my heart thumps with heavy beats. With fingers clenching into fists, I fight my natural urge to lash out.

For years, powerful people have tried to dictate how I live my life. And the more I've thought about Brad trying to intimidate me—and the way Ash flipped him off—the more I've realized how sick I am of walking on egg shells. Of being the one who always has to bend to others' wills.

The wash-in magenta color was the first thing I've done to defy Allendale expectations. I knew my grandparents would consider it trashy, but it was popular with the girls in my prep school and was—as Dad pointed out—only temporary, so I got away with it. Which gave me an intoxicating taste of freedom. I'm hoping for more of that once I get into the Briar Club and cement my own future.

Playing a slave girl in bed is fun, but the last thing I want is some guy trying to control every moment of my life. I get more than enough of that already.

"Jamie, I need to clarify something."

"What's that?" From his tone, I can tell he doesn't intend to meet me halfway.

Stiffening, I shake my head. "You know what? Never mind."

Jamie folds his arms across his chest and studies me. "You sure?"

"Look, if you expect to dictate what I do when I'm not with you, you're going to be disappointed."

"It's not about controlling you around the clock. But there were things in play last night that you know nothing about. And wouldn't want to. So, next time, I expect you to listen."

"Look, I've been a Tronex fan for a long time. Also, my roommate was going, and I would not have wanted her to go alone."

His grim expression hits me like a blow. "Remind me, are you the one who protected Ashling when she got in trouble? Or were you the cause of it? And needing to be rescued as well?"

My jaw drops. "That's so unfair!"

"Agreed. I needed to concentrate and keep the peace. Instead, I wanted to tear your brother's fucking head off."

"You didn't—"

"Don't say it," he snaps. "Do not fucking tell me I didn't need to follow you down dark hallways or knock your brother to the ground to stop him from doing whatever the fuck he was trying to do by unmasking you." His eyes narrow angrily. "And when I see your tits bouncing under a dress so thin I could tear it off with my goddamned teeth, all I want to do is shove you against a wall and fuck you. You're the worst kind of distraction, Sawyer. You're the one I can't resist." His breathing is harsh.

My brows rise, and I put my hand on his chest, trying to calm him, even though my own heart's beating wildly. No one's ever felt this strongly about me, and that is hard *for me* to resist.

He lowers his voice. "Don't push me to end things early. That's not what either of us wants."

"You're right. I don't want it to end. Next time, I'll do my best to get Ash to change gears."

"Don't worry about handling Ashling. My cousin is playing games, and you're not going to be able to stop her. You just keep yourself away and safe when I ask." Jamie pushes off the dresser to stand straighter, bringing our bodies close.

"It's hard not to worry about Ash, Jamie. Most girls know to be careful. But she's so—"

"Never concern yourself when she'll be with me. Years ago, that girl was the only one who got through to me when I needed it most. She could blow up a government building, and I'd have her back."

The tension in my shoulders eases. "Sure, of course." Licking my lips, I nod. "All right. I can't promise to always go along with everything you say, but I won't just ignore it. I'm willing to talk about anything that comes up."

One brow cocks skeptically. "There won't be anything to talk about, Sawyer. If I tell you to do something and you refuse, we'll be done."

I stiffen once again, but before I can say anything else, his thumb strokes my jaw and then presses against my lower lip.

"Now," he says. "If you're staying, get your clothes off."

Glaring at him does nothing to erase his smug expression.

"The Briar Club formal is next weekend."

Before I jump into bed for what promises to be a wild night, I need to know where we stand. The event organizer sent me a confirmation that she'd gotten the addition of my plus-one. Which was something Jamie apparently initiated on his own. When I heard, I'd been happy about it. I want to be sure he's not planning to bail at the last minute.

"I know about the club formal," he says. "I've already let them know I'm your escort."

"So, you're still planning to take me?"

"Of course. You've done what you promised. I'll do the same."

With a slow breath, I nod.

His intense focus moves from my eyes to my mouth. "Now strip, because I'm gonna use your body the way I wanted to use it last night."

Every one of my nerves screams at once. But instead of running, as I probably should, my fingers drop to the hem of my sweater so I can pull it over my head.

21

JAMIE

I lean back against the dresser, watching her slowly remove her clothes. At this pace, it's as though she's testing how long my control will hold. My body's primed, and my patience is wearing thin. Once the bra comes off and those incredible breasts are on display, I push off the dresser, unable to resist any longer.

Her stiff nipples jut out, begging to be sucked. I capture the soft slope of her breast and raise it. Bending, I run my tongue over the tip, enjoying the way her flesh quivers as she draws in a shaky breath.

Raising my head, I keep my gaze fixed on her tits. "Put your hands on your head, Sauce, and lower your eyes to the floor. Then arch your back."

After a beat, she complies. The pose makes her breasts an offering. And I'd happily worship at their altar. I squeeze her silky flesh before stepping back. Tonight is about more than slamming my cock into her for a quick release. We're going on a journey together.

Grabbing the steel circular nipple clamps from the bedside

table, I counsel my heartbeat to slow the fuck down. This is not a race. And yet, I sometimes feel as impatient as I was my first time, as though I haven't fucked scores of women and played wicked games many, many times.

I apply the first circular clamp, gently screwing it tighter and tighter until the pinch makes her gasp. Following suit on the other side, I watch the way her breasts sway as she takes deep breaths and tries to steady herself.

"Your body was made for these games. It's a shame filming is off the table. Watching you get fucked is something every man needs in his life."

She shudders, but her breathy response is terse. "I'm not a prop."

"No, but you should be." My teasing tone does nothing to disarm her.

Her shoulders move forward as if they can ease the pinch. Her right hand rises to a clamp but before her fingers can touch the screw, I push it away.

"Don't touch what doesn't belong to you." Running my fingertip along the undersurface of one heavy breast, I emphasize the point. "Your body is mine, not yours."

I lick her nipple and then blow on it, knowing that's little relief. If she wants to stop me, she'll have to use her safeword, and from the restless shifting of her hips, I doubt she'll do that before I make her come. Even without the restraints, she's trapped, and I think she's starting to realize it.

Her teeth sink into her lower lip, biting down as if to help distract from the erotic discomfort between her legs.

Leaning closer, I whisper, "Your body gives you away, Sauce. It won't be long before you're so far gone, you'd let me bend you over a table in a crowded room, pull your knickers down and fuck you raw amid the cheering."

The noise of her unsteady breathing fills the air, but she shakes her head.

Reaching between her legs, I cup her pussy and rub the heel

of my hand over her clit. "You would, yeah. We both know the way your pussy aches for my cock. I could convince you."

Her pupils are dilated to the size of saucers. Sawyer may wish she didn't want to play the whore for me, but she does.

"Get on your knees, little girl."

She remains rigid, seemingly begging me to punish her. Brushing my lips over the shell of her ear, I tease her clit with my fingers.

"If you want me to make you come, you'd better behave."

"I want to have sex right now." Sawyer licks her lips. "And play after."

"Not happening. On your knees, or I'll tease you and leave you on the brink all night."

Her tone is vicious as she lowers herself. "I hate you."

"Not as much as you will." My voice teases in the way that under other circumstances might invoke a junk punch. Turning serious again, I say, "Take out my cock and suck it like a good girl."

Her frustrated whine makes me smile. Her mouth is not where she wants me, but she nevertheless unzips my jeans and frees my dick. Swallowing hard, she leans forward and opens her pretty mouth.

SAWYER

IT'S IMPOSSIBLE TO UNDERSTAND WHY AROUSAL BURNS INSIDE me at the sight of his erection. Sucking him off isn't going to satisfy my needs, and yet, I'm hungry to get him in my mouth. With every move, the painful throb in my nipples grows stronger. I desperately want him to remove the pincers and replace them with his mouth.

I moisten my lips and then take his cock's smooth head between them. Enjoying the texture, I swirl my tongue over it before pushing my face forward. His blazing hot shaft fills my mouth and I trace the length of him, finding the ridges made by his veins.

"Mmm." With deep pleasure in his voice, he says, "Just like that."

I worship his cock as his hand slides into my hair and strokes my scalp in silent encouragement.

It doesn't take long for his grip to tighten on my hair. His thrusts take on a driving rhythm. Hollowing my cheeks, I concentrate on stroking him as he enters and pulls back.

"Fuck, that's good." Plunging deep, he chokes me on his cock until my eyes water and my vision blurs.

When he pulls back, I gasp for breath. A second later, he repeats the move. Soon, he's fucking my throat so deeply all I can do is concentrate on catching my breath in between his thrusts.

He sets a punishing pace, and my eyes water from the strain. My fingers grip his calves, squeezing as I start to become dizzy. And through it all, my pussy clenches like a fist. I am desperate to have him fuck me like a goddamned beast.

Without warning, he pulls me off his cock and sets me back on my heels. I drop onto my palms so the top of my head brushes his sac. For several long moments, my breathing is so harsh I can't hear anything else.

His hand under my chin pulls me up, so I'm kneeling with my butt on my heels. "Well done, Sauce." Exhaling audibly, he strokes my lower lip with his thumb. "Go lie on the bed."

Thank God.

I want him to hurry but resist the urge to say so. Rushing him isn't really in my best interest. From the other nights I've had sex with him, I know when I let go and lean into the loss of control, something incredible happens.

Lowering myself to the mattress between the black leather restraints, I wait.

Jamie sheds his clothes and climbs on the bed. When he

grips my left wrist, excitement overwhelms me. But I'm a little torn, too, as he secures it in the cuff. His golden body is so gorgeous, my fingers are greedy for his muscles. I love touching him. As the second restraint closes on my other wrist, I lose my chance.

He pulls the slack from the chains, and my arms are pulled overhead and locked in position. The tug on my muscles and joints causes butterflies in my stomach. This is serious. And seriously sexy.

Reaching over to the nightstand, he grabs a stainless steel bulb, a small silicone-capped vibrator, and a pump bottle of lube. Gooseflesh erupts over my entire body, and my breath becomes short.

"Spread your legs, little girl. It's time to really break you in."

I obey without a moment's hesitation. Whatever this is, I want it.

He drizzles silky oil onto the steel plug and anoints my asshole with it. I suck in a startled breath. For some reason, I'd thought that was going in front.

The smooth cold steel circles my ring.

My excitement falters, and I start to try to bring my legs together. "I'm not sure—"

"Get your knees apart." His tone is dark and demanding. "You're my toy. I can play with you however I want."

His ruthless filthy talk makes my pussy weep. Absolutely irresistible.

With a pounding pulse, I ease my knees apart until they're resting on the bed. Jamie takes advantage of how open I am. With steady pressure, he slides the plug into me, stretching my asshole and making me want to come unglued from how frazzled I feel. The sex toy doesn't hurt, but I'm acutely aware of its position inside me. And the fact that this is a warm up so he can eventually put something bigger there.

With slow sips of air, I stare at the ceiling, willing my mind to fly free. To reach that soaring place.

Jamie lies next to my left side and moves into my field of view. His blue eyes lock with my brown ones, and his fingers splay over my belly, which is knotted with nervousness and arousal.

There's a dark light in his eyes. "You like it, don't you?"

My voice is breathy and a little unsteady. "I don't know."

The corner of his mouth curves into a mocking smirk. "Don't lie, Cranberry Sauce."

"It makes me uneasy."

His hand moves down, and he slides two fingers into my pussy. "It also makes you drenched." As his smile widens, the shadows make his eyes look blue-gray. "You're almost too fucking perfect for me. It fills me with the urge to do things to you I've never done to anyone."

"Like what?" I whisper.

"None of your business, plaything." His teasing tone eases the tension slightly.

He unscrews one of the clamps, and the rush of blood into the blanched nipple makes me groan. Then he lowers his mouth and sucks it as he turns on the vibrator. When he slides the smooth vibrating head through my juices and it comes to rest on my clit, I scream from the trio of excruciating sensations... his mouth, the plug, and now the vibration. It's overwhelming.

My arms fight the chains, testing their strength. There's no give at all.

He ignores my struggles and my mounting desperation.

Using his left hand, he unscrews the other clamp and sucks the tip of my breast into his mouth. My nipples have never been so sensitive in my entire life.

The vibrator's relentless hum against my clit tips me over into a shockingly intense orgasm. My screams turn into guttural moans as I come.

Jamie moves between my open thighs and pushes his cock into my pussy while it's still spasming.

*Oh, God, **this**... This is what I want.*

Continuing to come while he fucks me with punishing thrusts, my mind unspools until the white ceiling turns colors.

Until my heart feels like it'll explode.

And like I'll die if he ever lets me go.

※

JAMIE

I CAN'T GET ENOUGH. OF HER. OF BEING INSIDE HER.

Late in the night, I position Sauce facedown over a bolster in four-point restraints that have her limbs forming an X and lay a black leather strap in front of her face.

"Ready for your punishment?"

Her teeth bite down on her full lower lip in a pose that vacates most rational thought from my mind. She is so fucking luscious. And has natural instincts for falling into a scene.

When she doesn't speak, I slap her ass a few times with my hand, raising color to warm her up.

"You can't listen to Ashling instead of me without paying for it." Picking up the strap, I make it sway.

Her voice is a hoarse whisper. "You're not playing fair."

"Never said I would." I stroke her spine with the strap. "I'm not sure you want me to. Let's find out."

The first pair of sharp spanks causes her to clench and cry out.

I pause, waiting to see if she'll use her safeword. Or stop grinding her pelvis in that telltale way, conveying how aroused she is.

Continuing in a steady rhythm, I watch her ass turn bright red as marks bloom over her flesh.

When it's time for her to stop me, she doesn't. Sauce must not realize she should, even though from the shaking of her shoulders I can tell she's breaking down.

I lay the warm strap across her back, surrendering the game. Sawyer can be stubborn as fucking hell.

"Look at me, Cranberry Sauce."

When she doesn't move, I grasp a handful of her hair, raise her head and turn it for her. I'm not rough, but there's no way she could resist, either.

There are tears spilling down her cheeks, but she presses her lips between her teeth, refusing to make a sound beyond the sniffling.

My thumb brushes away a tear that tracks down her cheek. "We're done." I catch a drop on my fingertip and suck it off. The salt dissolves on my tongue, and I wonder why I like it. "You could've stopped me anytime. You remember the safeword, right?"

After a nod, she whispers, "To hell with that."

My brows rise. Whatever sets some people apart and makes them hard to break, she has it. A willingness to play with fire... and never regret it.

The obsession I've barely been keeping at bay can no longer be denied. There is something inside Sawyer that I have to have.

Leaning closer, I give her a slow kiss on the mouth as I release her from the restraints. "If we aren't careful, hell may be exactly where we're headed." My throbbing cock is impatient to fuck her again, but I can't shirk my responsibility to provide some aftercare.

Rising, I go to the nightstand and grab the soothing lotion. After squeezing some onto her, my hand drops to massage it into her flaming cheeks.

With a hiss of pain, she pushes my hand away and rolls onto her right hip, so her swollen ass is out of reach.

"It'll make you feel better, Sauce."

"I feel fine," she lies.

After a moment, I set the bottle on the nightstand. "When you change your mind, let me know. Until then..." Grabbing her shoulder, I force her back onto her stomach and push her knees apart so I can kneel between them.

"Are you serious?" Her voice is laced with righteous skepticism.

"Indeed. Unless you say the word that'll stop me." I lick between her shoulder blades. Then I tease her pretty pink cunt, marveling at how hot and slick it is. My cock is so hard I could use it as a crow bar.

Lowering myself, I rest my pelvis against her ass, pushing the plug a little deeper as I enter her.

She groans, and her voice is raspy. "You're a fucking monster."

My fingers slide into her hair, and I lower my mouth to the side of her face. Sucking on her earlobe, I thrust deep inside her. With a plug in her ass, her pussy's even tighter than usual. From her gravelly moans, I know I'm not the only one enjoying that.

"Some women are made to be fucked, and you're one of them." After sliding my hand under her, I find her clit and stroke it in rough circles.

Her breathing grows jagged and raw.

"I'm gonna use you all night, until you're whimpering and sore. Then I'm going to fuck you all over again." Husking a breath into her ear, I thrust harder and deeper, banging against her cervix. "I hope you didn't have a workout planned for tomorrow because even walking is going to be difficult."

That threat tips her over. Her breath catches, and her pussy clenches around my cock, trying to get me to spill my seed.

I fuck her harder, and she squeezes my dick as she comes, biting down on the sheet to muffle her cries.

My pace intensifies in my quest to come inside her before she's done coming.

Breaking Sawyer with pain doesn't appeal to me. But breaking her with pleasure definitely does.

22

SAWYER

"Hey," Jamie murmurs against my hair. "Are you awake?"

I'm lying on my side, facing away but with my back pressed against his warm chest. His arms are wrapped tightly around me. This closeness is about more than sex, and I've just slept the deepest sleep of my entire life because of it.

"Kind of awake," I murmur against his arm.

"Turn this way." His low voice is sleep-roughened, which only makes it sexier.

I shift under the covers, untwisting myself enough so I can roll over. As promised, I'm sore between my legs and elsewhere, which sends a shiver of awareness through me as I move.

When I'm facing him, Jamie's eyes hold mine.

"Beautiful girl... How are you this morning?"

I nod with a small smirk. "I'm all the things."

"You are that. And more." His hand rests on the blanket above my shoulder.

I go one better and reach out to touch his bare chest.

"That was proper intense for a beginner. Wanna talk about anything?"

"I guess I want to know..." Licking my lips, I shrug. "When we can do it again?"

That draws a deep laugh from his chest. "Seriously? Do you not care at all that I'm an athlete in training? How do you expect me to make it to practice when I'm dead exhausted?"

I shrug with a small smile. "You had it right the first time. I don't care."

"Right, okay. I'm Sampson, and you're Delilah with your wee clippers, is it?"

That makes me laugh. "I guess? Isn't that a bible story? We're not religious, so I don't know them."

"Sacrilege," he says with mock disapproval. Then he strokes my hair in the sweetest way. "Despite your vicious tendencies and casual disregard for my athletic performance, I've got something for you."

After rising from the bed, he stalks out, muscled ass flexing magnificently. I wonder vaguely whether I actually could cause him to lose ground with his training. Then, I decide I wasn't kidding. I truly don't care.

Having these experiences is too important to me. I love when my mind blurs as he pushes me to the edge. I had no idea sex could feel this way. It's like being on fire and then plunging into cold water. Out of control and stunning. It takes my breath away in the best way.

I also love how soundly I sleep when I'm so spent I can barely move. It's amazing.

Jamie reappears with a white box. Before setting it down, he lifts the lid, revealing purple tissue paper secured with a gold foil logo sticker.

I sit up. "What's this?" Then I recognize the logo. It's from the vintage clothing store. Carefully pealing the sticker up, I open the folded tissue paper. Lying in the box is the black

Chanel dress. My audible gasp is followed by a sharp intake of breath.

When I glance up to meet his eyes, he's smiling.

"It's too much," I whisper. "You already got me the other dress."

He shrugs. "When you mentioned this one, I could tell you really wanted it."

Pushing the box aside, I knee-walk to the edge of the bed and throw my arms out. My eyes are stinging with grateful tears, and I should feel ridiculous, but I don't.

When I kiss and hug him, he leans into it.

"Best. Present. Ever. *Thank you*, Jamie."

"It's nothing," he murmurs, almost as if he's uncomfortable with this degree of gratitude.

I decide that's another thing I don't care about. For once, I'm going to show the emotions I've been trained to bury.

Kissing the side of his face again, I squeeze his arm. "It means a lot."

"Right, then. I'll expect blow jobs daily for a week, will I?"

I chuckle. "If you want." After climbing off the bed, I take the box and hang the dress in the closet. By the time I'm done admiring it, Jamie's lying on his back on the bed.

As I approach, he puts an arm behind his head. "Did you always suspect you'd like the sort of games we're playing, Sauce?"

"No. I didn't know anything about this." I lie down next to him.

"Usually people fantasize about things long before they experience them."

My fingers caress his chest muscles. "If I had dreams about wicked sex, I don't remember. Feels like I would. Pretty memorable." Moving my hand down to trace his ab muscles, I shrug. "When I was young I fantasized about being a mutant girl from comic books, so I could empty the bank account of anyone I wanted. And kick their asses in a fight. I wanted to beat the hell out of Brad until he begged for mercy. Could be why I have such a girl crush on Ash. She snatched that phone right out of Brad's hand, foiling his plans. I always wanted to be fast enough to keep him from taking my toys. Or to sidestep a punch so he'd break his fist on the wall."

"A punch?" Jamie echoes. "He hit you, Sauce?"

"Sometimes."

"Actually fucking hit you?" His scowl darkens. "When you were wee kids, you mean?"

"I think I was about fourteen the last time."

A stillness comes over him. The hardness in his expression takes on a dangerous edge, narrowing his eyes to slits and crinkling the skin around them. "When you were fourteen, he'd have been sixteen or seventeen? A grown man, physically." His expression shifts, becoming more shuttered. "And no one stopped him?"

"Nope." I lick my lips and chew on the lower one for a moment. "But I got good at ignoring him. Not breaking down is how I win."

"That's not winning, Sawyer."

"In a way, it was. You don't understand because you've never been in that kind of situation."

"Hmm." Jamie blows out a breath. "You should probably talk with a professional about what you've been through. And your brother needs a proper reckoning."

"No way," I scoff. "I've kept it a secret for a reason." My brows pinch together. "No one can know I told you, Jamie. I'll deny it."

"Relax," Jamie says in a calming tone, a distant expression developing on his features. "I wouldn't betray your trust, Sauce. Not ever."

The tension eases. "Anyway, it wasn't like I was really injured. He did it to prove he could. That he could get away with hurting me."

"Is that what went through your head last night during—?"

"Gross. No," I say emphatically. "The way you do things to

me… it's exciting. I know your intention is to turn me on. I can tell, and I like that." I run my hand over his skin. "I might not enjoy it as much if I wasn't so attracted to you. It's hard to separate the two things. I like getting to share scary, secret sex with the person everyone else wants." A small smirk emerges. "Fuck Clare Duffy, that little traitor."

A hint of a smile finally appears on Jamie's face. "All right."

I chuckle softly. "It's something Ash says."

"Ah. Our Ashling and her colorful expressions." Jamie's hand smooths my hair back. "I'm glad last night was good for you. If it's ever not, you have to tell me. This kind of relationship relies on communication to keep it from becoming abuse."

I nod. "That's not a problem—the communication part, I mean. I can talk to you."

"I hope so because last night you didn't say much."

"Well." I smirk. "Last night, I was pretending you'd have to kill me to break me."

"Jayzus. Don't even joke." He kisses me, tangling his fingers in my hair. "If that happened, it would be the end of us both. That much I can promise."

"Are you saying that if I died, it would kill you?"

"I'm saying if I was ever so out of control that I accidentally killed you during a scene, that yes, I would need to be put down like a rabid dog. And I would make sure it happened, one way or the other."

My brows rise at the seriousness in his tone. "Sounds like—have you actually thought about it?"

"I have, yeah. When I started having certain fantasies, I wasn't sure what that said about me. I decided if I started to get off on hurting innocent girls, ones who hadn't consented, or if I went too far, I would deal with myself accordingly. Then, over time, I realized these games are never one-sided for me. I like for the girl to want to play. I want her to want more of the same."

"The way I do?"

"Exactly that."

That causes me to smile. "So, we're a good match."

"More than good. In bed, I'd say we're a perfect match."

The smile that blossoms is one I can't suppress. "Does that mean I get to stay for breakfast? I'll cook."

"No way are you cooking. I'll make you breakfast and serve it to you in bed." He gives me a kiss before rising.

Stretching contentedly, I say, "I thought I was the slave?"

"You are." Jamie pulls on a pair of jeans. "But a master always has to feed and water his little pet so she stays strong enough to be useful." With a wink, he's out the door.

I continue to smile. I've never had breakfast in bed in my life. And while I know that having Jamie in bed is better than having breakfast here, I'm about to have both.

I may not have been born rich, but it feels like I'm living my best life now.

23

JAMIE

On the night of the Briar Club event, Ashling lets me into the lobby of Central Dorm when I arrive to collect Sawyer.

Ash wears no makeup and is dressed in thick, oversized sweats. She looks about fifteen.

"How is it with you, Ashling?"

She grins. "Right as rain. Nice outfit. Is that a designer tux?"

That I've relented and bought the tuxedo she suggested I would need at GU with all its formals causes me to roll my eyes. At the time she said it, I denied any intention of attending dances and the like, but plans have shifted.

As with all our family, Ash enjoys being right in the end and can't resist emphasizing it. Her cheeky smile remains.

"And what of your own plans? Bit of calisthenics, is it?"

She laughs. "No, just trying to decide if I'm going out tonight. I've got no boyfriend to Cinderella me around, so..." Her lips do a mock pout.

"I reckon the lack of boyfriend should tell you a bit about your personality. Time to do some work on yourself."

Her laughter causes me to smirk, too. Taking the mickey out of each other is standard among friends where I'm from, which she well knows. When she reciprocates it always gives me a bit of home.

Ash points her index finger in my direction. "Maybe I should take a page out of your book. Go overseas and act sad and lonely until someone takes pity on me."

My grin widens. "Is that what your little mate says about why she's dating me? Pity?"

"Maybe," she says with mock gravity. "Girl talk between roommates is private, *so it is*."

Her attempt at an Irish accent is, as usual, laughable. "Just so you're not spilling my secrets along with your own."

Her head cocks, sending her ponytail swinging. "What secrets?"

Mood sobering, I incline my head in her direction so I can lower my voice. "You've not told Sauce about Jude, have you?"

"No." Her brows rise as she turns serious. "Haven't you?"

My muscles tighten. "No. Not yet."

"Hmm." Her eyes assess me as though I'm a defective item that may need to be returned. Then though, her tone turns mellow and accepting. "Okay. I won't mention him."

"Grand."

Sharing confidences doesn't fit into my arrangement with Sawyer. Although, the other morning, she let me have a look behind the curtain of her life when she told me about her brother's violent tendencies. That set me on edge. A proper boyfriend would need to do something about him immediately, like beat him until he becomes familiar with the taste of his own blood.

My Crue sleeper cell, though, is trying to avoid notice. Public fights are therefore off the table.

Ash holds up a hand in a wave before heading toward the elevator. "Have fun tonight."

I nod, watching her until the door closes.

As a friend, Ash has good instincts—the best I've seen actually. At Jude's wake, Ash was Jude's age and looked almost exactly like him except for the long hair. While we were standing alone, she said to me, "If my brother died, I would want to die, too." Then her little arms wrapped around my waist in a tight hug. No one else reacted that way... or seemed to understand what losing my best friend of a brother was gonna mean for the rest of my life.

Over the years, on the anniversary of his death, an email or a text always came from America. The words were never anything special. *Dear Jamie. I was thinking about you and Jude. Hope you're okay. Love, your cousin Ash.* The words would be followed by heart emojis or a gif of kids hugging.

Fucking Ashling and her over-the-top sweet messages back when she was young. The year I thought she forgot because her message went into Spam, I was angry she'd forgotten. I found her email a week later and realized how important it still was to feel like there was another person who knew that some dark days would never be anything but black.

Of course, my parents and siblings remember Jude, too, but it's different. We never speak about it the way we should. No one's ever allowed to talk about what drove Jude to suicide. The old man and one of my sisters have even implied it was Jude's own choice to kill himself, so we're not under the same obligation to grieve as if he'd been hit by a car or something not his own fault.

Those comments ignite my rage, though I simmer in silence. A silent trip to the cemetery. The silent lighting of candles in church. Even when my immediate family is around me, remembering Jude, I often feel alone. Which, by the time I was a teenager, was how I wanted it. With the exception of hearing from Ash.

Ashling's grown-up messages don't carry heart emojis or hugging cartoon characters. Lately, they suggest we go to a pub to have a drink, which suits us now. Ash has always been the one person who seemed to want to be in this thing with me. Still can't understand why. But it's the reason Ashling could cause any amount of trouble to rain down, and I'd overlook it.

The memory surfaces of Brad Allendale grabbing my cousin. And of Sawyer's sad, resigned acceptance of the abuse she suffered at his hands as a young teenager. Allendale is going to bleed for those assaults. The thing I haven't decided yet is whether he's going to die for them.

Covering my tracks is trickier now, but it could be worth the risk.

Some murders are.

24

SAWYER

The Chanel dress is a little tight across my chest, but it still looks divine. It's exactly the confidence booster I want for a night like tonight.

Exiting the elevator, I spot Jamie. Handsome as a Bond actor, he stands near a tall window, needing to be photographed. I snap his pic as I walk over.

"Here," he says, taking my phone. He raises it and gets a selfie of us together. Passing the phone back, he smiles. "Text that to me as well."

The request spreads warmth through me. I like being with him and enjoy it even more when he lets slip that he likes it, too.

"You're gorgeous tonight," he says with a wink. "If you're after blending in so the other girls don't get jealous, lost fucking cause, Sauce."

My smile widens until I'm beaming. He's the ultimate charmer. Always sounds sincere. Is never sappy. Perfect, really.

"The others will be dressed up, too, so that won't be a problem. But thank you. And thank you for the dress. I love it so much." I rise onto my toes and pull him down by the neck to give him a lingering kiss. I catch the faint scent of his cologne. It's earthy and masculine, with a faint hint of spice. I wish we were going to his place, rather than out.

Once he helps me into my coat, we leave the dorm and walk along a path toward the parking lot. My breath emerges as fog as we pass in and out of the light from the lamp posts. The freezing temperature doesn't bother me. I'm too amped up to feel it.

"Care to drive, Cranberry Sauce?"

"Your new car?"

"Why not?"

That returns the smile to my face, and I nod.

He unlocks the Porsche, opens the driver's door and hands me the keys after I'm inside. As soon as I start the car, heat blasts. I pretend that's what causes the rush of pleasure.

Even over a short distance, the car is fun to drive. It's dark out, so despite clear roads, I don't push past the speed limit. I'd love to drive his car on a clear day.

After we reach the Briar Club house, I offer him back his keys.

Jamie shakes his head. "Hold onto them. I may have a nip of whiskey."

This is feeling more and more like a date, which makes me buoyantly happy. I tuck the keys into my clutch before exiting the car.

The Briar Club house is unabashedly peach-colored and frilly. It's a Queen Anne with turrets and delicate, ornate ivory trim adorning every edge and corner, like pastry frosting.

Even the steeply pitched black roof can't overcome its confectionary appearance. Obviously, like the club, the house is a piece of turn-of-the-century history, but for me, it's too over the top.

"Jesus, the Victorians really should've stopped at corsets. Their shite designs are enough to give me cavities."

Chuckling, I nod. "That's exactly what I was thinking."

Once inside the Briar house, I notice an immediate shift in

Jamie. It's like he's flipped a switch, turning on a light that radiates from inside him, drawing the whole club's attention.

As he works the room, he tells fishing and boating stories, zeroing in on the Briar Club president who's obsessed with sailing. After she's promised to come to the rowing team's regattas in spring and invites us for a sail once weather permits, Jamie seems satisfied.

Leaning close to me, he whispers, "Where's the VP? She's the one who takes cycling tours, right?"

"I'm not sure, but she's at the buffet."

I have no idea where Jamie got his advance knowledge of the club's most powerful players, but it's clearly a pro move. His promise to help me secure my acceptance obviously wasn't idle bullshit to get me into bed.

Jamie catches my hand and holds it as he migrates over to the food. He's so gorgeous people naturally turn toward him and include him in conversation. Within five minutes, he, the VP, and her date are discussing cross-country trips. Two years ago, Jamie drove his motorcycle halfway across the US, so the three of them exchange trip notes and recommendations.

Within two hours, he's worked his way up and down the club's leadership and senior roster. *With one exception.* Clare Duffy doesn't approach us when we're together. Instead, she finds me alone in the library while I'm searching for the club's scrapbook collection.

Clare's black dress has sharp angles and a wide black belt. It looks more like something a stylish lawyer would wear to court than what a coed should wear to a party.

She gestures around the library using her right hand where she's holding a tumbler of amber liquid. "What do you think you're doing?" Her tone is hard, but I try not to let it rattle me.

Keeping my voice light and friendly, I say, "Looking for scrapbooks from the years my mom was at GU. I wanted to see what pictures there were of her."

"The library is off limits for nonmembers. If you want access, you'd better go out and help O'Rourke work the room. His charm alone won't get you in, you know. You're the one who needs to make the grade, not him."

Forcing myself to smile the way I do at my fake Allendale grandparents, I incline my head. "I know, but his charm doesn't hurt. It got the president interested enough to read my essay while we were chatting in the parlor, and she said she was impressed. So, hopefully everything's on track." Infusing my voice with warmth, I say, "Thanks again for your mentorship."

One of her artificial-looking dark brown brows arches. "Get your lips off my ass, Allendale."

That ignites the kind of fury I have trouble controlling. "Just trying to be nice." My feigned friendliness is quickly draining away.

"You're right that my influence could've made you. It can also break you."

My eyes narrow. "Is that really who you want to become, Clare?"

She finishes her drink. "Don't flatter yourself. Nothing about you is worth a transformation of any kind. I am who I am."

"Someone who's spiteful for no good reason?"

"Fuck off." She stalks over to the door and holds it open. "Get out of the club library."

Despite becoming angrier by the second, I talk myself out of doing anything that could escalate things. Raised voices might draw a crowd, and an argument with a senior member would hurt my chances.

As I exit, I'm expecting her to follow me out. Instead, she closes the door, which immediately raises my suspicions. Would she hide or destroy the club's books with photographs of my adoptive mom? The thought causes my blood to run cold. Celine loved the club so much. I don't want her erased from its history.

No. Stop being paranoid, I tell myself. As a devoted member, Clare Duffy wouldn't destroy Briar Club property.

But after a few moments in the hall, I open the door slowly

and peer in. Clare stands in front of the local history shelf where I'd just been, and she's pulling items that definitely look like bound keepsakes from the shelf.

For fuck's sake. What is wrong with this woman?

Confronting her isn't the right strategy. When challenged, Clare Duffy digs in her heels. What I need is a distraction, something to draw her away and hopefully make her forget about the scrapbooks.

I stalk down the hall, determined to make the most of Jamie's help, though not exactly sure what I'll propose.

As I approach the group he's a part of, someone says, "With that underbite, Rawls looks like the rat he is."

"He does, yeah." Jamie's lovely accent seems just as irresistible to them as it is for me. "He's the kind of guy you want to punch in the jaw, but first you'd have to find it."

Laughter erupts, and Jamie takes a swig of whiskey.

When he spots me, however, his smile fades. He must sense something's wrong because he sets his glass on a tray and strolls over.

"Everything all right, Cranberry Sauce?"

I purse my lips as I shake my head. "Clare Duffy."

"Still?" He cocks his head, then shakes it. "Going down fighting, is she? That's the Irish."

"I tried being nice. Which landed poorly."

He glances over my shoulder. "Where is she?"

"In the library. Could you talk to her?"

"I will, yeah." He follows me down the hall. "Do me a favor, Sauce. Stand outside the door and keep watch. If someone comes over to you, knock once. If someone's coming in the room, knock twice."

My brows shoot up in surprise. "What are you intending to do? I don't want you to be *too* nice."

That causes a slight smile to appear. "Jealous?"

"Damn right. She's a bitch. I'm not sharing my boy toy with her."

His laughter makes me smile. "Boy toy, is it? As though I'd go along with that." Catching my arms in his hands, he pulls me to him. "There's no need to worry, Cranberry Sauce. There's only one girl in this house I'm gonna fuck tonight. And that's the one I *own*." He kisses me and then slowly wipes my lipstick off his lower lip. "Keep watch."

25

JAMIE

My body's feeling as good as if I were flying across the water on a windsurf board. Whiskey's partly to blame, for sure. But the taste of Sauce's lips lingering on mine is the biggest contributor. Berry flavored lip balm... Women don't need to carry guns when they can weaponize their smiles.

As I come around the corner of the bookshelves, I spot Clare standing near leather reading chairs with a collection of books stacked on an ottoman.

With a glance over her shoulder, she frowns. "The library is members only." Turning back to her task of flipping through pages, she feigns ignoring me.

I stroll over and lean against the bookcase. Her mood means that Plan A is unlikely to work, but I'm gonna float it anyway. For her sake.

"Clare, let's have a chat."

"Not interested."

"Did I ask if you were interested?" The chill in my voice

causes her head to turn toward me. Plan B is elbowing its way in. I'm impatient to have this settled.

Her scowl darkens, pinching her features. "I'm not going to recommend Allendale."

Drawing in a slow breath, I stare at her with a hard expression. She glares back, putting on her best impression of a high-powered lawyer. The trouble with posturing is there's nothing to back it up when facing off against someone who's not all talk.

My hand shoots out and grabs her throat. Her surprise takes a second to register as I squeeze, cutting off her voice and her breath.

I lean closer, so I'm whispering in her ear. "If you cross me, I will come for you. And you don't have the juice to stop me from retaliating in a way that will leave you dead or disfigured." I pause to let my words land like a hammer on the head of a nail.

Her eyes bulge, and her face reddens. As her fingers claw at my hand, I ease the pressure enough for her to suck in a breath. Then I tighten my grip again, letting air hunger induce another round of panic.

This time when I ease my grip she's gasping, with watery eyes smearing her mascara. I hold her in place with one hand as her body sags, ready to drop to the ground.

When I speak, it's with the finality of death. "You've got 'clever girl in a private club' power. The kind that lets you bully schoolgirls and get away with it. But I'm not a schoolgirl. I'm not even a clean-cut lad with a sport scholarship. That's *my cover*. Know the power I've really got?"

Her head jerks, and wide eyes stare at me. With terror, the world narrows. Neither fight or flight is an option for her now. All she can do is listen and hope this will be over soon.

With her full attention on my voice and message, I lay it out for her.

"I've got a bullet with your name on it. And the experience to bury it in your skull." Releasing her throat, I drop my hand. "Be smart. Or be dead."

26

SAWYER

When Jamie emerges from the Briar Club library, he winks and takes my hand. As he guides me to the closest door, I watch him out of the corner of my eye.

"It went okay?"

"Well enough," he says, opening the door to a bathroom and giving me a small push inside.

"Was she destroying anything when you went in?"

"Only my good mood." He locks the door. "Drop your knickers, Sauce. And bend over the sink."

My eyes widen.

"Be a good girl, and do it now."

Licking my lips, I turn toward the gold-and-pearl-framed mirror. I slide my undies down and plant my hands on the edges of the dark granite.

He lowers his zipper and frees his cock, then slides my dress up to my waist, exposing my ass and more. Drawing in a breath, his gaze locks onto his target.

"Fuck," he grounds out as he enters me. "Armageddon has a new look, and it's too pretty to resist by a fucking mile."

The next thrust hits the place inside me that makes my toes curl. I push back, so his soft wool-blend trousers tickle my bare ass. My lids drop, and my lips part on a sigh.

The fingers of his right hand clasp my shoulder, steadying me. His thumb strokes the back of my neck as he fucks me hard and deep until we're both breathless.

I expect it to be quick. Instead, it goes on and on. The muscles in the backs of my legs scream in protest from the way I'm holding myself on my toes.

"Oh, God," I whisper.

Dropping forward, I rest my forearms on the cool stone and plant my heels on the tile. As I bite my lower lip, I sink into the sensation of being taken by the most beautiful guy I've ever seen.

Above me, Jamie groans and tips his head back as he strains. A few moments later, his cum shoots into me like he intends to own me forever.

It feels as though he already may.

JAMIE

Fucking Cranberry Sauce is the ultimate reward for a night spent engaging with the club crowd as though I'm a seasoned politician looking for votes. In a way, I reckon I am on the campaign trail for her tonight.

I can't claim I haven't been rewarded, though. The feel of her soft flesh in my hands and finding the faint marks on her ass that I placed there... it's all perfect.

Once we put our appearances right and slip out to join the others, we act as though we never disappeared. Every now and then, Sauce and I share a glance that makes my heart bang like hail against a metal roof. She's game for my games. And has learned how to tease me and satisfy me. Now, we've got the best kind of secret—the hot, filthy sort that belongs only to lovers.

I catch a glimpse of Clare Duffy, but when she realizes I'm still in the house, she disappears upstairs. Casting a vote for smart. Good for her.

As the night wears on, Sawyer's shields drop, exposing the acerbic wit I've never seen her show in public. As she lashes out at overrated books and bureaucratic bullshit, the others reassess her. Her sarcastic quips quickly win over the sharp, privileged girls of the club. Nice is nice. Dangerously clever is better.

They can see her as one of them, which advances her cause much farther than having an athlete boyfriend. I could be gone in a minute, after all. But she'll still be clever.

The alcohol and the orgasm contribute to my sense of euphoria, but there's also something more. Sawyer's become a rip current I'm caught in. Only this time, I don't want to escape.

We stay until the end of the party, and the club VP walks us out herself, making us promise to have dinner with her and her boyfriend. It'll be an easy commitment to keep, so I accept.

When we reach the car, I open the driver's door for her.

She pauses a few feet away and tips her head back, stretching her arms wide as she stares up at the dark sky. "You told me so!" Shaking her head, she swallows and lowers her voice. "Thank you, Mom."

I can't resist a smile over that.

When she approaches the car, she grabs the lapels of my suit and tugs. After planting a kiss on my mouth, she says, "And thank you."

"You're welcome."

A few beats pass, and she gives me a small push so she can lift her purse and retrieve the Porsche's keys.

When we're both in the car with the motor running, she says, "Ash texted she's on her way to Boston and she's going to stay for a day or two. Wanna stay over in my dorm room tonight? Central's got one of the best dining halls for breakfast."

"What size bed do you have?"

"Cozy," she says with mock enthusiasm.

I laugh. "Right, okay." My thumb strokes her leg. "You're driving. Take us home."

27

SAWYER

Jamie and I are plastered together in my twin bed, and I'm laughing at his description of cleaning fish for the first time.

"Ma was showing us, but with twenty fish in the cooler and it being late, she's not messing about. She gets going and scales are flying everywhere and hitting us on the heads, and my wee brother Jude starts yelling. 'Fish rain. No! Stop getting on my head, fishy.' He climbs under the wood table for cover. As though we're under fire." Jamie chuckles. "I'm a clever lad, so I see an opportunity to avoid cleaning up the gruesome fish guts. I say, 'I'll get him, Ma.' Once I get under the table though, Jude and I start discussing what sweets we're going to eat as a reward for helping."

"How old were you guys?"

"I don't know. Four and three, I reckon. We were just a year and a half apart."

"Under five, though? And she gave you a knife to clean fish?"

"Nah, she was showing us the motion one at a time with her hand over each of ours. Until she got impatient. Then, what we were supposed to be doing was throwing away the remains and wrapping the cleaned fish in butcher paper. Usually she had the girls out there, not us. They were older and much more help, as you'd imagine. But Jude and I were so keen on fishing, and I think Ma reckoned she'd soon have three times as many fish to scale or fillet and wasn't having it. My mom doesn't actually care for fish the way most of the family does. Imagine you don't even like fish stew and you have to make a pot of it every week for your greedy family. Along with fish fillets and fish and chips. When the catch was good, we had fish more days than not. That suited my dad and me down to the toes, and we've not really changed. You know what my American cousins introduced me to that I could eat every week? Fish tacos. Absolutely brilliant."

He rises from the bed, flashing his perfect ass, as he grabs a packet of Scottish shortbread cookies from Ash's nightstand.

"Hey, those aren't from the dining hall."

"So?" he says, tearing open the package.

"They're Ash's stash, and I don't know where to get more to replace them. Don't—"

Jamie pops a cookie in his mouth and chews. "It's all right. Just tell her I ate them while reminiscing about my little brother. I could set fire to the beds, and she'd say, 'Oh, that's all right, Jamie. No problem.' She's the little sister I wish I had. The rest of my sisters put up with zed."

"You talk about your brother as though..." My voice trails off and I grimace, studying his face for signs I shouldn't ask. Finally, because he doesn't change the subject, I say, "Is he gone?"

With a lick of his lips, Jamie nods. His expression clouds for a moment, but he banishes the expression. "Long time now."

"I thought for a while I had a real brother. But no. So disappointing. I can't imagine growing up with a sibling and then... I mean I can imagine." I wince. "But it's obviously way more heartbreaking in your case."

Desperately wanting to know what happened to his little brother, I bite my tongue to keep myself from asking for details.

I, of all people, know that it's better not to ask intrusive personal questions.

After eating another cookie, Jamie holds out the packet to me in offering. I shake my head.

"Go ahead if you'd like one. I'll get Ash some more."

"I don't usually eat cookies for breakfast."

"No? Missed opportunity. Life is short, Sauce." The mock gravity in his tone makes me smile. "Explain about the brother you thought you had. How does that work?"

"Weirdly." I blow out a breath. "I don't usually talk about it." Holding my breath, I wait for him to let it pass. Which is what I want him to do. I think.

He sits on the side of the bed and finishes off the cookies before pitching the wrapper into the trash. When he looks at me, there's a speculative expression on his face. "You don't need to speak about it if you'd rather not. But if you want to say something, go ahead. I can keep it a secret if that's what you'd like."

Chewing on my lower lip, I shrug. "When I was young, there was a guy and a little boy living with us for a while. The little boy was a year or two older than me, I think. Someone must have joked that he was my brother or something."

"When was this?"

"I must've been about two or three when they moved in."

"This was before your mother married Allendale? So, he's not your real dad then?"

Pressing my lips between my teeth, I glance at the ceiling, then the window, then Jamie's chest. "Actually, I'm adopted. My dad's great, actually. We're close."

"Well, it worked out, then. I reckon you might be closer to him than I am to my father. We disagree on some fundamental things, and it's caused me to pull away. We may put it right one day but haven't so far."

"I hope you can. Family's important."

"It is, yeah. So, Brad Allendale? Brother or stepbrother?"

"Yeah, step. Well, adopted brother, but it doesn't feel like it."

"He resents it, does he? That's his rationale for what he does?"

"I guess. The family name is a big deal. Their money and family history are part of their identities. That's one of the reasons getting into the Briar Club is so important. My Allendale grandmother was a Briar Club member like my mom. If I get in, that'll go a long way to proving I'm like my mom Celine was. Someone with great potential who's going to be an asset to the family."

Jamie's hand slides over the side of my face. "Your mom's gone?"

"Yes. Cancer. Such an awful waste. She was a member of the US House of Representatives, and they put her on a really important committee during her second term. She was literally changing the world." Blowing out a breath, I blink my eyes several times to banish threatening tears. "The Allendale money and influence might've helped her get elected, but once she got there, every bit of respect was earned." Rubbing my eyes, I shake my head. "It's important that I live up to my potential and get her bracelet back."

My eyes narrow. "Wanna hear the fucked up thing my so-called brother did? Each member of the Briar Club gets a custom bracelet. When a member dies, they have the option of returning the bracelet to the club, so it can be passed on to a new member. My mom's had been passed down from one of the founders. It's *so* vintage and cool. I used to put it on my upper arm, like Cleopatra, and prance around. Mom wanted me to have it when I became a member. She was going to have a new one made for herself when I got in and give me hers. When she died, Brad took the bracelet and returned it to the club, instead of letting me keep it, which I totally could have. I would've brought it with me into the club. But no. So now, it's back in circulation and there's no guarantee I'll be the one to get my mom's. If I get in, I hope they'll let me have it. They're pretty big on legacy and tradition, so there's a good chance. Hope so."

Jamie nods with a serious expression. "It's important to have faith. And a plan. You're smart to have both."

"Am I?" I draw in a breath and shrug. "Just doing my absolute best every step of the way. Can't afford a misstep. But there's not exactly a plan."

"Sure, there is. And we executed it perfectly last night." He winks then leans over and kisses me. "Let's get up. I need caffeine."

"Same," I say with a small smile.

I should've told Jamie the whole truth, including about it being my bio mom, not Celine, who had live-in boyfriends. But explaining that I'm adopted and why I need to prove myself as worthy of the Allendale name is huge for me. If things keep going the way they are, I think I'll be able to tell him my whole life story eventually. Old shame is just hard to set aside.

When Brad told his prep school friends about my "jailbird" mom, "the Tennessee white trash," they either pitied me or became condescending assholes. One even blackmailed me into writing his final papers to keep my secret, so the popular girls at school wouldn't find out. That would've ruined me for sure. One day, I'm going to cross paths with that guy again. And when I do, I'm going to figure out a way to make him regret what he did.

A stab of concern erupts in my chest. A thirst for revenge is a nasty urge that hits me way too often. I worry I inherited it from my bio mom. She could be ruthless.

This morning though, I remind myself I'm my own person and I've gotten farther in life than my bio mom ever did. Even if I do have poison in my genes, I also have Celine's. She was a distant cousin to my biological mom, which is how she learned about my motherless plight in the first place.

Celine rose above her middle class roots and any blood ties she had to the Tennessee branch of the family. As long as I'm careful, I can, too.

28

SAWYER

The week before Thanksgiving is busy and kind of absurd. Jamie is so swamped I only meet up with him once for sex, at two o'clock on a Wednesday afternoon. Meanwhile, Ash and I are practically conjoined twins when not in class. We get coffee, study in the library, work out, eat meals and attend parties together. It's the most fun I've had on campus by far. She makes me laugh so much I forget to panic about the Briar Club vote and the upcoming holiday with the Allendale family.

On Friday morning, Ash and I are each lying in our beds, sipping hot chocolate and trying to study when my phone rings from an unknown number.

"Who?" Ash asks. I've come to realize she doesn't actually care who it is, nor is she truly interested in what they want. It's just her way of staying connected in the friendship.

"Unknown caller." I cock my head with mock curiosity. "Secret Admirer? Nigerian Prince?"

Doing a swiping motion with her index finger, she says, "Voicemail." Her attention goes back to her screen.

The number's local, so less likely to be a random scammer.

"What if I've inherited two million dollars, and I'm about to lose it because they don't have my banking information? Can't risk that." I swipe to answer. "Hello?"

"Sawyer?" It's a slightly squeaky female voice that sounds vaguely familiar.

"Yes, this is Sawyer."

"Hi, it's Billie Goggins, Briar Club VP."

All the air leaves my lungs in an instant. I try to speak but instead make a tiny croaking sound. Ash's head turns and, seeing my face, she sits up. The rushing sound in my ears is so loud, I only half hear Billie's next words.

"I wanted to call you personally to let you know, you're in."

Sucking in a breath, I mumble, "Sorry... couldn't hear. Did you say I've been accepted?"

"Yes. Congratulations. Welcome to the Briar Club."

"Oh, my God," I whisper. "Thank you! I'm so happy."

She chuckles. "You earned it. In a few minutes, you'll get an email with details about the Induction Ceremony. Members only."

"Perfect.... perfect." Sitting up, I exhale. "I'm—Is the Induction Ceremony where new members get their bracelets?"

"Let's not jump ahead, okay? The emails will have all the information you need."

My lips go dry, and my heart pounds. I really want to be able to wear the bracelet for the holiday get-together with my Allendale grandparents, but I force my voice to sound chill. "Of course. Thanks for the call, Billie."

"Happy to do it. See you soon."

The instant the call has safely ended, I fall back onto my bed and scream triumphantly.

Ash drops onto her side, facing me. "Two million Nigerian royal dollars? That's so awesome, babes."

We both laugh.

I tell her about my acceptance to the club, and we celebrate by adding an ounce of Bailey's to our hot chocolate and dancing to Tronex as we hang holiday lights around our window.

After we return to studying, I can't concentrate. I'm excited about the club, of course, but there's a downside. My deal with Jamie was that he would help me get in and *until then*, I would be his plaything. I can't help but wonder when the last time we'll have sex will be. With a plunging stomach, I realize I may already have had it.

As I'm opening my official email from the club, I wonder what the hell is up with me. I've worked for this for years. I'm about to be a new member of one of the most powerful feminist organizations in the country. But, at the same time, I have to admit, if only to myself, that I'm not tired of being the sex toy of an Irish rower.

29

JAMIE

The week is busy, and I only manage to hook up with Sawyer once. When she calls Friday morning, I kick my door shut and sit on the end of my bed, glad to hear her voice.

"I was just thinking about you, Cranberry Sauce. How are you keeping?"

"How am I keeping?" she teases. "You're very Irish today."

"And every day."

"Are you missing home?"

"Always. But less now that I'm talking to you, as the prospect of a great weekend looms."

"Well, I called because I have good news."

When she doesn't speak, I push, which she seems to be wanting. "Go on then."

"The Briar Club's VP called. I'm in."

My smile widens. "That's grand. We'll celebrate. You'll come here, so we can do it properly."

"I'd love to."

The eagerness in her voice is a hot wave crashing over me.

It's been a hard slog all week, and the only thing I truly enjoyed was having her in my bed for an hour.

"What's the word on your schedule, Sauce? Are you leaving town next week for the American Thanksgiving holiday?"

"Well, I thought I was, but my dad is going to be out of the country for work, and there's no way I'm going to Palm Beach if he won't be there. Ash actually invited me to come home with her."

That would be complicated. How would I play things in front of the family and the bosses? Sauce as just Ashling's friend? Or as something to me, too? I'll need to sort things first.

"No way does Ash get custody," I scoff. "She can have you when I'm busy. But I'm about to be free, so you'll stay here with me for the break."

"Won't your family be upset if you don't come home?"

"Why should they? It's not an Irish holiday, and I've been around the relatives plenty lately. Plus, there's Christmas next month as well, when we'll all be together for days before I head home. If anything, they're probably ready for a break from me."

"Sure, of course. Understandable." Sawyer's droll delivery and the way she slags me off is very Irish, which makes me smile. "So, to hell with family all around. Let's be rebels."

"Suits me." Unlike with her, there's no resentment on my end. The truth is I've gotten so comfortable among my American family I've decided I'll only go home to Ireland for part of the Christmas break. Being in the old house still feels bleak this time of year.

For a while, it was awful because I was staying in the room I shared with Jude when we were young. Later, my parents converted that room to storage, which infuriated me. I admit, if only to myself, there's no winning with me.

Sawyer chats on, but I'm only half listening as I think ahead to the Christmas holidays and whether I might want to cut my time in Ireland even shorter.

What usually happens when I go home to the island for two

weeks is I see family for a few days, including Christmas Eve and Christmas, and then take off to go surfing. I couldn't do that this year because big-wave surfing is one of the things I'm barred from doing under the terms of my athletic scholarship.

Which means if I want less time where anger eats me alive, I should stay in the States with a cranberry cream pastry in my bed. That would be no hardship at all.

So, if Sawyer won't be away the whole December break, I could split my US time between Coynston and being at Granthorpe with her.

Running a hand through my mussed hair, I glance around the room where there are scattered clothes. "War's leaving for Boston tomorrow, Sauce. So, you and I will have the house to ourselves for a whole week. Think you can bear it?"

"There's no telling until I try." Her deadpan response to my teasing makes me smile again. I fancy this girl more than I ever imagined I would.

With her entry into the Briar club, the arrangement is ending. It's time to redefine our situation, and I'm rethinking my position on girlfriends. Turns out I want one if Sawyer's the girl.

"Maybe we can get some groceries, Jamie, and I'll cook a Thanksgiving dinner for just us. You know, tradition dictates it comes with cranberry sauce."

"I always have a taste for that. Sure. A traditional feast it is."

We chat a while longer, and I arrange to pick her up in the afternoon.

After I toss my clothes in the wash, I walk through the kitchen and throw pizza boxes into the trash. War emerges in boxer briefs and sits on the barstool with his foot up, examining his thigh wound. Using a wee pair of scissors, he clips the stitches and pulls them free, cutting the black hair that's gotten caught up along the surface. Once he's cleared the patch, track marks are easily visible on either side of the healing scar. Being relatively fresh, it's still pink and violent-looking, but it's well closed.

"That'll be a proper battle scar."

He rolls his eyes. "A random ricocheting bullet makes for a shit story."

"Could dig deep into your Irish roots."

"You mean, make something up?"

I nod.

War shrugs and glances at the windows. "You and Killian can't work on the computer shit during Thanksgiving break, right? Because low network traffic will make it too easy to spot hacking?"

"Didn't realize you were paying attention when he was here. Thought you were out cold after the marathon you ran."

The marathon euphemism brings a small smirk to the edges of his mouth. While War had a lighter Crue workload, he brought his on-again off-again dancer submissive into his bed for a couple of nights. The girl is loud when she's being happily tortured, so I was very aware of what I was missing. After she left, War laid on the couch for hours, like all the energy had been drained from his body. Which I guess it had.

He swipes the black threads and hair into the trash. "What's the deal? You working or not over Thanksgiving?"

"As you heard, we won't hack in over break, but I want to monitor the pinhole cameras we put in the staff area of the computer labs and the software Killian installed on the night of the rave. The more passwords we get, the better."

Killian and I are both pursuing computer engineering degrees, so we can get access to old network storage data, but we don't have the clearance the two older guys who actually work for the IT department do.

GU is the place where tech billionaire Drew Ralston began his company and created the sophisticated encryption software used by financial institutions all over the world. Anyone with code that can be used to create a key that unlocks Ralston-encrypted data will have access to billions of dollars. It could lead to the ultimate digital heist.

Grabbing a glass of water, I add, "I'm going to do some reconnaissance on the living situations of the non-student IT guys, too. At least one of them was here when Ralston was."

"I should do surveillance since I'm not on the hacking and I keep later hours."

He's right that Killian and I crash early these days because team training is ramping up. The closer we get to the season, the more intense the schedule will become.

I shrug. "I'll have time on my hands while campus is running with a skeleton crew."

"No one should gather intel on houses next week when random extra family members may be coming and going from people's houses. You want an accurate picture? We should watch the IT guys during an ordinary week."

"Sure, but next week, extra cars driving slowly through neighborhoods will go unnoticed, precisely because of the holiday visitors."

"Yours wouldn't. Porsche?"

"Fair." I rest my hands on the counter, wondering why we're having this conversation. War can't really be that interested in the details of a low-risk surveillance operation.

"So," he says casually. "No reason to be here. Pack up and come to Boston."

"Nah, other plans."

His dark eyes flick to my hands as they clear away loose plastic bags and other debris. War nods and rises, grabbing the mustache scissors from the countertop.

It's the second time he's suggested I go to Boston for Thanksgiving, which I'm sure means something, but I don't know what.

For a time, he and I moved as a unit, working and playing hard in the off hours. While school and work haven't changed, the house dynamic has. War and I didn't have many hard boundaries until I started bringing Sawyer over. My moving to the downstairs bedroom with her was a clear message. *I'm keeping this one to myself. And out of your way.*

"Your mother's coming to town? For the holiday?" I ask.

He makes a nonspecific grunt of affirmation without turning around as he walks back to his room.

There's maybe a rift there. His mom's a four-hour drive away, give or take, but he hasn't gone to New York all year. When I went to Ireland right before starting uni, War flew to Eastern Europe, with the war waging, no less. He never said what he did during the trip, and I didn't ask.

Honestly, I don't give a toss what my friends get up to when it's got nothing to do with me, and he's the same. That's men for you. Meanwhile, Cranberry Sauce and Ash keep me updated on all their life events, both great and small, and also how they feel about them. It's a strange thing with girls. Not unwelcome, but odd.

I grab my laptop and walk to the couch. Speaking of hacking, there's another thing I need to get on with before Sauce arrives and I get distracted. After I open my computer, I enter my password.

Granthorpe used the same class ring company for fifteen of the target years and hacking into their network was easy. Old purchase data, however, was merged and archived. It took some work to uncover files with useful information.

Now, I've got to review the catalogues to find design names and write some code to scour the massive files to get the purchaser information I need.

I get to work, and a couple of hours later, I run the executable I've written. It spits out a table that includes everyone who ordered the style of signet ring I'm looking for. I sort by university, checking logos and crests as necessary.

In the end, I've got a handful of names.

Among them is one I don't expect.

Allendale.

30

SAWYER

After I've packed and submitted all the coursework that's due, I feel so free. There's one exam on Tuesday that I'll study a bit more for, but otherwise I'm basically on break.

My head buzzes with all the cool things Jamie and I could do during the week. My phone rings and a picture of Ash sticking her tongue out pops up on the screen, making me smirk.

I swipe to answer. "Hi, weirdo. Do you know what pic you've got as your profile?"

"Yeah, the tongue one. Hey, I need a favor."

"Okay."

"Crosby's been texting he needs his coat back before I leave for break, and I ignored him because I thought I didn't have it." She huffs out a breath. "Then I tossed my stuff in the back seat, and guess what I found."

"Fuck's sake."

"Yeah, he definitely planted it back there on purpose when I gave him and another guy a ride home from the tavern on

Wednesday. Listen, can you ride with me to return it? I'll drop you over at Jamie and War's right after."

"Are you afraid to go alone? Maybe Jamie should come with us?"

"Hell no, I'm not afraid. Crosby's monster strong, for sure, but I'm a little rain-forest PD frog. He doesn't know—or need to—but me scared of an aggressive frat guy? No way."

"You're a what frog?"

She laughs. "A golden poison dart frog. They're all little and sunny and cute. But even fully grown at four centimeters, they've got enough toxin to kill ten to twenty people. So, you know, predator beware."

"And how are you like one?"

"Seesaw! We don't have time for this discussion right now. If you're coming with me, I need you to say so, so I can text my cousin not to pick you up. And I need you to come down with your stuff, 'cause baby's gotta bounce."

My tone is full-on mock harassed, but I agree. "Yeah, sure, I'll ride with you. But I don't see why you need me if you're really a poisonous frog."

"It's strategy. I'll explain on the way. Come down!"

The phone goes silent, and I shake my head.

After I confirm Jamie isn't on his way to get me and doesn't mind Ash dropping me off, I grab my stuff and head downstairs.

On the passenger seat of Ash's car, I find an envelope full of parking tickets. She's so cavalier about the rules.

"Toss those in the glove box," she says. "Gotta pay them when I get back."

Slipping them away, I take my seat.

Ash pulls out of the parking spot and waits as the gated arm lifts.

"How do you get into this lot?"

"I bought an upperclassman's key card from him."

Staring at her, I cock an eyebrow. So sneaky. Maybe she is

part rain-forest tree frog. "You got a key card, yet you're still getting parking tickets?"

"Well, this is an unregistered car. But at least the parking fascists won't straight-up tow it, which they do in the un-gated lots if they run a plate and find it belongs to a freshman. You and I really need to get an apartment off campus. Maybe a townhouse?"

Moving off campus this year isn't an option for me, as I've told her, but still she persists. And next year, I'll hopefully get a room in the Briar Club house. A wave of satisfaction courses through me. *I'm in.* That thought has not gotten old.

As we drive, my good mood makes me admire the campus all the more. GU's old brick buildings are covered in ivy, the green threads crawling up the weathered walls and creeping along the windowsills. Afternoon sunshine has melted the morning's frost, so the bare tree branches are like spindly fingers. I love Granthorpe's creepiness as much as its storied history.

As we pull up in front of the large brick Beta fraternity house, I lean forward to look up at the Greek letters above the door.

A car on the street is pulling away as we arrive, so Ash parallel parks, expertly.

When I start to open my door, Ash's hand shoots out to grab my arm to stop me. "No, Seesaw. We're staying in the car." Her fingers slide over her phone as she sends a text, presumably to Crosby.

The phone rings and Ash answers, putting the call on speaker so she can reach into the back. "Hey, Cros, I'm here. Come out and get your coat."

"I need ya to bring it in. We're in the middle—"

"Hells no. I've got a friend I need to drop off who's already late. If you're not down here in one minute, your coat is coming home to Boston with me. And good luck ever getting it back after that because it's a nice coat, and I've got a cousin and buddies who are gonna be in my backseat this week."

"Ashling." His surly tone doesn't seem to make an impression, because her smile doesn't fade. "You have five minutes to come the fuck in. I've got a present for you."

"I love presents. Bring it down." Then she swipes, ending the call. A second later, her phone rings again. She sends Crosby to voicemail and gives the phone a voice command to set a timer for four minutes.

Cocking my head, I eye her. "You're diabolical. It's a really concerning quality."

She smirks and winks at me.

In the final minute on the timer, she starts the car. Ten seconds later, the front door of the fraternity house bangs open, and the stocky power lifter jogs outside. He's wearing jeans and a tight sweater and carries a small box.

Behind him, I spot my pseudo brother as Brad opens the storm door for a young woman to emerge. She's buttoned up in a green, plaid wool coat and shiny black boots. After a second, I realize it's Clare Duffy.

My body stiffens as I watch her. Why was she with Brad? Are they joining forces against me... maybe to get my acceptance to the Briar Club rescinded? No, if Clare wanted to sabotage me, she'd have done it before.

Stop being paranoid.

Crosby approaches the driver's door and holds out the box. "Here you go, beautiful."

"Thanks," Ash says, taking the box and dropping it in her lap. "Here's your coat. Happy Thanksgiving."

With one hand he takes the coat, but with the other, he grabs the steering wheel. "Come on. You have to open it now."

She slaps his hand. "I told you I don't have time." As if to punctuate the statement, her alarm goes off. "But I will make a video of me opening it and if I love the present, I'll send the video as a thank you. Fair?"

"Yeah." He releases the steering wheel, and his fingers detour to stroke her face as he withdraws his hand. "Text me when you get to Boston, so I know you got there safe."

"Nope. Not playing the girlfriend game. Now back up before my Camaro dents your foot bones."

A tap on my window causes my head to jerk toward it. Clare Duffy stands right next to the door.

Jesus.

I roll the window down halfway.

"Heard you got in. Congratulations." As she holds up her hand, I see what she wants me to see. There on her bony wrist is my mom's vintage Briar Club bangle.

What a fucking bitch.

31

JAMIE

When I see the name Allendale, everything stops. The world narrows down to a sense of dread.

I search the net for Sawyer's photogram account. Once I locate it, I start scrolling.

Years of searching for Jude's kidnapper ends with a single picture on her page. It's Sawyer's high school graduation. The asshole brother stands a couple of feet away, trying to get out of the frame. Next to her, with an arm around her shoulder and a smile that causes my guts to knot, is the man from the top of the hill. He's older, so there are deeper brackets around his mouth, and his hair has gray strands woven through it that weren't there in Ireland. But the eyes and face are still familiar. A whole lifetime passed in the time between when I locked eyes on him and the moment he grabbed Jude.

Thinking back, trying to compare every detail, my muscles contract in protest. I don't want to relive those moments. But I have to.

Some pieces are vague or lost. I can never remember dropping the fishing pole or scrambling up the hill. Time skips, like a rock across the surface of a lake. The parts I remember vividly never change... I see the intent in the man's expression as he looks at Jude. It starts an adrenaline rush of fear and dread inside me. He grabs my brother. In what seems to be an instant later, I am standing on the roadside, watching the car speed away.

I chase, following it with my eyes until it turns and disappears.

Bits of the long run are still with me. How quiet the road was. Praying for help. Praying I would get there in time. Or that I'd find Jude hiding on the side of the road because he'd jumped from the car to escape and was just waiting for me.

The blackness surrounds me again now.

I don't realize I've knocked a glass from the counter until War is standing a few feet away.

"J?" he barks.

Turning my head, I stare at him. "What?" My tone is as flat as the surface of the water that day.

With a narrow-eyed gaze, he shifts his attention to the shards of broken glass. "What's up?"

My own glance passes the laptop where it sits open on the counter, the offensive picture glaring at me. I flip the screen down, snapping the computer closed.

"Knocked a glass over," I say with a shrug I hope appears casual.

Something in my features gives me away. Or perhaps it's something else. He may have called my name a few times. I'm not sure.

War watches me like I'm an unknown quantity, which in this state, I am. My subconscious mind is five steps ahead of coherent thought. All my instincts are screaming at me to get the long rifle with the scope.

Calm the fuck down, I finally tell myself. *You have the man in your sights now. A picture on the computer is as good as having him in the room.*

Internally, I shake off my racing heart and racing thoughts.

Meanwhile, War is perfectly still. Like an animal scenting trouble in the distance. It's something I've seen before in him and admired. In moments of chaos, there is no wasted motion from War. No wasted energy.

Drawing in a breath, I frown. "Everything's all right." This time, I'm sure I've made my voice sound normal.

My shift toward calm is something he must recognize because he turns and walks away.

Good. I need to be alone to think.

In the time it takes me to clean up the broken glass, I've made my first decision.

Robert Allendale will lose his only son, and if his grief doesn't level him, I will keep going until I find something that does.

32

SAWYER

At Jamie's, I'm trying to pretend things are normal and that Clare Duffy didn't steal my mom's Briar Club bracelet out from under me. And also that fucking Brad didn't help her do it. Unfortunately, on and off, my mind reels from the pain and frustration. I don't know if it's too late to get it back somehow. I hope not. Though, I can't figure out how I'd pull that off.

There's no way I would whine about it to Briar Club leadership. They know that vintage bracelet was my mom Celine's, so if they let Clare trade hers in for it, they've already decided it should go to an accomplished senior rather than incoming-freshman me, who has yet to prove herself.

My hands are clasped in my lap as I sit on a barstool at the downstairs kitchen island. Jamie sits at the end, and as usual, War is standing. This time, however, War stands because he's cooking, rather than so he'll be at the ready to turn and stalk up the stairs.

War is dressed in jeans and a tight black t-shirt for a band called Five Finger Death Punch. As he cooks an Asian chicken stir fry, Jamie drinks whiskey and speaks with an accent so thick I can barely understand him.

I eat a pea pod as I watch them.

Jamie uses a string of words I don't recognize, and War murmurs, "If you take a nap like a five-year-old, you're out."

Jamie chuckles.

Studying him, I cock my head. "What did you just say?"

"Ah, sorry. War lived in Ireland for a time, so he understands me the way people from the island would. I just said I'm feeling exhausted. *Knackered*, we say."

I nod. He's never spoken with such a thick accent around me before. It's almost as though he's trying to shut me out or to emphasize to War that I'm no threat to the closeness of their friendship. Since I've never done anything that should make War have issues with me, I have to assume it's because he and Ash are at odds.

Picking up another loose pea pod, I study him. "Where else have you lived, War?"

War dumps a cutting board worth of veggies into a sizzling wok. "New York. Russia. Boston." His tone is slightly terse. Maybe he does have an issue with me for some reason.

We fall silent for a few moments as I watch him make a stir fry sauce with honey, soy sauce, and fresh ginger, among other things. He mixes the ingredients so fast it's as though he's whisking egg whites.

"Where did you learn to cook?"

"Where didn't I?" He glances at me. "When you eat nine thousand calories a day, flavor's a priority. I was sick of fuckin' omelets by the time I was ten, so I learned."

"This would up your rank in Ash's eyes. She's always saying she needs a boyfriend who cooks."

He doesn't look at me, but his attention sharpens, as evidenced by the sudden tension in his broad shoulders and the way he cocks his head. It's very similar to the subtle things Ash does when his name is mentioned.

War's lip curls with distaste. "She's so skinny and hyper, I figured her diet was all coffee and cocaine."

Jamie and I chuckle, but I shake my head.

"She does love coffee, but she loves food, too. Crosby Bergmann claims he's going to take a cooking class. I hope he's lying."

War and Jamie look at me, not trying to hide that I've got their full attention.

"You hope he's lying? Why's that, Sauce?" Jamie asks.

"I don't trust him."

Jamie leans closer, retrieving a leftover slice of carrot from the counter. "Did you tell her that?"

I nod. "I don't even think she's that attracted to him. He's just... unbelievably persistent."

The hardness around War's eyes intensifies before he turns his attention back to the wok.

"I should text her to see if she's had dinner," I say. "She's going to Boston today, but her last text said she got sidelined before leaving town. That girl is always traveling at Mach speed."

War flattens his hand on the stone counter next to the burner but otherwise doesn't move or speak.

"Nah," Jamie says, glancing at his friend and then back at me. "Dinner's almost ready. We'll invite her another time."

"Right, okay," I say, mimicking Jamie's accent as best I can.

He smirks. "Not too bad, that."

War exhales a derisive sound, making me lean back and flush with embarrassment.

"Don't pay attention to him." Jamie shakes his head. "I'm not having you on. It wasn't bad."

I shrug, locking eyes with Jamie. "It's my favorite thing... the way it sounds when you say it."

"When I say, 'right, okay'?"

Nodding, I smile.

"Because he's agreeing with you," War says, setting stoneware dishes on the counter.

"It doesn't hurt the cause." I raise a hand in a questioning gesture. "Who doesn't love being agreed with? But calling it the main thing? I suspect that says more about you, War, than about me." My tone is teasing, but he doesn't acknowledge it.

Instead, he pauses in spooning food onto his plate so his dark eyes can scowl at me.

"She has you there, mate." Jamie flashes a small smile. "You do like when members of the opposite sex behave the way you want them to."

"Not the same thing. Also..." War raises his middle finger and directs it at both of us before turning off the burners, grabbing his maximally full plate, and heading upstairs.

"Think it was an accident that he left us to clean up?" I ask.

"No." Jamie studies me for a moment between bites. "It wasn't an accident your bringing Ash into the conversation, either, was it? Why do that?"

"Testing a theory." When he doesn't ask, I change tack. "They need to make peace with each other. Mentioning another guy who's making an effort to get close to her is my attempt to motivate him."

"You need to leave off where they're concerned."

"He's your best friend on campus. She's mine. If we're going to be together, they will bump into each other. Are we going to accept their being at each other's throats every time they interact?"

"Cranberry Sauce," he says in a warning tone.

"Listen," I say, trying again to mimic his accent. Which earns me a tap on the arm. "I think they may be attracted to each other."

"I said leave off." His tone has hardened, and my lips purse into a pout. "And don't try to tempt me with those lips. It won't end well."

My brows rise. Something is definitely off.

Jamie finishes eating and puts the plate in the dishwasher. I'm not super hungry, so I finish too and put the extra food into a freezer bag. While we're tidying up, he pours himself another glass of whiskey. After draining half of it, he sets the glass on the stone island.

Reaching across, I put a hand on his arm. "Are you okay?"

Blowing out a breath, he studies me. "Well enough. But, listen..." His gaze falls to my hand and then he tugs his arm away.

My brows rise. "What's wrong?"

"Fuck this," he whispers, rubbing his jaw. "I want to ask you something." Grabbing his glass, he raises it and drinks the last of the whiskey. When he sets the tumbler down hard, there's a cracking sound that causes me to wince. "Do you know about the evil in your family, Sawyer?"

I freeze, my jaw dropping open a fraction. "I—what do you mean?"

After a beat, he winces and tilts his head. "You've gone white." He licks his lips then scowls. "Christ, you do know. How? From a police investigation? Or another way?"

I don't understand how he found out about my bio mom.

Or maybe I do. Brad told Clare, and Clare started spreading the rumors. Is this how she's already undermining me in the club? And how she convinced them to give her Celine's bracelet?

"For how long?" Jamie hisses.

I shake my head, starting to retreat.

He leans forward and grabs my forearm in a tight grip. "I asked how long?" His tone is like a slap.

Growing so stiff my body hurts, I'm overwhelmed by all the things I've been holding inside and trying to hide. I don't deserve to be attacked over things I can't control. Things that happened when I was a child.

There's no explanation as to why a lifetime of shame and fear becomes too much to take in an instant. Maybe because I feel so betrayed. I almost told him about my bio mom myself. Never in a million years did I expect Jamie to blame me.

"Why would it matter how long I knew?" I say, my tone angry and frustrated. "I'm not the person who did something wrong. Let go of my arm."

His eyes flame with rage that threatens to burn me alive. As soon as he releases me, I draw back.

"Right." His voice is blistering in its intensity. "This is us done, then." He stalks over to the stairs. "War!"

After a moment, the formidable housemate appears, towering from above like a barbarian on a cliff. "What?"

"The girl is going back to the dorm, and I'm too drunk to drive her. I need you to take her, mate."

War scowls and then disappears from view.

"Goodbye," Jamie says in a low voice before walking to one of the couches and sitting with his back to me.

There are a thousand things I want to scream at him, but what would be the point?

Mostly, I want to know why the shame of my bio mom is such a deal breaker. I don't even have the same last name. Unless he figures it'll get out because of my pseudo brother's spite, which is very likely. But why is that so deadly to our relationship? Jamie's not set to inherit a throne, and he's never said he plans to go into politics or public life. I can't see why it matters so much.

Maybe his brother overdosed? And he sees all drug dealers as the scum who are responsible? It's not a completely crazy sentiment. My bio mom did things to trick people into more powerful addictions. And the type of narcotics they laced the drugs with meant she's responsible for several people dying from accidental overdoses.

Knowing she deceived kids as young as thirteen into taking things that killed them is despicable. And yeah, a part of me despises her for it. But she went to jail for that.

There's no way I'm going to walk around with my head hanging in shame. My plan has always been to rise above the early part of my life, and *no one* is going to make me feel bad for trying to move on.

By the time War comes downstairs, I'm standing at the front door with my coat on and my bag in hand.

When he opens the door and walks out, I follow him.

No look back at Jamie.

No final goodbye.

33

JAMIE

My head is muddled with black thoughts and pent-up fury. Whatever I needed from that final fight—smashing glass, shouting, her weeping with remorse for not turning the bastard in—I didn't get and never will.

Not her problem, those were her words.

As I stew in rage, the chaos in my head drills down to one thing. I'm about to make it the problem of every person in her fucking family.

Lying on the couch, I grind my teeth when my phone rings. My hand snatches the device. It's Ash rather than Sawyer. I glare at the phone. After several rings, the call aborts. A moment later, it begins ringing again.

For fuck's sake.

I answer. "Yeah?"

"What is wrong with you?" Ash says in a grim voice.

Swallowing bile, I stare at the ceiling.

"You let her get all amped up about spending the holiday break with you and then dump her? Help me understand that."

"What's between Sawyer Allendale and me has nothing to do with you. Stay in your lane."

There's a prolonged beat of silence. "Yeah, well, she's my friend now, too, Jamie. And I'm pissed you set her up to take a fall like this. I'm halfway to Boston, and I'm guessing you don't want me to go back and get her? You expect me to leave her alone in the empty dorm all week?" Ash rarely takes a tone with me. Or anyone. Laid back and cheerful is her normal, so this is like her slamming a hammer on my thumb.

"Do whatever you want," I say, my terse tone matching her angry one.

"But let's be clear," Ash says. "If she comes home with me, you won't come, right?"

"Right. I don't want to see her."

"Tell me what happened."

"Ask her."

"For fuck's sake, Jamie." Ash's voice is impatient and frustrated, which only makes my own emotions burn hotter. "She didn't want to talk about it. Just said it's over."

"Right, there you have it." The whiskey is showing its hold because my words are slightly slurred.

"Tell me."

"Do you think this is what I wanted? Fuck off. She's not the girl I thought she was, and she's not to be trusted. Not by me."

At the sound of an alert and a main door opening, I glance over. War enters the house and stops at the kitchen island.

From the phone, Ash's voice rises. "Are you saying she played us? That she got close to us with ill intent?" The precision and formality of Ash's words are like a scalpel cutting through scar tissue to look inside at an old wound. One I don't particularly want to open up for the world. Or even for a family member I consider a friend.

"No, I'm saying she's not the girl *for me*. I can't say whether you'd give her a pass for... Listen, I don't want to talk. Do whatever you want. Swing back for her if you like. I won't be coming to Boston or Coynston anyway." After swiping to end the call, I drop the phone and rise.

I join War who's opened a cake holder. He cuts a slice of cinnamon cake and eats it over the sink.

"Thanks for dropping the girl off."

War watches me with an assessing gaze.

Resting my hands on the counter, I lean forward. "How committed are you to having a proper holiday with your family?"

"Not very." He waits a moment then adds, "Why?"

It's as I thought. War would like an excuse to bail. That still doesn't clear me to involve him in something that would be a danger to his freedom and his standing in the Crue.

I move to the opposite side of the kitchen counter and lower my voice. "I've a mind to step out of line. Could use help establishing an alibi."

"Step out of line how?"

After a moment of trying to read his face, I give that up as futile. A wee voice in my head warns me I'll regret talking about this while drunk. Blowing out a breath, I shake my head. "Never mind. I'm steamin', mate. Let sunrise and sleep sort me before I go on too much." I walk over to the couch that faces the window and drop onto it.

In a few minutes, War turns off the overheads and flicks on a single lamp. Then he joins me, sitting in a nearby chair and setting a bottle of vodka and a jar of olives in front of him.

Uncapping the bottle, he drinks like he's got a mind to catch up to me.

When there's half a liter of vodka gone, he pops a couple of olives in his mouth and swallows them whole. "Now," he murmurs, leaning back and kicking his feet onto the coffee table so it shudders. "Let's have it."

I stare at the river and can practically feel waves rolling over me. "There's something that needs doing. A marker I've been holding for too long." I lick my lips and close my eyes. "One murder, at least. Perhaps, two."

"The girl?"

That thought is like a blade driving straight through my heart till it nicks a shoulder blade on its way out the back. Pain snakes down my spine, and I shift in my seat, trying to shake it off.

"No." My mouth has gone dry. "She may deserve it, but no. Never." My lids open, and my gaze rises to the exposed beams.

War pops his knuckles absently. "Going against Crue law could get us ousted for good. Maybe worse. You all right with that?"

The word *yes* emerges as I exhale. "Needs must." I turn my head. "Listen, the drink's got me boilin' over." I rise. "I'll sleep off the Bushmills, and we'll call this conversation nothing but a dream because I've got no right to drag you into it."

War's dark eyes rest on my face. "No one drags me anywhere. How could they?" He taps his torso in a gesture that encompasses a lot, including the fact that it would probably take three or four men to drag him somewhere he didn't want to go. "By noon, we'll be sober. We'll circle back to this."

"Thanks, mate."

He nods, and I leave it at that.

When I'm face down on my bed, the regrets start in on me. I could've had a lovely holiday full of Sawyer's soft skin pressed against my body and her ragged breaths in my ear.

If only...

If only she wasn't the girl whose life I need to destroy.

34

SAWYER

Early on Saturday morning, I'm riding with the enemy. Stony silence fills Brad's Audi on the drive to the Boston international airport.

Ash, sweetheart that she is, would've come back to Foxgrove for me and taken me home to her family for the holidays, but Jamie's literally the last person I want to think about, so meeting and hanging out with his extended family is a hard pass.

The bitter sting of Jamie's rejection hits me again, and I can't keep the visceral response from happening... The sick feeling in my stomach. The desperate feeling of being tainted by my lowlife beginnings, and of perpetually being seen as low class when someone learns the truth about my life.

I let it all wash over me until it makes me angry instead of sad.

Fuck him. And *fuck anyone* else who tries to make themselves superior by putting me down.

The sole benefit of Jamie's proverbial slap in the face is it led to an epiphany moment. Fifteen years of carrying undeserved shame is long enough. Too long, in fact. I'm done. Letting it go won't be easy, but I'll never be happy in life if I don't.

"So what's the deal?" Brad's voice is half sullen, half accusatory sneer. "I thought you weren't coming to Palm Beach?"

"Plans change." The words are icy and clipped.

"You realize no one wants you there."

Staring out the windshield at the empty tree branches shaking from the wind, I raise a terse wall of silence. I refuse to be put on the defensive.

"You think getting into the Briar Club is a big triumph that'll finally impress Grandmother? When you barely made the cut? Even while riding my mom's coattails?"

My gaze flicks to the pinched expression on his face. "The nasal way you say grandmother makes you sound like a dickhead. You should rethink that."

After a beat, he swerves across two lanes of traffic and makes a turn into a random strip mall parking lot on the side of the feeder. His slamming on the brakes causes my seatbelt to lock so I rock forward and snap back at the screeching halt.

A second later, his fist nails me in the upper arm. A bitter gasp emerges before I can stop it. Pain explodes from the blow. I grit my teeth to keep from rubbing my arm and spewing rage.

"You're such a fucking cunt!" he snaps. To add to the humiliation, he slaps my face with enough force to turn my head and cause sharp, burning pain. I'm sure there will be a red mark. It might even stay visible and could raise questions, which he's never allowed before.

I blink stinging eyes and bite the inside of my cheek, fighting to stay calm. I want to slap him back. Or to scream at him, but I stop myself. He's dangerously out of control. After four and a half years of not hitting me, he's starting again.

A feeling of impending doom oozes over me, making the hair on the back of my neck stand like the hackles on a wolf.

"You think I'm afraid of your boyfriend? Fuck him. He's

about to have big problems. Ones that'll get him gone from GU."

I only half process his words because I'm reading his angry expression and body language. He's vibrating with rage. If I push back here and now with caustic taunts, he might snap and do more than hurt me.

My hand reaches the door handle and pulls. Light fills the small space, so I can see the harsh lines around his eyes. He grabs a clump of my hair and jerks me toward him. The pain in my scalp wipes away every thought. I shove at him, trying to escape.

"Close that fucking door or I swear to God—" He grabs my throat in a grip so hard I'm afraid he's about to break my neck.

My heartbeat jumps in my throat, making it difficult to breathe. Fear pours down like an avalanche. Brad's not just a bully. He's out of his mind.

Letting go, he reaches across and bangs my forearm with his closed fist. My hand wrenches off the door, and I let it hover over my lap as my mind races.

"I want to get out," I say, reaching for my seatbelt.

"Fuck you," he says, shifting the car into gear. In an instant, he propels us forward. "Shut that fucking door!"

I grab the armrest shakily, my breathing shallow and erratic.

"If you jump out. It'll be the last thing you ever do."

The thought that he might kill me is shocking, but I can't escape the feeling that things are spiraling, and my lifeless body could be found strangled in a nearby ditch.

A muscle in my jaw ticks as I stare at him. I can't tell if he's bluffing. He seems more in control now that he knows I'm scared, but I'm not sure I can trust his control to last.

He barrels onto the feeder, and the moment for jumping out of the car is gone. He enters the freeway going sixty.

"Dad asked me to bring you to the airport." His voice is calm now. Who but a psychopath can change gears that quickly? "You think I'm going to let him see a ride-share charge on your credit card?" The way he immediately thinks ahead to cover his tracks is sickening.

It's also something I need to learn. When I told my dad I was going to Palm Beach after all and was hoping he would come, too, I should've also said a friend would drive me to the airport. It was stupid to ride with Brad. But I'd honestly assumed he'd be over the rave party altercation by now, since he'd already retaliated by helping Clare get Celine's bracelet.

I rub my arm, which has grown its own painful heartbeat. That first punch was vicious.

As he drives, the car grows silent, and my mind tries to focus on next steps. The question becomes how am I going to handle things? When I was younger I would shrink off and hide. I avoided being near him.

My reasoning for going to Palm Beach for Thanksgiving was to start to face things head on. Ironic that the very thing that I thought would help me move forward has cast me back into the abuse I silently withstood in childhood.

"What do you want from me, Brad?" My voice is neutral and soft. I seriously want to know what he thinks his end game is.

"I want you gone for good."

Understanding dawns. Brad's driven by more than hatred. He's threatened by the prospect of my exerting my position in the family. There can only be one prince. One heir.

Watching him out of the corner of my eye, I recall the times when he punched a young me in the stomach so hard I worried about internal bleeding. I'd forgotten how dangerous he can be.

"I don't want to be around you, either." My voice is surprisingly level. Seemingly emotionless. "Maybe I will just stop coming to family things."

"You'd have to make excuses to avoid seeing my dad, too. Not just my grandparents. If you do it enough, they'll get the message that you don't want to have anything to do with us."

My not coming to several family functions must've given him hope I would do exactly what he's suggesting. That I would withdraw until the rift made me a distant memory. Remember that charity case we took in? What ever happened to her?

God knows my Allendale grandparents would probably be relieved, too, if I just disappeared.

"I won't come. I'll cancel my flight and take a ride-share back."

"No," he says bitterly. "He knows you're too much of a grasping freeloader to let an expensive last-minute ticket go to waste. Especially after you came all the way to the airport. No. It'll raise too many questions now."

Glancing at him out of the corner of my eye, I wonder why this concerns him. He wouldn't care whether I seem like a flake who can't make up her mind. Dad would be upset at me for wasting money. Unless my dad is suspicious of Brad's treatment of me and has said something to him about it.

Frowning, I shake my head. "I'm not going to be your punching bag all week. I'll say I got sick on the ride to the airport and couldn't fly."

"No." Brad's calm now as he rests back against his seat, one hand on the wheel, white knuckles gone. *Good.* Let him believe he's got the upper hand. "Nothing will happen to you during this trip. I swear to God, though, if you try to come to Christmas, you'll fucking regret it."

"I won't." I'm not sure what I'm saying. While I'm fine with skipping the next holiday, I'm not okay with cutting off contact with my dad. I have to figure out a way to stop Brad from getting near me in the future.

For some reason, getting Ash's advice springs to mind. Actually, not for no reason. She went to check on her friend who was apparently being hunted by bad people. She called herself a poisonous frog. That may have been false bravado, but I know she's clever. She might have good ideas for how to deal with this situation. Maybe, I'll see my dad separately? On the down low? Or secretly video Brad threatening or punching me? Ash could help me get documentation.

The image of Jamie and War jumping in to rescue us during the Tronex party flashes in my mind. I would love to be able to talk to Jamie about Brad.

Fuck no. Forget Jamie.

In response to that order, his handsome face appears in my mind, and a pang of longing surfaces.

Seriously, stop. It's pathetic.

Signs for Logan Airport flash overhead, bringing on a sense of relief. Once we're inside, Brad won't be able to touch me.

Pulling out my phone causes him to stiffen.

"Who are you texting?"

"No one," I lie, but there's a surge of satisfaction at the concern laced through his tone.

"It won't matter if you tell O'Rourke."

From his tone, it sure sounds like he thinks it *would* matter. Of course, I'm not going to, but it can't hurt for him to think Jamie would retaliate on my behalf. Another small protection against violence now that he seems to be thinking rationally again.

Putting my phone in my purse, I sit back. I'll wait to text until I'm no longer alone with him.

35

JAMIE

I wake at ten-thirty with echoes of a vague nightmare in my head. It's something to do with Clare Duffy pushing Sauce off the Kerry Cliffs in Ireland. Since I never dream about the girls I'm fucking, I have to wonder what the hell's up with my head.

Sweating whiskey, I grab my phone to text Sawyer before I remember the relationship's ended.

Yeah, over. Christ, that brings a raw sensation to my chest, as though someone's dragging glass across my heart.

Clenching my teeth, I shake my head at the urge I still have to text her.

Not happening.

Laying a hand over my replacement St. Christopher medal, I draw in a deep breath. The St. Chris medal I got from my grandparents is buried with Jude because he lost his on the day he was assaulted.

I'm close to avenging him. Until that's done, vengeance needs to be my focus.

When I get up and leave my room, I glance over at War's bedroom door, which is closed.

I hit the head and chug an electrolyte drink before pulling on clothes to go kayaking. I need to be outside to clear my head.

When I exit through the apartment door, the cold is bracing, and the air smells of salt and algae. *Perfect.*

I jog down the metal steps and grab the kayak from the shed. Within minutes, I'm on the water and paddling upstream at a hard clip. Nothing centers my mind faster than being on the water while sucking icy air into my lungs.

The workout is long enough for me to develop a warm, satisfying sweat under my clothes. It's so familiar, it takes the edge off my frustration.

By the time I re-enter the house, War's in the kitchen drinking a sports drink. Great minds think alike. I nod a greeting as I walk toward the hall.

"J—"

Pausing, I turn to look at him.

"Let's take a walk."

Walking outside to have a sensitive conversation is part of our training. And it hammers home my dilemma. Do I involve him in this? I shouldn't. War's a good mate, and this isn't his problem. It's mine and mine alone.

Pulling up the neck of my shirt, I use the fabric to wipe sweat from my temple. "Forget last night." I release the shirt, letting it fall back into place. "Seriously. Whiskey talk is nonsense."

"Let's take a walk."

In a low voice, I say, "Your uncle's grooming you for a larger role in the Crue. Last thing I want is to get you into something that ends that."

War grabs his coat and stalks over to the door "Might be a way around it."

I give him a meaningful look. "There isn't."

He shrugs and guzzles the rest of his drink before pitching the plastic bottle. It sails the distance and drops into the trash. "Yeah, well, I'm in anyway."

My reaction to his announcement is mixed. I always planned to carry out my revenge alone. But now that I have connections to the target's family, my alibi needs to be airtight. Accomplishing that on my own will be nearly impossible.

Grabbing my coat, I join War, and we leave the C Crue house.

Walking along the waterfront, War's silent as he waits for me to start speaking. There's a fist in my throat that prevents it.

Finally, I draw a deep breath and force myself to speak. "When he was young, my brother was taken. We got him back for a while. Then, he died, because of what happened while he was gone. I now know who took him." Stopping, I stare out at the water. "I'm gonna ruin the man's life. As I swore I would."

War's silence stretches outward, beckoning me to keep going.

"I'm gonna kill the man's son."

"When and where?"

"There's a complication. We know him. Had an altercation with him."

"Allendale?" The fact that War's mind works it out in an instant says a lot about how sharp he is.

I nod. "Allendale."

"Is that why you got involved with the girl? To confirm the family connection to your brother?"

"No." Swallowing, I shake my head. "When I met her, I had no idea. But she knows the family secrets. And she knows I know."

He gives me a hard look. "Why the fuck would you show her your hand?"

"Shouldn't have. I was looking for a different answer. I wanted her to be innocent—to have no idea."

War's eyes narrow thoughtfully. "The dad has a history as a sex offender?"

So, he's worked that part out too, from the little I said. "Never been caught."

"Then how would she know? And why would she admit knowing?"

I shrug. "We didn't get that far before I ended things and threw her out of the house."

Drawing in a breath and then blowing it out, he shakes his head. "Doing the brother now is dicey. You should let some time pass. Then it would be less likely anyone would believe her if she pointed a finger at you."

"I'm not waiting. The man who caused my brother's death has been living his life without consequences for too long already. But I will understand if you don't want any part of this."

War glances over at me. "I'm in. Unless you intend to get caught? So you can rub the dad's nose in it that you're avenging your brother? If so, you don't need me or anyone."

"No, not planning to get caught. One O'Rourke has already lost his life because of Robert Allendale. I want to take my life back, not forfeit it."

"So, Brad Allendale, when and where?"

"Florida. This week."

"Florida's better than Massachusetts, if we can cover our tracks well enough." War stares at the rocky embankment and nods. "Yeah. We can make it work."

Just like that, I'm no longer alone.

Now, it's a murder conspiracy.

I didn't realize how much it would mean for a mate to show that kind of loyalty. To risk his own freedom. And the future he's been building.

Blood will seal it. I'll owe War the same kind of loyalty. And one day, maybe when I'm back living a normal life in Ireland, I'll have to set that aside and step up for him. Am I willing to do it? Yeah, I am. There's no turning back for me. I'm already too far gone.

Besides, I'll never have the brother I grew up with. This has become the best alternative.

Brothers bound together by spilling the blood of others.

So be it.

36

SAWYER

The first two nights of the trip are better than expected. Except at meals when we can't, Brad and I avoid each other. Most of my free time is spent in solitude, where I'm either in my room reading, beach-combing for pretty seashells, or swimming in the heated pool.

I don't bring up the Briar Club, but when Grandmother Liz asks, it's nice to be able to tell her I've been accepted. We're alone in the sitting room, safely away from Brad, so he's not around to undermine the achievement with snide comments about my near failure to get in. Even if he had been there, I'm not sure whether I would've cared. What would it matter now when I'm planning to skip all future family holidays? I'll probably never see Liz Allendale again.

Ironically, upon hearing the news, Liz's small smile is warmer than any I can remember.

Sitting with her bony hands resting in her lap, she inclines her head. "That's excellent, Sawyer. Well done." As she leans forward, the strand of glowing white pearls around her throat sways. "All members are invited to the Induction Ceremony. I may attend. I would enjoy seeing my granddaughter get her bracelet."

I stare at her. She's never called me her granddaughter before. It's both satisfying and crushing. Just when I've finally made progress, it's become pointless.

"There will be a lot of photographs taken." She raises a small blue and white cup and takes a sip of coffee. "I can think of two I'd like to have. One of your receiving your bracelet. And another of the two of us together in front of the club's seal." After setting the cup down on its saucer, she taps a fingernail against the handle. "I'll hang the latter next to the one of Bobby and Brad at the golf classic."

I'm speechless. Is this some kind of cruel joke? Did Brad hint that I'll be gone from their lives soon? And Liz decided putting me on the family photo wall will be my parting gift?

I can't see that, though. If she's trying to erase me, why put up a reminder? The confusion on my face may be evident, but I try to cover it.

"I'm sorry Celine won't be with us." She sighs. "A picture of the three of us at the club would've made her very happy. And this is her triumph, too, isn't it?"

Tears burn my eyes, but I blink them away. Allendale women don't get weepy.

"May I ask you to consider something, dear?" Folding her hands in her lap again, she leans forward.

"Sure."

"Your hair." Her lips purse for a second. "The contrast is striking—even attractive—with your skin tone. But this moment in your life will be preserved in photographs forever, and I wonder if you'll be happy to have this style immortalized? You're an adult woman now who is just beginning to build her legacy."

At any other time, I would resent her trying to dictate my personal style, but at the moment, she sounds genuinely concerned that I'll be the one who has regrets. And it's not like I haven't had the same thoughts. I've already tried to gradually tone down the color, which was fun for high school when all the senior girls in my circle were doing bright colors. But it's not a popular look at GU. Plus, it's what caused Jamie to call me Cranberry Sauce, and I don't want reminders of that.

"Honestly, I have been thinking of changing my hair," I admit. "Do you know which salons in town are the best? Mom always said that for a big style change it's important to go to a great salon."

Liz clasps her hands around her trouser-clad knee. I always like when she takes this posture when talking with me. It feels casual and intimate. "The salon where I get my blowouts should suffice. They have quite a few young stylists and more importantly, clients your age. What change are you thinking of making?"

I finger the end of a strand. "Something more subtle and sophisticated. My natural color is that flat brown I don't really like."

Her lips press together. "Is that true, dear? Because I disagree. It's a rich shade of brown. Very lovely."

My brows rise. She has never complimented anything about my appearance. *Ever.*

"Well, thank you." Taken by surprise, I'm silent for a moment. "I thought I might go back to my natural color for the base with some light brown highlights. I might cut it quite short, too."

"A short cut can be very sophisticated." Her own silver hair is short and sleek. "My appointment is Tuesday. Would you like to join me?"

"I would. Yes, thank you." After a moment's consideration, I realize the problem with this plan. Brad will take note, and it might set him off. I'll need to backtrack, at least while he and I are both in Palm Beach.

I wonder if I could forge a new relationship with Liz privately. Maybe when she's at Granthorpe for the ceremony, we could have dinner. If he found out though… And it's not like I could ever confide in her about him. Allendale blood and his being the male heir would always win out.

Forcing a polite smile, I tilt my head. "You know what? I think I'd rather go to a Boston salon, so I can find a regular stylist. I need to go to the city for an Induction Ceremony outfit anyway. And it would be nice to surprise you with my new look on the day of the ceremony."

She smiles, and it may be the most genuine one I've seen from her yet. "I think that would be lovely. I look forward to it." When she rises, I do, too.

"Grandmother?" It's been a long time since I've used that word. It doesn't sound completely natural to my ears, but it's not totally awkward either.

"Yes, dear?"

"Are you planning to take a swim?" It's one of her daily rituals, and something she's always encouraged us to do. I used to bring my suit to placate her, but over the years, I've come to enjoy swimming each night.

"Unfortunately, I have an evening conference call for a fundraiser, so I'll have to see when that concludes. But you must go ahead, Sawyer. I insist. And I'll join you if I'm able."

"Of course."

After we leave the room, I watch her stride down the hall. I still don't know whether to trust that we've turned a corner in our relationship. Or whether I even care anymore. A part of me feels oddly numb.

While our conversation was pleasant enough, it pales in comparison to the connections I formed with Ash and Jamie in a tiny fraction of the time. The thing with Jamie wasn't real, of course, but while it lasted, it was still far better than anything I've had with my extended Allendale family.

Upstairs, I change out of my expensive navy trousers, silk blouse, and Mom's pearls. A staple of the holiday wardrobe. At least this time, I think Liz appreciated it.

Once I'm in my black one-piece swimsuit, I head downstairs

and grab a robe and towel from the tiled entry area that has a door directly to the pool.

This trip, I've been swimming for exercise rather than just floating to relax. I'm up to twenty-five laps in thirty minutes and want to see if I can push to thirty. That thought makes me think of Jamie's training regimen, which causes a pang of regret. Not only had I been looking forward to a lot of great sex with him, I wanted to watch him row for Granthorpe this spring. That won't happen now.

Because my mind's occupied as I exit the house, I don't realize Brad is in the pool until I'm halfway to it.

He spots me.

"Oh." I stop walking. "Didn't realize anyone was out here."

Although he seems in control of himself, I'd never willingly enter the pool while he's in it. The water in the deep end is well over my head, and he pulled me under a lot when we were kids, sometimes holding me underwater until I panicked.

Hard pass on ever getting within arm's reach of him again.

Brad, however, doesn't spare me a second glance as he walks toward the shallow end. "I'm done."

Interesting. Normally, he'd linger just to drive me away. His feeling that he'll soon be rid of me is making him unusually generous. He wouldn't be if he'd heard me calling Liz Allendale grandmother just now.

As he stops to grab his goggles from the ledge, my thoughts turn toward revenge. And to getting leverage over him so he can't force me out of my own family. Unfortunately, video of him beating me is probably the only evidence that would force him to back off. Would I be willing to risk serious injury just to obtain proof of his abuse? After all, if I actually had to use it to get him in trouble, the Allendale grandparents might end up blaming me for setting him up.

No, I'm not willing to risk getting hurt. They're not worth it. The only thing I care about now is maintaining a relationship with my dad, and that much I can do while also avoiding Brad.

My dad and I often have dinner on our own when Dad visits Granthorpe.

Remaining still in the shadows, I wait for Brad to leave. Once he's been inside the house for several minutes, I'll get in the water. But not before.

A popping sound causes me to gaze up at the sky. One of the party boats has been shooting off fireworks at the end of their tours. My eyes strain looking for colors, but it's dark over the ocean tonight. A smacking sound to my right draws my attention.

Brad's tripped coming out of the pool and is sprawled with his legs still in the water and his head and chest on the cement. His body twitches twice and then goes still.

"Brad?" My voice is low, and I'm not sure he hears me.

His face is turned away, so I don't know if he's playing or what. Did he really hit his head hard enough to knock himself out?

My general unease keeps me from approaching him. I don't want to be within arms' reach. What if this is some kind of trick to get at me?

"Bradley?" I repeat.

For several beats, I don't move.

Finally, I walk along the edge of the enclosure, keeping many feet away from him as I move to a position where I can see his face better.

As I start to circle him, goosebumps rise on my arms. Something isn't right.

Startled, I realize there's a dark liquid crescent spreading over the cement. Outward from beneath his head.

I'm frozen for a moment, uncomprehending and confused.

"Brad?"

He's utterly still.

Moving closer, I stare at the crimson liquid dripping from the back of his hair. Blood? He must have hit his head really hard. Except he's prone, so the place he struck when he fell is his right cheek, which is still against the pavement. Why is his scalp bleeding?

I move around him, so I can see his face.

Glassy eyes stare blankly out of his skull mere inches from a black hole between his brows.

Is that...?

Yes, he's been shot. In the head.

And he looks...

Dead.

37

JAMIE

Sawyer wasn't supposed to be here.
I wouldn't have pulled the trigger if I'd known she was in the pool area. I still don't understand how I didn't see her come outside. The curtains in front of the sliding glass door never moved.

After I break down the gun, I put the pieces in a black duffel bag. *Fuck*. Did she see the shot hit him? If so, that mental image is bound to stay with her forever.

As I'm climbing down from the neighbor's roof, a nearly overwhelming urge to go and get Sawyer hits me.

Taking her from the Allendale beach house would destroy the possibility of a clean exit, but I can't swear I would've been able to resist if War wasn't waiting on the street for me in a stolen car.

After pulling my hoody down over my forehead, I stride down the quiet street. I turn a corner at the same time the car does, and we meet in the middle.

I climb inside and glance over. War's dark hair is pulled back tight under a black baseball cap. He also wears a black-and-white athletic jersey for a Miami sports team, something he got specifically for this operation since it's nothing he would ever normally wear.

Sirens rise in the distance as we leave the area.

I keep watch in front of us and in the side mirror. We enter the expressway several miles from the scene, heading north toward the first waypoint, which is in Georgia.

I'm silent for the first leg, lost in my own thoughts. Trying to get a handle on why it was such a punch to the gut to see her there. If I'm done with her, what does it matter that she saw the brother die? Her PTSD, if she has any, won't be my problem to deal with.

And yet, every fucking cell in my body wants to turn the car around to go back for her.

To what end? I ask myself. There's no good answer. Just a bone deep feeling that after being through something traumatic, she belongs with me. In my bed. Where nothing else can touch her.

I frown. Thinking this way is pointless, but I can't stop myself.

It's not until War and I reach the first drop point that I allow myself to curse out loud over Sawyer being in the yard. War and I wipe down the outside of the car, remove the fake plates, and destroy the interior with fire.

As we walk to the second vehicle with flames still licking the sky, I exhale a frustrated breath. "Sawyer told me she wasn't going to Florida. There's a lot of bad blood in the family."

"Plans change." War opens the driver's side door, and I open the passenger one. "Doesn't matter. Unless you think she spotted you?"

We both climb in, and he glances over as he starts the car.

"No. I stayed low and watched her through the scope. From the way she looked around, she has no idea where the shot came from." I pinch the bridge of my nose. "She must've come out through a door that's not visible from the back of the house."

"Must have."

"If I'd spent another day watching..."

As he drives along the dirt road toward the highway, he shakes his head. "Then we'd have had a full day of our personal cells being dormant. That would look suspect as hell." He makes a dismissive gesture with his hand. "It's not optimal that she was there. Better if Allendale had been lying dead for hours before he was discovered. But we knew everything might not fall into place. It rarely does." He licks his lips and cocks his head, checking out the street signs. "We planned for this and worse."

I nod, but internally, a storm's brewing. As angry as I am that she didn't turn in her pedophile stepfather, it matters to me that she may be traumatized.

We drive another eight hours before reaching the second waypoint in South Carolina.

The adrenaline surge has worn off, and fatigue kicks in as we wipe down the stolen vehicle, before rolling it into a swamp and watching it sink.

After shedding our operation clothes and disposing of them elsewhere, along with our burn phones, we go to the rental car we left parked in a structure near a hotspot of bars and restaurants.

When we finally reach our vacation rental house, we've already run through our checklist twice. Everything we can do to protect ourselves from getting caught, we've done.

I answer a few texts, per the plan. Unfortunately, there are none from Ash. I'd been hoping she'd have heard from Sawyer and texted me, so I would have an opening to hear how Sawyer is.

War goes straight to bed and, from his snoring, is asleep in minutes. I lie down but it takes me longer to get my mind in order.

When I do drift off, I have nightmares Sawyer is caught in an eddy and drowning. I'm swimming hard to reach her, but can't.

Jerking awake, I wipe cold sweat from my chest. The irony is not lost on me. Committing murder could not concern me less, except for the one aspect.

Fucking hell. Apparently, I'm far from done with Sawyer Allendale.

38

SAWYER

Four days pass in a blur.

I'm questioned twice by the police but don't have anything helpful to tell them either time. The first night they grill me about what I saw and heard. I explain about mistaking the cracking sound—the gunshot—for fireworks. I share that I didn't see when or how the bullet struck Brad.

After repeating their questions in various ways and hearing the same useless answers, they move on to background information about the trip. I tell them about my change of plans and that Brad and I drove to the airport together, that we're at the same university but rarely saw each other. I don't mention his punching me or any of the times I'd seen him recently.

By the Friday after Thanksgiving, the police have gone through Brad's phone. Apparently, there are some very negative texts about me. I wonder if one of the people who received them is Clare Duffy because they ask repeatedly if he's done anything to me that I'm angry about, and of course, it was probably at Brad's suggestion that she took my mom's bracelet. He's one of the few people who knew how much that would hurt me.

To the police, I deny he did anything to upset me. I hope I sound convincing. The nagging soreness in my arm mocks me the entire time. I'm not sorry he's dead, but I don't want to land on their suspect list. I was alone with him. Maybe they'll think I killed him and stashed the gun somewhere.

I try to sound concerned. And maybe I really should be. I was only a few feet away when a sniper gunned him down. In addition to potentially being blamed, could I become a target for whoever murdered him? There's a lot of uncertainty.

During the second interview, the detective is interested in campus gossip and whether Brad seemed worried that someone was after him. It's hard to piece together why he would've been, but from their questions, I take it there was a scandal involving his fraternity that might have made someone want revenge.

Dad arrives, looking shell-shocked. I try to comfort him as best I can. But even when I try, I can't muster fake tears. I wonder if the police notice. My Allendale grandparents seem to.

On Sunday, I fly to Boston.

Ash picks me up from the airport, and after I get in the car, she reaches over to hug me. I accept the hug and return it, feeling awkward. She wears an enormous cobalt sweater that I could fit inside with her, gray leggings and a blue beanie. It's such a "bed hair don't care" look that I feel envious of her seemingly carefree life.

We exit the airport, and Ash shifts lanes and points us toward the highway.

"You don't have to talk if you don't want to, Sawyer."

I know why she says this. I texted her about the murder, but when she tried to call I didn't pick up. Partly because I didn't know what to say, and partly because I was paranoid someone might overhear my lack of emotion when telling the story.

"Okay, good," I murmur, rubbing the side of my neck. "Because I don't want to."

She glances at me. "Have you talked to Jamie?"

"No, why would I? I told you we broke up."

God, that seems a lifetime ago now. I've thought about Jamie, of course. Too much, and even in the midst of my brother's murder investigation. It's ridiculous.

"I thought he might have called." Ash glances at me again, her china blue eyes full of concern. "He's worried about you."

"You told him about the shooting?"

"Yeah."

I shrug. "He didn't call."

"Did you want him to?" When I don't answer, she speeds up. "I think we'll stop by his place. Just for a couple of minutes." Her tone is light and casual.

I want to see him. So badly. But I force myself to say, "There's no point. Just tell him I'm okay."

"You sure it's pointless? He's called me twice, wanting to know whether you're all right. And when you would be back on campus."

My insides twist in knots. There's pleasure and pain in hearing he's been worried.

"Jamie doesn't want me..." My jaws clench and release. "Because of something my mom did. And that, to me, is so unfair that I don't want him, either. Not anymore."

Ash's brows wrinkle. "Something your mom did?"

"She's in jail." I can't believe I blurt it out. My admission, more than anything, shows how off kilter I am.

"I thought your mom passed away?"

"That's my adopted mom. My bio mom is in prison in Tennessee."

"And Jamie told you he didn't want to be with you because of your former mom being in jail?" Her tone is so skeptical it almost makes me question what I heard.

"Yes."

She wrinkles her nose, looks over at me, and then shakes her head. "There's no way that's right."

"You weren't there, Ash. He was furious, too, because I didn't tell him."

"No way. There's some kind of disconnect." She blows out a breath. "Look up the name Scott Patrick on your phone."

"Your brother?"

She nods and points. "Do it."

I type the name into the search bar and click. Several articles surface related to him and his business partners renovating areas of Coynston, Massachusetts where they live. As I scroll, I find posts and columns about his wedding.

And then there are *others*. About him being arrested.

When I search by the arrests and click on images, there are two mugshots. In them, he's younger and, except for his short brown hair, he looks so much like Ash and Jamie, my brows rise.

"Find him?"

"Yes," I say softly. I'm so confused I'm at a loss.

"My brother's never been to prison, but he's been arrested a bunch of times. He's no angel. And Jamie and Scotty are close. We all are."

My mind reels, trying to remember exactly what Jamie said.

Ash shrugs, and her tone is certain. "There is zero chance Jamie broke up with you because your mom got sent to prison. *Zero.*"

39

JAMIE

My phone buzzes with an incoming text from Sawyer.

I'm sitting in the upstairs living room facing the windows but glance over my shoulder in the direction of the bathroom. War's in the shower after returning from the gym, and when he comes out, I'd rather he didn't hear me talking with her.

Switching seats so I can keep an eye on the hall, I unlock my phone.

> Sawyer: Ash is driving us back to GU. Wants to stop by yours. Is that ok?

There's not a second of hesitation.

> Jamie: Yes. Come.

Rising, I shake my head at the way my heart thumps faster at the thought of seeing her. I'm glad Ash is coming by, too. That way there's no chance Sawyer and I will start a deep conversation that's too honest to be safe. I'll just get to see her and make sure she's all right.

And if she needs me, I'll figure out a way to keep her close.

After I pull a sweatshirt on over my t-shirt, I get a text from Ash that they're downstairs. I grab my coat and gloves and keys. Then, I head outside, closing the door behind me.

Both women emerge from the car, and I join them. Ash puts an arm around my neck as she hugs me. Sawyer remains next to the car, several feet away. Though I should hold back too, I don't. Moving in, I pull her to me in a tight hug.

The familiar scent of spicy berries and Sawyer hits me like a express train.

In a low voice near her ear, I ask, "Are you all right?"

"Yeah, I'm fine. We weren't close. Or even on good terms. As you know." Her words are soft but clipped. Can't tell if she's angry or just guarded. Can't blame her either way.

Her fist presses into my ribs, signaling for me to let go.

With reluctance, I release her. "Glad you're well." Because she seems closed off, I glance over at Ash. "Want to come in?"

Ash's eyes rise to the second floor, and she narrows them. "No."

I glance over my shoulder and spot War's hulking figure as it recedes. He's seen what I'm about. Unfortunate, but not unexpected.

Sawyer reaches for the Camaro's door handle. At the same time, my palm presses against the door to prevent her from opening it.

Ash says, "Hang on, Seesaw. Don't you want to clear things up?"

My eyes return to Sawyer, studying her face for any hint at what they've been discussing during the drive. "What's that?"

"I told Ash why you broke up with me. She doesn't believe it."

So much for keeping things surface. "Let's not pull Ashling into it." I lick my lips. "But you and I should talk. There are aspects you're not seeing. And I was too quick to end things. Liquor and an Irish temper are not the best mates to turn loose together."

"Jamie," Ash says sharply. "Are you saying you really did break up with Sawyer because her biological mom's in prison? Because that's a straight-up hypocrite move no one—"

"Hold on, what?" My gaze cuts back and forth between the girls. "What's this about your mother?"

"My bio mother is in jail for dealing drugs and related crimes. It's why I had to go into foster care." Sauce stares at me with a hostile expression.

I give a nearly imperceptible shake of my head.

Ash's narrow-eyed gaze studies me. "You didn't know that?"

Sawyer's arms fold across her chest, but her expression becomes curious. "If not my mom... What the hell were you talking about? Who did you mean?"

I'm backed into a corner. Saying the brother did something is not an option, since he's just been murdered. And if I do tell her the truth about her father, it won't be in front of Ash.

At first, I say nothing.

Since I'm going after her father, what I should do is cover my tracks by claiming it *was* the biological mother's past that I took issue with. But as Sawyer stares up at me with her beautiful brown eyes, I just can't bring myself to do it.

"It's not the kind of conversation to have while we're freezing our arses off in a parking lot. Will you come in? Ash can go, and I'll drop you off later at your dorm."

Sawyer hesitates and then finally shakes her head. "It's been a long few days, and I'm all talked out." She turns and attempts to push my hand off the door.

I lean down, bringing us closer together. "Go then. We'll talk tomorrow. I'll come for you after class."

"I don't know." She shoves a hand back in a bid to push me away so she can open the car door.

My feet might as well be nailed to the ground.

Turning her head with fury flashing in her eyes, she stares at me. "You're seriously going to push the issue? Right now?"

I'm tempted to stop her from leaving. I want the misunderstanding behind us, so I can have her back. But it's not only us here. There's Ash. And there's War. Neither of them will be cool with my pulling Sawyer into the house.

"Right, no." Stepping back, I shove my hands in my pockets. "But tomorrow, Sauce. We *will* talk."

Ash appears next to me and gives me a gentle push to get me farther away. Then she opens the passenger door for Sawyer. "The men in my family are crazy. Really sorry about that."

Sawyer drops into the passenger seat, and Ash closes the door.

Ash turns and looks at me with a skeptical expression. "Sort yourself, James, or I'm going to stop helping you."

"You won't. But I will sort this out."

Ash gives me a brief, violent hug before she shoves me away and turns and stalks to the driver's side of the car.

I wait, watching as Ash gets in and the car starts. It's not until they pull away and completely disappear that I jog up the metal stairs to enter the house.

War sits on the couch, scrolling on his phone. Without looking up, he says, "You're fucking kidding, right?"

"I'll handle her."

His nearly black eyes rise. "That's the problem."

War's proven himself the best sort of mate a killer could have, so I don't fault him for a thing.

Avoiding Sawyer is in the interest of protecting myself *and him* from the hell-storm that would rain down if anyone found out what we'd just been up to.

It's a shame I can't do the smart thing.

Sawyer's mine, and I want her back.

40

SAWYER

When we get to the dorm, Ash and I eat in the dining hall, and then because it seems like everyone in the freaking dorm is doing her laundry after getting back from holiday travel, we go to our room and settle into our beds with laptops and Nutella lattes.

When Ash puts in earbuds to stream something, I'm finally able to concentrate and circle back to the encounter with Jamie. I've worked out that Brad must've done something really horrible for Jamie to blame me for not turning him in, but I have no idea what that was.

Online investigations reveal Brad's fraternity had a serious scandal two years ago. Apparently, guys took photos of sleeping or passed-out nude and semi-nude girls who stayed over. After, the guys shared the pics across campus, sometimes even selling them.

There were concerns the women might have been given sedatives to ensure they didn't wake while the guys removed their clothes and posed them for filming.

From the articles, the men whose involvement was proven

were expelled. In some cases however, the perpetrators couldn't be identified. The entire fraternity was sanctioned, and it narrowly missed being closed for good.

At least two irate fathers made threats against fraternity members.

Unlike some of his fraternity brothers, who'd been accused but whose involvement couldn't be confirmed, Brad wasn't named in any of the articles about the investigation or proceedings.

But since the only people in my family Jamie could've heard gossip or accusations about would've been Brad or my bio mom, Brad had to be the problem. The rest of my adopted family lives out of state and haven't been involved in any public scandals—or any private ones that I know about.

Flashing back to Jamie's fury on the night he accused me of covering for Brad makes me think Brad hurt someone Jamie cares about. *Like Ashling.* My stomach plummets at the thought. She did tell Crosby she never wanted to see Brad around. She claimed it was because of the way he treated me, but it might've been something more.

If Ash was the person who was hurt, Jamie isn't the only member of her family who might seek revenge. The articles about her brother said he started out working for an Italian crime family before forming a crime syndicate of his own with his closest friends. *A crime syndicate. God. And I'd had no idea.*

"Ash?"

She taps her iPad and removes an earbud. "Yeah, babes?"

"Can I ask you a sensitive question?"

"Sure." With a small smile, she cocks her head. "But I reserve the right to take the Fifth on behalf of myself and anyone else I care about."

"You told Crosby you didn't want to see him if Brad was with him. Did Brad do something to hurt or humiliate you?"

"No." Her expression is more perplexed than troubled. "Around me, he was just a garden-variety asshole."

"I've been thinking about the night Jamie broke up with me."

Ash watches me closely.

"He was really angry. Partly because he thought I was covering for someone. Since it wasn't my bio mom, it had to be Brad."

Ash shrugs, shifting her chameleon features into an innocent expression.

Lowering my voice to a whisper, I say, "If Brad did something to hurt you, and someone decided to hurt him in return, I wouldn't blame them."

"Good to know." Her smile is gentle, but there are no outward signs she's harboring anger or sadness below the surface. If she was the victim of something, she's world-class at compartmentalizing.

I pick at the edge of the blanket. "He was an elitist prick. And physically abusive at times."

"Toward you?"

I nod.

"Well then..." Her brows furrow, but her voice remains light. "Karma caught up with him." There's satisfaction in her tone. The shift is subtle but unmistakable. She despises him more now, so it's a pretty sure bet that she isn't hiding any trauma of her own.

"Karma... maybe. But for what? Have you heard any rumors about him? Something that would've made someone want to kill him?"

"I haven't." Ash climbs out of bed, grabs both our mugs, and re-heats our lattes. "But I'm sure he made a lot of enemies."

"Definitely." It occurs to me that admitting Brad assaulted me shows I had a motive to want him gone. Which is something I've been trying to keep secret. "You probably won't talk to the police, but if you do, would you mind forgetting I told you he was abusive?"

"You don't need to worry about that. I'll never speak to the police about your brother."

"Well... We're roommates and you go to school here, so they might come to talk to you. Or bump into you if they come to talk to me. They also might find out we were at the party at the Ruins and had an issue with Brad."

"Here's something a lot of people don't know, Seesaw. People aren't obligated to talk to the police. So, let's say the men in blue show up here and say, 'Miss Patrick, we'd like to talk to you about Brad Allendale yada, yada.' I would tell them, 'I don't have anything to say to you.' And then I'd just repeat that one line over and over until they went away. The police can't compel a person to speak, not even if you're under arrest. In fact, now that you've told them all the information you have about the night Brad died, you don't have to talk to them again, either."

Tilting my head, I ask, "Is that true?"

"Yep. Absolutely true."

"But since I was a witness, wouldn't I have to be interviewed as many times as they want to interview me?"

"No. You just say, 'I've told you all I know, and I don't want to talk to you anymore.' Unless they have grounds to arrest you, they can't force you to go anywhere with them. All you have to do is say no and close the door."

"Have you actually done that and had it work?"

She laughs softly. "No, but I've been coached by an expert."

"Your brother?"

"No. Better. His shark lawyer."

"Oh." My brows rise. "Why? Do you know things they don't want you to tell the police?"

She smirks and winks at me. "I have the right to remain silent. Gonna practice it right now."

"Sorry. I'm just—The thought of talking to the police again makes me nervous. The first time it was all about what I'd seen, and honestly, I was kind of in shock. The second interview, though, they were trying to get background information on him and any conflicts he had with people, including me."

"Did you mention me? Or my cousin?"

"No."

"War? The party at the Ruins?"

I shake my head.

"Good girl. It wouldn't lead anywhere if you had, but it could've become a hassle if the cops decided they wanted to talk about it."

"That's what I was thinking, too. I didn't want to cloud the picture." Blowing out a breath, I shrug. "I wonder if they could tell I wasn't telling them everything."

"Who cares?"

I blink.

"They will try anything to get people to spill everything they know, no matter how off-the-wall and unrelated it is. If you hesitate, they'll put tons of pressure on you by acting annoyed or trying to guilt you. To hell with that. Karma did its work. Why would we try to undermine it?" She raises her index finger, half pointing at me, half holding it up in a "number one" style. "I doubt they will, but if the police show up and try to bully you into talking to them again, just text me. I'll help you get rid of them."

I feel immense relief at not being alone. "You're a good friend, Ash."

"That's what I hear." She smirks and winks again. "You okay now, Seesaw? Because the streaming platform logged me out for taking so long to restart the movie."

"Tragic. How will you even cope?"

"I don't know. Gonna be tough." After putting her earbuds in, she raises her screen.

I finish my coffee and burrow down into my covers. The minute I start streaming a show myself though, I crash into a landscape of bloody nightmares.

Apparently, I'm not okay.

At least not yet.

41

SAWYER

The next day while I'm in class, I get a message from Clare Duffy asking me to come to the Briar Club at twelve-thirty. What the hell is this about?

Normally, a summons from her would make my heart kick into high gear, but I've been through too much lately for it to make an impact. Pushing my sweater's sleeve up so it's not draping over my knuckles onto my phone's screen, I wonder whether there's some way Clare could use Brad's death against me. The police never said, but I'm sure she was one of the people he sent terrible messages about me to.

A cracking sound makes me jump, and I look around sharply. It's not a gunshot, of course. Just a tablet dropped on a desktop.

Exhaling slowly, I grimace at myself. *Come on,* I think. The thing that happened to Brad happened because of something he did. Karma or revenge or whatever. Or if it wasn't, then it was random, and the Florida sniper is thirteen hundred miles away.

Sniper. Sometimes, I can't wrap my head around that. A sniper killed my brother.

I don't answer Clare's text.

She sends another, which I also ignore.

I will find out what she wants, but I'm not going to play the eager freshman inductee. My days of kissing Clare Duffy's ass are over.

When class ends, I walk to north campus and take a bus to the Briar Club's block. My phone buzzes as I exit the bus.

> Jamie: Done with class?

I'm happy to get his text. I don't even know why.

It's drizzling, so I don't stop to answer until I'm under an awning.

> Sawyer: Summoned to Briar Club by Clare Duffy. Going to see what's up.
>
> Sawyer: We can talk after. Pick me up?

> Jamie: definitely

When I ring the bell, Clare answers the door herself. She's wearing navy trousers and a navy and bronze GU knit shirt. Without makeup, the bluish shadows under her eyes make her look exhausted.

"Why am I here?" My voice's hard edge communicates plenty about my mood.

Clare's eyes narrow, and I can tell she wants to dress me down. A moment later, though, her expression shifts to neutral.

After crossing the empty foyer, she opens the drawer of a console table near the door. "I wanted to give you this." Her fingers shake slightly as she holds out my mom's vintage Briar bracelet. I wonder if Clare's shaky because she's furious. If so, why is she returning it?

"I don't understand." My gaze fixes on her face.

"You'll bring the bracelet with you on the day of the Induction Ceremony. Don't start wearing it until after."

"Why give it to me now? And why were you wearing it the other day?"

She starts to glance away but forces her eyes to meet mine. "I traded my modern one for this one because I prefer the vintage style. But it was your mother's..."

What bullshit. Clare's wardrobe is all sharp angles and modern. She's the last person you'd find in vintage or boho.

Her thin hand makes a vague gesture. "I realized it should go to you because of the family ties. So, here it is. You want it, right?"

More bullshit. Clare knew all along I was a legacy and that I was hoping to get my mom's bracelet back.

Taking it, I cock my head as I study her. The tension in my shoulders worsens. "What's going on, Clare?" Licking my dry lips, I grip the bracelet tightly. "I'm not in the mood for games."

Lowering her voice to a whisper, she says, "No games. If you were angry about the bracelet, now you don't need to be. Correct?"

"I guess."

She leans closer. "Just let it go, okay?" With a slow breath, she finally takes a step back. "If you complained to him, I expect you to let him know it's been returned to you."

"Complained to who?" For a moment, I think she's talking about Brad and that she hasn't heard he's dead.

"Jamie O'Rourke." Clare draws back as she says his name. *As if she's afraid.*

A shock rolls through me, stiffening my muscles. "Why are you worried about what Jamie thinks?"

"For the obvious reasons." The tone of her voice cools as she folds her arms across her chest.

"It's not obvious to me."

"No? Are you sure?"

I shake my head.

"Brad called you a cunt and apparently grabbed Ashling Patrick in front of members of the C Crue. Now, Brad is dead. It doesn't take a lot of imagination to figure out James O'Rourke is deeply involved with dangerous people. And that he doesn't make idle threats."

"Are you saying Jamie threatened Brad?" I stare at her, trying to work out if she's making things up to drive a wedge between Jamie and me.

She holds out her hands in a stop gesture. "You have the bracelet. From now on, I'll stay away from you. I'd appreciate if you'd do the same."

As if I had any other intention. Clare is the last person I want to spend time with anymore.

Still, an uneasiness settles in my chest because it's clear Clare knows things about my friends and my life that I don't.

42

JAMIE

Leaning against the car, I watch Sawyer emerge from the Briar Club house with a pensive expression. I look past her, scowling at the front door. If Duffy is giving her a hard time again, she's going to regret it.

Sauce zips her hooded black puffer coat up to her throat and puts on black gloves before leaving the wraparound porch. The wind whips her hair and pinks her cheeks, which reminds me of the way she looks while we're playing games. I miss everything about having her in my bed.

Halfway to the sidewalk, she sees me and slows. She didn't expect me to be waiting. I came because I didn't want to chance her changing her mind and going straight back to the dorm. Retrieving her from there would be a lot harder.

I push off the car and stride over to meet her on the sidewalk.

"I didn't mean for you to come and wait." Throwing a furtive look back at the house, she murmurs, "I would've texted when I was ready." A lock of hair drops in front of her eyes.

My fingers brush the strand back, and she tilts her head away. Not ready for me to touch her yet.

I raise my brow but lower my hand. "So, bad news or good from the club?"

"I don't know." Stepping around me, she goes toward the passenger side of the car. "Can you drop me off on campus?"

"I can. After we talk." I open her door, and she slides inside. "I'm starving. How about pizza at Hearth & Stone?"

Sawyer nods.

We're silent on the drive, with my gaze straying to her every chance it gets. She's too fucking pretty by half.

I know we need to talk, but she seems lost in her own thoughts, so I hold off on pushing my agenda.

The restaurant is south of campus in an old stone mansion on the water. They seat us in a back booth near the fireplace.

"It's nice here. My first time." She glances out the window at the water. "Eating outside in summer must be amazing."

"I'll bring you." Raising a glass of Guinness to my lips, I watch her face closely. "So, about what happened... You've got a right to be angry. The mistake I made was a significant one. It won't happen again."

Her eyes search my face. "What had you heard about Brad that made you so angry that night?"

So, as I thought she might, her assumption is now that Brad was the relative I had a problem with. Does she suspect I killed him? That would be suboptimal.

I glance around. "I'll tell you the truth. But not here."

She slides off her bench seat and moves to mine, sitting sideways.

This close, I can smell the winter wind on her and the hint of berry skin lotion. Sauce leans forward so she can whisper in my ear, and my body reacts like I'm a fucking teenage boy with his first girlfriend.

"I read some articles," she says softly. "You have a dangerous family, right?"

I shift in my seat so we're facing each other. "One member is, yes."

"What about you?"

Our eyes lock.

"Not to you." Sucking the stout from my lower lip for a moment, I shrug. "But on occasion, to those who deserve it, yes."

"Did my brother deserve it?"

I close her right hand in both of mine. "There are things I want to tell you." Raising her hand to my mouth, I drag her skin over my lower lip. It's a kiss. Of sorts. "I need a promise from you first, Sawyer."

"What promise?"

"To be mine."

"To be your what?"

"*Everything.*"

Her lips part in surprise, and we stare at each other for several beats. The way I want her in my life has shifted, and it's time to stop fucking about.

"Here's the thing." My thumb strokes hers. "I can't stop thinking about us. Before we broke up, I'd started to imagine a future with you. One where we'd trust each other with secrets and protect each other from outsiders. One where we might not last the four years at GU because maybe we'd transfer and finish uni in Ireland."

"Ireland?" The word pops out with a shocked breath.

"Why not? The island's beautiful. People are nice. You'd love it."

"Transferring to an Irish college, I couldn't do that on a whim. We'd have to be in a serious relationship... I'd have to feel sure of us."

"Agreed."

The fact that she doesn't balk outright speaks volumes. It's in her eyes that she's considering it. As she starts to tug on her hand, I tighten my grip. My pretty fish is on the line; I've no intention of letting her slip off.

"Listen, I know it's fast," I say. "But life got ahead of us. Things are happening, whether we want them to or not. So, as I see it, we either go our separate ways or we make the choice to ride out the storm together."

"I'm not saying I wouldn't want to try. I think about you constantly, too. But I barely know you. And there are *really* big unanswered questions." Her brows rise, challenging me to deny it, which of course I can't.

"Fair enough." My eyes hold hers, trying to convey my sincerity. "There's a story I'll tell you, and afterward, you'll know me. Then, you can decide."

The waitress approaches and slides a piping hot pizza onto a wooden cutting board in the center of the table. "Need anything else?"

"Thanks, no. We're good." I flash a polite smile in the waitress's direction. As she moves away, I slide a hand to the back of Sawyer's head. "Give me a kiss, Cranberry Sauce. It'll help me hold on."

Sawyer's got no idea what I'm working up to tell her, but she still gives me the sweetest kiss imaginable.

There'll be no end to the way I pursue her now. She's the one. God help her.

In a life with more than its share of darkness, I still can't resist holding on to an innocent girl. One who's got no business being caught up in the middle of a blood vendetta.

Feels as if it's meant to be, though. As if Sawyer and I were destined to meet. *Star-crossed lovers*, I think grimly.

And, as I've seen many times, there's no point trying to argue with fate.

43

SAWYER

After lunch, we head outside. Jamie takes my hand and tugs me toward an empty path along the river.

"Do you mind if we talk outside for a few minutes, Sauce?"

It's cold and overcast, but I sense something from him that makes me say, "No, I don't mind."

He removes his scarf and wraps it around my neck before zipping my coat up to my chin. Then, he raises my hood, effectively bundling me up like a child. My heartbeat stutters at the gesture. The way he's trying to protect me from the cold, at his own expense, can't fail to matter. Jamie takes my hand and puts it in his pocket with his own, tying us together.

"Once I start, don't say anything till I'm done." Jamie grimaces as he glances around. "It's the only way I'll be able to get to the end."

It's hard to imagine what would be so difficult that someone as tough as Jamie wouldn't be able to talk about it. I glance between him and the cobbled path where I'm trying to keep my feet so I don't step off into the mud. Drawing in a deep breath, I nod. If he's going to confide something important, I wouldn't dream of interrupting. I want him to let me in.

"My brother Jude and I were best mates our whole lives. We fought of course, on and off, as all brothers do, but on the whole, we got on. Less than two years apart in age, as I told you." Jamie tilts his head, staring into the middle distance with a small smile. "He could be really silly. At times, too much so for the others in our family, but not for me. Jude made me laugh like no one else could. I never went anyplace without him. It's just how it was." Jamie slows around a curve and pauses where the path is submerged in a murky puddle. Turning to face the water, he tightens his grip on my hand in his coat pocket. "The day it happened, we were meant to go fishing. Jude had to pee, so he stopped at a tree near the road. I climbed all the way down with the fishing poles and our tackle box."

Jamie's body is so rigid now, he could be a pole himself. "He was seven, by the way. But small for his age." He puts a hand out to gesture how tall that was. Not very. "There was a noise—I can't remember what. A shout from Jude or something. I looked up, and a man was standing over him, so close there was no way for Jude to get away in time. The guy snatched him up and carried him toward the road with Jude screaming and fighting to get free. Ever been in a car crash where you're hit from behind? Suddenly, the world's upended, and your mind struggles to understand what's happening. For a split second, that's how it was for me. Confusion. It was so surreal.

"When I saw the man's expression as he looked at Jude, I knew what he had it in his mind to do. I scrambled up to the road as fast as I could, hoping my brother would manage to break free. But he hadn't."

My heart cracks, and I feel sick, understanding, too, what's coming.

Jamie doesn't look at me. Instead, he stares at the brush on the side of the path, probably seeing nothing but his memories anyway. "I ran flat out. Once clear of the trees, it's easy to see the road for miles. I spotted the car in the distance and kept going, running as hard as I'd ever run. By the time I got there—to the abandoned stone cottage—the assault had already taken place. The man had gone. He left Jude tied to a pipe, planning to come back for more, I suppose. I've always wondered if the man had to leave so he wouldn't be missed. Maybe by family or business associates. Or if he left in case someone had summoned the guard—the police—and he was watching for the coast to be clear for him to come back. Doesn't matter. The damage was done. Though, I didn't understand how badly at the time."

Jamie's jaws work as he clenches his teeth. "In my mind, it was a rescue. Jude was found and came home alive that day, so I thought he would be all right. Yeah, of course, he was upset. But that would fade, surely."

He shrugs slowly. "Except, it didn't fade. It ate away at him. And I took some bad advice. My dad claimed Jude would be better off if we all pretended it never happened. So, when Jude tried to bring it up, I cut him off and swept it aside, changing the subject. I failed him on the day of the assault because I didn't get there soon enough to stop it. But I failed him way worse on all the days that followed. Every time I shut him down, he had to face those demons alone. The guilt and shame were killing him. And I—" Jamie's voice cracks, and he covers his eyes and rubs them with his free hand. "I let him die alone." Drawing in a breath, he shakes his head.

He doesn't cry, but it's there under the surface, threatening like storm clouds. "He hung himself. I found him, as I should do. He left me a note to tell me how sorry he was. *He* was sorry. That fucking gutted me. As if any of us deserved an apology. Least of all me."

I'm crying now, quietly but decidedly. I can't stop myself. Hopefully he understands he could cry in front of me, too, and I wouldn't think less of him.

Jamie jerks me to face him and wraps his arms around me in a hug, as though I'm the one who needs comforting. "Found the journal later." His voice is distant and steady, the recalling of it hard worn in his head, apparently. "Read the things the man said to him. About how he was the most beautiful boy. About how he'd been meant for him. Utter fucking rot. Things meant to twist a kid's mind into thinking he somehow deserved to be kidnapped and raped."

I press the heel of my hand against my eyelid, trying to get control of myself. I want to hear everything Jamie's telling me because the last thing I'd ever do is ask him to repeat anything that hurts him so much.

"Jude wrote about how our dad took him to buzz off his blond hair so he wouldn't look like such a 'pretty boy.' And how Da didn't want him to be in the school play. He wanted him to play rugby and told him he'd need to eat more so he wouldn't be so skinny. Jude felt ashamed and disgusted with himself. He was made to believe he liked 'the wrong things.' He even wondered if it was partly because of what happened—did he like acting in plays more than playing rugby because a man had forced him to be a girl for him? Those words, 'be a girl for him,' I don't think my brother came up with them on his own. Sounds like something Dad and my sister said, which... I'm the most to blame for losing him, but my whole fucking family shares in it. Those two especially."

Jamie's more in control of his grief now because he's angry. His voice is laced with the kind of fury you find in cornered animals. It takes several moments for his harsh breathing to ebb into a normal rhythm. My arms stay locked around him the whole time, as if he'll fly away if I don't.

"We thought the man who grabbed him might be American. It's why I came to the States. I'm hunting him. And he's not been the only one. I'm very good with computers and hacking. I got good because I wanted to find them." He exhales a mirthless sigh. "I catfished pedophiles using old pictures of me or Jude. Once I hooked one, I'd steal passwords, drain bank accounts, tip off the police to kiddie porn on their systems. Anything to ruin their lives the way they did to the kids they prey upon. As I got older and stronger, I tricked them into meeting me, so I could beat them into the fucking ground before I destroyed them with a hundred keystrokes. My rage against that kind of man is something that's very, very hard to control." His breath is hot against the top of my head.

After several moments, he whispers the word "sorry" into my hair. "You're half frozen, Sawyer. Come on. Let me get you inside."

44

JAMIE

It's only two in the afternoon, but it feels like four a.m. after a hard night of drinking. As I guide Sawyer into the house, I'm wrung out.

"Cup of tea?" I ask, slowing near the second set of downstairs couches.

"Sure." The sadness in the whispered word is the worst. We're in a death spiral to a major depressive episode.

Sawyer hovers near me as I put the kettle on. I can't see my way clear to drop the other bombshell, but we can't move forward till I do.

As she adds milk and sugar to her cup, I'm still at a loss. This is exactly why I never tell anyone about what happened to Jude. Afterward, it feels like it's always there, lingering like a festering sore that won't heal.

"There's something else," I say, forcing myself to go ahead. "It puts your family squarely in the middle of this."

Her cup freezes halfway to her mouth.

In for a penny, in for a pound now, I spit it out. "The man who took Jude, it's Robert Allendale."

Sawyer's cup clatters as it hits the island counter, splashing tea everywhere. Her head shakes as our eyes lock. "My dad? No, there's no way."

"Yes."

"Jamie, no." She takes a reflexive step back. "He's a good person. And I was never... He never—" Her head shakes, her eyes darting from side to side, avoiding mine. When she finally looks at me, she says, "You're not sure though, right?" Tears well in her eyes and spill over her lashes.

"Listen—" My fingers grip the lip of the counter until my knuckles whiten.

"Because I can't see it. He's so kind to kids... to me when I was little." Her voice cracks on the words. "He never hurt us."

Leaving my untouched tea, I move toward her. "Maybe he didn't want victims in his own house. More likely to get caught."

Glancing up at me, she meets my eyes with a stiffening spine. "What's your proof?"

"I recognize him."

"From seeing him for a second? Years ago?" She draws in a shaky breath. "Could you be wrong?"

Irritation creeps into my voice. "I'm not wrong."

"We live in Connecticut. What happened to your brother, that was in Ireland. That's not one of the places he travels for work."

"Sawyer," I say sharply. "Do not—"

"He's the only family I have left." Her voice is pitched high with alarm. "You can't expect me to just—eye witnesses often get identification wrong. The trauma and everything, it can distort memories. It's been years, right?"

"Thirteen years. And yeah, he does look different. He's older, but not so different that I can't see the connection."

"Maybe it was someone who looks like him. Plenty of men do. He's got male cousins. It could be one of them. Or someone else entirely."

"You need to fucking listen, Sawyer." My voice has risen so

much I'm almost shouting. The dam has broken for the second time today, but now it's fury rather than pain that's spilling out. "It's him. And he's going to pay for what he did. Along with anyone who protects him."

Sawyer stumbles backward, and I grab her arm to keep her from falling.

"Anyone who protects him? Why do you keep saying that? Is there—did Brad know something about it? Was that why something happened to him? Clare said—"

"Allendale's son got what he—"

"J," War barks.

We both turn as War jogs down the steps.

His thunderous expression is directed at both of us. "What the fuck?"

My heartbeat hammers like the hoofbeats of racing horses, and my muscles scream for release, wanting to smash something. But War's furious interruption is like having ice water dumped over my head.

"Let go of my arm." Sawyer winces as she tries to pull free. "You're hurting me."

My grip eases, allowing her to escape a few feet.

"You," War says, turning to face her. He points a finger. "Sit down on that couch."

"No." She starts to circle around the couch to head in the direction of the door.

I move quickly, grabbing her so War won't. "Hang on." My voice is measured now, calmer.

"Are you doing this?" She glares at me. "I said *let me go*. Are you forcing me to stay? The way someone forced Jude?"

"Don't fucking compare me to a disgusting pedophile."

"Then, stop using force to overpower me! You're scaring me."

I let go and hold out my hands in surrender. "Just sit down. We'll talk this out."

"I don't want to sit down. I'm going back to the dorm."

War moves with his signature economy and stealth to position himself between her and the exit.

When Sawyer spots him in her path, she says, "Stay out of this, War. It's got nothing to do with you."

I shift positions, so I'm near him and can whisper without being overheard. "You'll make it worse, mate."

His blazing anger stares daggers at me. He didn't want her here at all, let alone for us to have an explosive fight. Also, a woman ignoring War's order to do something never sits well with him.

"Leave it alone." My voice is low but steady.

War stands his ground.

Sawyer has taken the opportunity to grab her bag and phone. Her fingers slide across the device's screen. A moment later, the ping of an answering text message fills the air. "Ash is coming to get me."

War's narrowed eyes move from Sawyer to me. When he speaks, his tone is grim. "For fuck's sake." That War would like to slam his fist into my jaw is a given. Instead, he stalks past me to the stairs.

Sawyer opens the door and walks out. I follow her, hit full force by the cold the instant I cross the threshold.

"Sawyer."

As soon as I'm close enough to grab her, she spins to face me and puts out her hands. "Don't. Don't grab me again."

My outstretched arms and how long it takes me to lower them are a clear indication that that's exactly what I want to do.

"Someone implied something about my brother's murder." Her eyes bore into me like a drill. "That his death didn't have anything to do with things he'd done as a fraternity member. It was actually because he'd angered an organization called C Crue. Is that right? And are you part of that gang?"

It's as though the air is being siphoned from my lungs. C Crue is not something I can talk about with her, especially in the midst of a blowout argument.

"I want to show you something my brother drew. I'm pretty sure you'll—"

"Can you answer my question, Jamie? Are you working for some kind of organized crime syndicate?"

Clenching my jaw, I stare straight into her eyes. The silence stretches on until she grimaces.

"Are you... a killer?" Her whisper is almost lost in the wind. "Were you involved in what happened to my brother?"

"That's your biggest concern? Even after he denounced you publicly and abused you privately? Do you even consider him a brother?"

"I'm not—this is not about how I felt about Brad. You're right. He was a toxic person. That doesn't mean you or anyone had a right to murder him in front of me. I'm having nightmares about the back of his head being blown apart by a bullet. I can still see the blood."

"I'm sure whoever pulled the trigger never meant for there to be a witness. He probably didn't know you were there."

"Did he think I was still in Foxgrove?" she whispers. "Because I said I wasn't going to Florida? And so it was safe to go down there and do it then, when I should've been a thousand miles away?"

Shivering, I fold my arms across my chest. I need to get her back inside before I freeze to death. "I didn't say that."

She shudders and takes a step back. "Are they—my dad and my brother—the reason you got involved with me from the start? To get close to them?"

"No."

"You can answer that directly, huh? But not the rest?"

"Listen, if you stay, we can talk this through. Let me get my coat. Text Ash to say you don't need her to drive you. When we're finished speaking, *I'll* take you to the dorm if that's what you want."

The roar of a motor fills the air.

And Sawyer says the words I'm thinking late."

45

SAWYER

From the moment I get in the car, Ash can tell something's very wrong. Her easy smile disappears, and we drive in silence for several moments.

"Did you and Jamie have another fight?"

"Kind of. Can I ask you something?"

"Sure."

"Does Jamie work for your brother?"

Ash's brows rise, and she glances over at me. "I can't answer that." She licks her lips. "But here are some things anyone with an internet connection could learn. In Ireland, Jamie's family is working class—which is like blue collar. Jamie's got an athletic scholarship to attend GU, but it covers stuff like meals, dorm housing, and books, right?"

I stare at her profile.

"His beautiful new car, the Porsche 718 Cayman? It retails for about a hundred thousand dollars." Ash shrugs. "His work—whatever it is—must pay well."

Leaning forward, I put my face in my hands.

"Fuck. I'm sorry," she whispers, putting her hand on the back of my head for a moment before returning it to the gearshift. "But if certain occupations are a dealbreaker, it's better to know, right? Tough, though, I know." Her voice is so gentle. "You guys have really great chemistry. He's crazy about you."

My words are mumbled into my hands. "It's complicated."

"The best things are." Ash's bubbly personality has shifted, becoming serious. "I hope you and I can still be friends?"

"Yes." I lift my head to look at her. "Of course."

She smiles. "Good."

We finish the ride back to campus in silence. By some mutual unspoken agreement, we stop in the dining hall to get hot cocoas in to-go cups to take to our room. Once there, I settle into my bed with my laptop.

My dad tries to call for his weekly chat, but I let it go to voicemail. There is so much I want to ask, but I need to be careful. If Jamie's wrong about him, the last thing I want is for my dad to feel I'm falsely accusing him of something hideous.

And Jamie *must* be wrong. My dad isn't like Brad. My dad is kind. He's thoughtful.

With clenching muscles, I think about the way Brad could punch me and then walk out of the room with a smile and chat respectfully with our grandmother a minute later like nothing had happened. My brother was world-class at compartmentalizing. And at fooling the people he wanted to fool.

A slither of doubt creeps through me. Could Brad have inherited that ability?

No. Not from his dad. *My* dad. The only parent I've got left. The only person in the world who gives a shit about what happens to me.

My stomach knots, and I literally feel sick.

After climbing from the bed, I walk out of the room and down to the bathroom. The cool air in the hall helps. I lean against the wall until the sweats and nausea pass.

Jamie seems *very, very* sure.

What I really want is to crawl under my covers and pretend Jamie never uttered my dad's name.

But there is no way to unring the bell. I need to learn whether he's right or not.

Because if it is true, there might be another Jude O'Rourke standing too close to a road as my father drives by. I shudder, the sick feeling returning.

"Please don't let it be true," I whisper as I enter the bathroom stall to throw up.

No matter what the truth is, so many people have already lost.

※

JAMIE

As I pace my bedroom floor, the clock is ticking. The minute Sawyer asks the wrong question, Robert Allendale will know someone is investigating him. From then on, he'll be covering his tracks, potentially getting rid of trophies and destroying evidence.

That shouldn't matter to me since I know what he is, but Sawyer's skepticism nags at me. I rub my eyes. I'm angry she didn't take me at my word. And that she left, rather than staying to work things out.

I need to prove I'm right.

Going after evidence now, though, while the police are investigating the son's death— while Robert Allendale's probably still on edge and looking over his shoulder—makes the risk extremely high. All my training and common sense scream at me to stand down. To wait and be patient and follow through on my plans to be methodical and systematic as I crush him.

Waiting, though, would mean remaining in limbo with Sawyer, which I can't seem to accept.

For several long moments, I stand at the foot of my bed.

Maybe if I was less Irish—or less myself—I could take the path dictated by pragmatism. But in this moment, I'm the same as I ever was. I'm the man who asked for a wet suit at age seven so he could surf winter waves taller than him.

The way I feel when I'm with Sawyer is the new winter storm off Mullaghmore Head. A force so phenomenal she makes me forget everything outside of the current moment. I'm not losing her to him.

And standing still is not an option.

When I emerge from my room with a pair of duffel bags, War gives me a hard look from his position on the couch.

"What's the plan, J?"

There's no point trying to explain what I'm about to do. I already know it's reckless. Shaking my head, I walk to the locked closet where the weapons are stored.

War rises, folding his arms across his chest as he watches me put an unmarked pistol into the bottom of one of the bags.

"What the fuck?" War scoffs.

I stop in front of him and extend a hand. He knocks it away, and I extend it again. Finally, reluctantly, he shakes it.

"You're gonna get yourself caught over a girl who doesn't even give a shit."

"Mate, don't." We lock eyes a moment.

"Fuck's sake." War shoves me away from him with a bitter scowl.

"Listen, whatever happens, you're in the clear. Everything I did, or will do, I did alone."

"I'm not worried about myself. I trust you've got *my* back. Yours is the one that's in jeopardy."

"I'm grand. Back before anyone knows I'm gone."

We both know it's an empty promise.

46

SAWYER

There's no way I can concentrate. Not on school. Not on life. Not on anything, until I know.

The only chance I have of learning the truth is to go home, so that's what I decide to do.

Ash, the truest friend that ever was, drops me at the train station in Boston and gives me the tightest hug before she sends me off.

When I arrive in Connecticut, I'm trying to formulate a plan.

And shockingly—as if by dark magic—Jamie O'Rourke appears on the platform at the New Haven train station. Apparently, we were on the same two-hour train from Boston but sitting in different passenger cars.

Seeing him creates an ache in my chest. Why can't being sensible overpower everything else?

He wears black jeans and a black hoodie under a dark puffer coat. It's not a typical outfit for him. He looks American.

I'm drawn to him like a matching magnet. Without regard for the way we left things, I hurry across the platform. "Jamie."

He turns, and shock registers on his face. "Sauce. What are

you doing here?" His using the nickname causes warmth to spread through me. There's a part of me that just can't seem to stop wanting him. His gaze flicks toward the tracks. "Did you just arrive?"

"Yes. From Boston. Like you."

A stillness comes over him, and it's hard to interpret. After a beat, he says, "How are you?"

"All right." Exhaling a slow breath, I shrug. "Things really spiraled last night. I'm sorry for not—"

"No." His tone is firm. "More my fault than yours for rushing that conversation."

"I was overwhelmed. I wish I'd been able to stay longer to talk."

"You have a right to walk away from situations that scare you." His thumb strokes his stubbled jaw. "I'm sorry for that. I thought you understood I wouldn't hurt you. Or let anyone else do that either."

Leaning back slightly, I let his blue gaze cut through me like a laser. "Now that things have calmed down, maybe we should talk?"

"Yeah, I'd like that, Sawyer. But I can't right now." He licks his lips and glances around. "I have to catch a train to Philadelphia for work. We'll talk when we're back at school, all right? How many days will you be in Connecticut?"

"Um, I'm not sure. I sent my teachers notice I'd be taking a week of bereavement leave. They all said it was fine to turn coursework in when I return. I think a week here will be long enough, but I'm sure they'd allow me to extend it, so I'll see how things go."

"A week," he says. "And you're staying at your dad's house? Is that here in New Haven? Or elsewhere in Connecticut?"

"Yes, to my dad's." Studying his face, I try to work out why I feel something's off. "What are you doing here in Connecticut?" I glance at the duffel bags he's carrying.

"Just changing trains."

"Why? There's a direct route from Boston to Philly."

"The direct was sold out." His voice is smooth, despite the fact that he's lying.

"I don't think so," I say softly. "I bought my ticket last minute and remember looking at the board. None of the New England routes were sold out."

"Must have been a glitch." His tone is casual.

My hand reaches out to clasp his. "It's all right if you're here to investigate." My fingers squeeze for emphasis. "That's why I'm here, too. I know it seemed like I was dismissing everything you said, but I promise I wasn't. I just need to be sure. You can understand that, right? If I told you your dad did something unimaginable, wouldn't you want to be sure?"

"Sawyer, I don't want you digging into anything. You'll ask the wrong thing and tip him off. When a man feels cornered, there's no telling how he'll react. What if it becomes dangerous, and you're there with no one to protect you? No, I won't allow it."

Because it feels good when he's protective, I offer him a small smile. "You won't *allow* it?"

He blows out a breath and shrugs. "Seems I'm not ready to accept you're not mine anymore. And, if I'm being honest, the connection I feel to you is maybe something that's not going away for me. So, whether we're together or not, I won't let anyone hurt you."

Now we're crossing into territory that feels dangerous because he's never put limits on how far he would go in eliminating a threat.

He leans closer, so I catch the scent of spicy shower gel and winter wind. "What if I came with you to the house? We could say I'm your boyfriend."

"What about your work trip?"

"I'll reschedule or get someone to cover for me. I'd be an asset, Sauce. Not just as protection, but because I can get into electronics you wouldn't be able to access on your own."

"I don't think that's a good idea. What if you lost your temper? And then he turns out to be innocent? I wouldn't be okay with you hurting him."

"I won't lose control. You have my word."

Staring up into his bright blue eyes, everything in me wants to trust him. "There are questions you've never answered, Jamie."

"Right."

"Will you?"

"Depends." He tilts his head, assessing me. "Some information is on a 'need to know' basis and right now, you've got no need. A girlfriend, though, in a serious relationship with a man does need to understand who he is."

"Maybe I already know enough." My voice is little more than a whisper, but it's fierce. Our eyes lock. "My bio mom prioritized criminality over family. When she went to jail, it left me completely alone in the world. Now that I'm an adult, I wouldn't want to be in a relationship with someone whose work could force me to go through that again."

"My world is miles from what you lived before."

"Is it?"

"When I have a wife and kids, things will be in place to protect them. They wouldn't be alone and destitute if something happened to me. They'd be surrounded by the rest of my family. You've already seen what my people are like, right? Ash wanting to take you home for Thanksgiving? Do you imagine that girl would desert someone so important to me? And, for better or worse, she's the tip of the iceberg, Sauce. I'm Irish Catholic. There's a lot of family."

"Could you change careers if you wanted to? Tomorrow? Next week? Could you walk away?"

He smiles ruefully and glances around. "We've got other things to figure out first, wouldn't you say? Come on, let's go to your dad's place. I'll be there to keep you safe and to back your play as you look around. I'll even tell you what physical evidence we're looking for. And once we settle whether I'm right or not about Robert Allendale, we can figure out what to do next."

I slide my hand to the back of his neck, and he leans down at the beckoning touch.

"You have to promise me no matter what we learn, you won't hurt him after I've brought you into the house. We will call the police, but you won't touch him. Promise?"

He raises his head so we can look at each other. "If you bring me into the house, I won't touch him while we're there. I will *not* lose control." His words drip with grave sincerity.

I still don't know if he's telling the truth, but I want to trust him. I want it so much I'm willing to risk making a horrible mistake.

"Okay. But just so you know, if you break your word to me, Jamie, I won't protect you and become an accomplice. I will tell the police everything I know."

His eyes narrow, but he nods. "Grand. We know where we stand."

JAMIE

ON THE RIDE TO THE HOUSE, I'M OF TWO MINDS. ON ONE hand, this has worked out better than if I'd had to break in. This way, Allendale invites me in and, as an overnight guest, I'll have plenty of time to locate and access his electronics. Then, if the guy had help covering his tracks in Ireland or if he's a part of any pedophile rings that traffic kids, I'll be able to act on that information, too.

If it comes down to killing Allendale, I should hire someone to do that anyway. As much as I'd like to watch him die, I've got too many ties.

Glancing over at Cranberry Sauce twists my guts. She's beautiful today in her dove gray sweater, charcoal skirt, and black tights. Makes me wish we could make a detour to a hotel where we could pretend for a few hours that the past few days never happened.

We can't, though. Vengeance first.

When we arrive, the house isn't as large as I expected. Maybe three-thousand square-feet. Colonial colors with a pristine paint job that looks fresh. A wreath of pine and holly announces this is a place that celebrates the holidays.

I carry our bags, and as I wait for her to unlock the door, a fleeting doubt plagues me. I saw Jude's abductor from thirty or forty feet away, and it *was* only a glance. Could Sauce be right that my mind has filled in the blanks? God knows, I've been desperate to find the bastard.

When she pushes the door open and we step inside, an eerie sensation washes over me. With the curtains drawn, the entry is dark.

"Dad?" Sawyer opens the curtains and shades, revealing a small Christmas tree covered in wood ornaments and gold tinsel.

"Here," a male voice calls back.

When he emerges, the man looks like a fucking professor or the cover model for an English riding magazine. Wool trousers, tweed jacket. Affable smile. Maybe I *have* gotten it wrong.

Then our eyes meet, and I know. His eyes, his suddenly intent facial expression and flushed cheeks, and maybe the tilt of his head are all familiar. My muscles contract, ready to go after him the way he deserves.

You swore to her.

I lock my body down, becoming rigid and still as I watch him.

"Well, hello." His smile looks forced as he hugs Sawyer.

"Dad, this is my boyfriend Jamie. He's a rower like Brad, and he's been helping me cope. We decided at the last minute he should come home with me. I hope that's all right?"

"Of course." He extends a hand and I shake it, noting it's as cold as a deep water fish. "I just got back myself." His gaze travels from Sawyer to me and lingers. "Have you eaten?"

"No, and Jamie's probably starving."

Both of them look at me. It takes a moment for me to remember I'm hungry. All my concentration is focused on keeping myself in check so I don't reach out and grab the man by the throat. "I'm all right."

His brown eyes crinkle at the edges as he smiles. I manage not to recoil, but only just.

"Oh, I doubt that, Jamie," he says in an amiable tone. "Young men in training need fuel. My son was like a coal stove, always had to keep shoveling fuel in. Speaking of which, I'll bring some wood in for a fire, and after you drop your bags, you start on lunch, Sawyer."

"I'll get the wood," I hear myself say. Distance and cold air will do me good. At least my voice sounded steady enough. Everything I'm feeling is just below the surface, but I think I've kept it hidden so far. "Show me where you want it."

Allendale offers me a smile that turns my blood to ice. I've seen his pleased smile before. He had it when he scooped Jude up and hauled him to the road. Reflexively, my fingers close into a fist. I force my hand back open, hoping I manage to hide my bitter scowl.

"Here, Jamie," Sauce says, touching my arm. "Come with me, so we can unpack first."

"You in your room, Sawyer, and Jamie in the guest room with the burgundy bedspread."

I don't like the sound of my name from his mouth or that he uses it so freely.

"Of course, Dad," Sawyer says quickly. When she tries to reach for the handle of her suitcase, I shake my head and grab it.

Following her up the stairs, I continue to battle with myself. To be this close is even harder than I imagined.

She stops at a door. "This one is mine."

The minute I set her suitcase inside and turn, I've already forgotten what the room looks like. My entire focus is trapped between the past and what I need to do.

"Jamie?"

Looking over my shoulder, my gaze drops to her face. "Yes?"

"This way." She walks down the hall and opens the door to a guest room with a double bed with a white lace skirt hanging around its base like a barrister's collar.

I drop my duffles on the floor, and Sawyer puts a hand on my arm.

"Are you okay?"

With a sharp nod, I say, "Don't I seem all right?"

"You're quiet and distracted. I wondered whether you still think it's him? Or if you might be questioning that?"

My gaze flicks to the open doorway, and I shrug. "Show me the door to the backyard, so I can grab the wood."

Following my eye-line, she glances over her shoulder and then back at me. "Sure. The back door is downstairs."

After we head down, I go out and collect a stack of logs.

Once I've brought plenty of wood inside, I set some in the holder next to the hearth and a few in the fireplace.

"Thank you."

At the sound of Allendale's voice behind me, I rise from my knee and turn. I'm a few inches taller and much more fit. Comparing him to the memory I've got of him, he hasn't aged well. There are bags under his eyes that could store loose coins now, and he's thicker, especially around the middle. He may be stronger than he appears, but I reckon one good punch to the gut would bring him to his knees. I'd like to deliver it. Or a strong crack to the jaw to keep him from smiling for a good long time.

"Sawyer hasn't had a chance to tell me about you." His smile is hollow now. "How long have you been dating?"

"A few weeks. Feels longer, though. At least to me. She's a special girl."

"Your accent... is that Scottish? Fantastic golf courses there."

"Right, but no. Irish. Ever been to my country?"

"I have. Ireland has scenery that's the most beautiful in the world."

The words from Jude's journal come roaring back. *You're the most beautiful boy.* If I wasn't so furious, I might puke all over the floor.

Sawyer's voice saves me. "Are sandwiches all right with you guys? Keep it simple? I thought I'd try to make a steak-and-mushroom pie later from Great Grandma Allendale's old cookbook. Remember when Mom and I made it, Dad? It turned out so good."

"So well," Allendale corrects with a belated look at her.

Sawyer visibly deflates, and I have to redouble my efforts to keep from slamming a fist into his face.

"Yes." Sauce struggles to inject some cheer into her flat voice. "That's what I meant. It turned out so well. By the way—" She tugs up her sleeve and raises her forearm to show off a Briar Club bracelet.

"Oh, well done, Sawyer. Well done." The approval sounds genuine enough. "Have you let my mother know, yet?"

"She knows I was accepted but hasn't seen Mom's bracelet on me yet. With Brad and everything, it hasn't felt like the right time to send a picture."

Allendale's gaze returns to my face. "Yes, it's been terrible. And you've been helping my daughter cope?"

The lack of emotion in his voice hardens my anger to stone. "As much as anyone *can* help when a brother is lost."

Allendale holds my eyes, and I identify him as a reptile. Losing his son didn't destroy him. Far from it. He looks at me with a hopeful expression that seems to say he's anxious to go back to Ireland to find another Jude. Or maybe I'm reading things into his every move that aren't really there. It's hard to tell. Everything is surreal at the moment.

"Jamie, come with me?" Sawyer's hand reaches out toward me, the bracelet swaying on her wrist.

My hand takes hers and squeezes. "Sure." My eyes return to Allendale. "Excuse us."

If I hope to make it through the night without beating Allendale senseless, I need to hold onto Sawyer and what she means to me like a lifeline.

47

SAWYER

Initially, the vibe in the house is so tense I almost suggest we leave. I want to believe my dad seems strange because of Brad's death, but it feels like something else. The creepy way his eyes follow Jamie makes me uneasy.

Over lunch, though, things settle. My dad focuses the conversation on Granthorpe, asking how Jamie and I met and then about the rowing team and its prospects. Jamie's stiff at first and answers with one or two words rather than expounding. But over time—with my peppering him with additional questions—he eases into conversation. I learn all sorts of things I didn't know. Like that before Jamie left Ireland for the United States, he'd been on track to row for Ireland in the Olympics.

"I've hope it's still in my future, but time will tell," he says. "The coach wasn't best pleased when I left, and there's a great group of lads in the boat now. Stellar performances back to back. No guarantee I'll be on that level when I return. But in the GU Varsity boat this year, it's a monster crew of lads. You say to yourself, 'right, okay, maybe we've got a shot to place well in the standings.'"

"My son said the top Varsity 8 is as fast as the national champion boat from last year. And that the coach said it's the most competitive team he's ever seen at GU."

"Maybe so. We've got some strong lads for sure, but so do they all. I can say the chemistry in that boat is class. It's as much fun rowing as I've ever known. Every oar strikes as one, and the boat flies like we've got a sail up in perfect wind."

"You sail, too?"

"If it's to do with water, I'm in. Boating, swimming, surfing. My ma jokes that when I was a wee lad she checked behind my ears for gills. I took to the sea like I was born to it. I got my first wetsuit from Santa when I was seven, from sheer badgering." He winks. "Not a lad to get carried away, I wrote him about ten letters... in case a couple went astray or the wee elves dropped one or two."

I laugh, and he rolls his eyes at himself.

"Couldn't leave anything to chance as Santa was my last hope that year. I'd not gotten a wet suit for my birthday as I'd asked. Looking back, I think my parents had the sense to know how reckless I might be once I got it. And the example I'd set for my five-year-old brother who was straight after me in anything I tried."

Dad wipes his hands on a napkin. "The ocean's too cold to swim without one at the moment. But the pool's heated. You should take a swim after dinner. That's my kids' favorite pastime."

"Is it?" Jamie's hand strokes the back of my head as I nod. "Yeah, grand. Never tried swimming in hot water. Should be interesting."

When lunch is over, my dad gets his laptop to finish work from his recent business trip. Jamie asks for a tour of the house, which I'm sure isn't out of idle curiosity.

When we're outside my parents' room, Jamie stands in the hall peering inside. "Does your dad have a signet ring from his college graduation?"

"Yes."

"How about a St. Christopher medal? Smaller than the one I wear." He holds his index and thumb apart at about the width of a dime.

"No, he doesn't wear necklaces."

"Fair play. The ring though, grab it for me, will you?"

"What?"

"Or stand watch." Grabbing my arms, he lifts me and sets me in the center of the hall. Unknowingly, he's grabbed my still sore bruise from the ride to the airport. At my wince, he pauses. "What's wrong, Sauce?"

"Uh, nothing really." I rub my arm. "But, hey, don't go in there, okay? It's not—"

Jamie takes the end of my sleeve and pulls. Then he reaches under my sweater to pull my arm free. As he raises the sweater up onto my shoulder, he stares at the dark, raised bruise.

"For fuck's sake. Where did this come from?"

"It's from last week."

"That wasn't my question. How did you get this?"

Lowering my voice to a whisper, I say, "Brad hit me."

"What? When? Why didn't you tell me?"

"It happened during the break-up."

He blows out a breath and glances at the ceiling. I use the moment to put my arm back into my sleeve and straighten my sweater.

"That asshole is lucky he's dead."

The pure malice in his voice is both comforting and terrifying.

Jamie kisses my forehead. "Keep watch for me, Cranberry Sauce." Without waiting for a response, he moves into my parents' room and straight to the jewelry box on the dresser.

"Jamie, don't." My hiss of protest is low, but I'm certain he hears me.

He sifts through what is mostly my mom's jewelry. "Fucking

hell," he murmurs, and his body tenses. Jamie shakes his head as he pockets something and turns and stalks back out.

"Why would you take his ring?"

Jamie grabs my hand in his and leads me away from the doorway and to the stairs.

Once we're upstairs, he pulls me inside his guest room and closes the door. "Jesus Christ," he mutters to himself as he takes his phone out. "Right there... where he can look at it every fucking day." His breath is shaky and quick as he scrolls through a photo reel. "First the ring. Look here, Sawyer."

Staring at the screen, I study a picture that's clearly been drawn by a child. It's a ring with the letter *A* on top and a school logo on the side.

Jamie sets my dad's ring in my hand. It's the ring from the picture or something very much like it.

"My brother drew this ring from memory. The man was behind him, but his right hand was holding Jude's arm to keep him from getting away. Jude had to stare at the ring the entire time he was raped."

I suck in a breath and draw back, wincing. "I can't—"

"The angle and that script font made me think it was an *R*, but now that I see it clearly, of course it's an *A*. This one." He closes his fist around my hand like he wants to crush the metal into a nugget. "That's not all. One more thing."

Jamie slides his finger over the phone's screen, searching through pictures. "Here." He expands a pic to show its details. There's a small gold disc on a thin chain. "That's a St. Christopher medal. My grandfather gave us each one. Jude wore his all the time. Loved it. He had it on the day we went fishing. But he didn't have it afterward. He didn't remember it being taken. At first, we thought it must've been torn off in the struggle, but I searched. Never found it on the road or in that place he was taken to. Years later, I heard about serial killers and predators taking trophies and I wondered..." From his pocket, he holds up a chain with a small gold medal dangling from it. "It was right there in the jewelry box. With your mom gone, Allendale doesn't need to hide it—if he ever did."

The medal blurs before my eyes as all the blood drains from my head. My dad actually did it. He sexually assaulted a little boy. And kept a souvenir.

"I feel sick." Breathing hard through my mouth, I stagger away from Jamie.

He precedes me out of the room so he can yank open the bathroom door for me. I rush in and retch over the toilet bowl. My lunch splashes into the water until there's nothing left inside me. Even afterward, I keep heaving for what feels like a lifetime.

Finally, I sink down to sit on the floor with my back against the clawfoot tub.

"Here, Sauce." Jamie's voice is gentle as he hands me a damp cloth. "Easy now."

I reach behind him for a length of toilet paper and blow my nose. After I've thrown the tissue away, I wipe my face with the washcloth.

When I look up at him, tears fill my eyes. "I'm sorry. So, so sorry."

"You weren't to know." He rinses the washcloth and uses it to clean the strands of hair that are plastered to my face. "It's all right now. Your color's coming back." Jamie tosses the cloth into the sink and rests his hands on either edge.

With his eyes closed, he whispers, "Found it, Jude. Got it back." Opening his eyes, he brings his hand up and opens his palm to reveal the pendant, as if his young brother might be looking down at it. "You've mine with you, so that's all right. I'll just keep this one safe. Till we see each other again."

That fucking crushes me.

Jamie put his own St. Christopher medal on Jude to replace the one he'd lost. And it's buried deep in the ground with the boy who will never grow up.

I can't seem to cry quietly. The sounds are jagged and broken.

They're what they would've been for Brad, if he'd been worthy of it.

Jamie swallows and sits next to me. His arm curls around my shoulders and pulls me against his side. "That's been a long time coming, so you'll maybe forgive me for speaking to him in front of you." He licks his lips and seems to mentally shake himself from his thoughts of the past. Looking at me, he says, "I've dragged you down into a very dark hole, Sawyer. It was selfish, I know. Should've kept it from you—"

"*No*. No, Jamie." My tone has a fierce edge as I rub the tears from my face. "I'm heartbroken, but I *had* to know." Sucking in a breath, I brace myself, trying to pull what's left of my heart back together. "Of course I wish my dad was the person I thought he was. I'm ill that he's not. But that's not your fault. It's his."

He turns his head to kiss the top of my head. "Thank you for that." His arm squeezes me against his body. "I've never told anyone the whole story before. Couldn't bring myself to do it... Felt like it would be betraying Jude's confidence. But I reckon he understands why I had to this time." His breathing is deep, like he's trying to catch his breath. "You're someone I need to trust."

48

JAMIE

At her urging, I leave Sawyer alone to brush her teeth and compose herself.

After I photograph Allendale's signet ring, I return it to his wife's jewelry box. I don't return Jude's St. Christopher medal, though, not even temporarily. Allendale will never again have anything of Jude that I can take back. If he notices the necklace has gone missing and it puts him on guard, so be it.

I circle back to Sawyer, only to find the bathroom door standing open. She's gone to her bedroom. When she emerges, she's wearing a clean shirt. There's an underlying pallor to her freshly-washed face that hasn't completely receded.

She rubs her brows, smoothing them into place. "We need an excuse to leave tonight."

"Not tonight, no."

"That accent..." She steps forward so her fingers can trace my jaw. "It's the only bright spot in my whole fucking life right now." Dropping her hand, she glances around. "I don't think I can stay here and act like nothing's changed. Let's leave. We'll report him to the police so they can start an investigation."

I hug her to me, as though I could transfer some of my strength into her body by osmosis. "I need you to manage a little longer, Sauce. For the sake of other kids who may be in danger."

"What other kids? Once we've told the police, they'll be watching what he does."

"Maybe eventually. But law enforcement moves slowly and carefully. They might even question your motives for reporting him and drag their feet. There's no telling what the truth will be up against. I've a mind to give the police a smoking gun, as they say."

Rubbing her temples, she frowns. "So... we'll do what? I'll cook dinner like nothing's happened? We'll chat with him and go swimming and hang out here?"

"Right, exactly."

Her shoulders droop. "I can try, I guess." The voice she uses is soft and hesitant, not at all sure of herself. "But just for one night, okay? Tomorrow I need to leave, whether we've found any more evidence or not."

Hugging her to me, I whisper, "Agreed."

She shudders. "He fooled me for so fucking long. I thought he was so nice for chaperoning my class trips and events. What if he only did that to watch the other kids? Or worse?" Her teeth chatter as if she's standing in the cold. "It makes me so sick."

"Will you stand watch for me once more? This time outside the room where he's working and text me if he comes out?"

"What are you going to do?"

"Find and clone his personal computer. So later, I'll have proper time to go through it and find anything he's trying to hide."

Her brows furrow. "Like pictures of Jude?"

"Or any child."

Drawing in a breath, she steps back, growing pale again. "You mean porn, don't you? Child pornography?"

I frown, not wanting to tell her about the disgusting things

I've uncovered on the devices of men like him. "This can be pretty nasty business, yeah. It's why I'll go through it alone."

Balling her fists and clenching her jaw, I see her buck up. "Collecting images isn't worse than actually grabbing a child and sexually assaulting him, so there's no reason for me to be shocked. It's just... I've never thought about what men like him do in secret. If he has that kind of porn, then he paid someone for it. And the sellers exploited other kids to make it, bringing the damage he's caused to even higher levels. It's disgusting."

Disgusting... the exact word.

"Yeah. But when I uncover how he acquired it, I can track the others through the meta data and stop them, too."

Blowing out a breath, she nods. "I'll keep watch. Do what you need to do."

SAWYER

WE DON'T HAVE AS MUCH TIME AS WE'D LIKE BECAUSE MY DAD emerges from his study too quickly. At least I send a warning text in time.

Late afternoon passes in a blur.

Jamie and I have reversed roles. When we arrived at the house, I was the one who was able to engage normally with my dad, making small talk and smiling as though nothing was wrong. Now, I'm the one who's distracted and having a hard time forcing a smile.

As Jamie and I prepare dinner, my dad stands at the island, drinking red wine and peppering Jamie with questions about Ireland and his family. I don't understand how Jamie doesn't tell him to fuck off. Instead, he's cool and composed as he focuses on talking about his parents and sisters. Jamie never says Jude's name or mentions him. Not even when my dad tries to ask him if he has a brother.

My strangle grip on the knife is because I'm dangerously close to burying it in his hand to stop him from badgering Jamie for painful information. It's almost as if he knows... A chill runs down my spine. Jamie recognized my dad, but he was an adult at the time of Jude's abduction. Is it possible that, even though Jamie was only eight or nine at the time, that my dad recognizes him, too?

If so, it's beyond cruel to try to dig things up. The sour unrest in my stomach returns, and I have to excuse myself to the bathroom until I can overcome the urge to vomit.

When I'm back in the kitchen, I want to scream questions and accusations at my dad. Such as, *how could you!?* And, *what the fuck is in the locked secretary cabinet in your bedroom that Jamie couldn't get into before you emerged from your office?*

My dad offers Jamie, who's already refused wine, a cocktail.

"Nah, I'm grand," Jamie says with an easy smile as he chops carrots. "No liquor until we've put the knives away. I get a wee bit clumsy when I'm in my cups." He leans over and shakes some seasoning onto the steak cubes I'm tenderizing with a meat mallet. "Have you any Guinness, Mr. Allendale? Giving the meat a soak in stout will give it the best flavor."

"No Guinness. No beer at all, I'm afraid."

"If I were a better guest, I'd have brought some. Next time." Jamie opens the fridge and takes out steak sauce. He tosses the meat into a bowl and pours the sauce and red wine over the top of the meat.

"That's an expensive marinade," Dad says.

"Right, okay." Jamie holds up a hand in apology and sets the bottle back near my dad. "It was only a splash. Less than I'd have drunk to be sure if I were drinking."

"Are you a heavy drinker?"

"By island standards, no."

"Island standards?" Dad's brows pinch together in confusion.

"That's what he calls Ireland." My tone is flat and almost terse. Glancing at Jamie, I finally manage a real smile, albeit a small one. "Americans would never refer to Ireland that way. When we say island standards, we're thinking of tropical islands, like the ones in the Caribbean."

"Ah. Fair play."

While we let the pastry dough chill and the steak marinate, Jamie asks my dad about his travels, saying I'd mentioned he was traveling over the Thanksgiving holiday.

Dad leans against the counter. "Yes, a trip to San Diego to meet with some clients. I'd been hoping to extend my trip but we had the family emergency."

"Right, terrible. Very sorry about your son."

Dad nods. "It's hard to believe. Sometimes I forget he's gone."

"In the beginning, it doesn't seem real." Jamie draws in a breath, watchful.

"You lost someone close to you?"

Jamie's thinking about Jude, of course, but it's not what he says. "Grandparents. A while back."

This is starting to feel like a horrible cat-and-mouse game.

My dad takes a long swig of wine. "Luckily, it gets easier with time."

Jamie's head cocks, looking ready to deny that. Instead, he turns his attention back to food prep. Though he says nothing more, I picture the way he looked as he hung his head over the sink talking to his brother. The pain radiating from him in that moment is something I can never un-feel.

For the third time today, I feel like retching.

49

JAMIE

While my left hand sprinkles a crushed sleeping pill from Allendale's room into his food, my right hand pours mushroom gravy over the top to dissolve the powder.

All three of us will be eating off holiday china with Christmas trees around the edge, but the man's made it easy to identify his drugged portion because he's said no to baked apples with black walnuts, which both Sawyer and I are having.

I set Allendale's dish next to the full wine glass he's just refilled. I've been careful not to consume anything Allendale's handled. Working for my cousin's Crue has made me paranoid, as has the conversation of the past two hours where Allendale seemed determined to hear about the dead younger brother I haven't admitted I have.

Sawyer fills water glasses, and we join Allendale at the table. I'm craving a pint but need a clear head, so I resist when Allendale indicates again that I can help myself to any bottles on the bar cart.

His flushed face is puffy from alcohol and salty appetizers, making the hollows below his eyes more pronounced. He's lumbering through middle age. Something my brother will never get to do. A flash of Jude's small coffin fills my mind.

Just a little farther, Jude. This part is almost done.

Sawyer doesn't eat much and is noticeably on edge. Setting a hand between her shoulder blades, I massage her tight muscles as a subtle reminder to keep her game face on.

"If you're tired, Sawyer, why don't you lie down?" her dad says.

"I think I will. I've got a headache."

"I'll get you some medication," Allendale says, rising.

My eyes narrow, and I stand as well. She's not consuming anything from his hand. "You don't need meds, do you?"

Her head turns toward me sharply. Following my lead, she says, "No, just sleep."

Once she's set her dish on the counter and disappears upstairs, Allendale leans back in his chair.

"The food is delicious." Despite saying so, he's only eaten half a portion. Combined with the wine, it should still be enough to knock him out long enough for me to get into the cabinet he's keeping locked tight. I'd bet my last quid his dirty secrets are in there.

I finish my dinner, leaving the plate clean enough to see the ornaments on the trees. An army marches better with a full belly as my grandfather used to say.

Allendale leans forward. "Since Sawyer's gone to bed, maybe I'll join you for that swim?"

"Sure."

"Do you need to borrow swim trunks?"

"Nah, I'm grand. Not the first time I've swum in my *kex*. Won't be the last." I catch myself smirking and nearly curse. Being friendly is a habit and seeming relaxed is what I want, but it's a kick in the balls to think this man might get the impression I'm after being his friend.

Allendale says he'll bring the towels out.

An uneasy feeling causes me to head upstairs to check on Sawyer. It's a hard thing I'm asking of her, even if it is only for a night.

I enter her darkened room and sit next to her on the bed. "Cranberry Sauce, you still awake?"

"Yeah, just resting."

Setting my hand gently on the side of her head, I stroke her hair. "Almost done. I promise."

She turns her head and kisses my palm. "I'm all right. Just need a break from it."

"Take your break for as long as you like. Till it's time to pack if you want." I lean down and kiss her temple. "I can't say I'll be able to make up for this. Not sure anything could. But I will take you away for Christmas if you'll allow it. Anywhere you'd like and sparing no expense."

"Dangerous offer. I used to be an Allendale. I know the most expensive holiday destinations in the world."

"Do your worst. I plan to prove you won't miss a thing by trading them for me." Licking my lips, I study her. "I love you, Sauce."

Her eyes widen, and I nod to emphasize how serious I am.

She sits up and kisses me. "Same."

50

SAWYER

A crashing sound makes me jerk up in bed.

For a second, I'm not sure if I heard something or dreamed it.

When I remember what was happening before I laid down, all my uneasiness comes rushing back. I climb from bed and walk to the window to look outside.

It takes a moment for me to process that Jamie's passed out —or something. My breath catches. He's half on the end of a lounger that has one side cocked into the air from him landing on it.

Sucking in a startled breath, I scan the area. From several feet away, my dad wobbles toward Jamie.

What the fuck is happening?

Nothing good, that's for sure. My body lurches into motion. I need to get down there.

I rush from the room and down the stairs. Flinging the back door open, I propel myself outside.

Across the yard, my dad rolls Jamie over onto the lip of the pool. The lounger bangs back to the ground.

My dad doesn't notice me as I hurry toward them, so he continues, swaying unsteadily as he pulls Jamie onto his side so he's perched on the edge. Is he going to dump him in the fucking water?

"Stop!"

Dad's head jerks up to look at me as Jamie's body falls into the pool with barely a splash.

I rush forward and jump in. The water resists my running through it, and I have to swim. Jamie's sinking body is halfway to the bottom of the deepest point in the pool.

There's a loud splash as my dad jumps in, too.

I dive and grab Jamie's arm under the shoulder. As I'm dragging him to the surface, my dad's leg blocks our ascent.

Not wanting to waste time fighting against Dad's interference, I drag Jamie in the other direction. I expect my dad to grab us and prevent me from pulling away, but thank God, he doesn't.

When I reach the shallow end, I get my feet under me. As I stand, I move my chest under Jamie's back so I can prop his head and neck above the surface.

My dad swims to the edge of the pool, but his attempts to climb out fail. I guess he's extremely drunk. Lucky for me.

I manage to lay Jamie on the steps. His blue lips make my heart clench. What the hell? Is he dead?

I pinch his nose and blow breath into his mouth. There's so much resistance it's hard to get air into him. My seal on his mouth keeps breaking, so my breath escapes rather than going into his lungs.

Come on! I knee him in the side, trying to wake him as I continue to do my best to breathe life back in.

After a minute or two, I feel my breath being sucked inward. It's faint, but he's trying to breathe. I raise my head a couple of inches. His color is less blue.

"Jamie?"

His body twitches, but he doesn't draw a new breath. I give

him a couple more of mine, my heartbeat hammering in my throat. Why isn't he breathing? There's no blood or sign of injury. He looks perfect.

But he's dying.

His body tries to slide down the steps, and I have to stop rescue-breathing long enough to drag him back up.

Motion at the edge of my vision causes my eyes to jerk in Dad's direction. He pulls himself along the edge of the pool from the deep to the shallow end. He's only a few feet from us. I swear to God if he tries anything I will shove him under the water.

"What did you do to Jamie?"

My dad ignores my yelled question. Wobbling, he claws his way up the steps on his hands and knees. When he's out, he shoves his foot against Jamie's shoulder and pushes. He's trying to get Jamie back underwater.

My screech is more animal than human. I rise up over Jamie and slam my palms against my dad, causing him to fall onto the cement like a fish flopping onto the deck of a boat.

I shove his leg away from us. Fortunately, my dad's push was too weak to move Jamie, whose muscles are heavy, especially since he's dead weight.

As I lean over him and press my lips against his, I feel his mouth move under mine. Jerking my head up, I watch his lids flutter open.

Jamie pulls a deep breath in, and his brows pinch together in confusion. His body shifts under mine. In a hoarse voice, he mumbles, "Sauce?"

"Jamie, oh, my God. Can you get up?"

His head lolls slowly to the side and he looks around, his eyes squinting as he tries to focus. Dropping his hands underwater, he pushes off the steps to sit upright. My hands dart out to steady him as he sways.

"Feel strange." Shaking his head to clear it, he half crawls, half climbs up the steps. "Am I drunk?" he slurs.

As I help him, I spot a piece of plastic clinging to the skin between his shoulder blades. I think it's garbage that blew into the pool, but when I have to tug to pull it free, I realize there's adhesive around the edges.

Jamie looks over his shoulder.

I jerk it off his back and hold up the clear plastic. "What is this?"

He turns and leans over. Just as I read the word Fentanyl, my dad launches himself forward, slamming into me.

I fall backward, crashing into the water and landing on the bottom of the pool with him on top of me. A moment later, Dad is jerked off and Jamie lifts me up.

Sputtering, I blink water from my eyes.

Jamie twists to set me on my feet on the steps but stays where he is. After a beat, I realize he's standing on one foot and has the other planted in the middle of my dad's chest, holding him underwater.

"Jamie."

His determined, dark scowl sends chills through me.

My hand touches his arm in a bid to influence him. To pull him back to reality. "You can't. It's too dangerous." I'm not worried about my dad anymore. I just don't want Jamie to end up in jail for killing him. "Security cameras," I whisper. "I don't know where they're positioned."

Removing his foot slowly, Jamie stares down through the water at my father.

When Dad rises to the surface, he backpedals away from us. His chest heaves as he splutters for breath.

With a look of disgust, Jamie stalks up the steps. His hand catches my forearm as he passes and tugs me along with him.

Because of the adrenaline overload, I don't realize how cold I am until I'm inside the warm house. As I start to shiver, Jamie guides me upstairs. We track wet footprints as we walk, and I rub my arms.

"Do you use Fentanyl pain patches?" I ask.

"No." His frown deepens. "He slapped me on the back when I came outside. Played it off as a friendly gesture. Smart of him to smack that hard. Didn't feel that he'd stuck something on me. He's got fucking balls. I'll give him that."

I stop at a window to look outside. My dad has lain down a few feet from the door. "What's he doing?"

Jamie glances out and exhales a small, humorless laugh. "Maybe he'll fucking freeze to death." Turning to me, he says, "Take a shower, Sauce. Get warm."

I follow him into the bathroom where he strips out of his wet boxer-briefs and hangs them on a towel rack. After grabbing a towel, he locks the door before he walks out, still naked.

Deciding I'm too cold to do anything other than what he suggested, I step into the stall and turn on the water.

What the fuck is happening to my life? Now my dad is a murderer, too?

I just can't process this... Our entire life was a lie.

51

JAMIE

I stop in the guest room to dress and grab my gear. Then I get Allendale's keys from the kitchen drawer where I spotted them earlier. When I don't find a skeleton key for the locked cabinet on Allendale's key ring, I grab a paper clip from his office and go to work in the master bedroom. Antique locks aren't exactly high security.

Inside the secretary cabinet, there are two burn phones and a laptop. *Here we go.* I plug in my jiggler device to copy the computer's hard drive. Next, I suck phone data from those.

Rummaging through the cabinet's drawers and cubbies, I take photos of everything in case there are trophies hidden among his junk. Giving the jewelry box the same treatment, I move quickly. Then, I stalk back out to the hall and look in the yard. Allendale's unconscious and hasn't moved. Alcohol and the drug have finally kicked in.

"Jamie?"

Turning, I spot Sawyer standing at the top of the stairs. Christ, I need the rest of the pool water to drain from my ears. She's wrapped in a towel, looking pale and pensive.

Jogging up the stairs, I join her. "Hey, Sauce. He's out, but lock yourself in your room while you pack."

"So, we're leaving tonight?"

"We are, yeah." I guide her to her bedroom. "While you pack, there are a few other places I'll check for hidden evidence stashes. Won't take long. Then we're out."

She nods.

"You all right?" I ask.

Blowing out a slow breath, she shrugs.

Taking her face in my hands, I give her a kiss. "You saved my life, huh, Sauce?"

"Yes. I did." Her soft voice is slightly bemused. "Still can't believe that happened. That *any* of this is happening."

"I know." Hauling her against me, I wrap my arms around her. "It's tough, but you're going to be all right."

Her grip on me tightens. "Hope so." The steady voice impresses me. She's holding it together better than most people would.

After kissing her temple, I release her. "Right. Let's finish and go."

Drawing in a deep breath, she turns and walks away. Once she's in the bedroom, I confirm the door's locked before I head downstairs.

After this is over, I'm going to give that girl the fucking world.

※

SAWYER

I DRESS IN SWEATS AND AM PUTTING CLOTHES IN MY SUITCASE when I hear the door's lock click open. I whirl around and discover my dad in the doorway, wearing his bathrobe and holding a handgun. My breath catches in shock. What the hell? I had no idea there was a gun in the house.

He's pointing it in my general direction and looks very unsteady. Even if he doesn't intend to shoot me, he might by accident.

Becoming very still, I watch him. "What are you doing, Dad? Can you lower that please?"

Moving the gun's barrel toward the wall, he shakes his head. "He's using you, Sawyer." His voice sounds thick and slurred. "Do you know why he's dating you? It's to get access to this house."

"What are you talking about?" Trying to sound as innocent as possible, I hold up my hands in an "I surrender" gesture.

Dad narrows his glazed eyes. "He's trying to kill me."

"Jamie? No, he's not. Why would he?"

"Your brother owed him money and couldn't pay. That's why they killed him. And now he's threatening to do the same to me. He tried to drug and drown me. That's why I was trying to push him in the pool. I needed to do it before I passed out, and he killed me."

My stomach plummets, and for a split second, I consider whether he could be telling the truth. But no. If Jamie drugged him, it was only to search the house. "He didn't try to kill you."

"He would have. If you hadn't come out. He would've pushed me in the pool and made it look like an accidental drowning."

"No, that's what *you* tried to do."

"In self defense."

"You just happened to have a narcotic pain patch ready to drug him? Where did you even get it from?"

"Leftovers from Mom's cancer treatment. I'd forgotten all about them until I found one in the sink from his rifling through the medicine cabinet."

It's true that Mom had pain patches. Because of the gastric cancer, she couldn't eat or drink much at the end, so it was hard for her to take medications by mouth.

For a moment, I consider whether my dad could be telling

the truth about the reason Brad was killed. Could this all be about money Brad owed the C Crue?

No, it's ridiculous. If that was really the truth, when my dad suspected Jamie had poisoned him tonight, he would have called nine-one-one. Not try to murder the college student hitman the gangsters sent. It's insane.

Also, there was Jamie's brother's picture of the signet ring. And the Catholic medal in the jewelry box, which couldn't belong to anyone in our family. Am I supposed to believe the entire pedophile story is an elaborate ruse? No way. Using me would just make things messier. I can't see members of an organized crime syndicate involving innocent people unnecessarily.

"If you thought he was here to kill you, why not call the police? Who decides to drug someone with a pain patch?"

"These people are above the law. Who knows what cops and judges they have in their pocket."

Wow. He's a very good liar.

"In Connecticut? Jamie's from Ireland. His family lives near Boston."

He nods. "I figured you'd take his side. He's a good-looking kid... with seemingly good prospects. Do you feel lucky, Sawyer, to have gotten his attention? Because you're not. He's playing a game. At the end, he'll drop this. Drop you."

"If he does, he does. That's not a reason to kill anyone."

"You're right." He tucks the gun into the pocket of his robe, which still seems dangerous. "But let me show you something. *Proof.*" He gestures for me to come with him.

My mind races, and I hesitate. I don't trust him. "Get it and bring it to my room." While he's gone, I can sneak downstairs to get Jamie so we can leave.

"Can't. It's on the work computer. My office. Come downstairs."

I don't want him behind me. At least on the main floor, we'll be closer to where Jamie is. "You first, Dad." I gesture for him to go, and I'll follow.

He exits the room and I trail after him, leaving plenty of space between us.

Once we're downstairs in his office, he boots up his work laptop and clicks on a folder. When he backs away, I walk over to look at the picture on the screen.

I'm confused. The picture is of Jamie and Ash with two little boys. The dark-haired one who's sitting on Jamie's shoulders looks three or four years old. The blond toddler in Ash's arms is a little younger. He has the exact same blue eyes as the two of them. In the background, party decorations hang around the dining room, and helium balloons bob against the ceiling.

"What does this prove?" As I start to turn, something wraps around my throat and cinches tight.

Oh, my God!

My fingers claw at the braided cord, but it's so tight I can't get underneath it. My body bangs backwards into my dad, trying to get him to release me.

I try to scream, but I can't even speak. My mouth opens and closes as I try impotently to call for help. My dad is killing me!

The world starts to blur as I gouge at my throat, trying desperately to loosen the cord. There's no way to grip it. A searing pain in my neck radiates up and down. I can't breathe.

Reaching behind my head, I scratch his face. He jerks back, and the pressure on my throat is even tighter. It's digging into my flesh. I can't stop him!

My fingers scrabble over the surface of the desk, knocking over the desk organizer. The contents spill out, and as my legs start to buckle, I snatch the letter opener. My falling causes his grip to loosen, and my lungs manage to drag in a partial breath.

As the cord cuts into my neck again, I stab backward into his flesh. He squawks, losing his grip, and I land on the floor. While he crashes to his knees, I gasp for breath and try to scramble away.

Rolling onto my back as Dad lunges toward me, I manage to

get my knees up to block him. My hands cover my neck protectively as I pant and kick at him.

Suddenly, he's hauled backward, and Jamie's behind him. As I'm gasping, the cord jerks free of my dad's hands, and Jamie wraps it around Dad's neck.

The deadly blue of Jamie's eyes fills my own vision.

Dad falls to his knees, grasping desperately at his throat, his eyes bulging. He can't free himself, and I watch in horror as he experiences the same thing he just did to me. His hands reach down.

The gun.

As he starts to pull it out, I spring forward and knock the gun away. His hand gets a grip on the letter opener, but Jamie shoves him forward so he lands face down on the floor with the letter opener trapped beneath his body.

"Close your eyes, Sawyer." Jamie's voice is calm. Shockingly so.

My gaze locks with his, which is still full of cold determination.

Listening to him is the right call, but that's not something I can force myself to do. Instead, I scramble backward into the corner until my back hits the wall. As I watch, my dad's face turns purple, and his eyes bulge.

"Cranberry Sauce, don't watch." Jamie's voice is gentle but firm.

My gaze darts up to his face. "You promised not to kill him."

Jamie's expression hardens. "Sawyer—"

"You swore to me."

He loosens his grip, and my dad gasps for breath. He's not conscious yet, but his body shudders, trying to rouse.

I rub my sore neck, feeling the cord's bloody groove. Jamie has a knee planted on my dad's back, so he can't rise.

"I don't care anymore if you kill him, Jamie." Our eyes meet and hold. "I just don't want you to get caught." Licking my lips, I nod for emphasis. "It's you I don't want to lose."

"Right, understood." His accent comforts me. It's the voice I've come to trust more than anyone else's. Jamie's hands tighten the curtain cord once again. "Be a good girl, and close your eyes for me, Sauce. Do it now."

Licking parched lips, I allow my lids to drop closed. I can't understand why tears seep out from under them. It's not because the only parent I had left is dying. About that, I'm not even sorry.

Monsters don't deserve to live.

52

JAMIE

After pulling Sawyer into a tight embrace, we stand locked together. She's surprisingly calm as we talk and voices no resistance when I say we're not going to call the police.

Sawyer walks over to the computer and clicks the mouse to unlock the screen. The screenshot picture filling the monitor is one of me and Ash with Trick's sons at my aunt's birthday party. My muscles clench as I curse. Allendale must've grabbed it from social media. Which means he's known exactly who I am for a while.

Her voice is hollow as she says, "You should probably copy this computer, too."

When I close the screenshot from my aunt's party, I notice the picture icon next to the screenshot is named *Angel Boy*.

I brace myself as I click to open it. A cropped version of the birthday picture comes into view where only Trick's son Finn is in the frame. The blond hair, blue eyes and features all make him look like a young version of Jude.

Allendale's been stalking my family for a new target. I wish he wasn't already dead. I would kill him slowly.

Angel boy. Christ, it makes me feel like puking.

Leaning close, Sawyer whispers. "Who is that little boy?"

"My cousin. Ash's youngest nephew."

Sauce steps back, and a hardness enters her eyes as she glances at Allendale's body. "I'm glad he's dead." Looking at the blood on her hands, she shakes her head. "I don't want to deal with another investigation. I know I'll have to, but... it's unfair."

Putting an arm around her shoulders, I pull her against me and kiss the top of her head. "Wash up in his bathroom. Easier to explain traces of his blood in there. Could've cut himself shaving sometime. I'll clean up the scene here and decide what to do next."

When she goes into his bedroom, I copy Allendale's work drive and start to destroy evidence in the fireplace. The trophies I spotted in the basement, I'll leave for the cops to find.

His body is a problem. Our DNA will be on it. But disposing of a body is tricky business in the age of doorbell cameras. I want Sawyer away from the house as quickly as possible, but to clean the scene carefully, I need time.

I could escort Sawyer home to Foxgrove, establish an alibi and then sneak back here. Or... I could take advantage of being in C Crue and call in an expert. It would mean coming clean about the vendetta, which is dangerous, but it's the best option for having the murder scene handled properly.

SAWYER AND I KEEP UP APPEARANCES AS WE TRAVEL TO THE train station in a ride share. From our casual conversation about school and the holidays, no one would have a clue that a few hours earlier she witnessed me murder her father.

As soon as we're seated on the train, I text for reinforcements, asking Ash to pick us up from the Boston train station and letting Trick know, via coded message, I need to speak to him privately as soon as possible.

Trick calls and asks where I am. I tell him. Once he has my arrival time, he ends the call. In person, it'll be.

At the Boston train station, Ash waits for us wearing blue and green flannel pajama pants under her puffy coat. The pajamas, along with her fuzzy blue hat and wildly mussed hair cause me to cock a brow.

"Cracker look, Ash. Who are you meant to be? Wendy Darling just dropped off by Peter Pan after a trip to Neverland?"

Ash smirks and flips me off with good cheer before giving Sawyer a hug.

I pull Ash in for a hug, too, but I've got an ulterior motive. In her ear, I whisper, "Thanks for coming. Listen, I need another favor. If anything should happen to me, you'll look after Sawyer for me, yeah? I want your word you won't leave her alone. She belongs to us now."

Ash's grip tightens around my back. It's a credit to her that she doesn't ask a single question. "I swear."

"Grand. Off you go."

When I release her, Ash picks up Sawyer's tote. "Seesaw, do you feel like waffles because I—oh, hey!"

I follow her gaze and spot Trick's approach. His hair's brown, but otherwise we're cut from the same cloth. Same build and facial features. Even a similar gait.

He wears a vintage padded leather jacket with fleece lining over a knit shirt and jeans. His brown hiking boots tell a story, if only to me, about where we're headed when we leave the train station. Usually Trick wears trainers with jeans in a typical American fashion. Not today. So, once the girls are gone, he'll be taking me to the woods. Here's hoping we both emerge alive at the end of the meeting.

Oblivious to the serious mood, Ash launches herself at Trick, and he catches her in a hug. After, he looks her over with a wry smirk. "What the hell are you wearing, baby?"

She smirks back. "College clothes."

"Yeah, right."

Ash winks, still grinning. "Here, Scotty, meet my roommate." She pulls Sauce's sleeve to bring them together. "This is Sawyer."

Sawyer extends a hand, and Trick shakes it.

For her, he's got an easy smile. "Good to meet you."

"You, too. Ash quotes you all the time, and I've started to as well. You're a legend."

That causes him to chuckle.

"Have you had breakfast, Scotty?" Ash asks. "There's that great waffle place—"

"Can't this morning." Trick takes out his wallet. "But you girls, go. Have fun." He holds out a few hundred-dollar bills.

Ash puts her hands up in a "stop" gesture. "No. I have money."

Ignoring this, Trick slides the cash into Ash's coat pocket. "After breakfast, buy some real pants."

Ash's laughter bubbles out of her as she gives him a kiss on the cheek. "See ya." Then, she waves at me and hooks an arm through Sawyer's to tug her along.

Sawyer rolls her small case as she strolls away with Ash, but she looks back over her shoulder for a moment with concern. Maybe she senses the danger. I smile to put her at ease.

Once the girls disappear in the crowd, I drop the smile. Picking up the duffles, I follow Trick. There's no conversation, not even small talk. Apparently, he's not pleased about getting an unexpected emergency call from me and having to make the drive to Boston first thing in the morning.

Outside, I get into a black C Crue SUV with its bullet-proof windows. This is what serves as a company car for the successful crime syndicate these days.

Hip hop blares from the sound system when he drives out of the metropolitan area to a plot of land the organization owns.

In the woods, Trick parks on a dirt road that's dusted with snow.

We venture about three hundred yards into the trees. Unlike when the bosses call a meeting, there's no outdoor furniture, no fire pit, nothing.

Standing with his hands in his pockets, Trick says, "All right. I'm listening."

"I killed a man in Connecticut. I need to use the Crue's cleaner to deal with the body or I need to go back and do it myself."

Trick's expression turns as dark as I've ever seen it. "On whose authority, did you kill?"

"No one's." Silence stretches on. Finally, I add, "He was the pedophile who caused Jude's death. And he tried to kill me and Sawyer. Also, he had pictures of your boys on his computer. Finn's his favorite type. Blond-haired, blue-eyed, and looks just like Jude."

"How the fuck would he have pictures of my kids?"

"I don't know. Ash's socials are private, and I don't have any. But the pictures were from your mom's birthday party, so someone must have shared them publicly." I shrug. "I'm not sure when he got onto me. For all I know, he's kept tabs for years. I'll find out when I go through his files." I touch the duffle with my foot. "Cloned all his devices."

"Is he why you came to America?" Trick's analytical abilities are second to none.

Drawing in a slow breath, I nod.

"And you didn't bother to fucking tell me until now? When there's no moonlighting in our Crue. Which you know."

Again, I nod. "Whatever you decide to do, I'll accept."

"You're pretty fucking confident I'll cover for you. If I let C handle this the way we would any other Crue member who went off book to the tune of murder... Let's say we'd be dealing with more than one body this week."

I level my stare on him. "As I said, whatever you decide."

"The girl knows, right? Are you prepared for us to kill her, too?"

That causes my heart to clench in protest. "There's no need to hurt Sawyer. If I'm gone, I'm no longer a liability."

"If you're alive, she's a big fucking risk to you forever. The minute you break things off, or even if she just gets pissed enough, she could burn you."

"I know."

Trick scowls. "You work for us, so that's *our* problem, too."

"Leaving him alive would've been risky, too, Trick. While he was trying to kill Sawyer, she had to stab him. His going for medical care would've led to a record that police could've dug up later. Better to kill him as quickly and cleanly as possible."

"You wanna talk risk? It was a lot fucking riskier to go there alone with a civilian witness. We trained you better than that." He shakes his head. "Why the fuck didn't you confide in me? The planning for something like this should've been meticulous."

"Listen, I couldn't risk your telling me to leave him be. I made my promise to Jude over his fucking coffin." Licking my parched lips, I shrug. "If someone raped Ash and caused her to kill herself, would you let him live?"

"Don't waste time with stupid questions. My objection isn't to the murder. It's to the mess. If you'd told me the situation, your girl wouldn't have needed to get blood on her hands. Or in her head. Because she wouldn't have been anywhere near the scene."

I exhale. "I didn't go there to kill him. My original plan was different. I was going to destroy his life and make him suffer. Take everything, expose him, see him in jail and brutalized by grown men the way he liked to do." Clenching my jaws, I scowl. Allendale's death was too easy. "But when he tried to kill us, I couldn't risk leaving him alive. What if he'd run? He might've hurt someone else—even tried to grab Finn—while I was fucking about with cat-and-mouse games to find him. I couldn't have that on my head with Jude watching."

"With Jude watching?" Trick scoffs.

I exhale in frustration, holding up a hand to dismiss his skepticism. "I'm not mental." My teeth grind together. "Or maybe I am. Dunno."

Trick's expression becomes neutral again. "Give me the address of the scene."

I rattle it off. "Back door's open. Security system offline. He helped with that, actually. Turned it off so he could drown me and make it look like an accident. Almost worked."

"You knew what he was, and he got the drop on you?" Trick shakes his head, disgusted again.

"Aye, my guard was too low. But I'm not the type he usually targets. Fourteen years too old and ten stone too big. In a fair fight, he was no match for me."

"Any animal is dangerous when cornered. Especially a human one." Trick makes the call to send a man to New Haven to clean up. When he finishes, I nod my appreciation.

"Listen, I'm sorry, Trick. I meant to handle it alone and cleanly. With no ties to the Crue or anyone else."

Trick shrugs. "Man plans. God laughs. Which is why it's good to have a Crue that's got your back." Sliding his phone away, he studies me. "Tell me about the man. Everything you know."

For the next few minutes, I spill the intel I've gathered. When I tell him Allendale was Sawyer's father, his brows pinch together in a grim line. Still, he listens silently until I finish.

Trick appraises me with an expression that could freeze alcohol. "What's the story with you and the girl? Ash thinks it's serious."

"Serious enough that I'd die for her."

He makes a nonspecific sound that he's unimpressed by my declaration. Maybe it's because *all* the Crue leadership would die to protect what's theirs. Or maybe it's that he doubts me. Hard to tell with Trick.

"She was steady this morning," he says. "No outward signs of what happened." Trick glances around. "All right, marry her."

That grabs my attention, and my head jerks in surprise. I've already taken a notion about Sawyer. I want her to become a permanent fixture in my life, but she'd think I was mental if I proposed right after killing her dad. "She's just out of secondary school, Trick. At uni, sure, but still a schoolgirl."

Trick's eyes narrow. "The girl's eighteen, right?"

"Of course, yeah."

"Old enough then." Trick's hands emerge from the pockets of his coat, as though he's warmed up from the heat of his annoyance. "Law enforcement can't compel her to testify against you if she's your wife. You say you're willing to do anything to protect her. I'm telling you what to do."

The implied threat to Sawyer causes my fists to clench.

Trick wants her under my control where I can keep a close eye on her. And it's not the worst suggestion I've ever heard. I do want her, of course. But trying to lock her down quickly and suddenly might cause her to pull back.

"*Listen*, if I ask now, I doubt she'll even have me. We haven't been together long, and what she knows of me can't inspire much confidence about a happy future life."

Leveling me with a gaze, he says, "Convince her."

"Right." Drawing in a breath, I lean forward. "About the father, I have an idea that could make it look like he's gone on the run, rather than that something's happened to him."

"Tell me."

I run down my plans to schedule emails from his work account, including an incriminating one that will look like he sent it accidentally. "If the police think he's become afraid of being arrested, it'll muddy the waters."

"Yeah. We'll circle back to that in a couple of hours. Once I know the body's gone." He rubs the back of his neck. "If you had ideas about leaving the Crue now that your vendetta's complete, forget it. You'll be clearing your debt to us for a long time."

That brings me up short. I'd only promised the Crue one year's work after the training. "How long exactly?"

"I don't know. After I speak to C, he'll tell you." With that, Trick turns and heads back toward the truck.

Exhaling, I try to wrap my head around Trick's statements. It's tough to accept I won't be moving home to Ireland next year, but considering I've broken their rules and they're helping me cover up a murder... I'm lucky Trick values blood so much.

Nodding to myself, I reframe my expectations for the next few years. Right, so I'll only be visiting the island, not living there. I can deal with that. After all, a huge weight's been lifted from my shoulders. I've finally gotten vengeance for Jude, and in the bargain, I've found an excuse—albeit a dark one—to keep the girl I'm in love with.

On the whole, I'm getting a new life. I'd be a fool not to make the best of it.

53

SAWYER

The only way life could get more surreal would be if I dropped acid while wandering through a theme park.

It's been three days since New Haven, and the world is still turning as if my adopted father didn't die by violence. I'd probably be freaking out if it weren't for Jamie and Ash who never leave me alone for a second.

When we're taking a walk outside, Jamie gives me instructions. "I reckon it's been the right amount of time now, Sauce. Tomorrow, you'll call your grandparents to ask if they've heard from him and say you haven't. You can ask their advice about whether they think you should call the police. If they've noticed he's been out of touch, they may decide to do it for you, which is even better. If not, you'll wait another day and then call the police to go by. You'll say you're worried because he seemed so depressed over the death of his son. It'll plant the seed he may have disappeared because he decided to harm himself."

It's clever. And carefully considered. Jamie seems to sense I'm at a loss as to what to say next because he cups my cheek and strokes it reassuringly.

"Your plan sounds perfect," I say. My eyes dart from his to the path. "Sorry for acting rattled. I promise I can handle this."

"Listen," he says slowly. "You've been brilliant altogether. From the house to the train station and ever since."

Licking my dry lips, I shrug. "I'm trying."

"Lean into me on this. You know how when we're playing games in bed, you let go of trying to maintain control and just let me lead?"

"Sure."

"Do that now." Licking his lips, he tips his forehead until it touches mine. "I swear I'll get you through this."

After a shudder, I hug him. "I want us *both* through it."

"I know." He takes my face in his hands and kisses me. His tongue caresses mine slowly, tasting me.

A mouth that kisses like his is rare, and all the doubts that were eating me up dissolve.

We'll be all right.

JAMIE

ALLENDALE HAS BEEN REPORTED MISSING, AND A SLOW-MOVING police investigation has started. The cops are already hypothesizing the man left town of his own free will... to lie low, for reasons they aren't willing to share. A pedophile on the run is exactly what I want them to see him as, so that's a win.

War is scarce around the house, which has me wondering whether his uncle ordered him to give me a wide berth. Sawyer and I carry out a normal routine to keep up appearances, which I hope is also helping her distance herself mentally from Connecticut.

Trick's sons are both Christmastime babies, and he and the wife are having an early December birthday party for them, separate from the actual holiday week. When Trick texts to invite me, he suggests I bring Sawyer so everyone can meet her. I accept immediately. Keeping Sauce occupied and distracted is my highest priority right now.

It's midafternoon but looks later because storm clouds are spitting down freezing rain. I call Ash to suggest she drive the three of us to Coynston for the upcoming party. As usual, she's game for a group road trip.

Within the hour, she's in the lot, engine idling, windows fogged from the blasting heat and the chatter between her and Sawyer. When I open the passenger door, Sawyer gets out.

I give her a quick kiss. "Sit in back with me, Sauce."

Ash scoffs. "Am I the chauffeur?"

"You are, yeah." Guiding Sawyer into the back, I wink at Ash.

She smirks and shakes her head. "You're lucky you're my favorite cousin."

As soon as I'm settled, she backs out of the spot and swivels the wheel. Leaving the lot, the car fishtails slightly. She's a deft hand at keeping control, but I tell her to mind the road anyway.

"No backseat driving allowed." Ash's hearty chuckle is shameless.

Sawyer rolls her eyes. As we turn a corner, her hand squeezes my thigh to keep from sliding.

The girls talk about school. I learn Sawyer brought two formal dresses back from Connecticut. One for the Briar Club Induction Ceremony and one for a GU holiday party.

"Did you bring the burgundy dress for the birthday party?" I ask. "Because *that's* the outfit I'd like to see again."

Sawyer clucks her tongue skeptically. "Of course not. I brought the Chanel dress and a pantsuit."

"It's a kids' party," Ash says, glancing at us in the rearview mirror like we're insane. "I'm probably wearing jeans and a sweatshirt."

Cocking my brow, it's my turn to look skeptical. "A sweatshirt?"

"Well, maybe not that," Ash concedes. "Why? Did Trick say we should dress up? He told me casual clothes."

I shake my head. "The last birthday party he threw had fireworks and a professional photographer. I've been to weddings that were more low-key."

Ash laughs, and Sawyer appears thoughtful.

"Shut up, James. I told Sawyer our family is laid back and cool. And that she doesn't need to be nervous. Why are you making us sound so bougie?"

"That's me exaggerating, is it? Were there staged photo areas at your ma's party or not?" My phone buzzes in my pocket, and I slide it free.

> War: Hit me back when you're alone.

As I start to put my phone away, it buzzes again.

> C: When you get to Coins, come see me.

A summons from C. That's bound to be a reckoning.

Sawyer's brows pinch together. "What's wrong?"

Putting my arm around her shoulders, I kiss her temple. "Not a thing."

She settles against my side, which feels right. But I realize I may have miscalculated. Trick wouldn't do anything to scare Sawyer. That's not his style. But his partners are hard men, and they scare people without even trying. Bringing her to the heart of C Crue territory right now might not have been the best idea after all.

SAWYER

JAMIE'S COUSIN'S MODERN GRAY-AND-WHITE HOUSE LOOMS above a stone enclosure. Ash puts her thumb on the security keypad. The tall gate slides open, revealing an Asian-inspired front landscape with smooth dark stone borders curving up to the front door.

We emerge from the car, and Jamie grabs the suitcases while Ash and I take the handle bags that have wrapped presents for the little boys.

The front door opens, and a pretty woman with long dark hair waves at us. She's wearing wide-legged black trousers with a jade-colored cashmere sweater. She belongs in a J Crew ad.

"Hey," Ash says, hurrying up to the door and raising the bags. "We need to sneak these inside."

From behind the woman comes the sound of children playing, and a small blond head appears from around her legs.

"Too late," the dark-haired woman says with a smile.

Seeing the boy from the picture on my dad's computer gives me a jolt.

Spotting Ash, the boy makes an excited sound and darts around his mom's legs, trying to get outside to us.

Ash bends down and scoops him up. "Hey, where are you going without shoes, mister?"

The boy talks excitedly while trying to get into the shopping bags.

"I missed you, Finn," Ash says, giving him a kiss while deftly handing off the bag as she enters the house. "Wanna meet my friend?" Ash turns to the mom as I approach. "Laurel, this is my roommate, Sawyer."

I extend a hand and marvel at the woman's practically translucent green eyes. They're like sea glass.

"Hi, Sawyer. Really nice to meet you. Come on in." She opens a front closet and sets the bags with the presents inside and then hangs our coats.

The adorable brown-haired brother stands at the end of the hall, watching us.

"Hi, Sean," Ash says, walking toward him. "What are you doing?" She bends so she can hug him.

"Want cookies?" Sean asks.

"Definitely." Ash gives him a kiss and lets the squirming Finn escape her arms. "Did you help Chef Chris make them?"

"Yep," Finn says, darting away.

"Come on." Sean takes Ash's hand to guide her. "Three flavors."

"Hi, Jamie," Laurel says, giving him a one-sided embrace since he's got the luggage. "You can put your bags up in the guest rooms and then come through to the kitchen."

"Grand. Sawyer, go ahead with Laurelyn. I'll be right there." He heads down the hallway and breaks right.

Laurel offers me a warm smile as we go through stunning rooms to an open kitchen with bright white walls, stone counters and glossy navy cabinets. There's a thirty-something guy with a blue bandana tied around his forehead who appears to be the chef. He's manning a panini grill.

On the island, there's a spread of veggies and hummus, cheese, crackers, and mustards, and a three-tier serving stand of cookies.

"Ash texted that you hadn't eaten yet. We're making paninis."

"I'll take ham and cheddar," Ash says as Sean outlines the cookie flavors, and Finn demands a chocolate chip one, calling it a chip.

"No more right now. You've had enough cookies," Laurel says, shaking her head at Finn.

"I want." The little boy tugs on her pant leg. "Chip."

Then Ash's brother Scott comes in wearing faded Levis and a gray t-shirt. He hugs Ash, then gives her a suspicious look. "Roads are bad. How'd you make such good time?"

"I'm an excellent driver," she says in a robotic voice that causes him to roll his eyes with a chuckle.

He extends a hand to me. "Hey, Sawyer, nice to see you."

I shake the hand as his younger son pulls on his pant leg.

"Dada, chip cookie." His little fist opens and closes. "I need one. No, two." He points up at the counter. "Two chips."

Scott's shrewd eyes shift from the little boy's hopeful face to his wife's. "How many has he had?"

"Too many," she says mildly. "I already said no."

Finn stamps his foot. "Yes! Chip-cookie!"

In a cheerful voice that draws everyone's attention, Ash says, "Oh my gosh! You know what I need, guys? I need to know what your animals are up to. Have they been getting along or are they fighting?"

"Fighting!" Finn announces. "Dray jail now."

"Really? Draco the dragon's in jail?" She scoops him up. "I'd better go and see. Dragons have wings, you know. He could be escaping right this minute because no one's watching. Let's go check."

As she hurries from the room carrying his little brother, Sean jumps off the step stool he's standing on and rushes out after her.

I drift toward the doorway, unable to keep from smiling. It's been a long time since I've been around small children. I'm drawn to the sounds of their excitement, instantly feeling lighter and happier than I have in days.

Scott pulls a pair of Guinnesses from the fridge. "Sawyer, what'll you take to drink?" He pushes the door open wider for me to choose from a deep shelf of beverages.

Jamie enters and extends his hand, which Scott shakes. Nodding toward the beers, he says, "I'll pour, shall I?"

Scott's eyes narrow. "Meaning what?"

Jamie's lips twitch into a small smirk. "Meaning, half head and overflowing last time, and I'd rather not risk it."

"Fuck off," Scott says. "That was four in the morning with Ash banging my chair."

"Right, sure." Jamie slides an empty Guinness glass towards himself. "How about to each his own?"

Laurel chuckles, and Scott turns his scowl on her. "Whose side are you on?"

Ash saunters back in and spots the pints as Scott sets them on the counter. "Oh, good, Guinness. Can I pour?"

"No," the men say in unison.

That causes all of us to laugh, including Ash. "I'm an excellent bartender," she says in the robotic voice from earlier.

"What's this now?" Jamie opens his can.

"Rain Man. Old movie," Scott says dryly while scrutinizing the way Jamie tilts his glass.

As Jamie pours, he slowly decreases the angle of the glass so it's upright by the time it's full. There's a perfect layer of foam on top. "That's all right, that is." With the devil in his eyes, he glances at Ash. "Ash, love, you best stand next to your brother while he gives it a go. That way, if things go awry, he can blame you for knocking his arm."

Scott cocks a brow. "This is what comes of letting the poor relations come to stay. Shit manners from start to finish."

Grinning, Ash pokes Scott's arm as he pours.

Brows rising, Scott stops and sets the beer down to stare at her. "Are you kidding?"

"I am," she says, throwing her arms around his neck.

"Get off," he says with mock disgust. "After all I've done? To hell with you."

With a laugh and a kiss, she finally lets go. "Yay, my panini's ready."

Scott returns to pouring his Guinness. In the end, it doesn't overflow, but the thick foam must not be right because Scott slides the glass to Ash. "That's yours."

"Awesome," she says, taking the glass and her dish to the table.

"If you need more practice, mate, your wife and my girlfriend still need one." Jamie takes a swig from his glass. "What do you reckon? Make it best of four?"

Scott tips his head back and laughs.

I can't stop smiling, and the warm sensation in my chest at hearing Jamie call me his girlfriend eats me up. This is just what I need to forget about all the Allendale drama.

Jamie's phone buzzes, and he checks it. Rising, he takes another drink from his glass before setting it in front of me. "Have some, Sauce." To Scott, he says, "I need to step out."

"Yeah, go. Good riddance." Scott takes another Guinness from the fridge.

Glancing at me, Jamie gestures toward the chef. "I'll take two of whatever he's making." His tone is light, but there's a subtle pinch between his brows that makes me wonder what's up.

As Jamie exits, the boys come barreling past him and run to Ash's chair.

"He's out!" Finn grabs her arm and tries to drag her from her seat.

She swallows her bite of food and nods. "Don't worry. We'll capture him. But I bet he's gonna be hiding somewhere sneaky."

At these words, Sean, who's near the doorway, turns and trots off.

She lifts Finn, who's still trying to pull her from the chair, onto her lap. "You want a bite of this panini, Finn? It's so good."

"No pih-nee-oh. You come, Nash!"

"Hey, Finn," Scott says in a stern voice. "No yelling."

Finn's outrage turns to consternation. As if the world has gone insane for not realizing the urgency of the dragon situation he's got going on. He leans forward and announces, "Dray got free!"

Scott finishes his pour, which looks perfect to me. "He's gonna be the only one if you land in time-out."

Ash winks at me. "It's a dragon emergency."

With a smile, I say, "So I understand."

After taking a drink, Scott nods and says to me, "The little one inherited patience from his aunt Ash. Which is to say, none at all."

"Pot, kettle, Scotty. *Pot. Kettle.*" Ash kisses the head of the squirming toddler before setting him on the floor. "Go help Seany, Finn. I'll be right there."

Outside, Jamie passes by the windows. My smile fades. He seems to be texting someone, and from his grim expression, something is wrong.

54

JAMIE

Stopping at the koi pond, I glance around to be sure I'm alone.

The Crue bosses bought about seven house lots to build their gated compound. Trick and Anvil share their massive backyard, which has a swimming pool with a rock waterfall, a fairy house, the koi pond, and enough flower beds and landscaping to rival any city park.

I'm on the cobblestone path to the gate that leads to C's place. Before approaching the gate, I call War.

"Yeah," he says.

"Hey, mate. I'm at Trick's and headed to C's."

"He asked for a meet?"

"He did, yeah." Licking my lips, I glance around. I haven't told War about killing Robert Allendale, but he'll guess as soon as word that the man's missing surfaces.

War makes a nonspecific sound of displeasure. "Anvil's in the Foxgrove house."

My body goes stiff, and my mind races. "Are you home?"

"Nah, but C and Trick are, right? And Killian and your cousin aren't there. So that only leaves Anvil as the person who entered the code and went in."

My head cocks. "I didn't get an alert."

"Someone turned off notifications. I'm guessing Trick."

As I stand in the cold, my blood runs to ice. I'd been feeling pleased that Trick had gone back to normal, joking around with me like we're the best of friends. "Anvil's in the house and they don't want us tipped to that? What do you make of it?" Turning my back to the wind, I stare at Trick's house where he's holding court like there's nothing fucking amiss.

"I assume he's checking something out. C knows I'm in Boston, and he told me to head to Coynston. I think he's going to come at us about our trip to the Carolinas."

"Maybe," I say slowly, my mind quickly clicking through what Anvil could be looking for in the house. "Right, well, there's nothing to find in Foxgrove, so he's wasted a trip."

"I doubt that." War's voice is grim.

"Let's take this conversation offline, mate."

War and I know better than to say anything incriminating while talking on our personal phones on Crue property. The feds have been after this Crue for years. While I didn't spot any surveillance vans on the street outside the house, War and I would never risk talking murder when I'm in Trick and Anvil's yard.

"No time. You're heading to C's now, and I'm telling you, his questions are already ready."

"Listen, he's got other reasons for talking to me. That have nothing to do with our last minute vacation to the Carolinas, mate."

"No?" War's voice is skeptical. "He called me in from Boston."

"Maybe to see what you know about other things." I walk a few more feet toward the gate to C's. "I need to head there."

"If you get jammed up about the vacation, don't cover."

That brings me up short. He's telling me if C corners me and

I have to admit to killing Brad Allendale, I shouldn't try to cover up his involvement. "Mate, no way. That's decided."

"J," War says grimly. "If the vacation isn't what he's after, good. Don't mention it. But if it is, and he gets you cornered, do *not* lie."

Looking up at the sky, I curse under my breath. If this is a trap, I brought Sawyer right into it. My first instinct is to go back into Trick's to get her the hell out of Coynston.

But if this really is a trap, that won't work. Trick will block any move I make. I trust Trick won't do anything to Sawyer with his family in the house and awake, but later...

"Right, okay." My frown deepens. "If a confrontation's coming, I'll face it. But listen, I need a last favor. A contingency for if I can't get back to Trick's. I'm texting Sawyer's number to you. Lure her out and send her somewhere safe."

"She's with you, and you think they wanted it that way?" War's voice is dead calm. "If that's true, there's nowhere safe to send her."

"I won't go to C's unless I know you'll try to get her out. I'll go back to Trick's for her myself."

"You're not fast enough. He'll be waiting for your move, and he'll drop you."

Exhaling, I shake my head. "Your word, or I go back."

"She's not worth this. You barely fucking know her." The sharpness of his voice tells me he's considering it. If he wasn't, he'd be calm while he refused. When I don't speak, he finally says, "If I even attempt to do this, you will owe me."

"I already owe you."

"Not like you will for this. If you and I both get out of this alive, you will *owe* me. Anything I ask. No matter what."

My eyes drift shut as warnings swirl in my head. Then, I think about Sawyer sitting innocently at my cousin's kitchen counter, where I brought her like a lamb to the slaughter. I can't leave her to her fate. "Right. Any payment, it's yours."

"Fucking suicide mission," War mutters under his breath just before the call goes dead.

With a slow exhalation, I slide my phone away and walk the rest of the way to the gate.

❦

SAWYER

Ash offers to set me up in the family room to watch movies or play video games while she plays with her nephews, but the boys are so cute and happy I opt to join her instead.

The boys' bedroom is huge, and in one corner there is a life-sized teddy bear with his legs on the mattress of a daybed, which has been removed from its frame. On the mattress is what must be a two-foot-tall mound of smaller stuffed animals.

Sean and I, along with a stuffed elephant, search the pile for the dragon escapee. Ash and a babbling Finn, search the closet.

When I ask what the dragon did to end up in jail in the first place, Sean and his little brother show me the treasure chest behind Sean's boat-framed bed. Inside the chest are a collection of plastic gold doubloons and jewels.

I have a hard time understanding some of the words Finn uses, but apparently seeing my confusion, Sean helpfully interprets, saying the dragon burned the lock with his breath to steal the treasure.

While we're discussing fire-breathing dragons, there's a knock on the door. The boys turn as the door opens and their mom appears.

"Guys, look who came over to play."

The boys race toward her as two little girls enter. One has such pretty, delicate features she looks like a doll. She's dressed in a black, glittery brocade tunic shirt and leggings, with a sparkly black ribbon around her dark ponytail. Her onyx-and-sapphire antique drop earrings look like they belong in the treasure chest. She's carrying an e-reader with a black glossy cover that matches her outfit.

Behind her is a girl with lopsided pigtails who's dressed in a dark t-shirt and leggings. Loose hair at the nape of her neck flutters as she runs in.

The girl with the e-reader hugs Ash and then extends her small hand toward me. A silver-and-sapphire bangle bracelet sways as we shake.

"Hello. I'm Irina Stroviak. That's my sister Makayla. Are you another cousin of the Patricks?" Despite being as small as Sean, her speech is crystal clear.

"Hi. No, I'm not related. My name's Sawyer."

"This is my friend from school," Ash says. "Irina, you look so cute in this outfit. Let me see your bracelet."

"Thank you." Irina holds up her arm.

"Gorgeous."

A few feet away, the boys are explaining about the missing dragon. Sean conveys that they suspect the bear might have helped with the prison break. Unlike the other kids, Makayla doesn't say a word. Instead, she turns and narrows her eyes at the bear. Then with a running leap, she jumps onto the bear's chest and punches him in the head.

It's so ferocious and hilarious that both Ash and I laugh.

"Oh, my goodness. Makayla," Irina says in a long-suffering tone more suited to a parent. "Be careful. If you break his stitching, Aunt Laurelyn and Uncle Trick will probably be upset. Remember you're supposed to be gentle?"

Makayla glances over briefly as she climbs onto the end of a dresser.

"Oh, my gosh." Irina turns quickly toward Ash. "If she jumps on him, it might knock out his stuffing. It's happened at our house."

Ash strolls over and catches Makayla mid-leap. The little girl's momentum is so powerful, Ash falls backward onto the mattress and stuffed toys.

The boys find the crash-landing hilarious and are still laughing as Ash sits up with Makayla.

"Wow." Ash's hair flies around her face. If she'd had pigtails, they would definitely have become lopsided. "You're getting too big for me to catch you when you jump!" Ash's tone is a mix of admiration and reproach. "Come on, Makayla." Standing up, she takes the girl's hand. "Can you help Finn and I search the closet for Draco? He's a pretty sneaky dragon, and we need the help."

Makayla nods amiably and pushes up her sleeves. Finn hooks an arm around Makayla's and says something about their being a team.

We continue searching the room, and it's Irina who discovers the adorable black-and-red stuffed dragon crammed behind Sean's bed.

The kids all gather around the toy and discuss what sort of new prison to put him in so he won't be able to escape.

There's a banging knock on the door that causes us to jump. When the door swings open to reveal War, clad in head-to-toe black and looming like a gothic tower, the kids freeze, like bunnies scenting a lion.

Makayla launches herself forward like a rocket. When she's a foot from War, she raises her fist. My jaw drops as Makayla punches his leg with more force than should be contained in such a small body.

"The hell?" he says, looking down.

Undeterred, Makayla draws her fist back and shuffles her feet into what may be a boxer's stance.

War reaches down, but Ash springs forward and snatches Makayla, then backpedals out of reach. In a low, cool voice, Ash says, "I would kill you."

Rolling his eyes, War makes a sound of derision. "Right." He points at me and then wags his finger for me to come over.

"No," Ash says, stepping in front of me. "Why are you here?" Her firing the question at War in no way means he will answer. He does not.

Putting a hand on Ash's shoulder, I try to reassure her. "It's fine." I walk around them, noticing that Makayla has almost twisted out of Ash's grip.

Irina comes over, her brows crinkled with concern. When she addresses her sister by name, the little girl stops trying to writhe free, instead focusing all her attention on Irina.

My brows rise as the older girl speaks to her in what sounds like Russian.

"Good advice," War says.

Makayla glares at War and redoubles her efforts at escape, swinging her body so hard she breaks free of Ash's hold. Ash tries to grab her but lands on one knee and a palm instead.

Makayla barrels forward, but this time War plucks her up before she can land a punch. She does manage to kick his chest in a move a ninja might envy.

Unconcerned, he tosses her into the pile of stuffed animals.

I gasp because she's flown so far through the air. But she pops up immediately and explodes out of the pile like lava from a volcano.

"Don't you dare do that again," Irina snaps at War before whirling around to face her sister. Throwing up her hand, she yells, "Stop." Then, Irina launches into what sounds like a sharp rebuke in Russian.

Makayla halts in front of Irina, and despite the fact that she's apparently younger, she's a bit taller, and they're eye-to-eye.

With furrowed brows, Makayla whispers a couple words, also in Russian. It's the first time I've heard her speak since she arrived, and she looks as grave as a general about to go into battle.

War's brows rise in surprise at whatever she says, then he laughs. The entire room is shocked at the deep, rich sound.

"Enemy?" War says, amusement still playing at the edges of his mouth. "I'll remember that."

Ash's nephews crowd around the girls, with Sean and Finn both asking questions.

"Sawyer," War says, all amusement gone. "I need to speak to you."

Deciding I should show at least as much courage as a three-year-old, I cross the room to face Jamie's giant housemate.

"Hallway." He ushers me out the door and closes it before Ash can follow.

JAMIE

C's place has turrets and a stone facade, so it's nicknamed The Castle. After ringing the bell, I wait, glancing at the circle drive where an SUV with CRUE 1 stamped on its license plate sits front and center.

The door opens, and C fills the doorway. At an inch or two under six feet, he's not short, but he's so muscular he doesn't look as tall as he is.

"Good," he says, pushing the storm door open. He's recently buzzed his hair close to the scalp, revealing a barbed-wire C tattoo on his head. Marked for life. It's a Crue edict.

I notice C doesn't offer his hand for me to shake. That's a breach of protocol and hints at where things stand.

Following him in, I remain silent. From the entry, we're heading past the living room when C stops next to a side table.

"Any electronics you've got on you, leave here. Coat, too."

I empty my pockets of my phone and key ring and lay my coat over the back of a couch. C drops his phone onto a cushion as well, then strides to a metal door with a keypad. He places his left thumb on the scan pad and then types in a code. The sounds of locks clicking can be heard just before he opens the door.

"Go down."

I precede him down the steps, glancing back when I'm halfway to the bottom. C slides a metal crossbar into a slot in the wall. If anyone wants to get downstairs before it's removed, they'll need a medieval ram capable of breaching an actual castle stronghold.

The basement isn't what I expect. For some reason, I'd been picturing a waterboarding set up, bare cement floor, and milk crates as seating. Instead, the floor's sealed dove gray concrete and the furnishings could do as well upstairs as down. There's a table whose top looks like a mixed media art project, with shellacked overlapping pieces of black and burgundy leather. The chairs are carved wood with red leather padded seats.

There's a dark gray couch with burgundy pillows and a heavy mahogany coffee table. Plus, a wood-and-marble bar cabinet that Napoleon might've gone to war for. C grabs ice from a black chest and mixes himself a whiskey and Coke.

He tilts his head toward the booze, but I shake mine. For this conversation, a clear head is critical. So, while a few swallows of Guinness are medicinal, I wouldn't touch whiskey on a million-dollar dare.

C sits at the table, and I take the seat across from him. "I heard about why Robert Allendale had to die. And that you knew you'd kill him before you came to work for us." Hazel eyes always seem the warmest to me, until now that is. "To me that means you were never a part of this Crue. So, every penny you were paid will come back to the organization. If you weren't who you are, you'd be in the ground, but your cousins have covered your debt and then some to keep you alive and out of the hospital."

My brows draw together. I think I heard an *s* on the end of the word *cousin*. Is he talking about Ashling, in addition to Trick? And if so, why?

"Are you saying—?"

"Don't interrupt." C's voice is low, but there's an unmistakable edge.

He's armed, and we're barricaded in an underground bunker. C has been a gangster for most of his life. I know better than to give him an excuse to ventilate my chest when that's precisely what he would like to do.

After a swig of whiskey, he sets his glass on the table. "To understand the extent of the potential damage, I need information. Anytime you lie to me, you lose something you care about. Like your ability to ever row again. Or the pretty young girl you made a witness to a murder we covered up for you."

I tense, watching him warily.

C leans forward. "Why did the son have to die?"

My mouth goes dry as I stare back at him. "To destroy the father. And because he was hurting the girl."

"Who pulled the trigger? You or War?"

"Me."

"War was what? Lookout? Getaway driver?"

"No, I never said that."

"We already know he was there. We've taken inventory. The gun and burn phones you stole from the Foxgrove house and ultimately destroyed are on the tab. Who unlocked the closet and took those out? You or him?"

"Me. Everything that was done, I did."

"The only reason you needed two burn phones was so you could communicate with each other. And his personal phone traveled with yours as far as the Carolinas. And then the burn phones traveled together the rest of the way."

My grimace is so fierce it makes my entire head hurt.

"He was supposed to be at Thanksgiving dinner here in Coynston. Bailed at the last minute. You both had to know there would be questions."

"War goes off without a word plenty. As you know, he's not big on social gatherings. Changed his mind about Thanksgiving, I guess."

"What was his share in the Brad Allendale murder?"

Shaking my head, I shrug. "No share. Everything that was done, I did."

"But not alone. You're not telling me you went to Palm Beach by yourself?"

Blowing out a breath, I rub the bridge of my nose. I'd sacrifice the bones in my hand, sure, which is what I think he was threatening when he said I'd never row again. But Sawyer's life?

After grinding my teeth together, I suck in a breath. "Listen, this vendetta dates back to when I was a boy. It's got nothing to do with anyone I've gotten close to in the past year." The thing my mind can't stop wondering about is whether War has gotten Sawyer out of Trick's house and away. If I knew she was gone, I would lie until the fucking end and to hell with life.

"Did you not fucking hear me say I already know War was with you? I want to hear what part he had in the execution of Brad Allendale."

Swallowing, I shake my head. "Brad Allendale died because my brother Jude died."

C's eyes narrow and bore into me. "It had nothing to do with you guys wanting Allendale dead because he got rowdy and grabbed Ash by the throat at the rave?"

"No." Leaning on my elbows, I stare him straight in the eyes. "I won't say I wouldn't have taken the chance to beat him down if the opportunity had arisen sometime in an alley outside a GU bar. I would have happily beaten him bloody. But killing him? No. If I'd wanted to murder him as retaliation for what he'd done to Sawyer and Ash, I'd have come to you and Trick to see if I could get cleared to do it."

"And War gave no indication he wanted to kill Allendale?"

"Christ, no. None." I tap my fingertip against the tabletop. "Killing Brad Allendale was a choice I made alone. Everything from taking the gun to pulling the trigger, it was a hundred percent me and no one else."

C picks up his glass and leans back. Sucking down whiskey, he watches me the way a hawk watches a rat. "It's time you fuck off back to Ireland. Out of my Crue and out of my sight for good. Don't show up on this side of the Atlantic for shit. You're not welcome."

"Hang on." I rest my elbows on the table. "Trick said I would stay in the Crue longer. As payback."

"I don't need you. Never did. Trick's already covered the cost of the Connecticut cleanup and for training you. You can work out a way to pay him back if that's what he wants. And since it's too soon for you to marry the girl, you'll break things off with her. We'll keep an eye on her to make sure she stays silent."

I'm not going to break up with Sawyer and be banned from the States while she's still here.

What the fuck is this?

55

SAWYER

War lures me out of the house by telling me Jamie needs us to meet him. Then, he drives to a toy store on the outskirts of town where he says he has to make a stop. It's full dark and practically closing time when we arrive.

His stride is so long I have to hurry to keep up.

Inside, he grabs a giant box containing a water slide and carries it to the front. When he pays with hundred-dollar bills, the young guy at the register appears confused by having to handle actual money. Looking at the crisp bills suspiciously, he hesitates. War glares at him, and the guy finally deposits them in the register.

War carries the large box outside and shoves it in the back of the SUV. He walks around the truck and stops next to me at the passenger door.

"Phone."

I stare at his massive outstretched hand. "Why?"

"Hand it over."

"Or what?"

He jerks my purse from my arm and then opens the door. "Get in."

"What's going on?"

"Get in, or I'll stick you in back."

My brows shoot up. "What the hell are you talking about? Are we actually meeting Jamie?"

"No, I'm fucking kidnapping you while I run errands." War rolls his eyes as he grabs my arm and drags me toward the back of the vehicle.

"What the fuck? Stop." Trying to pull away, I glare at him.

He drops my purse on the ground at his feet while he opens the back hatch with his left hand. After he pushes the waterslide box to the side, War sweeps me up and sets me inside.

I scream as he slams the back down and clicks the lock.

As I'm trying to open the back, he closes the passenger door and stalks around to the truck's driver's side. While he's getting in, I climb over the barrier and land on the back seats.

My heart feels like it'll pound out of my chest as I try to open a side door. Child locks must be enabled, because the door won't budge.

For fuck's sake. What is happening?

Unperturbed, War opens my purse, extracts my phone, and presses the side button to power it down. When he jerks his own phone out and turns it off too before tossing both devices onto the passenger seat with my purse, I go still.

"What are you doing?"

"Making it so we can't be tracked."

"The truck has GPS." I regret the words as soon as they're out of my mouth. I want him to see the futility of what he's doing, but I'm not trying to assist in my own abduction.

He starts the truck and swings it in a wide arc to exit the parking lot.

"Look, it doesn't cost you anything to explain yourself," I say.

"Situation is fluid. He'll tell you what he wants you to know. Unless he can't, and then I will."

Falling back against the seat, I feel as though all the air deflates from my lungs. *Unless he can't.* Does that mean someone will order Jamie not to share details? Or that he'll be too injured to speak?

Crossing my arms over my chest, I grow increasingly surly. "Jamie went to talk to one of your bosses, didn't he? If they sent him to do something dangerous, why the hell aren't you with him?"

War ignores me. I swallow the lump in my throat with a racing heart. What possible reason could War have for pulling me out of Scott's home? Where Jamie left me to drink Guinness and play with his little cousins?

I stare suspiciously at the back of War's head. Maybe he took me as leverage. If so, he's working against Jamie, not with him. And I need to try to get away.

When we're about thirty minutes outside Coynston, he pulls off the expressway and into the parking lot of a weathered motel that needs a coat of paint. And about a thousand other things.

War turns in the seat to look at me with his signature scowl. "This is a precaution." He gestures at the motel office. "I'm getting you a room. We can't use our cell phones here. But in a while, I'll go offsite so I can contact him."

With my arms still crossed over my chest, I glare at him.

He's unmoved by my discontent. "Get down so no one sees you when the interior lights come on." War grabs the phones and shoves them in his pockets. When I make no move to lie down, he shakes his head. "Your fucking funeral."

I stare after him as he exits the truck and locks the doors again with the fob, trapping me inside, before he stalks away.

There are a few cars in the dark lot, but no one's around. The only movement comes from passing headlights on the highway.

A few minutes later, War returns and opens one of the side doors.

I don't move toward him. "The truck has GPS, and there will

be surveillance footage of us walking around the toy store. There's no way you'll be able to—"

"GPS is disabled on all Crue trucks. It's the first thing that's done." He glances around the parking lot, then opens the front passenger door to grab my purse, which he holds out to me. "Come on."

I'm torn. I want out of the truck with its creepy kidnapping-enabled locks. But I have no idea what awaits me in the motel room.

"I can't believe Jamie agreed to your doing this."

"Agreed to it? This is a favor *for him*."

My brows furrow. "He told you to abduct me? To a seedy motel? I don't think so."

War grabs me and slides me out of the truck. "There wasn't time to discuss specifics." He flings the doors shut and grabs my arm again when I try to move away. "And no, he won't like the way this went down. But when you act like a fucking brat, I've gotta improvise."

With a slack-jawed expression, I stare at him.

"You gonna walk? Or do you need to be carried like a baby doll?"

He's out of his mind. Does he really expect me to believe Jamie—who knows him—would have him take me anywhere?

"I'll walk." My gaze scans the motel room windows. All the curtains are closed, but two have slivers of light framing the curtains. It's only nine-thirty. If I start screaming, I should be heard. The question is... should I?

War points. "Room 103."

My shuffling gait is slow but steady as I walk toward the door. I reason that if War wanted to take me to a location where no one would hear me scream, that's what he would've done. So maybe he's telling the truth?

War unlocks the motel room door and flicks on the light.

I enter and sit at the cheap dinette table. He swings the door shut and sits on the end of the bed, consulting his watch. A stillness settles over him. So, at least the part where he said we'd wait in the room seems credible.

After several moments of silence, I tilt my head. "Why the water slide?"

He looks up, staring at the wall rather than looking at me. "It's cover."

Studying his profile, I say, "I don't know what that means."

After a beat, he turns so his body's angled in my direction. Flipping a hand in a vague gesture, he says, "Needed an excuse to come upstairs to get you. Said I was coming to the kids' party tomorrow and needed to talk to you about the joint gift we were gonna get." His dark eyes rake over me. "If the situation goes right. We'll wrap the fucking box and give it to Trick's sons tomorrow."

"A water slide? It's the middle of winter."

"So?" His brow cocks. "It's not fucking Narnia. Summer's coming eventually."

"Big C.S. Lewis fan?"

He sighs heavily, as though conversation is the biggest waste of time since doomscrolling. After checking his watch, he pops his knuckles. "What did J tell you about his work?"

"Nothing." Licking my lips, I shake my head. "But I know about his cousin's past arrests from the net. And that C Crue is a criminal organization."

"Yeah?" He leans forward, resting his arms on his thighs. "So, what the fuck's a good girl still doing hanging out with him?"

"Maybe I'm not that good."

A black brow rises again, communicating his skepticism. "What happened in Connecticut?"

"Information being on a 'need to know' basis cuts both ways." My voice sounds hard and slightly smug. Which pleases me. "Anything Jamie wants you to know, he'll tell you."

The corner of War's mouth twitches, like he's close to smirking.

Resting my elbows on the table, I lean forward. "Stroviak, that's the last name of one of Scott's partners, right?"

"Scott?"

"Scott Patrick. Ash's brother."

"Ah. No one calls him that."

"Is Stroviak the name of his partner?"

War stands and stretches. He's so tall his fingers graze the ceiling. "Yeah. Anvil's last name is Stroviak."

"You think it was a good idea to throw his daughter across a room?"

An evil smirk curves his lips. "Impulsive decision."

"She could've been hurt."

His dark gaze slides to my face. "I could bench three hundred at fifteen."

"Meaning?"

"Did I break any bones when I put you in the back of the truck?" War shakes his head as he walks over to the small flatscreen that's mounted in the corner of the room. "When I hurt people, it's no accident."

"Still, you might have scared her."

He murmurs some words in Russian before turning to face me.

"What?"

"The princess one told the violent one she's not allowed to hit people, even if they're mean. And especially not if they're so big." For a brief moment, a smile appears, and War looks almost human. He rests his hands on his head, huge muscles straining the sleeves of his shirt. Then he sits on the end of the bed again. "What I said just now was 'born fighters fight.'" His head tilts as he looks over at me. "Ever meet Anvil?"

I shake my head.

"Yeah, well... the younger one, she's all Stroviak. About the only thing that kid got from the mother is a fucking X chromosome that's dormant." He checks his watch. "She was looking for a fight, and I gave her the closest thing anyone ever has. She look scared to you when she hit that mattress pile of stuffed animals?" Staring down at the floor, he allows himself another flash of a smile.

The idea that he thinks he was providing a child with fun by tossing her across a room is crazy. And yet, Makayla did erupt like a volcano without an ounce of fear or regret.

"Her father may not view your version of play-fighting as casually as you do."

"May not." He stands. "And then you and Blondie can cheer my demise."

"Blondie is Ash?"

Without answering, he rolls his massive shoulders as though he needs to keep his muscles loose. "It's been long enough. I'm gonna roll out to a safe distance to check for messages from J." He pulls my phone from his pocket and sets it on the end of the bed. "Give me an hour for the round trip. If I'm not back by then, it's safe to turn your phone on."

"What makes you think I won't turn it on the instant you leave?"

"Nothing." His gaze sweeps over me. "Nor do I really give a shit. By now, you should realize the *only* way I'd do what I just did for you is as a favor to him. From here on out, if you don't cooperate with being helped, you're on your fucking own."

I lose our stare-down, and he stalks over to the door. Without another word, he walks out and slams the door behind him.

So, I'm alone.

Free to participate in my kidnapping. Or not.

56

JAMIE

"C," I say slowly. "I learned things I needed to learn during Crue training, and that was always with the intention of using those skills both to carry out my revenge and to do whatever operations you put in front of me. I'm not looking to get out of C Crue early. I'm committed to being an investment that pays dividends."

"We've got no Ireland-based operations. And that's always been the goal, right? To go back?"

"Not if it means cutting all ties here and leaving things hanging." I splay my fingers on the table. "I'm in a position to help with the on-campus operation. I want to see it through. And to do any other work you think I'm suited to. I'm ready."

"There's no half in," C says. "I never should've agreed to let you do a one-year contract. This isn't a tour in the fucking military. It's a life sentence. And the guys you're working with need to know you've got their backs, not some hidden agenda that's more important than their lives. In their place, I would want you gone."

"Listen, I was fully focused during operations. My personal

mission of destroying Jude's attacker never interfered with my work for the Crue." Blowing out a breath, I feel things slipping away, and the idea rips me open.

The Crue training and operations were so intense that a part of me feels as much a member of C Crue as a citizen of Ireland. Also, I've never not paid a debt before. The thought of walking away... of losing the family I've bonded with in the States. Not to mention losing Sawyer. If I'm gone, she's alone in the world, and I've got no way to protect her. That cannot happen.

Tapping my thumb against the table, I lean forward. "Given the choice between leaving or staying, there's no contest. Here."

"Is that right." His mouth forms a hard line. "You ready to be all in? Even if it means living where we tell you to live, indefinitely?"

My body's so full of adrenaline the new spike doesn't even register. "I am, yeah."

C's hard stare bores into me. "Step out of line even once, and I will put you in the fucking ground myself, blood or not."

"Understood."

"All right. Pour yourself a drink and knock it back. We're celebrating."

It doesn't exactly feel like a celebration, but I'll have the drink as ordered.

C rises and pours himself another drink, too. Standing next to the bar, he cocks his head, assessing me. "Refusing to name War as an accomplice on the first murder was a gamble. Might have gotten you killed."

Setting the glass down, I shrug. "There are worse things than dying."

"Truer words were never spoken."

SAWYER

THE MOTEL ROOM'S EERIE QUIET UNSETTLES ME. I PACE TO FILL the silence, if only with the sound of my breath and my feet shuffling against the cheap carpet. I'd trade almost anything to be back in the playroom with Ash and the rambunctious kids and for Jamie to be there with us.

Every time Jamie enters my head, I tense. He's been so protective of me the past week, making sure I'm never alone and soothing my worries about Connecticut, that I've grown used to always being near him or knowing exactly when I will be again.

The sudden detachment feels grim, especially at night, which is when I normally feel the closest to him. In bed, there's the heart-pounding intimacy of sex when we're literally fused into one body. But there's also the conversations we have in low voices before we fall asleep. Sometimes, he's more talkative than I am. When he describes Ireland in his stories, I can practically feel the misty rain on my skin. I've never longed for a place I've never been before, but I'm desperate to experience Ireland with Jamie. To walk over ancient rocks at the edge of the world as he calls it.

I stop, sighing, and hug my arms around my chest.

Please be okay.

Drawing in a shaky breath, I bite down on my lower lip and blink my eyes, which keep threatening to tear up. I won't let myself cry. That would be ridiculous when I'm not even sure anything is wrong.

But the nagging fear returns like swarming bees from a hive I've accidentally overturned. Jamie wouldn't have had War move me to a secret location unless he wasn't able to do it himself. Which raises so many horrible questions.

Every few minutes, I pick up my phone, tempted to turn it on so I can text him. If he didn't answer, I could text Ash that I'm worried about him and for her to come and get me so we can start the process of tracking him down. Ash could ask her brother where Jamie is and if he's all right. Scott should easily be able to find out Jamie's status.

Thinking about Scott, I have mixed feelings. In person, I like him so much. I could see Jamie and I visiting Scott and Laurel's house as often as we're invited over. But I'm frustrated Scott isn't more careful about Jamie's safety. Why would he send him to see one of his partners who would then send Jamie out to work when we're in town for a party? If it's an entire organization, they must have other people who could work tonight.

The television drones on with a cooking show. I'm not paying attention, but I've got it on so I can check the time, which feels as though it's moving at a glacial pace. Forty minutes feels more like forty years.

War said an hour. I'm not giving him a minute more.

The speed of my pacing increases until the exertion coupled with my anxiety makes my heart pound.

Around the edges of the patterned pull curtain, light flashes. *A new car's arrived.* Pulling the corner of the curtain back, I peek out. My heart leaps when I spot Ash's Camaro pulling into a spot right in front of the room.

I rush over to the door, my fingers fumbling to flip the security bar back and yank it open.

Jamie emerges from the car, looking none the worse for wear, thank God.

When he reaches the doorway, grudging relief explodes from inside me. "Jesus Christ." My tone is harsh, and my brows pinch together as I glare at him. "You scared me to death. Why would you have War bring me here?"

As he enters, I'm forced to step back. Without a word, he catches my face in his hands and kisses me. He tastes of liquor and sweet soda. Apparently, his work assignment wasn't as bad as I was imagining.

I kiss him for a second, then shove at his chest until he releases me. "I need an explanation, James."

"James, is it?" Amusement colors his features for a moment. "There's a sure sign we're getting serious." He winks and turns to flip the security latch. When he faces me again, the lightness in his expression is gone. "I ran into a bit of trouble."

My brows furrow, and my voice lowers. "What kind exactly?"

"Not the Connecticut kind," he says softly. "But I thought it might go that way."

Balling my fists as though I could punch his bosses in the throat, I say, "For you or someone else?"

"Me."

That causes my stomach to drop like I'm falling. "But everything's okay now?"

"It is, yeah."

"Did War bring me here for them as leverage to force you to do something? Or was he really doing you a favor?"

"Favor."

"Well, he fucking sucks at being a bodyguard because I thought he was kidnapping me." Rubbing Jamie's arms, I exhale a shaky breath. "I was so worried about you. I'm glad you're okay."

"Thanks." He pulls me into a tight hug and kisses the top of my head. "Sorry I worried you."

"Seriously though, you need to give me a heads-up the next time War's going to be my designated getaway driver. When I was hesitant to leave town with him, he locked me in the back of the SUV with the rest of the cargo. If there had been a trunk, I'm positive he'd have put me in it."

"Jayzus." Jamie shakes his head with a grimace, his thumb stroking my jaw to soothe my nerves. "For a barbarian, he's a surprisingly good mate. But a light touch he is not."

I exhale a small amused sound that's more born out of relief than real amusement. "Why did I need to leave your cousin's house?"

"That was just a precaution in case anyone was overzealous."

Holding his sides, I stare up at his eyes, trying to fill in the holes he's not. "I don't understand. I need you to explain what happened tonight."

"I'd like to, sure. Maybe one day, but not right now. Here's the thing you need to know. I work for some dangerous people. They're not all bad, but I can't walk away."

My heart thumps harder in my chest, and I feel the uneasiness rising again.

"And through no fault of your own, you're in this with me, Sauce. Do you want me to try to get you out? Well and truly? It would mean moving and hiding." He sucks on his lower lip as he stares at me as though he'd like to hear my deepest thoughts.

"What? When you say moving away and hiding, do you mean me alone?"

With a grim expression, he nods.

"You swore I wouldn't be alone." I slam my palm against his ribs. "You fucking promised."

"I know, and I meant it. Still do." When I start to hit him again, he grabs my wrists and shoves them behind my back, stepping forward so our bodies touch and my hands are pinned behind me. "If you plan to stay with me for good, you'll never be alone again. But for the next few years, we'll be here in the States. Not living some happy fairy tale in Ireland that I was peddling outside the Hearth and Stone. Before Connecticut, I owed less than a year to this work. Could've gone home next fall term if I wanted. That's not the case anymore. So now, this is the life you'd be signing on for. Where I might go out in the middle of the night without warning to do dangerous work."

"And you expect me to do what? Roll with being shoved into car trunks? Visit you in jail?"

"Maybe. Yeah. Being with me from here on, it's not for the feint of heart. It means staying, come hell or high water." His expression is gravely serious now. "I love you, and I don't want to let you go. But the bright future you've been working toward might be leveled. Collateral damage."

Tears burn in my eyes. This is the choice. Him. Or trying to follow in Celine's footsteps—the Allendales and politics and a marriage to someone like the guys I dated in school. Bland. Boring. Blue-blooded, yet bloodless.

Swallowing, I shake my head. "Is that why you took me to your cousin's? To tempt me with the huge, gorgeous house and adorable children?"

"To show you, yeah. That there are good parts."

"I'd still want to go to law school. Maybe I won't end up in politics, but—"

"You'll go to law school for sure. I'll see to that. And you might become a politician, too. I'm just saying there's a bigger risk that people won't accept you. Or vote you in if you've got a dark albatross around your neck."

"Welcome to my whole life." Grinding my teeth, I try to tug my wrists free.

Jamie holds them tighter, unwilling to let me go. Which is as reassuring as it is unnerving.

"Your family will accept me, though, right?" I fire the question at him as though it's an accusation that they're about to betray me. "Because I wouldn't be the darkest dark sheep now." My tone is defiant.

"By comparison, you're Snow White, Sauce. And of course, they accept you. That part's done."

"You know…" My pulse slows to a jagged thump in the back of my throat. "Today was the best family day I've ever had. The entire time I felt like I could be myself and enjoy myself. Other than being kidnapped and dragged to a shady motel, it was pretty much perfect."

A startled chuckle escapes from low in his chest. "Right, okay. I'll keep the abductions to a minimum." He tips his head down, so our faces are closer. "I'll take a kiss if you're ready to give one up."

"You don't deserve it."

"Aye, I know. But you may as well get used to that." His lips brush mine. "Come on."

Rising onto my toes, I kiss him.

Our tongues tangle together, and he pulls my body flush with his until I'm breathless.

"Well, that's a silver lining." Licking his lips, he nods, his blue eyes trapping mine. "To hell with regrets when there's this." He releases my wrists, rubbing my back for a second before he steps back. "Ready to leave this shite place, Cranberry Sauce? Because I want to take you to bed, but not this one."

"I've been ready." A relieved smile emerges as I gather my purse and phone. "That's another beef I've got with War. He couldn't spring for better than this? If he'd gone for just one more star, it would've doubled the rating."

Jamie laughs and shakes his head as we go outside. "Don't doubt War's decision-making. He chose here because he could pay cash, and the guy at the desk wouldn't ask questions when War gave a fake name for the register."

"Hmm."

"Not convinced, huh?" Jamie opens the passenger door of the Camaro.

I slide inside. "Not unconvinced. Just still annoyed about being toted about like baggage."

"Right. Understood."

With the radio and the heat blasting, he drives back to Coynston. When we arrive in town, however, he doesn't take the same route to his cousin Scott's that Ash did. Instead, Jamie drives to the top of a hill and pulls onto the shoulder. The pretty town glitters below, including the town square with its ferris wheel.

"Zip up your coat, Sauce. I want to get out for a minute."

"Always outside in the freezing cold." My voice is mock annoyed. "What is with you?"

"I like fresh air. And I want to show you the view."

The view? At nearly midnight on a winter night? He's lost his mind.

After I climb out, he uses his phone as a flashlight to guide me down several stone steps to a gazebo that's on a hillside platform. During the day, I'm sure it's lovely, but this…

349

Once we step through the arch, motion-activated lights threaded through the woodwork flick on. It's magical.

Looking around, my reluctance fades. Jamie turns me by the shoulders, so I'm facing him, with the town and hill still in the periphery.

He tucks his phone away and steps back. "Sawyer, I've got a question for you." When he lowers himself to one knee, my breath catches.

There is no way.

Jamie pulls out a white box. "Will you stay with me come hell or high water?"

My heart hammers against my ribs as he opens the box. A huge oval diamond glitters like the twinkling lights.

"Will you marry me, Sauce?"

My racing thoughts crash into each other. This can't be happening.

Too soon. Too reckless.

Completely *insane*.

57

JAMIE

I half expect her to do the sensible thing and say no. Or at least, not yet.

Instead, Sawyer smiles and holds out her hand, whispering, "Hell or high water."

Fuck's sake, *yes*.

I don't realize I'm holding my breath until I exhale. Bringing her hand to my mouth, I kiss her knuckles fiercely and then slide the ring on her finger.

So, that's it. My new life underway with a gorgeous American girl with no good sense in her. The surreal quality of the whole night wrecks my head.

When Sauce bends down to kiss me, I realize I'm still on bended knee.

Christ's sake. Collect yourself and get on.

Rising, I give her a sound kiss.

"Jamie, it's freezing."

"I know. Though I can't feel it just now." I wink.

After I take her back up to the road, I tuck her into Ash's hotrod.

As I circle the car, I glance up at the black sky and its sprinkling of stars. "Got it," I whisper, half in prayer. "Right, that's me accepting this gift and swearing I'll take care of her." After a solemn moment, I climb into the driver's seat.

Sauce is giddy on the drive back to Trick's, more talkative than I've ever seen her. Which makes me smile.

Ash lets us into the house and spots the sparkler straight off, giving us hugs and kisses and promising to help with the wedding prep. It's grand altogether.

When we get to the guest room and start to undress, Sawyer pauses near the edge of the bed to admire the ring. "It's incredible. I love it."

My cock's too preoccupied with her bare breasts to take up the cause of a touching moment, but I manage a nod to convey I'm glad she likes the ring.

Looking up from her hand, she glances at the door. "We can have sex here, right?"

"We can, yeah. Just not so loud that we wake the house."

Drawing in a breath, she drops her knickers and climbs in bed. "Now that you have me for life, I hope you're not planning to slack off."

It takes me a second to catch her meaning. Then, I laugh. "Of the two of us, your interest in sex is likely to fade long before mine."

"No, it won't."

That brings a smile to my face as I climb in bed. "A competition, is it? To see who tires first?" My hand slides between her legs.

Her fingers slip along my collarbone, over my shoulder, and into the hair at the nape of my neck. Her voice is a tantalizing whisper. "Sounds good to me."

And so, I'm free to fuck her for two relentless hours.

In the end, she calls for a break before I do. I doubt she's more knackered than I am, though. It's more that a girl has less to prove when it comes to stamina.

Putting her palm on the side of my face, she stares into my eyes. "I love you, and we're going to have a great life together."

"Seems like it," I say dryly, making her laugh. "Try to sleep now, Sauce. Tomorrow's going to be a marathon, too."

"Good." She kisses me softly, then lies back.

Deep under the covers, I find her hand and thread our fingers together. I'm sated and content, but there's a part of me that doesn't want to let go. Ever.

58

JAMIE

The next day passes faster than I'd like. From breakfast to a houseful of guests, including a dozen excited kids playing noisy party games, it's all entertaining.

The funniest moment is when War arrives late with a big box that looks like a drunk on a bender wrapped it. There are three different types of wrapping paper, and they've been applied at an angle.

Sawyer and Trick both cock their heads as they examine it.

In a dubious voice, Sauce says, "Tell me about this."

Trick laughs.

War rolls his eyes as he stalks past. "Store only had one of each kind of paper."

Sawyer's brows crinkle in mock confusion. "Is there just the one store in Massachusetts now? When did that happen?"

Trick's head tips back, and he laughs so hard other people start to walk over.

"Fuck off," War mutters under his breath, but not so low that the three of us miss it.

Shaking my head, I smirk. "It'll be smooth sailing from here with my best mate and future wife such good friends."

"Yeah, good luck." To Sawyer, Trick says, "Bet that's the last time you put him in charge of wrapping anything."

She takes a sip of hard cider and shakes her head. Deadpan tone, she says, "Yeah, he's fired."

With a smirk, Trick winks at her and says, "Welcome to the family. You're gonna fit right in." Then he leads Sauce over to meet his older sister Kat, who lived with us in Ireland for a while. I can't remember much of that time since I was so young, but I do appreciate never having to tone down my accent when talking to her.

War returns to stand next to me. "A ring already?"

"World's in need of more Irish babies. Gotta do my part."

His eyes narrow as he looks Sauce over. "You think the time's right for kids?"

"Up to her."

Ash joins them and puts her arm around Sawyer's shoulders.

A part of me may always miss living in Ireland, but as I watch Sawyer with my family, I know I would've missed more if I'd taken C's offer to leave.

No regrets.

The future is now.

* * *

Want to see Sawyer & Jamie in Ireland?

To unlock access to free bonus content, subscribe to Marlee's newsletter at www.MarleeWray.com

There are many pages of FREE bonus scenes available for Marlee's newsletter subscribers, including *New Life With the Irish,* which has extra epilogue scenes for this book.

Subscribe at www.marleewray.com

READING ORDER

The *Knights* Dark College Romances are set in the same universe as the *Ruthless Kings* series of Dark Mafia Romances. The C Crue founders who are mentioned and/or appear in this book, each have a book of their own.

Recommended Reading Order

Held (Ruthless Kings 1)
Pursued (Ruthless Kings 2)
Used: (Ruthless Kings 3)
C Crue Afters (Ruthless Kings Related Content)
His Prize (Ruthless Kings 4)

Indecent Demands (Dark Knights 1)
(Bonus > Xmas Eve Among Killers)

Wicked Demands (Dark Knights 2)
(Bonus > New Year Among Billionaires)

Twisted Demands (Dark Knights 3)
(Bonus > Sunrise Among Newlyweds)

(Bonus > Coffee With a Kingpin)

READING ORDER

Ruthless Heart (Ruthless Kings 5)

Pretty Threats (Knights of Wrath 1)
(Bonus > Road Trip With a Killer)

Pretty Vengeance (Knights of Wrath 2)
(Bonus > New Life Among the Irish)

Pretty Wrath (Knights of Wrath 3) - Coming Soon

PRETTY WRATH

He's a raging alpha-hole who hates me. And I'm trapped with him.

Something sinister is happening behind the ivy-covered walls of our university. When a predatory frat guy drags me into it, it becomes my problem.

This is not the first time I've been kidnapped. Usually, I take these things in stride. But with the enraged six-foot-six monster, War, trapped with me, I'm losing my way. Our captors vow to force him to do unspeakable things to me. He hates me, so maybe he will.

No matter what they do, though, I'll never admit I'm scared.
    And if they make even one mistake, it will be their last.

THE MARLEE-VERSE COMPANION

All of Marlee's contemporary romances take place in the same universe, and she includes character updates in her newsletters. There is also a companion document that includes images and other material from the interconnected books. Visit www.marleewray.com to subscribe and get your copy today!

Made in the USA
Coppell, TX
27 January 2026

69206077R10203